East Coast Ghosts

East Coast Ghosts

EDITED BY
CHARLES G. WAUGH
AND
MARTIN H. GREENBERG

THE MIDDLE ATLANTIC PRESS
Wilmington, Delaware

Table of Contents

Anonymous—The Lighthouse Keeper's Secret   5

Mary Wilkins Freeman—Luella Miller   9

Henry James—The Ghostly Rental   25

Elia W. Peattie—The Crime of Micah Rood   63

O. Henry—The Furnished Room   79

Josephine Daskam Bacon—The Children   87

F. Marion Crawford—The Upper Berth   111

Henry Van Dyke—The Night Call   137

Frank R. Stockton—The Transferred Ghost   155

John A. Foote—The Mystery of Shaft No. 6   169

Richard F. Woods—The Ringing of the Bell   181

Ambrose Bierce—A Tough Tussle   199

Elizabeth Coatsworth—Caleb Thorne's Day   209

William Gilmore Simms—Grayling: or,
  "Murder Will Out."   221

Mrs. F. W. Dawson—A Tragedy of South Carolina   257

John William DeForest—A Strange Arrival   275

John D. MacDonald—The Legend of Joe Lee   297

INTRODUCTION

East Coast Ghosts

When Horace Greeley said "Go west, young man," he hadn't read *East Coast Ghosts*. If he had, he'd have gone west too. For this spirited blend of recognized classics and forgotten treasures leaves the haunting impression that habitation athwart the eastern shores is a grave mistake for all but a couple of "wild and crazy poltergeists."

Thrills, tears, and laughter await you in these devilish delights by John D. MacDonald, Henry James, O. Henry, Ambrose Bierce, Elizabeth Coatsworth, Frank R. Stockton, F. Marion Crawford, Mary Wilkins Freeman, and others.

On the rocky coast of Maine you step into horror as a peg-legged lighthouse keeper stalks his boss's secret. In the primordial swamps of Florida, you itch with excitement as an elusive hotrodder knifes through roadblocks like a phantom. In between, you dodge a small town psychic vampire in New England, are confounded by the premature ghost of your fiancee's father in New Jersey, explore rumors of a luminscent presence lurking within an abandoned Pennsylvania coal mine, wrestle with a rebel incorporeal on a civil war battlefield in Virginia, and sign articles with the accursed "Flying Dutchman" to escape a sinking Jamaica bound schooner.

1

*   *   *

I'm not afraid,'' says the heroine of a Broadway play,
Ladies in Retirement, ''to go out alone on the moors at night.
I believe there is Someone who watches over us.''

''I believe that too,'' says her scared friend, ''but I'm not
so sure who that Someone is.''

Such an idea produces an eerie little chill.

Is it for such thrills people enjoy reading ghost stories? Of
course. But there is more to it than that.

Ghosts have shadowed humanity since the dawn of time.
First whispered about over flickering campfires, they perme-
ate legends and lore of every time and place, and even appear
in the greatest literary works.

In Shakespeare's plays, for example, ghosts manifest themselves to Macbeth, usurper of the throne of Scotland, who
kills Banquo and finds his friend has deceased but not
desisted: and to Hamlet, Prince of Denmark, who is implored
to avenge a murder most familial.

The appeal of the ghost story is universal. The fact that so
many show ghosts interceding in the affairs of people they
knew, to settle matters such as love or justice left undone at
death, provides a clue to this allure. For, beneath the supernatural horror lies a different and deeper theme—hope.

The ghost story, by its very nature, tells us that our loved
ones do not die; that somewhere, in some strange, interdi-
mensional part of the universe, they remain somehow alive,
as involved and interested spectators to our ''hour upon the
stage.''

*   *   *

For our particular stage, we have chosen (including near
miss Pennsylvania) the fifteen east coast states abutting the
Atlantic Ocean. Geographically, they occupy nearly four hundred thousand square miles of varied terrain and stretch
across approximately twenty-five degrees of latitude, or more

than one thousand five hundred crow-flown miles. Historically, they were settled first, have backdropped important national events such as the civil war, and still constitute our country's most densely populated sector.

With more people, the east coast presumably produces more ghosts. With more dramatic events, there must be more unfinished business for ghosts to handle. With more writers as residents, more ghost stories are centered here. Finally, with more occupants, there is a larger potential audience of readers.

The lure of the sea and the coast in so many east coast ghost stories is harder to account for; possibly these settings may be only ploys to intensify suspense, mood and atmosphere, but then again they may offer something else.

Perhaps, deep between the lines, the writers are trying to tell us something. "Storytellers," said Sigmund Freud, "are valuable allies (for the psychological investigator), and their testimony is to be rated high, for they usually know many things not yet dreamed of in our philosophy . . . because they draw from (unconscious) sources that have not yet been made accessible to science."

The sea is, after all, our ancestral home, where life evolved from nothingness millennia ago and the beaches are where our phylogenetic predecessors thrust themselves ashore as pointmen on the road to civilization. When mists arise and fogs engulf these settings, the borders of time and space seem insubstantial, and we are perhaps more willing to believe certain fundamental laws of the universe can be altered.

* * *

In short, this anthology is composed of seventeen fascinating stories exploring one of literature's most popular themes—ghosts—and featuring the east coast—at the risk of *east*nocentrism, our country's most important region. So if your vacation is being stiffed by a rainy night at the shore, settle down to turn these pages one by one—and if you hear a gentle tapping, tapping, tapping on the windowpane, remember it's only the wind-whipped branches of a bush or tree . . . and nothing more.

Well, isn't it?

CHARLES G. WAUGH AND FRANK D. MCSHERRY, JR.

THE LIGHTHOUSE KEEPER'S SECRET

Anonymous

"My man, do you want a berth?" said he.

"Aye, aye, cappen," said I. "I want one badly. I'm half-starved and half-frozen."

He made no answer but just a sign to follow him. He stalked away towards Casco Bay and I pegged after him. He kept close along the shore as we walked, and for a while he said nothing. At last he turned and pointed seaward.

He indicated a lighthouse on a lonely rock. "I'm the keeper," said he. "I want you to cook my meals and keep my bachelor's hall for me. Now and then I shall want you to row in and buy provisions. The work won't be hard. I think the pay will suit you. Do you know why I chose you?"

"No, Cappen," said I.

"Because I saw that hope was at an end with you," he said. "It's only a man who had come to that who could live with me in a lighthouse."

I'd been in a lighthouse before; it was no new thing to me, but after I'd been there for a few hours I wondered what my master hired me for. It was like being pensioned off; there was nothing to do. But, mark ye, when it came night, and the wind began to moan about the lighthouse, and the lamps were lit and all outside was black as pitch, and all the sound

5

we heard was the swash, swash, swash of the waves, my
master mixed some grog and called me to sit along with him.
That looked sociable, but I can't say he did. He sat glowering
over his glass for a while, and opening his mouth as if to
speak, and shutting it again. Then said he:

"What's your name?"

"Ben Dare," said I.

"Would you mind calling yourself Brace?"

"I've no reason to be ashamed of my name," said I.

"Look here," said he, "I am a gentleman born and bred. I
never came to earning my bread before. I'm ashamed of it.
This is what I mean: If any strangers come out here and ask
for William Brace, why, you can say you are the man. You
claim to be lighthouse keeper. It's easy. I don't suppose
much company will call, but I choose not to see them if they
do. That's what I hired you for."

"Oh," said I.

"You see," said he, "I got this place through a rich man
who had influence. Those who gave it to me never saw me.
If I die some day, why, here you are in the place. If I go off,
and I may, here you are still."

"Well, it's shamming," said I, "but, after all, what does
any one care what my name is; and what shall I call you?"

"Call me nothing," said he. "Call me Captain."

Gentleman or no, he wasn't lazy. He didn't care how he
worked. The lamps were as bright as jewels. There wasn't a
speck of dirt in the whole tower. But let any boat come nigh
us, away he went and hid himself, and came out with a
white, scared face and a shaking hand. At night he was afraid
to go up to the lamps alone, and he'd look over his shoulder
and turn white as we stood together. At last he took a new
turn. He stood staring for awhile. Then he spoke to me in a
low voice: "Brace, do you believe in ghosts?"

"I hadn't considered the question," I answered.

"Well," he said, softlier than before, "look into that
corner," and he pointed. I looked.

"Don't you see anything?" he asked.

"No," said I; "no, Cappen."

But that wasn't nothing to what happened the very next night. We slept in two bunks nigh each other, and naturally when he woke up with a yell I woke too. He was shrieking and shaking and wringing his hands.

"The woman! the woman!" he said. "She stood here just now, all red with blood. It dripped down the white ruffles. It dripped on her hands. Stop her! She has gone to call them. Stop her! stop her!"

"Where did she go?" I asked.

He stared at me with his wide-open eyes.

"She couldn't have been here," said he. "It was a dream." So we went asleep. But I heard of the woman so often after that that I grew used to her. The Cappen, as I called him, got to be worse and worse every day. I wanted to go ashore and fetch the doctor, but he would not hear to it.

At last there came a hot, hot night in June. It was burning hot all day, and a dead calm at night. About dark the Cappen went to sleep, and I went and sat where I could see the water and hear the sailors in a Spanish ship moored not far away singing in their foreign lingo. And I was sort of quiet and dreamy-like, when something happened that waked me mighty wide and sudden. Something was standing on the steps below me, something white. Something came toward me.

It was a little, slender figure, with long hair all about its shoulders. I couldn't see its face. I don't think I really saw it plainly at all. But it went past me softly while I looked, and I knew it was a woman in a white, ruffled gown, and that she had gone to the room where my master lay. I shook too hard for a moment to move; but as soon as I could I started to go to him. Just then a voice cried: "Lighthouse, ahoy!"

I answered, "Aye, aye," and stopped a bit.

A boat lay at the foot of the steps, and four men jumped out of it.

"We want William Brace, keeper of this lighthouse," said one, a big man in a linen overcoat.

"I'm one that answers to the name," says I. He swung a lantern over my head.

"Search the place, my men," said he.

"I've got a sick friend aloft," says I. "Don't disturb him. I'm afraid the woman will skeer him, anyhow, he's so low."

"No woman came with us," he snarled.

"Stand aside. Men, do your duty."

Then went upstairs. I followed. I saw them walk into the Cappen's room. I heard them cry out and stand still. When I got to the door they stood in a row looking down on the bed. I looked, too. Man nor woman couldn't frighten the Cappen more. He was dead.

"What had he done?" I asked the officer.

"Killed his wife," said he, "that's all. No doubt she deserved it; but it's not allowed by law when they do."

"God help him," said I.

LUELLA MILLER

Mary Wilkins Freeman

Close to the village street stood the one-story house in which Luella Miller, who had an evil name in the village, had dwelt. She had been dead for years, yet there were those in the village who, in spite of the clearer light which comes on a vantage-point from a long-past danger, half believed in the tale which they had heard from their childhood. In their hearts, although they scarcely would have owned it, was a survival of the wild horror and frenzied fear of their ancestors who had dwelt in the same age with Luella Miller. Young people even would stare with a shudder at the old house as they passed, and children never played around it as was their wont around an untenanted building. Not a window in the old Miller house was broken: the panes reflected the morning sunlight in patches of emerald and blue, and the latch of the sagging front door was never lifted, although no bolt secured it. Since Luella Miller had been carried out of it, the house had had no tenant except one friendless old soul who had no choice between that and the far-off shelter of the open sky. This old woman, who had survived her kindred and friends, lived in the house one week, then one morning no smoke came out of the chimney, and a body of neighbors, a score strong, entered and found her dead in her bed. There were dark whispers as to the cause of her death, and there were those who testified to an expression of fear so exalted that it showed forth the state of the departing soul upon the dead face. The old woman had been hale and hearty when she entered the house, and in seven days she was dead; it seemed that she had fallen a victim to some uncanny power. The minister talked in the pulpit with covert severity against the sin of superstition; still the belief prevailed. Not a soul in the village but would have chosen the almshouse rather than that dwelling. No vagrant, if he heard the tale, would seek shelter beneath that old roof, unhallowed by nearly half a century of superstitious fear.

There was only one person in the village who had actually known Luella Miller. That person was a woman well over eighty, but a marvel of vitality and unextinct youth. Straight as an arrow, with the spring of one recently let loose from the bow of life, she moved about the streets, and she always went to church, rain or shine. She had never married, and had lived alone for years in a house across the road from Luella Miller's.

This woman had none of the garrulousness of age, but never in all her life had she ever held her tongue for any will save her own, and she never spared the truth when she essayed to present it. She it was who bore testimony to the life, evil, though possibly wittingly or designedly so, of Luella Miller, and to her personal appearance. When this old woman spoke—and she had the gift of description, although her thoughts were clothed in the rude venacular of her native village—one could seem to see Luella Miller as she had really looked. According to this woman, Lydia Anderson by name, Luella Miller had been a beauty of a type rather unusual in New England. She had been a slight, pliant sort of creature, as ready with a strong yielding to fate and as unbreakable as a willow. She had glimmering lengths of straight, fair hair, which she wore softly looped round a long, lovely face. She had blue eyes full of soft pleading, little slender, clinging hands, and a wonderful grace of motion and attitude.

"Luella Miller used to sit in a way nobody else could if they sat up and studied a week of Sundays," said Lydia Anderson, "and it was a sight to see her walk. If one of them willows over there on the edge of the brook could start up and get its roots free of the ground, and move off, it would go just the way Luella Miller used to. She had a green shot silk she used to wear, too, and a hat with green ribbon streamers, and a lace veil blowing across her face and out sideways, and a green ribbon flyin' from her waist. That was what she came out bride in when she married Erastus Miller. Her name before she was married was Hill. There always was a sight of "l's" in her name, married or single. Erastus Miller was good lookin', too, better lookin' than Luella. Sometimes I used to think that Luella wa'n't so handsome after all. Erastus just about worshiped her. I used to know him pretty well. He lived next door to me, and we went to school together. Folks used to say he was waitin' on me, but he wa'n't. I never thought he was except once or twice when he said things that some girls might have suspected meant somethin'. That was before Luella came here to teach the district school. It was funny how she came to get it, for folks said she hadn't any education, and that one of the big girls, Lottie Henderson, used to do all the teachin' for her, while she sat back and did embroidery work on a cambric pocket-handkerchief. Lottie Henderson was a real smart girl, a splendid scholar, and she just set her eyes by Luella, as all the girls did. Lottie would have made a real smart woman, but she died when Luella had been here about a year—just faded away and died: nobody knew what ailed her. She dragged herself to that schoolhouse and helped Luella teach till the very last minute. The committee all knew how Luella didn't do much of the work herself, but they winked at it. It wa'n't long after Lottie died that Erastus married her. I always thought he hurried it up because she wa'n't fit to teach. One

of the big boys used to help her after Lottie died, but he
hadn't much government, and the school didn't do very well,
and Luella might have had to give it up, for the committee
couldn't have shut their eyes to things much longer. The boy
that helped her was a real honest, innocent sort of fellow, and
he was a good scholar, too. Folks said he overstudied, and
that was the reason he took crazy the year after Luella
married, but I don't know. And I don't know what made
Erastus Miller go into consumption of the blood the year after
he was married: consumption wa'n't in his family. He just
grew weaker and weaker, and went almost bent double when
he tried to wait on Luella, and he spoke feeble, like an old
man. He worked terrible hard till the last trying to save up a
little to leave Luella. I've seen him out in the worst storms on
a wood-sled—he used to cut and sell wood—and he was
hunched up on top lookin' more dead than alive. Once I
couldn't stand it: I went over and helped him pitch some
wood on the cart—I was always strong in my arms. I wouldn't
stop for all he told me to, and I guess he was glad enough for
the help. That was only a week before he died. He fell on the
kitchen floor while he was gettin' breakfast. He always got
the breakfast and let Luella lay abed. He did all the sweepin'
and the washin' and the ironin' and most of the cookin'. He
couldn't bear to have Luella lift her finger, and she let him
do for her. She lived like a queen for all the work she did.
She didn't even do her sewin'. She said it made her shoulder
ache to sew, and poor Erastus's sister Lily used to do all her
sewin'. She wa'n't able to, either; she was never strong in
her back, but she did it beautifully. She had to, to suit
Luella, she was so dreadful particular. I never saw anythin'
like the fagottin' and hemstitchin' that Lily Miller did for
Luella. She made all Luella's weddin' outfit, and that green
silk dress, after Maria Babbit cut it. Maria she cut it for
nothin', and she did a lot more cuttin' and fittin' for nothin'
for Luella, too. Lily Miller went to live with Luella after
Erastus died. She gave up her home, though she was real

attached to it and wa'n't a mite afraid to stay alone. She rented it and she went to live with Luella right away after the funeral.''

Then this old woman, Lydia Anderson, who remembered Luella Miller, would go on to relate the story of Lily Miller. It seemed that on the removal of Lily Miller to the house of her dead brother, to live with his widow, the village people began to talk. This Lily Miller had been hardly past her first youth, and a most robust and blooming woman, rosy-cheeked, with curls of strong, black hair overshadowing round, candid temples and bright dark eyes. It was not six months after she had taken up her residence with her sister-in-law that her rosy color faded and her pretty curves became wan hollows. White shadows began to show in the black rings of her hair, and the light died out of her eyes, her features sharpened, and there were pathetic lines at her mouth, which yet wore always an expression of utter sweetness and even happiness. She was devoted to her sister; there was no doubt that she loved her with her whole heart, and was perfectly content in her service. It was her sole anxiety lest she should die and leave her alone.

"The way Lily Miller used to talk about Luella was enough to make you mad and enough to make you cry," said Lydia Anderson. "I've been in there sometimes toward the last when she was too feeble to cook and carried her some blanc-mange or custard—somethin' I thought she might relish, and she'd thank me, and when I asked her how she was, say she felt better than she did yesterday, and asked me if I didn't think she looked better, dreadful pitiful, and say poor Luella had an awful time takin' care of her and doin' the work—she wa'n't strong enough to do anything'—when all the time Luella wa'n't liftin' her finger and poor Lily didn't get any care except what the neighbors gave her, and Luella eat up everythin' that was carried in for Lily. I had it real straight that she did. Luella used to just sit and cry and do nothin'. She did act real fond of Lily, and she pined away

considerable, too. There was those that thought she'd go into
a decline herself. But after Lily died, her Aunt Abby Mixter
came, and then Luella picked up and grew as fat and rosy as
ever. But poor Aunt Abby began to droop just the way Lily
had, and I guess somebody wrote to her married daughter,
Mrs. Sam Abbot, who lived in Barre, for she wrote her
mother that she must leave right away and come and make a
visit, but Aunt Abby wouldn't go. I can see her now. She
was a real good-lookin' woman, tall and large, with a big,
square face and a high forehead that looked of itself kind of
benevolent and good. She just tended out on Luella as if she
had been a baby, and when her married daughter sent for her
she wouldn't stir one inch. She'd always thought a lot of her
daughter, too, but she said Luella needed her and her daughter didn't. Her daughter kept writin' and writin', but it didn't
do any good. Finally she came, and when she saw how bad
her mother looked, she broke down and cried and all but
went on her knees to have her come away. She spoke her
mind out to Luella, too. She told her that she'd killed her
husband and everybody that had anythin' to do with her, and
she'd thank her to leave her mother alone. Luella went into
hysterics, and Aunt Abby was so frightened that she called
me after her daughter went. Mrs. Sam Abbot she went away
fairly cryin' out loud in the buggy, the neighbors heard her,
and well she might, for she never saw her mother again live.
I went in that night when Aunt Abby called for me, standin'
in the door with her little green-checked shawl over her head.
I can see her now. "Do come over here, Miss Anderson,"
she sung out, kind of gasping for breath. I didn't stop for
anythin'. I put over as fast as I could, and when I got there,
there was Luella laughin' and cryin' all together, and Aunt
Abby trying to hush her, and all the time she herself was
white as a sheet and shakin' so she could hardly stand. "For
the land sakes, Mrs. Mixter," says I, "You look worse than
she does. You ain't fit to be out of your bed."

" 'Oh, there ain't anythin' the matter with me,' says

she. Then she went on talkin' to Luella. 'There, there, don't, don't, poor little lamb,' she says. 'Aunt Abby is here. She ain't goin' away and leave you. Don't, poor little lamb.' ''

" 'Do leave her with me, Mrs. Mixter, and you get back to bed,' says I, for Aunt Abby had been layin' down considerable lately, though somehow she contrived to do the work.

" 'I'm well enough,' says she. 'Don't you think she had better have the doctor, Miss Anderson?' ''

" 'The doctor,' says I, 'I think *you* had better have the doctor. I think you need him much worse than some folks I could mention.' And I looked right straight at Luella Miller laughin' and cryin' and goin' on as if she was the center of all creation. All the time she was actin' so—seemed as if she was too sick to sense anythin'—she was keeping a sharp outlook to see how we took it out of the corner of one eye. I see her. You could never cheat me about Luella Miller. Finally I got real mad and I run home and I got a bottle of valerian I had, and I poured some boilin' hot water on a handful of catnip, and I mixed up that catnip tea with most half a wineglass of valerian, and I went with it over to Luella's. I marched right up to Luella, a-holdin' out that cup, all smokin'. 'Now,' says I, 'Luella Miller, *you swaller this!*'

" 'What is—what is it, oh, what is it?' she sort of screeches out. Then she goes off a-laughin' enough to kill.

" 'Poor lamb, poor little lamb,' says Aunt Abby standin' over her, all kind of tottery, and tryin' to bathe her head with camphor.

" '*You swaller this right down,*' says I. And I didn't waste any ceremony. I just took hold of Luella Miller's chin and I tipped her head back, and I caught her mouth open with laughin', and I clapped that cup to her lips, and I fairly hollered at her: 'Swaller, swaller, swaller!' and she gulped it right down. She had to, and I guess it did her good. Anyhow, she stopped cryin' and laughin' and let me put her to bed, and she went to sleep like a baby inside of half an hour. That was more than poor Aunt Abby did. She lay awake all that night and I stayed with her, though she tried not to have me; said she wa'n't sick enough for watchers. But I stayed, and I made some good cornmeal gruel and I fed her a teaspoon every little while all night long. It seemed to me as if she was jest dyin' from bein' all wore out. In the morning as soon as it was light I run over to the Bisbees and sent Johnny Bisbee for the doctor. I told him to tell the doctor to hurry, and he come pretty quick. Poor Aunt Abby didn't seem to know much of anythin' when he got there. You couldn't hardly tell she breathed, she was so used up. When the doctor had gone, Luella came into the room lookin' like a baby in her ruffled nightgown. I can see her now. Her eyes were as blue and her face all pink and white like a blossom, and she looked at Aunt Abby in the bed sort of innocent and surprised. 'Why,' says she, 'Aunt Abby ain't got up yet?'

" 'No, she ain't,' says I, pretty short.

" 'I thought I didn't smell the coffee,' says Luella.

" 'Coffee,' says I. 'I guess if you have coffee this mornin' you'll make it yourself.'

" 'I never made the coffee in all my life,' says she, dreadful astonished. 'Erastus always made the coffee as long as he lived, and then Lily she made it, and then Aunt Abby made it. I don't believe I *can* make the coffee, Miss Anderson.'

" 'You can make it or go without, jest as you please,' says I.

" 'Ain't Aunt Abby goin' to get up?' says she.

" 'I guess she won't get up,' says I, 'sick as she is.' I was gettin' madder and madder. There was somethin' about that little pink-and-white thing standin' there and talkin' about coffee, when she had killed so many better folks than she was, and had jest killed another, that made me feel 'most as if I wished somebody would up and kill her before she had a chance to do any more harm.

" 'Is Aunt Abby sick?' says Luella, as if she was sort of aggrieved and injured.

" 'Yes,' says I, 'she's sick, and she's goin' to die, and

then you'll be left alone, and you'll have to do for yourself
and wait on yourself, or do without things.' I don't know but
I was sort of hard, but it was the truth, and if I was any
harder than Luella Miller had been I'll give up. I ain't
never been sorry that I said it. Well, Luella, she up and
had hysterics again at that, and I just let her have 'em.
All I did was to bundle her into the room on the other
side of the entry where Aunt Abby couldn't hear her, if
she wa'n't past it—I don't know but she was—and set her
down hard in a chair and told her not to come back into
the other room, and she minded. She had her hysterics
in there till she got tired. When she found out that nobody
was comin' to coddle her and do for her she stopped. At
least I suppose she did. I had all I could do with poor
Aunt Abby tryin' to keep the breath of life in her. The
doctor had told me that she was dreadful low, and give
me some very strong medicine to give to her in drops real
often, and told me real particular about the nourishment.
Well, I did as he told me real faithful till she wa'n't able to
swaller any longer. Then I had her daughter sent for. I had
begun to realize that she wouldn't last any time at all. I
hadn't realized it before, though I spoke to Luella the way
I did. The doctor he came, and Mrs. Sam Abbot, but when
she got there it was too late; her mother was dead. Aunt
Abby's daughter just give one look at her mother layin'
there, then she turned sort of sharp and sudden and looked
at me.

" 'Where is she?' says she, and I knew she meant Luella.

" 'She's out in the kitchen,' says I. 'She's too nervous to
see folks die. She's afraid it will make her sick.'

"The Doctor he speaks up then. He was a young man. Old
Doctor Park had died the year before, and this was a young
fellow just out of college. 'Mrs. Miller is not strong,' says
he, kind of severe, 'and she is quite right in not agitating
herself.'

" 'You are another, young man; she's got her pretty claw on you,' thinks I, but I didn't say anythin' to him. I just said over to Mrs. Sam Abbott that Luella was in the kitchen, and Mrs. Sam Abbot she went out there, and I went, too, and I never heard anythin' like the way she talked to Luella Miller. I felt pretty hard to Luella myself, but this was more than I ever would have dared to say. Luella she was too scared to go into hysterics. She jest flopped. She seemed to jest shrink away to nothin' in that kitchen chair, with Mrs. Sam Abbot standin' over her and talkin' and tellin' her the truth. I guess the truth was too much for her and no mistake, because Luella presently actually did faint away, and there wa'n't any sham about it, the way I always suspected there was about them hysterics. She fainted dead away and we had to lay her flat on the floor, and the Doctor he came runnin' out and he said somethin' about a weak heart dreadful fierce to Mrs. Sam Abbot, but she wa'n't a mite scared. She faced him jest as white as even Luella was layin' there lookin' like death and the Doctor feelin' of her pulse.

" 'Weak heart,' says she, 'weak heart; weak fiddlesticks! There ain't nothin' weak about that woman. She's got strength enough to hang onto other folks till she kills 'em. Weak? It was my poor mother that was weak: this woman killed her as sure as if she had taken a knife to her.'

"But the Doctor he didn't pay much attention. He was bendin' over Luella layin' there with her yellow hair all streamin' and her pretty pink-and-white face all pale, and her blue eyes like stars gone out, and he was holdin' onto her hand and smoothin' her forehead, and tellin' me to get the brandy in Aunt Abby's room, and I was sure as I wanted to be that Luella had got somebody else to hang onto, now Aunt Abby was gone, and I thought of poor Erastus Miller, and I sort of pitied the poor young Doctor, led away by a pretty face, and I made up my mind I'd see what I could do.

"I waited till Aunt Abby had been dead and buried about a month, and the Doctor was goin' to see Luella steady and folks were beginnin' to talk; then one evenin', when I knew the Doctor had been called out of town and wouldn't be round, I went over to Luella's. I found her all dressed up in a blue muslin with white polka dots on it, and her hair curled jest as pretty, and there wa'n't a young girl in the place could compare with her. There was somethin' about Luella Miller seemed to draw the heart right out of *me*. She was settin' rocking in the chair by her sittin'-room window, and Maria Brown had gone home. Maria Brown had been in to help her, or rather to do the work, for Luella wa'n't helped when she didn't do anythin'. Maria Brown was real capable and she didn't have any ties; she wa'n't married, and lived alone, so she'd offered. I couldn't see why she should do the work any more than Luella; she wa'n't any too strong; but she seemed to think she could and Luella seemed to think so, too, so she went over and did all the work—washed, and ironed, and baked, while Luella sat and rocked. Marie didn't live long afterward. She began to fade away just the same fashion the others had. Well, she was warned, but she acted real mad when folks said anythin': said Luella was a poor, abused woman, too delicate to help herself, and they'd ought to be ashamed, and if she died helpin' them that couldn't help themselves she would—and she did.

" 'I s'pose Maria has gone home,' says I to Luella, when I had gone in and sat down opposite her.

" 'Yes, Maria went half an hour ago, after she had got supper and washed the dishes,' says Luella, in her pretty way.

" 'I suppose she has got a lot of work to do in her own house to-night,' says I, kind of bitter, but that was all thrown away on Luella Miller. It seemed to her right that other folks that wa'n't any better able than she was herself should wait on her, and she couldn't get it through her head that anybody could think it *wa'n't* right.

" 'Yes,' says Luella, real sweet and pretty, 'yes, she said

she had to do her washin' tonight. She has let it for a
fortnight along of comin' over here.'

" 'Why don't she stay home and do her washin' instead of
comin' over here and doin' *your* work, when you are just as
well able, and enough sight more so, than she is to do it?'
says I.

"Then Luella she looked at me like a baby who has a rattle
shook at it. She sort of laughed as innocent as you please.
'Oh, I can't do the work myself, Miss Anderson,' says she.
'I never did. Maria *has* to do it.'

"Then I spoke out: 'Has to do it!' says I. 'Has to do it!'
She don't have to do it, either. Maria Brown has her own
home and enough to live on. She ain't beholden to you to
come over here and slave for you and kill herself.'

"Luella she jest set and stared at me for all the world like
a doll-baby that was so abused that it was comin' to life.

" 'Yes,' says I, 'she's killin' herself. She's goin' to die
just the way Erastus did, and Lily, and your Aunt Abby.
You're killin' her jest as you did them. I don't know what
there is about you, but you seem to bring a curse,' says I.
'You kill everybody that is fool enough to care anythin'
about you and do for you.'

"She stared at me and she was pretty pale.

" 'And Maria ain't the only one you're goin' to kill,' says
I. 'You're goin' to kill Doctor Malcom before you're done
with him.'

"Then a red color came flamin' all over her face. 'I ain't
goin' to kill him, either,' says she, and she begun to cry.

" 'Yes, you *be!*' says I. Then I spoke as I had never spoke
before. You see, I felt it on account of Erastus. I told her that
she hadn't any business to think of another man after she'd
been married to one that had died for her: that she was a
dreadful woman; and she was, that's true, but sometimes I
have wondered lately if she knew it—if she wa'n't like a
baby with scissors in its hand cuttin' everybody without
knowin' what it was doin'.

"Luella she kept gettin' paler and paler, and she never took her eyes off my face. There was somethin' awful about the way she looked at me and never spoke one word. After awhile I quit talkin' and I went home. I watched that night, but her lamp went out before nine o'clock, and when Doctor Malcom came drivin' past and sort of slowed up he see there wa'n't any light and he drove along. I saw her sort of shy out of meetin' the next Sunday, too, so he shouldn't go home with her, and I begun to think maybe she did have some conscience after all. It was only a week after that that Maria Brown died—sort of sudden at the last, though everybody had seen it was comin'. Well, then there was a good deal of feelin' and pretty dark whispers. Folks said the days of witchcraft had come again, and they were pretty shy of Luella. She acted sort of offish to the Doctor and he didn't go there, and there wa'n't anybody to do anythin' for her. I don't know how she *did* get along. I wouldn't go in there and offer to help her—not because I was afraid of dyin' like the rest, but I thought she was just as well able to do her own work as I was to do it for her, and I thought it was about time that she did it and stopped killin' other folks. But it wa'n't very long before folks began to say that Luella herself was goin' into a decline jest the way her husband, and Lily, and Aunt Abby and the others had, and I saw myself that she looked pretty bad. I used to see her goin' past from the store with a bundle as if she could hardly crawl, but I remembered how Erastus used to wait and 'tend when he couldn't hardly put one foot before the other, and I didn't go out to help her.

"But at last one afternoon I saw the Doctor come drivin' up like mad with his medicine chest, and Mrs. Babbit came in after supper and said that Luella was real sick.

" 'I'd offer to go in and nurse her,' says she, 'but I've got my children to consider, and maybe it ain't true what they say, but it's queer how many folks that have done for her have died.'

"I didn't say anythin', but I considered how she had been

Erastus's wife and how he had set his eyes by her, and I
made up my mind to go in the next mornin', unless she was
better, and see what I could do; but the next mornin' I see her
at the window, and pretty soon she came steppin' out as spry
as you please, and a little while afterward Mrs. Babbit came
in and told me that the Doctor had got a girl from out of
town, a Sarah Jones, to come there, and she said she was
pretty sure that the Doctor was goin' to marry Luella.

"I saw him kiss her in the door that night myself, and I
knew it was true. The woman came that afternoon, and the
way she flew around was a caution. I don't believe Luella
had swept since Maria died. She swept and dusted, and
washed and ironed; wet clothes and dusters and carpets were
flyin' over there all day, and every time Luella set her foot
out when the Doctor wa'n't there there was that Sarah Jones
helpin' of her up and down the steps, as if she hadn't learned
to walk.

"Well, everybody knew that Luella and the Doctor were
goin' to be married, but it wa'n't long before they began to
talk about his lookin' so poorly, just as they had about the
others; and they talked about Sarah Jones, too.

"Well, the Doctor did die, and he wanted to be married
first, so as to leave what little he had to Luella, but he died
before the minister could get there, and Sarah Jones died a
week afterward.

"Well, that wound up everything for Luella Miller. Not
another soul in the whole town would lift a finger for her.
There got to be a sort of panic. Then she began to droop in
good earnest. She used to have to go to the store herself, for
Mrs. Babbit was afraid to let Tommy go for her, and I've
seen her goin' past and stoppin' every two or three steps to
rest. Well, I stood it as long as I could, but one day I see her
comin' with her arms full and stoppin' to lean against the
Babbit fence, and I run out and took her bundles and carried
them to her house. Then I went home and never spoke one
word to her though she called after me dreadful kind of

pitiful. Well, that night I was taken sick with a chill, and I was sick as I wanted to be for two weeks. Mrs. Babbit had seen me run out to help Luella and she came in and told me I was goin' to die on account of it. I didn't know whether I was or not, but I considered I had done right by Erastus's wife.

"That last two weeks Luella she had a dreadful hard time, I guess. She was pretty sick, and as near as I could make out nobody dared go near her. I don't know as she was really needin' anythin' very much, for there was enough to eat in her house and it was warm weather, and she made out to cook a little flour gruel every day, I know, but I guess she had a hard time, she that had been so petted and done for all her life.

"When I got so I could go out, I went over there one morning. Mrs. Babbit had just come in to say she hadn't seen any smoke and she didn't know but it was somebody's duty to go in, but she couldn't help thinkin' of her children, and I got right up, though I hadn't been out of the house for two weeks, and I went in there, and Luella she was layin' on the bed, and she was dyin'.

"She lasted all that day and into the night. But I sat there after the new doctor had gone away. Nobody else dared to go there. It was about midnight that I left her for a minute to run home and get some medicine I had been takin', for I begun to feel rather bad.

"It was a full moon that night, and just as I started out of my door to cross the street back to Luella's, I stopped short, for I saw something."

Lydia Anderson at this juncture always said with a certain defiance that she did not expect to be believed, and then proceeded in a hushed voice:

"I saw what I saw, and I know I saw it, and I will swear on my death bed that I saw it. I saw Luella Miller and Erastus Miller, and Lily, and Aunt Abby, and Maria, and the Doctor, and Sarah, all goin' out of her door, and all but

Luella shone white in the moonlight, and they were all helpin' her along till she seemed to fairly fly in the midst of them. Then it all disappeared. I stood a minute with my heart poundin', then I went over there. I thought of goin' for Mrs. Babbit, but I thought she'd be afraid. So I went alone, though I knew what had happened. Luella was layin' real peaceful, dead on her bed.''

This was the story that the old woman, Lydia Anderson, told, but the sequel was told by the people who survived her, and this is the tale which has become folklore in the village.

Lydia Anderson died when she was eighty-seven. She had continued wonderfully hale and hearty for one of her years until about two weeks before her death.

One bright moonlit evening she was sitting beside a window in her parlor when she made a sudden exclamation, and was out of the house and across the street before the neighbor who was taking care of her could stop her. She followed as fast as possible and found Lydia Anderson stretched on the ground before the door of Luella Miller's deserted house, and she was quite dead.

The next night there was a red gleam of fire athwart the moonlight and the old house of Luella Miller was burned to the ground. Nothing is now left of it except a few old cellar stones and a lilac bush, and in summer a helpless trail of morning glories among the weeds, which might be considered emblematic of Luella herself.

THE GHOSTLY RENTAL

Henry James

I was in my twenty-second year, and I had just left college. I was at liberty to choose my career, and I chose it with much promptness. I afterward renounced it, in truth, with equal ardor, but I have never regretted those two youthful years of perplexed and excited, but also of agreeable and fruitful experiment. I had a taste for theology, and during my college term I had been an admiring reader of Dr. Channing. This was theology of a grateful and succulent savor; it seemed to offer one the rose of faith delightfully stripped of its thorns. And then (for I rather think this had something to do with it), I had taken a fancy to the old Divinity School. I have always had an eye to the back scene in the human drama, and it seemed to me that I might play my part with a fair chance of applause (from myself at least), in that detached and tranquil home of mild casuistry, with its respectable avenue on one side, and its prospect of green fields and contact with acres of woodland on the other. Cambridge, for the lovers of woods and fields, has changed for the worse since those days, and the precinct in question has forfeited much of its mingled pastoral and scholastic quietude. It was then a College-hall in the woods—a charming mixture. What it is now has nothing to do with my story; and I have no doubt that there are still doctrine-haunted young seniors who, as they stroll near it in the summer dusk, promise themselves, later, to taste of its fine leisurely quality. For myself, I was not disappointed. I established myself in a great square, low-browed room, with deep window-benches; I hung prints from Overbeck and Ary Scheffer on the walls; I arranged my books, with great refinement of classification, in the alcoves beside the high chimney-shelf, and I began to read Plotinus and St. Augustine. Among my companions were two or three men of ability and of good fellowship, with whom I occasionally brewed a fireside bowl; and with adventurous reading, deep discourse, potations conscientiously shallow, and long country walks, my initiation into the clerical mystery progressed agreeably enough.

With one of my comrades I formed an especial friendship, and we passed a great deal of time together. Unfortunately he had a chronic weakness of one of his knees, which compelled him to lead a very sedentary life, and as I was a methodical pedestrian, this made some difference in our habits. I used often to stretch away for my daily ramble, with no companion but the stick in my hand or the book in my pocket. But in the use of my legs and the sense of unstinted open air, I have always found company enough. I should, perhaps, add that in the enjoyment of a very sharp pair of eyes, I found something of a social pleasure. My eyes and I were on excellent terms; they were indefatigable observers of all wayside incidents, and so long as they were amused I was contented. It is, indeed, owing to their inquisitive habits that I came into possession of this remarkable story. Much of the country about the old College town is pretty now, but it was prettier thirty years ago. That multitudinous eruption of domiciliary pasteboard which now graces the landscape, in the direction of the low, blue Waltham Hills, had not yet taken place; there were no genteel cottages to put the shabby meadows and scrubby orchards to shame—a juxtaposition by which, in later years, neither element of the contrast has gained. Cer-

tain crooked cross-roads then, as I remember them, were
more deeply and naturally rural, and the solitary dwellings on
the long grassy slopes beside them, under the tall, customary
elm that curved its foliage in mid-air like the outward dropping ears of a girdled wheat-sheaf, sat with their shingled
hoods well pulled down on their ears, and no prescience
whatever of the fashion of French roofs—weather-wrinkled
old peasant women, as you might call them, quietly wearing
the native coif, and never dreaming of mounting bonnets, and
indecently exposing their venerable brows. That winter was
what is called an "open" one; there was much cold, but little
snow; the roads were firm and free, and I was rarely compelled by the weather to forego my exercise. One gray December afternoon I had sought it in the direction of the
adjacent town of Medford, and I was retracing my steps at an
even pace, and watching the pale, cold tints—the transparent
amber and faded rose-color—which curtained, in wintry fashion, the western sky, and reminded me of a sceptical smile
on the lips of a beautiful woman. I came, as dusk was
falling, to a narrow road which I had never traversed and
which I imagined offered me a short cut homeward. I was
about three miles away; I was late, and would have been
thankful to make them two. I diverged, walked some ten
minutes, and then perceived that the road had a very unfre-
quented air. The wheel-ruts looked old; the stillness seemed
peculiarly sensible. And yet down the road stood a house, so
that it must in some degree have been a thoroughfare. On
one side was a high, natural embankment, on the top of
which was perched an apple-orchard, whose tangled boughs
made a stretch of coarse black lace-work, hung across the
coldly rosy west. In a short time I came to the house, and I
immediately found myself interested in it. I stopped in front
of it gazing hard, I hardly knew why, but with a vague
mixture of curiosity and timidity. It was a house like most of
the houses thereabouts, except that it was decidedly a handsome specimen of its class. It stood on a grassy slope, it had

its tall, impartially drooping elm beside it, and its old black
well-cover at its shoulder. But it was of very large proportions, and it had a striking look of solidity and stoutness of
timber. It had lived to a good old age, too, for the woodwork on its door-way and under its eaves, carefully and
abundantly carved, referred it to the middle, at the latest, of
the last century. All this had once been painted white, but the
broad back of time, leaning against the door-posts for a
hundred years, had laid bare the grain of the wood. Behind
the house stretched an orchard of apple-trees, more gnarled
and fantastic than usual, and wearing, in the deepening dusk,
a blighted and exhausted aspect. All the windows of the
house had rusty shutters, without slats, and these were closely
drawn. There was no sign of life about it; it looked blank,
bare and vacant, and yet, as I lingered near it, it seemed to
have a familiar meaning—an audible eloquence. I have always thought of the impression made upon me at first sight,
by that gray colonial dwelling, as a proof that induction may
sometimes be near akin to divination; for after all, there was
nothing on the face of the matter to warrant the very serious
induction that I made. I fell back and crossed the road. The
last red light of the sunset disengaged itself, as it was about
to vanish, and rested faintly for a moment on the time-
silvered front of the old house. It touched, with perfect
regularity, the series of small panes in the fan-shaped window above the door, and twinkled there fantastically. Then it
died away, and left the place more intensely somber. At this
moment, I said to myself with the accent of profound
conviction—"The house is simply haunted!"

Somehow, immediately, I believed it, and so long as I was
not shut up inside, the idea gave me pleasure. It was implied
in the aspect of the house, and it explained it. Half an hour
before, if I had been asked, I would have said, as befitted a
young man who was explicitly cultivating cheerful views of
the supernatural, that there were no such things as haunted

houses. But the dwelling before me gave a vivid meaning to
the empty words; it had been spiritually blighted.

The longer I looked at it, the intenser seemed the secret
that it held. I walked all round it, I tried to peep here and
there, through a crevice in the shutters, and I took a puerile
satisfaction in laying my hand on the door-knob and gently
turning it. If the door had yielded, would I have gone in?
—would I have penetrated the dusky stillness? My audacity,
fortunately, was not put to test. The portal was admirably
solid, and I was unable even to shake it. At last I turned
away, casting many looks behind me. I pursued my way,
and, after a longer walk than I had bargained for, reached the
high-road. At a certain distance below the point at which the
long lane I have mentioned entered it, stood a comfortable,
tidy dwelling, which might have offered itself as the model
of the house which is in no sense haunted—which has no
sinister secrets, and knows nothing but blooming prosperity.
Its clean white paint stared placidly through the dusk, and its
vine-covered porch had been dressed in straw for the winter.
An old, one-horse chaise, freighted with two departing visitors, was leaving the door, and through the undraped windows, I saw the lamp-lit sitting-room, and the table spread
with the early ''tea,'' which had been improvised for the
comfort of the guests. The mistress of the house had come to
the gate with her friends; she lingered there after the chaise
had wheeled creakingly away, half to watch them down the
road, and half to give me, as I passed in the twilight, a
questioning look. She was a comely, quick young woman,
with a sharp, dark eye, and I ventured to stop and speak to
her.

''That house down that side-road,'' I said, ''about a mile
from here—the only one—can you tell me whom it belongs
to?''

She stared at me a moment, and, I thought, colored a little.
''Our folks never go down that road,'' she said, briefly.

''But it's a short way to Medford,'' I answered.

She gave a little toss of her head. "Perhaps it would turn out a long way. At any rate, we don't use it."

This was interesting. A thrifty Yankee household must have good reasons for this scorn of time-saving processes. "But you know the house, at least?" I said.

"Well, I have seen it."

"And to whom does it belong?"

She gave a little laugh and looked away, as if she were aware that, to a stranger, her words might seem to savor of agricultural superstition. "I guess it belongs to them that are in it."

"But is there any one in it? It is completely closed."

"That makes no difference. They never come out, and no one ever goes in." And she turned away.

But I laid my hand on her arm, respectfully. "You mean," I said, "that the house is haunted?"

She drew herself away, colored, raised her finger to her lips, and hurried into the house, where, in a moment, the curtains were dropped over the windows.

For several days, I thought repeatedly of this little adventure, but I took some satisfaction in keeping it to myself. If the house was not haunted, it was useless to expose my imaginative whims, and if it was, it was agreeable to drain the cup of horror without assistance. I determined, of course, to pass that way again; and a week later—it was the last day of the year—I retraced my steps. I approached the house from the opposite direction, and found myself before it at about the same hour as before. The light was failing, the sky low and gray; the wind wailed along the hard, bare ground, and made slow eddies of the frost-blackened leaves. The melancholy mansion stood there, seeming to gather the winter twilight around it, and mask itself in it, inscrutably. I hardly knew on what errand I had come, but I had a vague feeling that if this time the door-knob were to turn and the door to open, I should take my heart in my hands, and let them close behind me. Who were the mysterious tenants to

whom the good woman at the corner had alluded? What had
been seen or heard—what was related? The door was as
stubborn as before, and my impertinent fumblings with the
latch caused no upper window to be thrown open, nor any
strange, pale face to be thrust out. I ventured even to raise
the rusty knocker and give it half-a-dozen raps, but they
made a flat, dead sound, and aroused no echo. Familiarity
breeds contempt; I don't know what I should have done next,
if, in the distance up the road (the same one I had followed),
I had not seen a solitary figure advancing. I was unwilling to
be observed hanging about this ill-famed dwelling, and I sought
refuge among the dense shadows of a grove of pines near by,
where I might peep forth, and yet remain invisible. Presently,
the new-comer drew near, and I perceived that he was making straight for the house. He was a little old man, the most
striking feature of whose appearance was a voluminous cloak,
of a sort of military cut. He carried a walking-stick, and
advanced in a slow, painful, somewhat hobbling fashion, but
with an air of extreme resolution. He turned off from the
road, and followed the vague wheel-track, and within a few
yards of the house he paused. He looked up at it, fixedly and
searchingly, as if he were counting the windows, or noting
certain familiar marks. Then he took off his hat, and bent
over slowly and solemnly, as if he were performing an
obeisance. As he stood uncovered, I had a good look at him.
He was, as I have said, a diminutive old man, but it would
have been hard to decide whether he belonged to this world
or to the other. His head reminded me, vaguely, of the
portraits of Andrew Jackson. He had a crop of grizzled hair,
as stiff as a brush, a lean, pale, smooth-shaven face, and an
eye of intense brilliancy, surmounted with thick brows, which
had remained perfectly black. His face, as well as his cloak,
seemed to belong to an old soldier; he looked like a retired
military man of a modest rank; but he struck me as exceeding
the classic privilege of even such a personage to be eccentric
and grotesque. When he had finished his salute, he advanced

to the door, fumbled in the folds of his cloak, which hung
down much further in front than behind, and produced a key.
This he slowly and carefully inserted into the lock, and then,
apparently, he turned it. But the door did not immediately
open; first he bent his head, turned his ear, and stood listening, and then he looked up and down the road. Satisfied or
re-assured, he applied his aged shoulder to one of the deep-
set panels, and pressed a moment. The door yielded—opening
into perfect darkness. He stopped again on the threshold, and
again removed his hat and made his bow. Then he went in,
and carefully closed the door behind him.

Who in the world was he, and what was his errand? He
might have been a figure out of one of Hoffmann's tales.
Was he vision or a reality—an inmate of the house, or a
familiar, friendly visitor? What had been the meaning, in
either case, of his mystic genuflexions, and how did he
propose to proceed, in that inner darkness. I emerged from
my retirement, and observed narrowly, several of the windows. In each of them, at an interval, a ray of light became
visible in the chink between the two leaves of the shutters.
Evidently, he was lighting up; was he going to give a party—a
ghostly revel? My curiosity grew intense, but I was quite at a
loss how to satisfy it. For a moment I thought of rapping
peremptorily at the door; but I dismissed this idea as unman-
nerly, and calculated to break the spell, if spell there was. I
walked round the house and tried, without violence, to open
one of the lower windows. It resisted, but I had better
fortune, in a moment, with another. There was a risk, certainly, in the trick I was playing—a risk of being seen from
within, or (worse) seeing, myself, something that I should
repent of seeing. But curiosity, as I say, had become an
inspiration, and the risk was highly agreeable. Through the
parting of the shutters I looked into a lighted room, a room
lighted by two candles in old brass flambeaux, placed upon
the mantel-shelf. It was apparently a sort of back parlor, and
it had retained all its furniture. This was of a homely, old-

fashioned pattern, and consisted of hair-cloth chairs and sofas, spare mahogany tables, and framed samplers hung upon the walls. But although the room was furnished, it had a strangely uninhabited look; the tables and chairs were in rigid positions, and no small, familiar objects were visible. I could not see everything, and I could only guess at the existence, on my right, of a large folding-door—the shadow, evidently, of a figure in the adjoining room. It was apparently open, and the light of the neighboring room passed through it. I waited for some time, but the room remained empty. At last I became conscious that a large shadow was projected upon the wall opposite the folding-door—the shadow, evidently, of a figure in the adjoining room. It was tall and grotesque, and seemed o represent a person sitting perfectly motionless, in profile. I thought I recognized the perpendicular bristles and far-arching nose of my little old man. There was a strange fixedness in his posture; he appeared to be seated, and looking intently at something. I watched the shadow a long time, but it never stirred. At last, however, just as my patience began to ebb, it moved slowly, rose to the ceiling, and became indistinct. I don't know what I should have seen next, but by an irresistible impulse, I closed the shutter. Was it delicacy?—was it pusillanimity? I can hardly say. I lingered, nevertheless, near the house, hoping that my friend would re-appear. I was not disappointed; for he at last emerged, looking just as when he had gone in, and taking his leave in the same ceremonious fashion. (The lights, I had already observed, had disappeared from the crevice of each of the windows.) He faced about before the door, took off his hat, and made an obsequious bow. As he turned away I had a hundred minds to speak to him, but I let him depart in peace. This, I may say, was pure delicacy;—you will answer, perhaps, that it came too late. It seemed to me that he had a right to resent my observation; though my own right to exercise it (if ghosts were in the question) struck me as equally positive. I continued to watch him as he hobbled softly down the bank, and along the lonely road. Then I musingly retreated in the opposite direction. I was tempted to follow him, at a distance, to see what became of him; but this, too, seemed indelicate; and I confess, moreover, that I felt the inclination to coquet a little, as it were, with my discovery—to pull apart the petals of the flower one by one.

I continued to smell the flower, from time to time, for its oddity of perfume had fascinated me. I passed by the house on the cross-road again, but never encountered the old man in the cloak, or any other wayfarer. It seemed to keep observers at a distance, and I was careful not to gossip about it: one inquirer, I said to myself, may edge his way into the secret, but there is no room for two. At the same time, of course, I would have been thankful for any chance side-light that might fall across the matter—though I could not well see whence it was to come. I hoped to meet the old man in the cloak elsewhere, but as the days passed by without his reappearing, I ceased to expect it. And yet I reflected that he probably lived in that neighborhood, inasmuch as he had made his pilgrimage to the vacant house on foot. If he had come from a distance, he would have been sure to arrive in some old deep-hooded gig with wheels—a vehicle as venerably grotesque as himself. One day I took a stroll in Mount Auburn cemetery—an institution at that period in its infancy, and full of a sylvan charm which it has now completely forfeited. It contained more maple and birch than willow and cypress, and the sleepers had ample elbow room. It was not a city of the dead, but at the most a village, and a meditative pedestrian might stroll there without too importunate reminder of the grotesque side of our claims to posthumous consideration. I had come out to enjoy the first foretaste of Spring— one of those mild days of late winter, when the torpid earth seems to draw the first long breath that marks the rupture of the spell of sleep. The sun was veiled in haze, and yet warm, and the frost was oozing from its deepest lurking-places. I had been treading for half an hour the winding ways of the cemetery, when suddenly I perceived a familiar figure seated

on a bench against a southward-facing evergreen hedge. I call
the figure familiar, because I had seen it often in memory and
in fancy; in fact, I had beheld it but once. Its back was turned
to me, but it wore a voluminous cloak, which there was no
mistaking. Here, at last, was my fellow-visitor at the haunted
house, and here was my chance, if I wished to approach him!
I made a circuit, and came toward him from in front. He saw
me, at the end of the alley, and sat motionless, with his
hands on the head of his stick, watching me from under his
black eyebrows as I drew near. At a distance these black
eyebrows looked formidable; they were the only thing I saw
in his face. But on a closer view I was re-assured, simply
because I immediately felt that no man could really be as
fantastically fierce as this poor old gentleman looked. His
face was a kind of caricature of martial truculence. I stopped
in front of him, and respectfully asked leave to sit and rest
upon his bench. He granted it with a silent gesture, of much
dignity, and I placed myself beside him. In this position I
was able, covertly, to observe him. He was quite as much an
oddity in the morning sunshine, as he had been in the dubious twilight. The lines in his face were as rigid as if they had
been hacked out of a block by a clumsy wood-carver. His
eyes were flamboyant, his nose terrific, his mouth implaca-
ble. And yet, after awhile, when he slowly turned and looked
at me, fixedly, I perceived that in spite of this portentous
mask, he was a very mild old man. I was sure he even would
have been glad to smile, but, evidently, his facial muscles
were too stiff—they had taken a different fold, once for all. I
wondered whether he was demented, but I dismissed the
idea; the fixed glitter in his eye was not that of insanity.
What his face really expressed was deep and simple sadness;
his heart perhaps was broken, but his brain was intact. His
dress was shabby but neat, and his old blue cloak had known
half a century's brushing.

I hastened to make some observation upon the exceptional
softness of the day, and he answered me in a gentle, mellow

voice, which it was almost startling to hear proceed from such bellicose lips.

"This is a very comfortable place," he presently added.

"I am fond of walking in graveyards," I rejoined deliberately; flattering myself that I had struck a vein that might lead to something.

I was encouraged; he turned and fixed me with his duskily glowing eyes. Then very gravely,—"Walking, yes. Take all your exercise now. Some day you will have to settle down in a graveyard in a fixed position."

"Very true," said I. "But you know there are some people who are said to take exercise even after that day."

He had been looking at me still; at this he looked away.

"You don't understand?" I said, gently.

He continued to gaze straight before him.

"Some people, you know, walk about after death," I went on.

At last he turned, and looked at me more portentously than ever. "You don't believe that," he said simply.

"How do you know I don't?"

"Because you are young and foolish." This was said without acerbity—even kindly; but in the tone of an old man whose consciousness of his own heavy experience made everything else seem light.

"I am certainly young," I answered; "but I don't think that, on the whole, I am foolish. But say I don't believe in ghosts—most people would be on my side."

"Most people are fools!" said the old man.

I let the question rest, and talked of other things. My companion seemed on his guard, he eyed me defiantly, and made brief answers to my remarks; but I nevertheless gathered an impression that our meeting was an agreeable thing to him, and even a social incident of some importance. He was evidently a lonely creature, and his opportunities for gossip were rare. He had had troubles, and they had detached him from the world, and driven him back upon himself; but the social chord in his antiquated soul was not entirely broken, and I was sure he was gratified to find that it could still feebly resound. At last, he began to ask questions himself; he inquired whether I was a student.

"I am a student of divinity," I answered.

"Of divinity?"

"Of theology. I am studying for the ministry."

At this he eyed me with peculiar intensity—after which his gaze wandered away again. "There are certain things you ought to know, then," he said at last.

"I have a great desire for knowledge," I answered. "What things do you mean?"

He looked at me again awhile, but without heeding my question.

"I like your appearance," he said. "You seem to me a sober lad."

"Oh, I am perfectly sober!" I exclaimed—yet departing for a moment from my soberness.

"I think you are fair-minded," he went on.

"I don't any longer strike you as foolish, then?" I asked.

"I stick to what I said about people who deny the power of departed spirits to return. They *are* fools!" And he rapped fiercely with his staff on the earth.

I hesitated a moment, and then, abruptly, "You have seen a ghost!" I said.

He appeared not at all startled.

"You are right, sir!" he answered with great dignity. "With me it's not a matter of cold theory—I have not had to pry into old books to learn what to believe. *I know!* With those eyes I have beheld the departed spirit standing before me as near as you are!" And his eyes, as he spoke, certainly looked as if they had rested upon strange things.

I was irresistibly impressed—I was touched with credulity.

"And was it very terrible?" I asked.

"I am an old soldier—I am not afraid!"

"What was it?—where was it?" I asked.

He looked at me mistrustfully, and I saw that I was going too fast.

"Excuse me from going into particulars," he said. "I am not at liberty to speak more fully. I have told you so much, because I cannot bear to hear this subject spoken of lightly. Remember in future, that you have seen a very honest old man who told you—on his honor—that he had seen a ghost!" And he got up, as if he thought he had said enough. Reserve, shyness, pride, the fear of being laughed at, the memory, possibly, of former strokes of sarcasm—all this, on one side, had its weight with him; but I suspected that on the other, his tongue was loosened by the garrulity of old age, the sense of solitude, and the need of sympathy—and perhaps, also, by the friendliness which he had been so good as to express toward myself. Evidently it would be unwise to press him, but I hoped to see him again.

"To give greater weight to my words," he added, "let me mention my name—Captain Diamond, sir. I have seen service."

"I hope I may have the pleasure of meeting you again," I said.

"The same to you, sir!" And brandishing his stick portentously—though with the friendliest intentions—he marched stiffly away.

I asked two or three persons—selected with discretion—whether they knew anything about Captain Diamond, but they were quite unable to enlighten me. At last, suddenly, I smote my forehead, and, dubbing myself a dolt, remembered that I was neglecting a source of information to which I had never applied in vain. The excellent person at whose table I habitually dined, and who dispensed hospitality to students at so much a week, had a sister as good as herself, and of conversational powers more varied. This sister, who was known as Miss Deborah, was an old maid in all the force of the term. She was deformed; and she never went out of the house; she sat all day at the window, between a bird-cage and

a flower-pot, stitching small linen articles—mysterious bands
and frills. She wielded, I was assured, an exquisite needle,
and her work was highly prized. In spite of her deformity and
her confinement, she had a little, fresh, round face, and an
imperturbable serenity of spirit. She had also a very quick
little wit of her own, she was extremely observant, and she
had a high relish for a friendly chat. Nothing pleased her so
much as to have you—especially, I think, if you were a
young divinity student—move your chair near her sunny
window, and settle yourself for twenty minutes' "talk."
"Well, sir," she used always to say, "what is the latest
monstrosity in Biblical criticism?"—for she used to pretend
to be horrified at the rationalistic tendency of the age. But
she was an inexorable little philosopher, and I am convinced
that she was a keener rationalist than any of us, and that, if
she had chosen, she could have propounded questions that
would have made the boldest of us wince. Her window
commanded the whole town—or rather, the whole country.
Knowledge came to her as she sat singing, with her little,
cracked voice, in her low rocking-chair. She was the first to
learn everything, and the last to forget it. She had the town
gossip at her fingers' ends, and she knew everything about
people she had never seen. When I asked her how she had
acquired her learning, she said simply—"Oh, I observe!"
"Observe closely enough," she once said, "and it doesn't
matter where you are. You may be in a pitch-dark closet. All
you want is something to start with; one thing leads to
another, and all things are mixed up. Shut me up in a dark
closet and I will observe after a while, that some places in it
are darker than others. After that (give me time), and I will
tell you what the President of the United States is going to
have for dinner." Once I paid her a compliment. "Your
observation," I said, "is as fine as your needle, and your
statements are true as your stitches."

Of course Miss Deborah had heard of Captain Diamond.

He had been much talked about many years before, but he had survived the scandal that attached to his name.

"What was the scandal?" I asked.

"He killed his daughter."

"Killed her?" I cried. "How so?"

"Oh, not with a pistol, or a dagger, or a dose of arsenic! With his tongue. Talk of women's tongues! He cursed her—with some horrible oath—and she died!"

"What had she done?"

"She had received a visit from a young man who loved her, and whom he had forbidden the house."

"The house," I said—"ah yes! The house is out in the country, two or three miles from here, on a lonely cross-road."

Miss Deborah looked sharply at me, as she bit her thread.

"Ah, you know about the house?" she said.

"A little," I answered; "I have seen it. But I want you to tell me more."

But here Miss Deborah betrayed an incommunicativeness which was most unusual.

"You wouldn't call me superstitious, would you?" she asked.

"You?—you are the quintessence of pure reason."

"Well, every thread has its rotten place, and every needle its grain of rust. I would rather not talk about that house."

"You have no idea how you excite my curiosity!" I said.

"I can feel for you. But it would make me very nervous."

"What harm can come to you?" I asked.

"Some harm came to a friend of mine." And Miss Deborah gave a very positive nod.

"What had your friend done?"

"She had told me Captain Diamond's secret, which he had told her with a mighty mystery. She had been an old flame of his, and he took her into his confidence. He bade her tell no one, and assured her that if she did, something dreadful would happen to her."

"And what happened to her?"

"She died."

"Oh, we are all mortal!" I said. "Had she given him a promise?"

"She had not taken it seriously, she had not believed him. She repeated the story to me, and three days afterward, she was taken with inflammation of the lungs. A month afterward, here where I sit now, I was stitching her grave-clothes. Since then, I have never mentioned what she told me."

"Was it very strange?"

"It was strange, but it was ridiculous too. It is a thing to make you shudder and to make you laugh, both. But you can't worry it out of me. I am sure that if I were to tell you, I should immediately break a needle in my finger, and die the next week of lock-jaw."

I retired, and urged Miss Deborah no further; but every two or three days, after dinner, I came and sat down by her rocking-chair. I made no further allusion to Captain Diamond; I sat silent, clipping tape with her scissors. At last, one day, she told me I was looking poorly. I was pale.

"I am dying of curiosity," I said. "I have lost my appetite. I have eaten no dinner."

"Remember Bluebeard's wife!" said Miss Deborah.

"One may as well perish by the sword as by famine!" I answered.

She still said nothing, and at last I rose with a melodramatic sigh and departed. As I reached the door she called me and pointed to the chair I had vacated. "I never was hard-hearted," she said. "Sit down, and if we are to perish, may we at least perish together." And then, in very few words, she communicated what she knew of Captain Diamond's secret. "He was a very high-tempered old man, and though he was very fond of his daughter, his will was law. He had picked out a husband for her, and given her due notice. Her mother was dead, and they lived alone together. The house had been Mrs Diamond's own marriage portion; the Captain, I believe, hadn't a penny. After his marriage

they had come to live there, and he had begun to work the
farm. The poor girl's lover was a young man with whiskers
from Boston. The Captain came in one evening and found
them together; he collared the young man, and hurled a
terrible curse at the poor girl. The young man cried that she
was his wife, and he asked her if it was true. She said, No!
Thereupon Captain Diamond, his fury growing fiercer, repeated his imprecation, ordered her out of the house, and
disowned her forever. She swooned away, but her father
went raging off and left her. Several hours later, he came
back and found the house empty. On the table was a note
from the young man telling him that he had killed his daughter, repeating the assurance that she was his own wife, and
declaring that he himself claimed the sole right to commit her
remains to earth. He had carried the body away in a gig!
Captain Diamond wrote him a dreadful note in answer, saying
that he didn't believe his daughter was dead, but that, whether
or not, she was dead to him. A week later, in the middle of
the night, he saw her ghost. Then, I suppose, he was convinced. The ghost reappeared several times, and finally began regularly to haunt the house. It made the old man very
uncomfortable, for little by little his passion had passed
away, and he was given up to grief. He determined at last to
leave the place, and tried to sell it or rent it; but meanwhile
the story had gone abroad, the ghost had been seen by other
persons, the house had a bad name, and it was impossible to
dispose of it. With the farm, it was the old man's only
property, and his only means of subsistence; if he could
neither live in it nor rent it he was beggared. But the ghost
had no mercy, as he had had none. He struggled for six
months, and at last he broke down. He put on his old blue
cloak and took up his staff, and prepared to wander away and
beg his bread. Then the ghost relented, and proposed a
compromise. 'Leave the house to me!' it said; 'I have marked
it for my own. Go off and live elsewhere. But to enable you
to live, I will be your tenant, since you can find no other. I

will hire the house of you and pay you a certain rent.' And
the ghost named a sum. The old man consented, and he goes
every quarter to collect his rent!''

I laughed at his recital, but I confess I shuddered too, for
my own observation had exactly confirmed it. Had I not been
witness of one of the Captain's quarterly visits, had I not all
but seen him sit watching his spectral tenant count out the
rent-money, and when he trudged away in the dark, had he
not a little bag of strangely gotten coin hidden in the folds of
his old blue cloak? I imparted none of these reflections to Miss
Deborah, for I was determined that my observations should
have a sequel, and I promised myself the pleasure of treating
her to my story in its full maturity. ''Captain Diamond,'' I
asked, ''has no other known means of subsistence?''

''None whatever. He toils not, neither does he spin—his
ghost supports him. A haunted house is valuable property!''

''And in what coin does the ghost pay?''

''In good American gold and silver. It has only this
peculiarity—that the pieces are all dated before the young
girl's death. It's a strange mixture of matter and spirit!''

''And does the ghost do things handsomely; is the rent
large?''

''The old man, I believe, lives decently, and has his pipe
and his glass. He took a little house down by the river; the
door is sidewise in the street, and there is a little garden
before it. There he spends his days, and has an old colored
woman to do for him. Some years ago, he used to wander
about a good deal, he was a familiar figure in the town, and
most people knew his legend. But of late he has drawn back
into his shell; he sits over his fire, and curiosity has forgotten
him. I suppose he is falling into his dotage. But I am sure, I
trust,'' said Miss Deobrah in conclusion, ''that he won't
outlive his faculties or his powers of locomotion, for, if I
remember rightly, it was part of the bargain that he should
come in person to collect his rent.''

We neither of us seemed likely to suffer any especial

penalty for Miss Deborah's indiscretion; I found her, day
after day, singing over her work, neither more nor less active
than usual. For myself, I boldly pursued my observations. I
went again, more than once, to the great graveyard, but I was
disappointed in my hope of finding Captain Diamond there. I
had a prospect, however, which afforded me compensation. I
shrewdly inferred that the old man's quarterly pilgrimages
were made upon the last day of the old quarter. My first sight
of him had been on the 31st of December, and it was
probable that he would return to his haunted home on the last
day of March. This was near at hand; at last it arrived. I
betook myself late in the afternoon to the old house on the
cross-road, supposing that the hour of twilight was the appointed season. I was not wrong. I had been hovering about
for a short time, feeling very much like a restless ghost
myself, when he appeared in the same manner as before, and
wearing the same costume. I again concealed myself, and
saw him enter the house with the ceremonial which he had
used on the former occasion. A light appeared successively in
the crevice of each pair of shutters, and I opened the window
which had yielded to my importunity before. Again I saw the
great shadow on the wall, motionless and solemn. But I saw
nothing else. The old man re-appeared at last, made his
fantastic salaam before the house, and crept away into the
dusk.

One day, more than a month after this, I met him again at
Mount Auburn. The air was full of the voice of Spring; the
birds had come back and were twittering over their Winter's
travels, and a mild west wind was making a thin murmur in
the raw verdure. He was seated on a bench in the sun, still
muffled in his enormous mantle, and he recognized me as
soon as I approached him. He nodded at me as if he were an
old Bashaw giving the signal for my decapitation, but it was
apparent that he was pleased to see me.

"I have looked for you here more than once," I said.
"You don't come often."

"What did you want of me?" he asked.

"I wanted to enjoy your conversation. I did so greatly when I met you here before."

"You found me amusing?"

"Interesting!" I said.

"You didn't think me cracked?"

"Cracked?—My dear sir—!" I protested.

"I'm the sanest man in the country. I know that is what insane people always say; but generally they can't prove it. I can!"

"I believe it," I said. "But I am curious to know how such a thing can be proved."

He was silent awhile.

"I will tell you. I once committed, unintentionally, a great crime. Now I pay the penalty. I give up my life to it. I don't shirk it; I face it squarely, knowing perfectly what it is. I haven't tried to bluff it off; I haven't begged off from it; I haven't run away from it. The penalty is terrible, but I have accepted it. I have been a philosopher!

"If I were a Catholic, I might have turned monk, and spent the rest of my life in fasting and praying. That is no penalty; that is an evasion. I might have blown my brains out—I might have gone mad. I wouldn't do either. I would simply face the music, take the consequences. As I say, they are awful! I take them on certain days, four times a year. So it has been these twenty years; so it will be as long as I last. It's my business; it's my avocation. That's the way I feel about it. I call that reasonable!"

"Admirably so!" I said. "But you fill me with curiosity and with compassion."

"Especially with curiosity," he said, cunningly.

"Why," I answered, "if I know exactly what you suffer I can pity you more."

"I'm much obliged. I don't want your pity; it won't help me. I'll tell you something, but it's not for myself; it's for your own sake." He paused a long time and looked all round him, as if for chance eavesdroppers. I anxiously awaited his revelation, but he disappointed me. "Are you still studying theology?" he asked.

"Oh, yes," I answered, perhaps with a shade of irritation. "It's a thing one can't learn in six months."

"I should think not, so long as you have nothing but your books. Do you know the proverb, 'A grain of experience is worth a pound of percept'? I'm a great theologian."

"Ah, you have had experience," I murmured sympathetically

"You have read about the immortality of the soul; you have seen Jonathan Edwards and Dr. Hopkins chopping logic over it, and deciding, by chapter and verse, that it is true. But I have seen it with these eyes; I have touched it with these hands!" And the old man held up his rugged old fists and shook them portentously. "That's better!" he went on; "but I have bought it dearly. You had better take it from the books—evidently you always will. You are a very good young man; you will never have a crime on your conscience."

I answered with some juvenile fatuity, that I certainly hoped I had my share of human passion, good young man and prospective Doctor of Divinity as I was.

"Ah, but you have a nice, quiet little temper," he said. "So have I—now! But once I was very brutal—very brutal. You ought to know that such things are. I killed my own child."

"Your own child?"

"I struck her down to earth and left her to die. They could not hang me, for it was not with my hand I struck her. It was with foul and damnable words. That makes a difference; it's a grand law we live under! Well, sir, I can answer for it that *her* soul is immortal. We have an appointment to meet four times a year, and then I catch it!"

"She has never forgiven you?"

"She has forgiven me as the angels forgive! That's what I can't stand—the soft, quiet way she looks at me. I'd rather she twisted a knife about in my heart—O Lord, Lord, Lord!"

and Captain Diamond bowed his head over his stick, and leaned his forehead on his crossed hands.

I was impressed and moved, and his attitude seemed for the moment a check to further questions. Before I ventured to ask him anything more, he slowly rose and pulled his old cloak around him. He was unused to talking about his troubles, and his memories overwhelmed him. "I must go my way," he said; "I must be creeping along."

"I shall perhaps meet you here again," I said.

"Oh, I'm a stiff-jointed old fellow," he answered, "and this is rather far for me to come. I have to reserve myself. I have sat sometimes a month at a time smoking my pipe in my chair. But I should like to see you again." And he stopped and looked at me, terribly and kindly. "Some day, perhaps, I shall be glad to be able to lay my hand on a young, unperverted soul. If a man can make a friend, it is always something gained. What is your name?"

I had in my pocket a small volume of Pascal's "Thoughts," on the fly-leaf of which were written my name and address. I took it out and offered it to my old friend. "Pray keep this little book," I said. "It is one I am very fond of, and it will tell you something about me."

He took it and turned it over slowly, then looked up at me with a scowl of gratitude, "I'm not much of a reader," he said; "but I won't refuse the first I present I shall have received since—my troubles; and the last. Thank you, sir!" And with the little book in his hand he took his departure.

I was left to imagine him for some weeks after that sitting solitary in his arm-chair with his pipe. I had not another glimpse of him. But I was awaiting my chance, and on the last day of June, another quarter having elapsed, I deemed that it had come. The evening dusk in June falls late, and I was impatient for its coming. At last, toward the end of a lovely summer's day, I revisited Captain Diamond's property. Everything now was green around it save the blighted orchard in its rear, but its own immitigable grayness and

sadness were as striking as when I had first beheld it beneath
a December sky. As I drew near it, I saw that I was late for
my purpose, for my purpose had simply been to step forward
on Captain Diamond's arrival, and bravely ask him to let me
go in with him. He had preceded me, and there were lights
already in the windows. I was unwilling, of course, to disturb
him during his ghostly interview, and I waited till he came
forth. The lights disappeared in the course of time; then the
door opened and Captain Diamond stole out. That evening he
made no bow to the haunted house, for the first object he
beheld was his fair-minded young friend planted, modestly
but firmly, near the door-step. He shopped short, looking at
me, and this time his terrible scowl was in keeping with the
situation.

"I knew you were here," I said. "I came on purpose."

He seemed dismayed, and he looked round at the house
uneasily.

"I beg your pardon if I have ventured too far," I added,
"but you know you have encouraged me."

"How did you know I was here?"

"I reasoned it out. You told me half your story, and I
guessed the other half. I am a great observer, and I had
noticed this house in passing. It seemed to me to have a
mystery. When you kindly confided to me that you saw
spirits, I was sure that it could only be here that you saw
them."

"You are mighty clever," cried the old man. "And what
brought you here this evening?"

I was obliged to evade this question.

"Oh, I often come; I like to look at the house—it fasci-
nates me."

He turned and looked up at it himself. "It's nothing to
look at outside." He was evidently quite unaware of its
peculiar outward appearance, and this odd fact, communicated to me thus in the twilight, and under the very brow of

the sinister dwelling, seemed to make his vision of the strange things within more real.

"I have been hoping," I said, "for a chance to see the inside. I thought I might find you here, and that you would let me go in with you. I should like to see what you see."

He seemed confounded by my boldness, but not altogether displeased. He laid his hand on my arm. "Do you know what I see?" he asked.

"How can I know, except as you said the other day, by experience? I want to have the experience. Pray, open the door and take me in."

Captain Diamond's brilliant eyes expanded beneath their dusky brows, and after holding his breath a moment, he indulged in the first and last apology for a laugh by which I was to see his solemn visage contorted. It was profoundly grotesque, but it was perfectly noiseless. "Take you in?" he softly growled. "I wouldn't go in again before my time's up for a thousand times that sum." And he thrust out his hand from the folds of his cloak and exhibited a small agglommeration of coin, knotted into the corner of an old silk pocket handkerchief. "I stick to my bargain no less, but no more!"

"But you told me the first time I had the pleasure of talking with you that it was not so terrible."

"I don't say it's terrible—now. But it's damned disagreeable!"

This adjective was uttered with a force that made me hesitate and reflect. While I did so, I thought I heard a slight movement of one of the window-shutters above us. I looked up, but everything seemed motionless. Captain Diamond, too, had been thinking; suddenly he turned toward the house. "If you will go in alone," he said, "you are welcome."

"Will you wait for me here?"

"Yes, you will not stop long."

"But the house is pitch dark. When you go you have lights."

He thrust his hand into the the depths of his cloak and

produced some matches. "Take these," he said. "You will find two candlesticks with candles on the table in the hall. Light them, take one in each hand and go ahead."

"Where shall I go?"

"Anywhere—everywhere. You can trust the ghost to find you."

I will not pretend to deny that by this time my heart was beating. And yet I imagine I motioned the old man with a sufficiently dignified gesture to open the door. I had made up my mind that there was in fact a ghost. I had conceded the premise. Only I had assured myself that once the mind was prepared, and the thing was not a surprise, it was possible to keep cool. Captain Diamond turned the lock, flung open the door, and bowed low to me as I passed in. I stood in the darkness, and heard the door close behind me. For some moments, I stirred neither finger nor toe; I stared bravely into the impenetrable dusk. But I saw nothing and heard nothing, and at last I struck a match. On the table were two old brass candlesticks rusty from disuse. I lighted the candles and began my tour of exploration.

A wide staircase rose in front of me, guarded by an antique balustrade of that rigidly delicate carving which is found so often in old New England houses. I postponed ascending it, and turned into the room on my right. This was an old-fashioned parlor, meagerly furnished, and musty with the absence of human life. I raised my two lights aloft and saw nothing but its empty chairs and its blank walls. Behind it was the room into which I had peeped from without, and which, in fact, communicated with it, as I had supposed, by folding doors. Here, too, I found myself confronted by no menacing specter. I crossed the hall again, and visited the rooms on the other side; a dining-room in front, where I might have written my name with my finger in the deep dust of the great square table; a kitchen behind with its pots and pans eternally cold. All this was hard and grim, but it was not formidable. I came back into the hall, and walked to the foot of the staircase,

holding up my candles; to ascend required a first effort, and I
was scanning the gloom above. Suddenly, with an inexpress-
ible sensation, I became aware that this gloom was animated;
it seemed to move and gather itself together. Slowly—I say
slowly, for to my tense expectancy the instants appeared
ages—it took the shape of a large, definite figure, and this
figure advanced and stood at the top of the stairs. I frankly
confess that by this time I was conscious of a feeling to
which I am in duty bound to apply the vulgar name of fear. I
may poetize it and call it Dread, with a capital letter; it was at
any rate the feeling that makes a man yield ground. I mea-
sured it as it grew, and it seemed perfectly irresistible; for it
did not appear to come from within but from without, and to
be embodied in the dark image at the head of the staircase.
After a fashion I reasoned—I remember reasoning. I said to
myself, "I had always thought ghosts were white and transparent; this is a thing of thick shadows, densely opaque." I
reminded myself that the occasion was momentous, and that
if fear were to overcome me I should gather all possible
impressions while my wits remained. I stepped back, foot
behind foot, with my eyes still on the figure and placed my
candles on the table. I was perfectly conscious that the proper
thing was to ascend the stairs resolutely, face to face with the
image, but the soles of my shoes seemed suddenly to have
been transformed into leaden weights. I had got what I
wanted; I was seeing the ghost. I tried to look at the figure
distinctly so that I could remember it, and fairly claim,
afterward, not to have lost my self-possession. I even asked
myself how long it was expected I should stand looking, and
how soon I could honorably retire. All this, of course, passed
through my mind with extreme rapidity, and it was checked
by a further movement on the part of the figure. Two white
hands appeared in the dark perpendicular mass, and were
slowly raised to what seemed to be the level of the head.
Here they were pressed together, over the region of the face,
and then they were removed, and the face was disclosed. It

was dim, white, strange, in every way ghostly. It looked
down at me for an instant, after which one of the hands was
raised again, slowly, and waved to and fro before it. There
was something very singular in this gesture; it seemed to
denote resentment and dismissal, and yet it had a sort of
trivial, familiar motion. Familiarity on the part of the haunting Presence had not entered into my calculations, and did
not strike me pleasantly. I agreed with Captain Diamond that
it was "damned disagreeable." I was pervaded by an intense
desire to make an orderly and, if possible, a graceful retreat.
I wished to do it gallantly, and it seemed to me that it would
be gallant to blow out my candles. I turned and did so,
punctiliously, and then I made my way to the door, groped
a moment and opened it. The outer light, almost extinct as it
was, entered for a moment, played over the dusty depths of
the house and showed me the solid shadow.

Standing on the grass, bent over his stick, under the early
glimmering stars, I found Captain Diamond. He looked up at
me fixedly for a moment, but asked no questions, and then
he went and locked the door. This duty performed, he dis-
charged the other—made his obeisance like the priest before
the altar—and then without heeding me further, took his
departure.

A few days later, I suspended my studies and went off for
the summer's vacation. I was absent for several weeks, during which time I had plenty of leisure to analyze my impressions of the supernatural. I took some satisfaction in the
reflection that I had not been ignobly terrified; I had not
bolted nor swooned—I had proceeded with dignity. Nevertheless, I was certainly more comfortable when I had put
thirty miles between me and the scene of my exploit, and I
continued for many days to prefer the daylight to the dark.
My nerves had been powerfully excited; of this I was particularly conscious when, under the influence of the drowsy air
of the sea-side, my excitement began slowly to ebb. As it
disappeared, I attempted to take a sternly rational view of

my experience. Certainly I had seen *something*—that was not fancy; but what had I seen? I regretted extremely now that I had not been bolder, that I had not gone nearer and inspected the apparition more minutely. But it was very well to talk; I had done as much as any man in the circumstances would have dared; it was indeed a physical impossibility that I should have advanced. Was not this paralyzation of my powers in itself a supernatural influence? Not necessarily, perhaps, for a sham ghost that one accepted might do as much execution as a real ghost. But why had I so easily accepted the sable phantom that waved its hand? Why had it so impressed itself? Unquestionably, true or false, it was a very clever phantom. I greatly preferred that it should have been true—in the first place I did not care to have shivered and shaken for nothing, and in the second place because to have seen a well-authenticated goblin is, as things go, a feather in a quiet man's cap. I tried, therefore, to let my vision rest and to stop turning it over. But an impulse stronger than my will recurred at intervals and set a mocking question on my lips. Granted that the apparition was Captain Diamond's daughter; if it was she it certainly was her spirit. But was it not her spirit and something more?

The middle of September saw me again established among the theologic shades, but I made no haste to revisit the haunted house.

The last of the month approached—the term of another quarter with poor Captain Diamond—and found me indisposed to disturb his pilgrimage on this occasion; though I confess that I thought with a good deal of compassion of the feeble old man trudging away, lonely, in the autumn dusk, on his extraordinary errand. On the thirtieth of September, at noonday, I was drowsing over a heavy octavo, when I heard a feeble rap at my door. I replied with an invitation to enter, but as this produced no effect I repaired to the door and opened it. Before me stood an elderly Negress with her head bound in a scarlet turban, and a white handkerchief folded across her bosom. She looked at me intently and in silence; she had that air of supreme gravity and decency which aged persons of her race so often wear. I stood interrogative, and at last, drawing her hand from her ample pocket, she held up a little book. It was the copy of Pascal's "Thoughts" that I had given to Captain Diamond.

"Please, sir," she said, very mildly, "do you know this book?"

"Perfectly," said I, "my name is on the fly-leaf."

"It is your name—no other?"

"I will write my name if you like, and you can compare them," I answered.

She was silent a moment and then, with dignity—"It would be useless, sir," she said, "I can't read. If you will give me your word that is enough. I come," she went on, "from the gentleman to whom you gave the book. He told me to carry it as a token—a token—that is what he called it. He is right down sick, and he wants to see you."

"Captain Diamond—sick?" I cried. "Is his illness serious?"

"He is very bad—he is all gone."

I expressed my regret and sympathy, and offered to go to him immediately, if his sable messenger would show me the way. She assented deferentially, and in a few moments I was following her along the sunny streets, feeling very much like a personage in the Arabian Nights, led to a postern gate by an Ethiopian slave. My own conductress directed her steps toward the river and stopped at a decent little yellow house in one of the streets that descend to it. She quickly opened the door and led me in, and I very soon found myself in the presence of my old friend. He was in bed, in a darkened room, and evidently in a very feeble state. He lay back on his pillow staring before him, with his bristling hair more erect than ever, and his intensely dark and bright old eyes touched with the glitter of fever. His apartment was humble and scrupulously neat, and I could see that my dusky guide was a faithful servant. Captain Diamond, lying there rigid and pale on his white sheets, resembled some ruggedly carven figure on the lid of a Gothic tomb. He looked at me silently, and my companion withdrew and left us alone.

"Yes, it's you," he said, at last, "it's you, that good young man. There is no mistake, is there?"

"I hope not; I believe I'm a good young man. But I am very sorry you are ill. What can I do for you?"

"I am very bad, very bad; my poor old bones ache so!" and, groaning portentously, he tried to turn toward me.

I questioned him about the nature of his malady and the length of time he had been in bed, but he barely heeded me; he seemed impatient to speak of something else. He grasped my sleeve, pulled me toward him, and whispered quickly:

"You know my time's up!"

"Oh, I trust not," I said, mistaking his meaning. "I shall certainly see you on your legs again."

"God knows!" he cried. "But I don't mean I'm dying; not yet a bit. What I mean is, I'm due at the house. This is rent-day."

"Oh, exactly! But you can't go."

"I can't go. It's awful. I shall lose my money. If I am dying, I want it all the same. I want to pay the doctor. I want to be buried like a respectable man."

"It is this evening?" I asked.

"This evening at sunset, sharp."

He lay staring at me, and, as I looked at him in return, I suddenly understood his motive in sending for me. Morally, as it came into my thought, I winced. But, I suppose I looked unperturbed, for he continued in the same tone. "I can't lose my money. Some one else must go. I asked Belinda; but she won't hear of it."

"You believe the money will be paid to another person?"

"We can try, at least. I have never failed before and I don't know. But, if you say I'm sick as a dog, that my old bones ache, that I'm dying, perhaps she'll trust you. She don't want me to starve!"

"You would like me to go in your place, then?"

"You have been there once; you know what it is. Are you afraid?"

I hesitated.

"Give me three minutes to reflect," I said, "and I will tell you." My glance wandered over the room and rested on the various objects that spoke of the threadbare, decent poverty of its occupant. There seemed to be a mute appeal to my pity and my resolution in their cracked and faded sparseness. Meanwhile Captain Diamond continued, feebly:

"I think she'd trust you, as I have trusted you; she'll like your face; she'll see there is no harm in you. It's a hundred and thirty-three dollars, exactly. Be sure you put them into a safe place."

"Yes," I said at last, "I will go, and, so far as it depends upon me, you shall have the money by nine o'clock tonight."

He seemed greatly relieved; he took my hand and faintly pressed it, and soon afterward I withdrew. I tried for the rest of the day not to think of my evening's work, but, of course, I thought of nothing else. I will not deny that I was nervous; I was, in fact, greatly excited, and I spent my time in alternately hoping that the mystery should prove less deep than it appeared, and yet fearing that it might prove too shallow. The hours passed very slowly, but, as the afternoon began to wane, I started on my mission. On the way, I stopped at Captain Diamond's modest dwelling, to ask how he was doing, and to receive such last instructions as he might desire to lay upon me. The old Negress, gravely and inscrutably placid, admitted me, and, in answer to my inquiries, said that the Captain was very low; he had sunk since the morning.

"You must be right smart," she said, "if you want to get back before he drops off."

A glance assured me that she knew of my projected expedition, though, in her own opaque black pupil, there was not a gleam of self-betrayal.

"But why should Captain Diamond drop off?" I asked.

"He certainly seems very weak; but I cannot make out that he has any definite disease."

"His disease is old age," she said, sententiously.

"But he is not so old as that; sixty-seven or sixty-eight, at most."

She was silent a moment.

"He's worn out; he's used up; he can't stand it any longer."

"Can I see him a moment?" I asked; upon which she led me again to his room.

He was lying in the same way as when I had left him, except that his eyes were closed. But he seemed very "low," as she had said, and he had very little pulse. Nevertheless, I further learned the doctor had been there in the afternoon and professed himself satisfied. "He don't know what's been going on," said Belinda, curtly.

The old man stirred a little, opened his eyes, and after some time recognized me.

"I'm going, you know," I said. "I'm going for your money. Have you anything more to say?" He raised himself slowly, and with a painful effort, against his pillows; but he seemed hardly to understand me. "The house, you know," I said. "Your daughter."

He rubbed his forehead, slowly, awhile, and at last, his comprehension awoke. "Ah, yes," he murmured, "I trust you. A hundred and thirty-three dollars. In old pieces—all in old pieces." Then he added more vigorously, and with a brightening eye: "Be very respectful—be very polite. If not—if not—" and his voice failed again.

"Oh, I certainly shall be," I said, with a rather forced smile. "But, if not?"

"If not, I shall know it!" he said, very gravely. And with this, his eyes closed and he sunk down again.

I took my departure and pursued my journey with a sufficiently resolute step. When I reached the house, I made a propitiatory bow in front of it, in emulation of Captain

Diamond. I had timed my walk so as to be able to enter
without delay; night had already fallen. I turned the key,
opened the door and shut it behind me. Then I struck a light,
and found the two candlesticks I had used before, standing on
the tables in the entry. I applied a match to both of them,
took them up and went into the parlor. It was empty, and
though I waited awhile, it remained empty. I passed then
into the other rooms on the same floor, and no dark image
rose before me to check my steps. At last, I came out into the
hall again, and stood weighing the question of going upstairs.
The staircase had been the scene of my discomfiture before,
and I approached it with profound mistrust. At the foot, I
paused, looking up, with my hand on the balustrade. I was
acutely expectant, and my expectation was justified. Slowly,
in the darkness above, the black figure that I had seen before
took shape. It was not an illusion; it was a figure, and the
same. I gave it time to define itself, and watched it stand and
look down at me with its hidden face. Then, deliberately, I
lifted my voice and spoke.

"I have come in place of Captain Diamond, at his re-
quest," I said. "He is very ill; he is unable to leave his bed.
He earnestly begs that you will pay the money to me; I will
immediately carry it to him." The figure stood motionless,
giving no sign. "Captain Diamond would have come if he
were able to move," I added, in a moment, appealingly;
"but, he is utterly unable."

At this the figure slowly unveiled its face and showed me a
dim, white mask; then it began slowly to descend the stairs.
Instinctively I fell back before it, retreating to the door of the
front sitting-room. With my eyes still fixed on it, I moved
backward across the threshold; then I stopped in the middle
of the room and set down my lights. The figure advanced; it
seemed to be that of a tall woman, dressed in vaporous black
crape. As it drew near, I saw that it had a perfectly human
face, though it looked extremely pale and sad. We stood

gazing at each other; my agitation had completely vanished; I was only deeply interested.

"Is my father dangerously ill?" said the apparition.

At the sound of its voice—gentle, tremulous, and perfectly human—I started forward; I felt a rebound of excitement. I drew a long breath, I gave a sort of cry, for what I saw before me was not a disembodied spirit, but a beautiful woman, an audacious actress. Instinctively, irresistibly, by the force of reaction against my credulity, I stretched out my hand and seized the long veil that muffled her head. I gave it a violent jerk, dragged it nearly off, and stood staring at a large fair person, of about five-and-thirty. I comprehended her at a glance; her long black dress, her pale, sorrow-worn face, painted to look paler, her very fine eyes,—the color of her father's,—and her sense of outrage at my movement.

"My father, I suppose," she cried, "did not send you here to insult me!" and she turned away rapidly, took up one of the candles and moved toward the door. Here she paused, looked at me again, hesitated, and then drew a purse from her pocket and flung it down on the floor. "There is your money!" she said, majestically.

I stood there, wavering between amazement and shame, and saw her pass out into the hall. Then I picked up the purse. The next moment, I heard a loud shriek and a crash of something dropping, and she came staggering back into the room without her light.

"My father—my father!" she cried; and with parted lips and dilated eyes, she rushed toward me.

"Your father—where?" I demanded.

"In the hall, at the foot of the stairs."

I stepped forward to go out, but she seized my arm.

"He is in white," she cried, "in his shirt. It's not he!"

"Why, your father is in his house, in his bed, extremely ill," I answered.

She looked at me fixedly, with searching eyes.

"Dying?"

"I hope not," I stuttered.

She gave a long moan and covered her face with her hands.

"Oh, heavens, I have seen his ghost!" she cried.

She still held my arm; she seemed too terrified to release it. "His ghost!" I echoed, wondering.

"It's the punishment of my long folly!" she went on.

"Ah," said I, "it's the punishment of my indiscretion—of my violence!"

"Take me away, take me away!" she cried, still clinging to my arm. "Not there"—as I was turning toward the hall and the front door—"not there, for pity's sake! By this door—the back entrance." And snatching the other candles from the table, she led me through the neighboring room into the back part of the house. Here was a door opening from a sort of scullery into the orchard. I turned the rusty lock and we passed out and stood in the cool air, beneath the stars. Here my companion gathered her black drapery about her, and stood for a moment, hesitating. I had been infinitely flurried, but my curiosity touching her was uppermost. Agitated, pale, picturesque, she looked, in the early evening light, very beautiful.

"You have been playing all these years a most extraordinary game," I said.

She looked at me somberly, and seemed disinclined to reply. "I came in perfect good faith," I went on. "The last time—three months ago—you remember?—you greatly frightened me."

"Of course it was an extraordinary game," she answered at last. "But it was the only way."

"Had he not forgiven you?"

"So long as he thought me dead, yes. There had been things in my life he could not forgive."

I hesitated and then—"And where is your husband?" I asked.

"I have no husband—I have never had a husband."

She made a gesture which checked further questions, and
moved rapidly away. I walked with her round the house to
the road, and she kept murmuring—"It was he—it was
he!" When we reached the road she stopped, and asked
me which way I was going. I pointed to the road by which I
had come, and she said—"I take the other. You are going to
my father's?" she added.

"Directly," I said.

"Will you let me know to-morrow what you have found?"

"With pleasure. But how shall I communicate with you?"

She seemed at a loss, and looked about her. "Write a few
words," she said, "and put them under that stone." And she
pointed to one of the lava slabs that bordered the old well. I
gave her my promise to comply, and she turned away. "I
know my road," she said. "Everything is arranged. It's an
old story."

She left me with a rapid step, and as she receded into the
darkness, resumed, with the dark flowing lines of her drapery, the phantasmal appearance with which she had at first appeared to me. I watched her till she became invisible, and
then I took my own leave of the place. I returned to town at a
swinging pace, and marched straight to the little yellow
house near the river. I took the liberty of entering without a
knock, and, encountering no interruption, made my way to
Captain Diamond's room. Outside the door, on a low bench,
with folded arms, sat the sable Belinda.

"How is he?" I asked.

"He's gone to glory."

"Dead?" I cried.

She rose with a sort of tragic chuckle.

"He's as big a ghost as any of them now!"

I passed into the room and found the old man lying there
irredeemably rigid and still. I wrote that evening a few lines
which I proposed on the morrow to place beneath the stone,
near the well; but my promise was not destined to be exe-
cuted. I slept that night very ill—it was natural—and in my

restlessness left my bed to walk about the room. As I did so I caught sight, in passing my window, of a red glow in the northwestern sky. A house was on fire in the country, and evidently burning fast. It lay in the same direction as the scene of my evening's adventures, and as I stood watching the crimson horizon I was startled by a sharp memory. I had blown out the candle which lighted me, and my companion, to the door through which we escaped, but I had not accounted for the other light, which she had carried into the hall and dropped—heaven knew where—in her consternation. The next day I walked out with my folded letter and turned into the familiar cross-road. The haunted house was a mass of charred beams and smoldering ashes; the well-cover had been pulled off, in quest of water, by the few neighbors who had had the audacity to contest what they must have regarded as a demon-kindled blaze, and the loose stones were completely displaced, and the earth had been trampled into puddles.

THE CRIME OF
MICAH ROOD

Elia W. Peattie

In the early part of the last century there lived in eastern
Connecticut a man named Micah Rood. He was a solitary
soul, and occupied a low, tumble-down house, in which
he had seen his sisters and his brothers, his father and his
mother, die. The mice used the bare floors for a play-ground;
the swallows filled up the unused chimneys; in the cellar the
gophers frolicked, and in the attic a hundred bats made their
home. Micah Rood disturbed no living creature, unless now
and then he killed a hare for his day's dinner, or cast bait for
a glistening trout in the Shetucket. For the most part his food
came from the garden and the orchard, which his father had
planted and nurtured years before.

Into whatever disrepair the house had fallen, the garden
bloomed and flourished like a western Eden. The brambles,
with their luscious burden, clambered up the stone walls,
sentineled by trim rows of English currants. The strawberry
nestled among its wayward creepers, and on the trellises
hung grapes of varied hues. In seemly rows, down the sunny
expanse of the garden spot, grew every vegetable indigenous
to the western world, or transplanted by colonial industry.
Everything here took seed, and bore fruit with a prodigal
exuberance. Beyond the garden lay the orchard, a labyrinth

of flowers in the spring-time, a paradise of verdure in the summer, and in the season of fruition a miracle of plenty.

Often the master of the orchard stood by the gate in the crisp autumn mornings, with his hat filled with apples for the children as they passed to school. There was only one tree in the orchard of whose fruit he was chary. Consequently it was the bearings of this tree that the children most wanted.

"Prithee, Master Rood," they would say, "give us some of the gold apples?"

"I sell the gold apples for silver," he would say; "content ye with the red and green ones."

In all the region there grew no counterpart to this remarkable apple. Its skin was of the clearest amber, translucent and spotless, and the pulp was white as snow, mellow yet firm, and without a flaw from the glistening skin to the even brown seeds nestling like babies in their silken cradle. Its flavor was peculiar and piquant, with a suggestion of spiciness. The fame of Micah Rood's apple, as it was called, had extended far and wide, but all efforts to engraft it upon other trees failed utterly; and the envious farmers were fain to content themselves with the rare shoots.

If there dwelt any vanity in the heart of Micah Rood, it was in the possession of this apple tree, which took the prize at all the local fairs, and carried his name beyond the neighborhood where its owner lived. For the most part he was a modest man, averse to discussions of any sort, shrinking from men and their opinions. He talked more to his dog than to any human being. He fed his mind upon a few old books, and made Nature his religion. All things that made the woods their home were his friends. He possessed himself of their secrets, and insinuated himself into their confidences. But best of all he loved the children. When they told him their sorrows, the answering tears sprang to his eyes; when they told him of their delights, his laugh woke the echoes of the Shetucket as light and free as their own. He laughed frequently when with the children, throwing back his great head, while the tears of mirth ran from his merry blue eyes.

His teeth were like pearls, and constituted his chief charm. For the rest he was rugged and firmly knit. It seemed to the children, after a time, that some cloud was hanging over the serene spirit of their friend. After he had laughed he sighed, and they saw, as he walked down the green paths that led away from his place, that he would look lovingly back at the old homestead and shake his head again and again with a perplexed and melancholy air. The merchants, too, observed that he began to be closer in his bargains, and he barreled his apples so greedily that the birds and the children were quite robbed of their autumnal feast. A winter wore away and left Micah in this changed mood. He sat through the long, dull days brooding over his fire and smoking. He made his own simple meals of mush and bacon, kept his own counsels, and neither visited nor received the neighboring folk.

One day, in a heavy January rain, the boys noticed a strange man who rode rapidly through the village, and drew rein at Micah Rood's orchard gate. He passed through the leafless orchard, and up the muddy garden paths to the old dismantled house. The boys had time to learn by heart every good point of the chestnut mare fastened to the palings before the stranger emerged from the house. Micah followed him to the gate. The stranger swung himself upon the mare with a sort of jaunty flourish, while Micah stood heavily and moodily by, chewing the end of a straw.

"Well, Master Rood," the boys heard the stranger say, "thou'st till the first of next May, but not a day of grace more." He had a decisive, keen manner that took away the breath of the boys used to men of slow action and slow speech. "Mind ye," he snapped, like an angry cur, "not another day's grace." Micah said not a word, but stolidly chewed on his straw while the stranger cut his animal briskly with the whip, and mare and rider dashed away down the dreary road. The boys began to frisk about their old friend and pulled savagely at the tails of his coat, whooping and whistling to arouse him from his reverie. Micah looked up and roared:

"Off with ye! I'm in no mood for pranks."

As a pet dog slinks away in humiliation at a blow, so the boys, hurt and indignant, skulked down the road speechless at the cruelty of their old friend.

The April sunshine was bringing the dank odors from the earth when the village beauties were thrown into a flutter of excitement. Old Geoffry Peterkin, the peddler, came with such jewelry, such stuffs, and such laces as the maidens of Shetucket had never seen the like of before.

"You are getting rich, Geoffry," the men said to him.

"No, no!" and Geoffry shook his grizzled head with a flattered smile. "Not from your women-folk. There's no such bargain-drivers between here and Boston town."

"Thou'lt be a-setting up in Boston town, Geoffry," said another. "Thou'rt getting too fine to travel pack a-back amongst us simple country folk."

"Not a bit of it," protested Geoffry. "I couldn't let the pretty dears go without their beads and their ribbons. I come and go as reg'lar as the leaves, spring, summer, and autumn."

By twilight Geoffry had made his last visit, and with his pack somewhat lightened he tramped away in the raw dusk. He went straight down the road that led to the next village, until out of sight of the windows, then turned to his right and groped his way across the commons with his eye ever fixed on a deeper blackness in the gloom. This looming blackness was the orchard of Micah Rood. He found the gate, entered, and made his way to the dismantled house. A bat swept its wing against his face as he rapped his stick upon the door.

"What witchcraft's here?" he said, and pounded harder.

There were no cracks in the heavy oaken door through which a light might filter, and old Geoffry Peterkin was blinded like any owl when the door was flung open, and

Micah Rood, with a forked candle-stick in his hands, appeared, recognized him, and bade him enter. The wind drove down the hallway, blew the flame an inch from the wicks, where it burned blue a moment, and then expired, leaving the men in darkness. Geoffry stepped in, and Micah threw his weight against the door, swung the bar into place, and led Geoffry into a large bare room lit up by a blazing hickory fire. When the candles were relit, Micah said:

"Hast thou supped this night, friend Peterkin?"

"That have I, and royally too, with Rogers the smith. No more for me."

Micah Rood stirred up the fire and produced a bottle of brandy from a cupboard. He filled a small glass and offered it to his guest. It was greedily quaffed by the peddler. Micah replaced the bottle, and took no liquor himself. Pipes were then lit. Micah smoked moodily and in silence. The peddler, too, was silent. He hugged his knee, puffed vigorously at his pipe, and stared at the blazing hickory. Micah spoke first.

"Thou hast prospered since thou sold milk-pans to my mother."

"I've made a fortune with that old pack," said the peddler, pointing to the corner where it lay. "Year after year I have trudged this road, and year after year has my pack been larger and my stops longer. My stuffs, too, have changed. I carry no more milk-pans. I leave that to others. I now have jewels and cloths. Why, man! There's a fortune even now in that old pack."

He arose and unstrapped the leathern bands that bound his burden. He drew from the pack a variety of jewel-cases and handed them to Micah. "I did not show these at the village," he continued, pointing over his shoulder. "I sell those in towns."

Micah clumsily opened one or two, and looked at their contents with restless eyes. There were rubies as red as a serpent's tongue; silver, carved as daintily as hoar-frost, gleaming with icy diamonds; pearls that nestled like precious eggs in fairy golden nests; turquois gleaming from beds of enamel, and bracelets of ebony capped with topaz balls.

"These," laughed Geoffry, dangling a translucent necklace of amber, "I keep to ward off ill-luck. She will be a witch indeed that gets me to sell these. But if thou'lt marry, good Master Rood, I'll give them to thy bride."

He chuckled, gasped, and gurgled mightily; but Micah checked his exuberance by looking up fiercely.

"There'll be never a bride for me," he said. "She'd be killed here with the rats and the damp rot. It takes gold to get a woman."

"Bah!" sneered Geoffry. "It takes youth, boy, blue eye, good laugh, and a strong leg. Why, if a bride could be had for gold, I've got that."

He unrolled a shimmering azure satin, and took from it two bags of soft, stout leather.

"There is where I keep my yellow boys shut up!" the old fellow cried in great glee; "and when I let them out, they'll bring me anything I want, Micah Rood, except a true heart. How have things prospered with thee?" he added, as he shot a shrewd glance at Micah from beneath his eyebrows.

"Bad," confessed Micah, "very bad. Everything has been against me of late."

"I say, boy," cried the peddler, suddenly, "I haven't been over this old house for years. Take the light and show us around."

"No," said Micah, shaking his head doggedly. "It is in bad shape and I would feel that I was showing a friend who was in rags."

"Nonsense!" cried the peddler, bursting into a hearty laugh. "Thou need'st not fear, I'll ne'er cut thy old friend."

He had replaced his stuffs, and now seized the branched candle-stick and waved his hand toward the door.

"Lead the way," he cried. "I want to see how things look," and Micah Rood sullenly obeyed.

From room to room they went in the miserable cold and

the gloom. The candle threw a faint gleam though the unkept apartments, noxious with dust and decay. Not a flaw escaped the eye of the peddler. He ran his fingers into the cracks of the doors, he counted the panes of broken glass, he remarked the gaps in the plastering.

"The dry rot has got into the wainscoting," he said jauntily.

Micah Rood was burning with impotent anger. He tried to lead the peddler past one door, but the old man's keen eyes were too quick for him, and he kicked the door open with his foot.

"What have we here?" he cried.

It was the room where Micah and his brothers had slept when they were children. The little dismantled beds stood side by side. A work-bench with some miniature tools was by the curtainless window. Everything that met his gaze brought with it a flood of early recollections.

"Here's a rare lot of old truck," Geoffry cried. "The first thing I should do would be to pitch this out of doors."

Micah caught him by the arm and pushed him from the room.

"It happens that it is not thine to pitch," he said.

Geoffry Peterkin began to laugh a low, irritating chuckle. He laughed all the way back to the room where the fire was. He laughed still as Micah showed him his room—the room where he was to pass the night; chuckled and guffawed, and clapped Micah on the back as they finally bade each other good-night. The master of the house went back and stood before the dying fire alone.

"What can he mean, in God's name?" he asked himself. "Does he know of the mortgage?"

Micah knew that the peddler, who was well off, frequently negotiated and dealt in the commercial paper of farmers. Pride and anger tore at his heart like wild beasts. What would the neighbors say when they saw his father's son driven from the house that had belonged to the family for generations? How could he endure their surprise and contempt? What would the children say when they found a stranger in possession of the famous apple-tree? "I've got no more to pay it with," he cried in helpless anguish, "then I had the day the cursed lawyer came here with his threats."

He determined to find out what Peterkin knew of the matter. He spread a bear's skin before the fire and threw himself upon it and fell into a feverish sleep, which ended long before the purple dawn broke.

He cooked a breakfast of bacon and corn cake, made a cup of coffee, and aroused his guest. The peddler, clean, keen, and alert, noted slyly the sullen heaviness of Micah. The meal was eaten in silence, and when it was finished, Geoffry put on his cloak, adjusted his pack, and prepared to leave. Micah put on his hat, took a pruning-knife from a shelf, remarking as he did so:

"I go early about my work in the orchard," and followed the peddler to the door. The trees in the orchard had begun to shimmer with young green. The perfume, so familiar to Micah, so suggestive of the place that he held dearer than all the rest of the world beside, wrought upon him till his curiosity got the better of his discretion.

"It is hard work for one man to keep up a place like this and make it pay," he remarked.

Geoffry smiled slyly, but said nothing.

"Bad luck has got the start of me of late," the master continued with an attempt at real candor.

The peddler knocked the tops off some gaunt, dead weeds that stood by the path.

"So I have heard," he said.

"What else didst thou hear?" cried Micah, quickly, his face burning, and shame and anger flashing from his blue eyes.

"Well," said the peddler, with a great show of caution. "I heard the mortgage was a good investment for any one who wanted to buy."

"Perhaps thou know'st more about it than that," sneered Micah.

Peterkin blew on his hands and rubbed them with a knowing air.

"Well," he said, "I know what I know."

"D—— you," cried Micah, clinching his fist, "out with it!"

The peddler was getting heated. He thrust his hand into his breast and drew out a paper.

"When May comes about, Master Rood, I'll ask thee to look at the face of this document."

"Thou art a sneak!" foamed Micah. "A white-livered, cowardly sneak!"

"Rough words to call a man on his own property," said the peddler, with a malicious grin.

The insult was the deepest he could have offered to the man before him. A flood of ungovernable emotions rushed over Micah. The impulse latent in all angry animals to strike, to crush, to kill, came over him. He rushed forward madly, then the passion ebbed, and he saw the peddler on the ground. The pruning-knife in his own hand was red with blood. He gazed in cold horror, then tried in a weak, trembling way to heap leaves upon the body to hide it from his sight. He could gather only small handfuls, and they fluttered away in the wind.

The light was getting brighter. People would soon be passing down the road. He walked up and down aimlessly for a time, and then ran to the garden. He returned with a spade and began digging furiously. He made a trench between the dead man and the tree under which he had fallen; and when it was finished he pushed the body in with his foot, not daring to touch it with his hands.

Of the peddler's death there was no doubt. The rigid face and the blood-drenched garments over the heart attested the fact. So copiously had the blood gushed forth that all the soil, and the dead leaves about the body, and the exposed roots of the tree were stained with it. Involuntarily Micah looked up at the tree. He uttered an exclamation of dismay. It was the tree of the gold apples.

After a moment's silence he recommenced his work and tossed back the earth in mad haste. He smoothed the earth so carefully that when he had finished not even a mound appeared. He scattered dead leaves over the freshly turned earth, and then walked slowly back to the house.

For the first time the shadow that hung over it, the gloom deep as despair that looked from its vacant windows, struck him. The gloss of familiarity had hidden from his eyes what had long been patent to others—the decay, the ruin, the solitude. It swept over him as an icy breaker sweeps over a drowning man. The rats ran from him as he entered the hall. He held the arm on which the blood was rapidly drying far from him, as if he feared to let it touch his body with its confession of crime. The sleeve had stiffened to the arm, and inspired him with a nervous horror, as if a reptile was twined about it. He flung off his coat, and finally, trembling and sick, divested himself of a flannel undergarment, and still from finger-tip to elbow there were blotches and smears on his arm. He realized at once the necessity of destroying the garments; and, naked to the waist, he stirred up the dying embers of the fire and threw the garments on. The heavy flannel of the coat refused to burn, and he threw it deeper and deeper in with a poker till he saw with dismay that he had quenched the fire.

"It's fate!" he cried. "I can not destroy them."

He lit a fire three times, but his haste and his confused horror made him throw on the heavy garments every time and strangle the infant blaze. At last he took them to the garret and locked them in an old chest. Starting at the shadows among the rafters, and the creaking of the boards, he crept back through the biting chill of the vacant rooms to the one that he occupied, and washed his arm again and again, until the deep glow on it seemed like another blood-stain.

After that for weeks he worked in his garden by day, and at night slept on the floor with the candles burning, and his hand on his flint-lock.

Meanwhile in the orchard the leaves budded and spread, and the perfumed blossoms came. The branches of the tree of the gold apples grew pink with swelling buds. Near that spot Micah never went. He felt as if his feet would be grasped by spectral hands.

One night a swelling wind arose, strong, steady, warm, seeming palpable to the touch like a fabric. In the morning the orchard had flung all its banners to the air. It dazzled Micah's eyes as he looked upon the tossing clouds of pink and white fragrance. But as his eye roamed about the waving splendor he caught sight of a thing that riveted him to the spot with awe.

The tree of the gold apples had blossomed blood-red.

That day he did no work. He sat from early morning till the light waned in the west, gazing at the tree flaunting its blossoms red as blood against the shifting sky. Few neighbors came that way; and as the tree stood in the heart of the orchard, fewer yet noticed its accursed beauty. To those that did Micah stammeringly gave a hint of some ingenious ingrafting, the secret of which was to make his fortune. But though the rest of the world wondered and wagged its head and doubted not that it was some witchcraft, the children were enraptured. They stole into the orchard and pilfered handfuls of the roseate flowers, and bore them away to school; the girls fastened them in their braids or wore them above their innocent hearts, and the boys trimmed their hat-bands and danced away in glee like youthful Corydons.

Spring-time passed and its promises of plenty were fulfilled. In the garden there grew a luxury of greenness; in the orchard the boughs lagged low. Micah Rood toiled day and night. He visited no house, he sought no company. If a neighbor saw him in the field and came for a chat, before he had reached the spot Micah had hidden himself.

"He used to be as ready for the news as the rest of us," said they to themselves, "and he had a laugh like a horse. His sweetheart has jilted him, most like."

When the purple on the grapes began to grow through the amber, and the mellowed apples dropped from their stems, the children began to flock about the orchard gate like buzzards about a battle-field. But they found the gate padlocked and the board fence prickling with pointed sticks. Micah they saw but seldom, and his face, once so sunny, was as terrible to them as the angel's with the flaming sword that kept guard over the gates of Eden. So the sinless little Adams and Eves had no choice but to turn away with empty pockets.

However, one morning, accident took Micah to the bolted gate just as the children came trooping home in the early autumn sunset; for in those days they kept students of any age at work as many hours of the day as possible. A little fay, with curls as sunny as the tendrils of the grape, caught sight of him first. Her hat was wreathed with scarlet maple leaves; her dress was as ruddy as the cheeks of the apples. She seemed the sprite of autumn. She ran toward him, with arms outstretched, crying:

"Oh, Master Rood! Do come and play. Where hast thou been so long? We have wanted some apples, and the plaguy old gate was locked."

For the first time for months the pall of remembrance that hung over Micah's dead happiness was lifted, and the spirit of that time came back to him. He caught the little one in his brawny arms and threw her high, while she shrieked with terror and delight. After this the children gave no quarter. The breach begun, they sallied in and stormed the fortress. Like a dream of water to a man who is perishing of thirst, who knows while he yet dreams that he must wake and find his bliss an agony, this hour of innocence was to Micah. He ran, and leaped, and frolicked with the children in the shade of the trees till the orchard rang with their shouts, while the sky changed from daffodil to crimson, from crimson to gray, and sank into a deep autumn twilight. Micah stuffed their little pockets with fruit, and bade them run home. But they lingered dissatisfied.

"I wish he would give us of the golden apples," they whispered among themselves. At last one plucked up courage.

"Good Master Rood, give us of the gold apples, if thou please."

Micah shook his head sternly. They entreated him with eyes and tongues. They saw a chance for a frolic. They clung to him, climbed his back, and danced about him, shouting:

"The gold apples! The gold apples!"

A sudden change came over him; he marched to the tree with a look men wear when they go to battle.

"There is blood in them!" he cried hoarsely. "They are accursed—accursed!"

The children shrieked with delight at what they thought a jest.

"Blood in the apples! Ha! ha! ha!" and they rolled over one another on the grass, fighting for the windfalls.

"I tell ye 'tis so!" Micah continued. He took one of the apples and broke it into halves.

"Look," he cried, and in his eyes there came a look in which the light of reason was waning. The children pressed about him, peeping over each other at the apple. On the broken side of both halves, from the rind to the core, there was a blood-red streak the width of a child's little finger. An amazed silence fell on the little group.

"Home with ye now!" he cried huskily. "Home with ye, and tell what ye have seen! Run, ye brats."

"Then let us take some of the apples with us," they persisted.

"Ha!" he cried, "ye tale-bearers! I know the tricks ye'd play! Here then——"

He shook the tree like a giant. The apples rolled to the ground so fast that they looked like strands of amber beads. The children, laughing and shouting, gathered them as they fell. They began to compare the red spots. In some the drop of blood was found just under the skin, and a thin streak of carmine that penetrated to the core and colored the silvery pulp; in others it was an isolated clot, the size of a whortle-berry, and on a few a narrow crescent of crimson reached half-way around the outside of the shining rind.

Suddenly a noise, not loud but agonizing, startled the little ones. They looked up at their friend. He had become horri-ble. His face was contorted until it was unrecognizable; his eyes were fixed on the ground as if he beheld a specter there. Shrieking, they ran from the orchard, nor cast one fearful glance behind.

The next day the smith, filled with curiosity by the tales of the children, found an odd hour in which to visit Micah Rood's house. He invited the tailor, a man thin with hunger for gossip, to go with him. The gate of the orchard stood open, flapping on its hinges as the children had left it. The visitors sauntered through, thinking to find Micah in the house, for it was the noon hour. They tasted of this fruit and that, tried a pear, now an apricot, now a pippin.

"The tree of the gold apples is right in the center," said the smith.

He pointed. The tailor looked; then his legs doubled under him as naturally as they ever did on the bench. The smith looked; his arm dropped by his side. After a time the two men went on, clinging to each other like children in the dark.

Micah Rood, with his sunny hair tangled in the branches, his tongue black and protruding, his face purple, and his clinched hands stained with dirt, hung from the tree of the golden apples. Beneath him, in a trench, from which the ground had been clawed by human hands, lay a shapeless, discolored bundle of clothes. A skull lay at one end of the trench, and beneath it a moldy pack was found with precious stones amid the decaying contents.

THE FURNISHED ROOM

O. Henry

Restless, shifting, fugacious as time itself is a certain vast bulk of the population of the red brick district of the lower West Side. Homeless, they have a hundred homes. They flit from furnished room to furnished room, transients forever—transients in abode, transients in heart and mind. They sing "Home, Sweet Home" in ragtime; they carry their *lares et penates* in a bandbox; their vine is entwined about a picture hat; a rubber plant is their fig tree.

Hence the houses of this district, having had a thousand dwellers, should have a thousand tales to tell, mostly dull ones, no doubt; but it would be strange if there could not be found a ghost or two in the wake of all these vagrant guests.

One evening after dark a young man prowled among these crumbling red mansions, ringing their bells. At the twelfth he rested his lean hand-baggage upon the step and wiped the dust from his hatband and forehead. The bell sounded faint and far away in some remote, hollow depths.

To the door of this, the twelfth house whose bell he had rung, came a housekeeper who made him think of an unwholesome, surfeited worm that had eaten its nut to a hollow shell and now sought to fill the vacancy with edible lodgers.

He asked if there was a room to let.

"Come in," said the housekeeper. Her voice came from her throat; her throat seemed lined with fur. "I have the third-floor back, vacant since a week back. Should you wish to look at it?"

The young man followed her up the stairs. A faint light from no particular source mitigated the shadows of the halls. They trod noiselessly upon a stair carpet that its own loom would have forsworn. It seemed to have become vegetable; to have degenerated in that rank, sunless air to lush lichen or spreading moss that grew in patches to the stair-case and was viscid under the foot like organic matter. At each turn of the stairs were vacant niches in the wall. Perhaps plants had once been set within them. If so they had died in that foul and tainted air. It may be that statues of the saints had stood there, but it was not difficult to conceive that imps and devils had dragged them forth in the darkness and down to the unholy depths of some furnished pit below.

"This is the room," said the housekeeper, from her furry throat. "It's a nice room. It ain't often vacant. I had some most elegant people in it last summer—no trouble at all, and paid in advance to the minute. The water's at the end of the hall. Sprowls and Mooney kept it three months. They done a vaudeville sketch. Miss B'retta Sprowls—you may have heard of her—Oh, that was just the stage names—right there over the dresser is where the marriage certificate hung, framed. The gas is here, and you see there is plenty of closet room. It's a room everybody likes. It never stays idle long."

"Do you have many theatrical people rooming here?" asked the young man.

"They comes and goes. A good proportion of my lodgers is connected with the theatres. Yes, sir, this is the theatrical district. Actor people never stays long anywhere. I get my share. Yes, they comes and they goes."

He engaged the room, paying for a week in advance. He was tired, he said, and would take possession at once. He counted out the money. The room had been made ready, she said, even to towels and water. As the housekeeper moved away he put, for the thousandth time, the question that he carried at the end of his tongue.

"A young girl—Miss Vashner—Miss Eloise Vashner—do you remember such a one among your lodgers? She would be singing on the stage, most likely. A fair girl, of medium height and slender, with reddish, gold hair and a dark mole near her left eyebrow."

"No, I don't remember the name. Them stage people has names they change as often as their rooms. They comes and they goes. No, I don't call that one to mind."

No. Always no. Five months of ceaseless interrogation and the inevitable negative. So much time spent by day in questioning managers, agents, schools and choruses; by night among the audiences of theatres from all-star casts down to music halls so low that he dreaded to find what he most hoped for. He who had loved her best had tried to find her. He was sure that since her disappearance from home this great, water-girt city held her somewhere, but it was like a monstrous quicksand, shifting its particles constantly, with no foundation, its upper granules of to-day buried to-morrow in ooze and slime.

The furnished room received its latest guest with a first glow of pseudo-hospitality, a hectic, haggard, perfunctory welcome like the specious smile of a demirep. The sophistical comfort came in reflected gleams from the decayed furniture, the ragged brocade upholstery of a couch and two chairs, a foot-wide cheap pier glass between the two windows, from one or two gilt picture frames and a brass bedstead in a corner.

The guest reclined, inert, upon a chair, while the room, confused in speech as though it were an apartment in Babel, tried to discourse to him of its diverse tenantry.

A polychromatic rug like some brilliant-flowered, rectangular, tropical islet lay surrounded by a billowy sea of soiled

matting. Upon the gay-papered wall were those pictures that
pursue the homeless one from house to house—The Huguenot
Lovers, The First Quarrel, The Wedding Breakfast, Psyche at
the Fountain. The mantel's chastely severe outline was inglo-
riously veiled behind some pert drapery drawn rakishly askew
like the sashes of the Amazonian ballet. Upon it was some
desolate flotsam cast aside by the room's marooned when a
lucky sail had borne them to a fresh port—a trifling vase or
two, pictures of actresses, a medicine bottle, some stray
cards out of a deck.

One by one, as the characters of a cryptograph became
explicit, the little signs left by the furnished rooms' procession of guests developed a significance. The threadbare space
in the rug in front of the dresser told that lovely women had
marched in the throng. The tiny fingerprints on the wall spoke
of little prisoners trying to feel their way to sun and air. A
splattered stain, raying like the shadow of a bursting bomb,
witnessed where a hurled glass or bottle had splintered with
its contents against the wall. Across the pier glass had been
scrawled with a diamond in staggering letters the name
"Marie." It seemed that the succession of dwellers in the
furnished room had turned in fury—perhaps tempted beyond
forbearance by its garish coldness—and wreaked upon it their
passions. The furniture was chipped and bruised; the couch,
distorted by bursting springs, seemed a horrible monster that
had been slain during the stress of some grotesque convul-
sion. Some more potent upheaval had cloven a great slice
from the marble mantel. Each plank in the floor owned its
particular cant and shriek as from a separate and individual
agony. It seemed incredible that all this malice and injury had
been wrought upon the room by those who had called it for a
time their home; and yet it may have been the cheated home
instinct surviving blindly, the resentful rage at false household gods that had kindled their wrath. A hut that is our own
we can sweep and adorn and cherish.

The young tenant in the chair allowed these thoughts to

file, soft-shod, through his mind, while there drifted into the room furnished sounds and furnished scents. He heard in one room a tittering and incontinent, slack laughter; in others the monologue of a scold, the rattling of dice, a lullaby, and one crying dully; above him a banjo tinkled with spirit. Doors banged somewhere; the elevated trains roared intermittently; a cat yowled miserably upon a back fence. And he breathed the breath of the house—a dank savor rather than a smell—a cold, musty effluvium as from underground vaults mingled with the reeking exhalations of linoleum and mildewed and rotten woodwork.

Then suddenly, as he rested there, the room was filled with the strong, sweet odor of mignonette. It came as upon a single buffet of wind with such sureness and fragrance and emphasis that it almost seemed a living visitant. And the man cried aloud: "What, dear?" as if he had been called, and sprang up and faced about. The rich odor clung to him and wrapped him around. He reached out his arms for it, all his senses for the time confused and commingled. How could one be peremptorily called by an odor? Surely it must have been a sound. But, was it not the sound that had touched, that had caressed him?

"She has been in this room," he cried, and he sprang to wrest from it a token, for he knew he would recognize the smallest thing that had belonged to her or that she had touched. This enveloping scent of mignonette, the odor that she had loved and had made her own—whence came it?

The room had been but carefully set in order. Scattered upon the flimsy dresser scarf were half a dozen hairpins—those discreet, indistinguishable friends of womankind, feminine of gender, infinite mood and uncommunicative of tense. These he ignored, conscious of their triumphant lack of identity. Ransacking the drawers of the dresser he came upon a discarded, tiny, ragged handkerchief. He pressed it to his face. It was racy and insolent with heliotrope; he hurled it to the floor. In another drawer he found odd buttons, a theatre programme, a pawn-broker's card, two lost marshmallows, a book on the divination of dreams. In the last was a woman's black satin hair bow, which halted him, poised between ice and fire. But the black satin hair bow also is femininity's demure, impersonal common ornament and tells no tales.

And then he traversed the room like a hound on the scent, skimming the walls, considering the corners of the bulging matting on his hands and knees, rummaging mantel and tables, the curtains and hangings, the drunken cabinet in the corner, for a visible sign, unable to perceive that she was there beside, around, against, within, above him, clinging to him, wooing him, calling him so poignantly through the finer senses that even his grosser ones became cognizant of the call. Once again he answered loudly: "Yes, dear!" and turned, wild-eyed, to gaze on vacancy, for he could not yet discern form and color and love and outstretched arms in the odor of mignonette. Oh, God! whence that odor, and since when have odors had a voice to call? Thus he groped.

He burrowed in crevices and corners, and found corks and cigarettes. These he passed in passive contempt. But once he found in a fold of the matting a half-smoked cigar, and this he ground beneath his heel with a green and trenchant oath. He sifted the room from end to end. He found dreary and ignoble small records of many a peripatetic tenant; but of her whom he sought, and who may have lodged there, and whose spirit seemed to hover there, he found no trace.

And then he thought of the housekeeper.

He ran from the haunted room downstairs and to a door that showed a crack of light. She came out to his knock. He smothered his excitement as best he could.

"Will you tell me, madam," he besought her, "who occupied the room I have before I came?"

"Yes, sir. I can tell you again. 'Twas Sprowls and Mooney, as I said. Miss B'retta Sprowls it was in the theatres, but Missis Mooney she was. My house is well known for respectability. The marriage certificate hung, framed, on a nail over—"

"What kind of a lady was Miss Sprowls—in looks, I mean?"

"Why, black-haired, sir, short, and stout, with a comical face. They left a week ago Tuesday."

"And before they occupied it?"

"Why, there was a single gentleman connected with the draying business. He left owing me a week. Before him was Missis Crowder and her two children, that stayed four months; and back of them was old Mr. Doyle, whose sons paid for him. He kept the room six months. That goes back a year, sir, and further I do not remember."

He thanked her and crept back to his room. The room was dead. The essence that had vivified it was gone. The perfume of mignonette had departed. In its place was the old, stale odor of mouldy house furniture, of atmosphere in storage.

The ebbing of his hope drained his faith. He sat staring at the yellow, singing gaslight. Soon he walked to the bed and began to tear the sheets into strips. With the blade of his knife he drove them tightly into every crevice around windows and door. When all was snug and taut he turned out the light, turned the gas full on again and laid himself gratefully upon the bed.

It was Mrs. McCool's night to go with the can for beer. So she fetched it and sat with Mrs. Purdy in one of those subterranean retreats where housekeepers foregather and the worm dieth seldom.

"I rented out my third-floor-back this evening," said Mrs. Purdy, across a fine circle of foam. "A young man took it. He went up to bed two hours ago."

"Now, did ye, Mrs. Purdy, ma'am?" said Mrs. McCool, with intense admiration. "You do be a wonder for rentin' rooms of that kind. And did ye tell him, then?" she concluded in a husky whisper laden with mystery.

"Rooms," said Mrs. Purdy, in her furriest tones, "are furnished for to rent. I did not tell him, Mrs. McCool."

" 'Tis right ye are, ma'am; 'tis by renting rooms we kape alive. Ye have the rale sense for business, ma'am. There be many people will rayjict the rentin' of a room if they be tould a suicide has been after dyin' in the bed of it."

"As you say, we has our living to be making," remarked Mrs. Purdy.

"Yis, ma'am; 'tis true. 'Tis just one wake ago this day I helped ye lay out the third-floor-back. A pretty slip of a colleen she was to be killin' herself wid the gas—a swate little face she had, Mrs. Purdy, ma'am."

"She'd a-been called handsome, as you say," said Mrs. Purdy, assenting but critical, "but for that mole she had a-growin' by her left eyebrow. Do fill up your glass again, Mrs. McCool."

THE CHILDREN

Josephine Daskam Bacon

It all came over me, as you might say, when I began to
tell the new housemaid about the work. Not that I hadn't
known before, of course, what a queer sort of life was
led in that house; it was hard enough the first months,
goodness knows. But then, a body can get used to anything.
And there was no harm in it—I'll swear that to my dying
day! Although a lie's a lie, any way you put it, and if all I'm
told—but I'll let you judge for yourself.

As I say, it was when I began to break Margaret in that it
all came over me, and I looked about me, in a way of
speaking, for how I should put it to her. She'd been house-
parlor maid in a big establishment in the country and knew
what was expected of her well enough, and I saw from the
first she'd fit in nicely with us; a steady, quiet girl, like the
best of the Scotch, looking to save her wages, and get to be
housekeeper herself, some day, perhaps.

But when Hodges brought the tray with the porringers on it
and the silver mugs and said,

"I suppose this young lady 'll take these up, Mrs.
Umbleby?" and when Margaret looked surprised and said,

"I didn't know there were children in the family—am I
supposed to wait on them, too?"—then, as I say, it all came

over me, and for the first time in five years I really saw
where I stood, like.

I stared at Hodges and then at the girl, and the tray nearly
went down amongst us.

"Do you mean to say you haven't told her, Sarah?" says
Hodges (and that was the first time that ever he called me by
my given name).

"She's told me nothing," Margaret answers, rather short,
"and if it's invalid children or feeble-minded, I take it most
unkind, Mrs. Umbleby, for I've never cared for that sort of
thing, and could have had my twenty-five dollars a month
this long time if I'd wanted to go out as nurse."

"Take the tray up this time yourself, Mr. Hodges, please,"
I said, "and I'll have a little talk with Margaret;" and I sat
down and smoothed my black silk skirt (I always wore black
silk, of an afternoon) nervously enough, I'll be bound.

The five years rolled away like yesterday—as they do now
. . . as they do now.

I saw myself, in my mind's eye, new to the place, and
inclined to feel strange, as I always did when I made a
change, though I was twenty-five and no chicken, but rather
more settled than most, having had my troubles early and got
over them. I'd just left my place—chambermaid and seamstress
—in a big city house, and though it was September, I was
looking out for the country, for I was mortal tired of the
noise and late hours and excitement that I saw ahead of me.
It was parties and balls every night and me sitting up to
undress the young ladies; for they kept no maid, like so many
rich Americans, and yet some one must do for them. There
was no housekeeper either, and the mistress was not very
strong, and we had to use our own responsibility more than I
liked—for I wasn't paid for that, do you see, and that's what
they forget in this country.

"I think I've got you suited at last, Sarah," the head of the
office had said to me, "a nice, quiet place in the country,
good pay and light work, but everything as it should be, you

understand. Four in help besides the housekeeper, and only one in family. Church within a mile, and every other Sunday for yourself.''

That was just what I wanted, and I packed my box thankfully and left New York for good, I hoped; and I got my wish, for I've never seen the inside of it since.

A middle-aged coachman in good, quiet country livery met me at the little station, and though he was a still-mouthed fellow and rather reserved, I made out quite a little idea of the place on the way. The mistress, Mrs. Childress, was a young widow, deep in her mourning, so there was no company. The housekeeper was her old nurse, who had brought her up. John, who drove me, was coachman-gardener, and the cook was his wife—both Catholics. Everything went on very quiet and regular, and it was hoped that the new upstairs maid wouldn't be one for excitement and gayety. The inside man had been valet to Mr. Childress, and was much trusted and liked by the family. I could see that old John was a bit jealous in that direction.

We drove in through a black iron gate with cut-stone posts and old black iron lanterns on top, and the moment we were inside the gates I began to take a fancy to the place. It wasn't kept up like the places at home, but it was neat enough to show that things were taken thought for, and the beds of asters and dahlias and marigolds as we got near the house seemed so home-like and bright to me I could have cried for comfort. Childerstone was the name of the place; it was cut into a big boulder by the side of the entrance, and just as we drove up to the door John stopped to pick some dahlias for the house (being only me in the wagon), and I took my first good look at my home for eight years afterward.

There was something about it that went to my heart. It was built of gray cut stone in good-sized blocks, square, with two windows each side the hall door. To some it might have seemed cold-looking, but not to me, for one side was all over ivy, and the thickness of the walls and the deep sills looked

solid and comfortable after those nasty brownstone things all
glued to one another in the city. It looked old and respectable
and settled like, and the sun, just at going down, struck the
windows like fire and the clean panes shone. There was that
yellow light over everything and that stillness, with now and
then a leaf or so dropping quietly down, that makes the fall
of the year so pleasant, to my mind.

The house stood in beeches, and the trunks of them were
gray, like the house, and the leaves all light lemon-colored,
like the sky, and that's the way I always think of Childerstone—
gray and clean and still. Just a few rooks (you call them
crows here) went over the house, and except for their cry as
they flew, there wasn't a sound about the place. I can see
how others might have found it sad, but it never seemed so to
me.

John set me down at the servants' entrance, and there,
before ever I got properly into the hall, the strangeness
began. The cook in her check apron was kneeling on the
floor in front of the big French range with the tears streaming
down her face, working over her rosary beads and gabbling
to drive you crazy. Over her stood a youngish but severe-
appearing man in a white linen coat like a ship's steward,
trying to get her up.

"Come, Katey," he was saying, "come, woman, up with
you and help—she'll do no harm, the poor soul! Look after
her, now, and I'll send for the doctor and see to madam—it's
only a fit, most like!"

Then he saw me and ran forward to give a hand to my box.

"You're the chambermaid, miss, I'm sure," he said. "I'm
sorry to say you'll find us a bit upset. The housekeeper's
down with a stroke of some sort, and the madam's none too
strong herself. Are you much of a hand to look after the
sick?"

"I'm not so clumsy as some," I said; "let me see her,"
and so we left the cook to her prayers and he carried my box
to my room.

I got into a print dress and apron and went to the house-keeper's room. She was an elderly person, and it looked to me as if she was in her last sickness. She didn't know any one, and so I was as good as another, and I had her tidy and comfortable in bed by the time the doctor came. He said she would need watching through the night and left some medicine, but I could see he had little hope for her. I made up a bed in the room, and all that night she chattered and muttered and took me for different ones, according as her fever went and came. Toward morning she got quiet and, as I thought, sensible again.

"Are you a nurse?" she says to me.

"Yes, Mrs. Shipman; be still and rest," I told her, to soothe her.

"I'm glad the children are sent away," she went on, after a bit; " 'twould break their mother's heart if they got the fever. Are the toys packed?"

"Yes, yes," I answered, "all packed and sent."

"Be sure there's enough frocks for Master Robertson," she begged me; "he's so hard on them and his aunties are so particular. And my baby must have her woolly rabbit at night or her darling heart will be just broken!"

"The rabbit is packed," I said, "and I saw to the frocks myself."

There's but one way with the sick when they're like that, and that's to humor them, you see. So she slept, and I got a little nap for myself. I was glad the children were away by next morning, for she was worse; the cook lost her head, and managed to break the range, so that the water-back leaked, and John and Hodges were mopping and mending all day. The madam herself had a bad turn, and the doctor brought a nursing Sister from a Catholic convent near there to look after her; she wasn't allowed to know how bad her old nurse was.

So it turned out that I'd been a week in the house without ever seeing my mistress. The Sister and I would meet on the stairs and chat a little evenings, and once I took a turn in the grounds with her.

"It's a good thing the children are sent away," I said; "they always add to the bother when there's sickness."

"Why, are there children?" says she.

"Oh yes, a boy and a girl," I answered. "'Poor old Mrs. Shipman is forever talking about them. She thinks she's their nurse, it seems, as she was their mother's."

"I wish they were here, then," says she, "for I don't like the looks of my patient at all. She doesn't speak seven words a day, and there's really little or nothing the matter with her that I can see. She's nervous and she's low and she wants cheering, that's all. I wonder the doctor doesn't see it."

That night, after both patients were settled, she came up to my room and took a glance at the old lady, who was going fast.

"Mrs. Childress will soon have to know about this," she said; and then, suddenly, "Are you sure about the children, Sarah?"

"Sure about them?" I repeated after her. "In what way, Sister?"

"That there are any?" says she.

"Why, of course," I answered. "Mrs. Shipman talks of nothing else. They're with their aunty, in New Jersey, somewhere. It's a good thing there are some, for, from what she says when she's rambling, the house and all the property would go out of the family otherwise. It's been five generations in the Childress family, but the nearest now is a cousin who married a Jew, and the family hate her for it. But Master Robertson makes it all safe, Mrs. Shipman says."

"That's a queer thing," said the Sister. "I took in a dear little picture of the boy and girl this afternoon to cheer her up a bit, and told her to try to think they were the real ones, who'd soon be with her, for that matter, and so happy to see their dear mamma, and she went white as a sheet and fainted in my arms. Of course I didn't refer to it again. She's quiet now, holding the picture, but I feared they were dead and you hadn't known.''

"Oh no," said I, "I'm sure not," and then I remembered that I'd been told there was but one in family. However, that's often said when there's a nurse to take care of small children (though it's not quite fair, perhaps), and I was certain of the children, anyway, for there were toys all about Mrs. Shipman's room and some seed-cookies and "animal-crackers," as they call those odd little biscuits, in a tin on her mantel.

However, we were soon to learn something that made me, at least, all the more curious. The doctor came that morning and told the Sister that her services would be no longer required, after he had seen her patient.

"Mrs. Childress is perfectly recovered," he said, "and she has unfortunately conceived a grudge against you, Sister. I need you, anyway, in the village. Poor old Shipman can't last the night now, and I want all that business disposed of very quietly. I have decided not to tell Mrs. Childress until it is all over and the funeral done with. She is in a very morbid state, and as I knew her husband well I have taken this step on my own responsibility. Hodges seems perfectly able to run things; and, to tell the truth, it would do your mistress far more good to attend to that herself," he said, turning to me.

"It would be a good thing for the poor lady to have some one about her, doctor," the Sister put in, quietly. "If there were children in the house, now—"

"Children!" he cried, pulling himself up and staring at her. "Did you speak to her about them? Then that accounts for it! I should have warned you."

"Then they *did* die!" she asked him. "That's what I thought."

"I'm afraid not," he said, shaking his head with a queer sort of sad little smile. "I forgot you were new here. Why, my dear Sister, didn't you know that—"

"Excuse me, sir, but there's no sign of your mare about—

did you tie her?'' says Hodges, coming in a great hurry, and
the doctor swore and ran off, and I never heard the end of the
sentence.

Well, I'm running on too long with these little odds and
ends, as I'm sure Margaret felt when I started telling her all
about it. The truth is, I dreaded then, just as I dread now, to
get at the real story and look our conduct straight in the face.
But I'll get on more quickly now.

Old Mrs. Shipman died very quiet in her sleep, and madam
wasn't told, which I didn't half like. The doctor was called
out of those parts to attend on his father very suddenly, and
Hodges managed the funeral and all. It was plain to see he
was a very trusty, silent fellow, devoted to the family. I took
as much off him as I could, and I was dusting the drawing-
room the day of the funeral, when I happened to pick up a
photograph, in a silver frame, of the same little fellow in the
picture the Sister had shown me—a dear little boy in short
kilts.

"That's Master Robertson, isn't it?" I said, very care-
lessly, not looking at him—I will own I was curious. He
gave a start.

"Yes—yes, certainly, that's Master Robertson—if you
choose to put it that way," he said, and I saw him put his
hand up to his eyes and his mouth twitched and he left the
room.

I didn't question him again, naturally; he was a hard man
to cross and very haughty, was William Hodges, and no one
in the house but respected him.

That day I saw Mrs. Childress for the first time. She was a
sweet, pretty thing, about my own age, but younger-looking,
fair, with gray eyes. She was in heavy crêpe, and her face all
fallen and sodden like, with grief and hopelessness—I felt for
her from the moment I saw her. And all the more that I'd
made up my mind what her trouble was: I thought that the
children were idiots, maybe, or feeble-minded, anyhow, and
so the property would go to the Jew in the end, and that his

family were hating her for it! Folly, of course, but women will have fancies, and that seemed to fit in with all I'd heard.

She'd been told that Shipman was away with some light, infectious fever, and she took it very mildly, and said there was no need to get any one in her place at present.

"Hodges will attend to everything," she said, in her pretty, tired way; "not that there's much to do—for one poor woman."

"Things may mend, ma'am, and you'll feel more like having some friends about you, most likely, later on," I said, to cheer her a bit.

She shook her head sadly.

"No, no, Sarah—if I can't have my own about me, I'll have no others," she said, and I thought I saw what she meant and said no more.

That night the doctor and the legal gentleman that looked after the family affairs were with us, and my mistress kept them for dinner. I helped Hodges with the serving, and was in the butler's pantry after Mrs. Childress had left them with their coffee and cigars, and as Hodges had left the door ajar I couldn't help catching a bit of the talk now and then.

"The worst of it is this trouble about the children," said the doctor. "She will grieve herself into a decline, I'm afraid."

"I suppose there's no hope?" said the other gentleman.

"No hope?" the doctor burst out. "Why, man, Robertson's been dead six months!"

"To be sure—I'd forgotten it was so long. Well, well, it's too bad, too bad," and Hodges came back and closed the door.

I must say I was thoroughly put out with the doctor. Why should he have told me a lie? And it was mostly from that that I deliberately disobeyed him that night, for I knew from the way he had spoken to the Sister that he didn't wish children mentioned. But I couldn't help it, for when I came to her room to see if I could help her, she was sitting in her black bedroom gown with her long hair in two braids, crying over the children's picture. "Hush, hush, ma'am!" I said, kneeling by her and soothing her head. "If they were here, you may be sure they wouldn't wish it."

"Who? Who?" she answers me, quite wild, but not angry at all. I saw this and spoke it our boldly, for it was plain that she liked me.

"Your children, ma'am," I said softly but very firm; "and you should control yourself and be cheerful and act as if they *were* here—as if it had pleased God to let you have them and not Himself!"

Such a look as she gave me! But soon she seemed to melt like, and put out her arm over my shoulders.

"What a beautiful way to put it, Sarah!" says she, in a dreamy kind of way. "Do you really think God has them— somewhere?"

"Why, of course, ma'am," said I, shocked in good earnest. "Who else?"

"Then you think I might love them, just as if—just as if—" here she began to sob.

"Why, Mrs. Childress," I said, "where is your belief? That's all that's left to mothers. I know, for I've lost two, and their father to blame for it, which you need never say," I told her.

She patted my shoulder very kindly. "But, oh, Sarah, if only they *were* here!" she cried, "really, really here!"

"I know, I know," I said, "it's very hard. But try to think it, ma'am—it helped me for weeks. Think they're in the room next you here, and you'll sleep better for it."

"Shall I?" she whispered, gripping my hand hard. "I believe I would—how well you understand me, Sarah! And will you help me to believe it?"

I saw she was feverish, and I knew what it means to get one good refreshing night without crying, and so I said, "Of course I will, ma'am; see, I'll open the door into the next room, and you can fancy them in their cribs, and I'll sleep in there as if it was to look after them, like."

Well, she was naught but a child herself, the poor dear! and she let me get her into bed like a lamb, and put her cheek into her hand and went off like a baby. It almost scared me to see how easy she was to manage, if one did but get hold of the right way. She looked brighter in the morning, and as Hodges had told me that Shipman used to do for her, I went in and dressed her—not that I was ever a lady's-maid, mind you, but I've always been one to turn my hand easily to anything I had a mind to, and I was growing very fond of my poor lady—and then I was a little proud, I'll own, of being able to do more for her than her own medical man, who couldn't trust a sensible woman with the truth!

She clung to me all the morning, and after my work was done I persuaded her to come out for the air. The doctor had ordered it long ago, but she was obstinate, and would scarcely go at all. That day, however, she took a good stroll with me, and it brought a bit of color into her cheeks. Just as we turned toward the house she sat down on a big rock to rest herself, and I saw her lip quiver and her eyes begin to fill. I followed her look, and there was a child's swing, hung from two ropes to a low bough. It must have been rotted with the rains, for it looked very old and the board seat was cracked and worn. All around—it hung in a sort of little glade—were small piles of stones and bits of oddments that only children get together, like the little magpies they are.

There's no use to expect any one but a mother or one who's had the constant care of little ones to understand the tears that come to your eyes at a sight like that. What they leave behind is worse than what they take with them; their curls and their fat legs and the kisses they gave you are all shut into the grave, but what they used to play with stays there and mourns them with you.

I saw a wild look come into her eyes, and I determined to quiet her at any cost.

"There, there, ma'am," I said quickly, " 'tis only their playthings. Supposing they were there now and enjoying them!

You go in and take your nap, as the doctor ordered, and leave me behind. . . ."

She saw what I meant in a twinkling, and the color jumped into her face again. She turned and hurried in, and just as she went out of sight she looked over her shoulder, timid like, and waved her hand—only a bit of a wave, but I saw it.

Under a big stone in front of me—for that part of the grounds was left wild, like a little grove—I saw a rusty tin biscuit-box, and as I opened it, curiously, to pass the time, I found it full of little stoneware platters and cups. Hardly thinking what I did, I arranged them as if laid out for tea, on a flat stone, and left them there. When I went to waken her for lunch, I started, for some more of those platters were on the table by her bed, and a white woolly rabbit and a picture-book! She blushed, but I took no notice, and after her luncheon I spied her going quickly back to the little grove.

"Madam's taking a turn for the better, surely," Hodges said to me that afternoon. "She's eating like a Christian now. What have you done to her, Miss Umbleby?" (I went as "Miss," for it's much easier to get a place so.)

"Mr. Hodges," I said, facing him squarely, "the doctors don't know everything. You know as well as I that it's out of nature not to mention children, where they're missed every hour of the day and every day of the month. It's easing the heart that's wanted—not smothering it."

"What d'you mean?" he says, staring at me.

"I mean toys and such like," I answered him, very firm, "and talk of them that's not here to use them, and even pretending that they are, if that will bring peace of mind, Mr. Hodges."

He rubbed his clean-shaven chin with his hand.

"Well, well!" he said at last; "well, well, well! You're a good girl, Miss Umbleby, and a kind one, that's certain. I never thought o' such a thing. Maybe it's all right, though. But who could understand a woman, anyway?"

"That's not much to understand," said I shortly, and left him staring at me.

She came in late in the afternoon with the rabbit under her arm, and there was Mr. Hodges in the drawing-room laying out the tea—we always had everything done as if the master was there, and guests, for the matter of that; she insisted on it. He knew his place as well as any man, but his eye fell on the rabbit, and he looked very queer and nearly dropped a cup. She saw it and began to tremble and go white, and it came over me then that now or never was the time to clinch matters, or she'd nearly die from shame and I couldn't soothe her any more.

"Perhaps Hodges had better go out and bring in the rest of the toys, ma'am," I says, very careless, not looking at her. "It's coming on for rain. And he can take an umbrella . . . shall he?"

She stiffened up and gave a sort of nod to him.

"Yes, Hodges, go," she said, half in a whisper, and he bit his lip, and swallowed hard, and said,

"Very good, madam," and went.

Well, after that, you can see how it would be, can't you? One thing led to another, and one time when she was not well for a few days and rather low, I actually got the two little cribs down from the garret and ran up some white draperies for them. She'd hardly let me leave her, and indeed there was not so much work that I couldn't manage very well. She gave all her orders through me, and I was well pleased to do for her and let Mr. Hodges manage things, which he did better than poor old Shipman, I'll be bound. By the time we told her about Shipman's death she took it very easy—indeed, I think she'd have minded nothing by that time, she had grown so calm and almost healthy.

Mr. Hodges would never catch my eye, and I never talked private any more with him, but that was the only sign he didn't approve, and he never spoke for about a month, but joined in with me by little and little, and never said a word but to shrug his shoulders when I ordered up a tray with porringes on it for the nursery (she had a bad cold, and got restless and grieving). I left her in the nursery with the tray and went out to him, for I saw he wished to speak to me at last.

"Doctor Wilmet would think well of this, if he was here? Is that your idea, Miss Umbleby?" he said to me, very dry. (The doctor had never come back, but gone to be head of a big asylum out in the West.)

"I'm sure I don't know, Mr. Hodges," I answered. "I think any doctor couldn't but be glad to see her gaining every day, and when she feels up to it and guests begin to come again, she'll get willing to see them and forget the loss of the poor little things."

"The loss of *what*?" says he, frowning at me.

"Why, the children," I answered.

"What children?"

"Master Robertson, of course, and Miss Winifred," I said, quite vexed with his obstinacy. (I had asked her once if the baby was named after her, and she nodded and went away quickly.)

"See here, my girl," says he, "there's no good keeping this up for my benefit. *I'm* not going into a decline, you know. I know as well as you do that she couldn't lose what she never had!"

" 'Never had'!" I gasped. "She never had any children?"

"Of course not," he said, steadying me, for my knees got weak all of a sudden. "That's what's made all the trouble—that's what's so unfortunate! D'you mean to say you didn't know?"

I sank right down on the stairs. "But the pictures!" I burst out.

"If you mean that picture of Mr. Robertson Childress when he was a little lad and the other one of him and his sister that died when a baby, and chose to fancy they was hers," says he, pointing up-stairs, "it's no fault of mine, Miss Umbleby."

And no more it was. What with poor old Shipman's ramblings and the doctor's words that I had twisted into what they never meant, I had got myself into a fine pickle.

"But what shall I do, Mr. Hodges?" I said, stupid like, with the surprise and the shock of it. "It'd kill her if I stopped now."

"That's for you to decide," said he, in his reserved, cold way. "I have my silver to do."

Well, I did decide. I lay awake all night at it, and maybe I did wrong, but I hadn't the heart to see the red go out of her cheek and the little shy smile off her pretty mouth. It hurt no one, and the mischief was done, anyway—there'd be no heir to Childerstone now. For five generations it had been the same—a son and a daughter to every pair, and the old place about as dear to each son, as I made out, as ever his wife or child could be. General Washington had stopped the night there, and some great French general that helped the Americans had come there for making plans to attack the British, and Colonel Robertson Childress that then was had helped him. They had plenty of English kin and some in the Southern States, but no near friends near them, on account of my mistress' husband having to live in Switzerland for his health and his father dying young (as he did), so that his mother couldn't bear the old place. But as soon as Mr. Robertson was told he was cured and could live where he liked, he made for Childerstone and brought his bride there—a stranger from an American family in Switzerland—and lived but three months. If anybody was ever alone, it was that poor lady, I'm sure. There was no big house like theirs anywhere about—no county families, as you might say—and those that had called from the village she wouldn't see, in her mourning. And yet out of that house she would not go, because he had loved it so; it was pitiful.

There's no good argle-bargling over it, as my mother used

to say. I'd do the same again! For I began it with the best of
motives, and as innocent as a baby myself of the real truth,
you see.

I can shut my eyes now and it all comes back to me as it
was in the old garden of autumn afternoons—I always think
of Childerstone in the autumn, somehow. There was an old
box hedge there, trimmed into balls and squares, and beds
laid out in patterns, with asters and marigolds and those little
rusty chrysanthemums that stand the early frosts so well. A
windbreak of great evergreens all along two sides kept it
warm and close, and from the south and west the sun streamed
in on the stone dial that the Childress of General Washington's time had had brought over from home. It was set for
Surrey, Hodges told me once, and no manner of use consequently, but very settled and homelike to see, if you understand me. In the middle was an old stone basin all mottled
and chipped, and the water ran out from a lion's mouth in
some kind of brown metal, and trickled down its mane and
jaws and splashed away. We cleaned it out, she and I, one
day *pretending we had help*, and Hodges went to town and
got us some goldfish for it. They looked very handsome
there. Old John kept the turf clipped and clean and routed out
some rustic seats for us—all gray they were and tottery, but
he strengthened them, and I smartened them up with yellow
chintz curtains I found in the garret—and I myself brought
out two tiny armchairs, painted wood, from the loft in the
coach-house. We'd sit there all the afternoon in September,
talking a little, me mending and my mistress embroidering on
some little frocks I cut out for her. We talked about the
children, of course. They got to be as real to me as to her,
almost. Of course at first it was all what they *would* have
been (for she was no fool, Mrs. Childress, though you may
be thinking so), but by little and little it got to be what they
were. It couldn't be helped.

Hodges would bring her tea out there, and she'd eat heart-
ily, for she never was much of a one for a late dinner, me

sewing all the time; for I always knew my place, though I believe in her kind heart she'd have been willing for me to eat with her, bless her! Then she'd look at me so wistful like, and say, "I'll leave you now, Sarah—eat your tea and don't keep out too late. Good-by—good-by . . ." Ah, dear me!

I'd sit and think, with the leaves dropping quiet and yellow around me and the water dripping from the lion's mouth, and sometimes I'd close my eyes and—I'll swear I could hear them playing quietly beyond me! They were never noisy children. I'll say now something I never mentioned, even to her, and I'd say it if my life hung by it. More than once I've left the stoneware tea-set shut in the biscuit-box and found it spread out of mornings. My mistress slept in the room next me with the door open, and am I to think that William Hodges, or Katey, crippled with rheumatism, or that lazy old John came down and set them out? I've taken a hasty run down to that garden (we called it the children's garden after a while) because she took an idea, and seen the swing just dying down, and not a breath stirring. That's the plain gospel of it. And I've lain in my bed, just off the two cribs, and held my breath at what I felt and heard. She knew it, too. But never heard so much as I, and often cried for it. I never knew why that should be, nor Hodges, either.

There was one rainy day I went up in the garret and pulled the old rocking-horse out and dusted it and put it out in the middle and set the door open and went away. It was directly over our heads as we sat sewing, and—ah, well, it's many years ago now, a many and a many, and it's no good raking over too much what's past and gone, I know. And as Hodges said afterward, the rain on the roof was loud and steady. . . .

I don't know why I should have thought of the rocking-horse, and she not, that was always thinking and planning for them. Hodges said it was because I had had children. But I could never have afforded them any such toy as that. Still, perhaps he was right. It was odd his saying that (he knew the facts about me, of course, by that time), being such a dry

man, with no fancy about him, you might say, and disliking
the whole subject, as he always did, but so it was. Men will
often come out with something like that, and quite astonish
one.

He never made a hint of objection when I was made
housekeeper, and that was like him, too, though I was, to say
so, put over him. But he knew my respect for him, black silk
afternoons or no black silk, and how we all leaned on him,
really.

And then Margaret came, as I said, and it was all to tell,
and a fine mess I made of it, and William Hodges that settled
it, after all.

For Margaret wanted to pack her box directly and get off,
and said she'd never heard of such doings, and had no liking
for people that weren't right.

"Not right?" said Hodges—"not right? Don't you make
any such mistake, my girl. Madam attends to all her law
business and is at church regularly, and if she's not for much
company—well, all the easier for us. Her cheques are as
sensible as any one's, I don't care who the man is, and a lady
has a right to her fancies. I've lived with very high families
at home, and if I'm suited, you may depend upon it the place
is a good one. Go or stop, as you like, but don't set up above
your elders, young woman."

So she thought it over, and the end of it all was that she
was with us till the last. And gave me many a black hour,
too, poor child! meaning no harm; but she admired Hodges,
it was plain, and being younger than I and far handsomer in a
dark, Scotch way, it went hard with me, for he made no sign,
and I was proud and wouldn't have showed my feelings for
my life twice over.

Well, it went on three years more. I made my little frocks
longer and the goldfish grew bigger and we set out new
marigolds every year, that was all. It was like some quiet
dream, when I've gone back and seemed a girl again in the
green lanes at home, with mother clear-starching and the

rector's daughter hearing my catechism, and Master Law-
rence sent off to school for bringing me his first partridge.
Those dreams seem long and short at one and the same time,
and I wake years older, and yet it has not been years that
passed, but only minutes. So it was at Childerstone. The
years went by like the hours went in the children's garden, all
hedged in like, and quiet, and leaving no mark. We all
seemed the same to one another, and one day was like
another, full, somehow, and busy and happy, too, in a quiet
gentle way.

When old Katey lay dying she spoke of those days for the
first time to me. She'd sent up the porringers and set out
glasses of milk and made cookies in heart shapes, with her
mouth tight shut for all that time, and we never knowing if
she sensed it rightly or not. But on her death-bed she told me
that she felt the Blessed Mary (as she called her) had given
those days to my poor mistress to make up to her for all she'd
lost and all she'd never had, and that she'd confessed her part
in it and been cleared long ago. I never loved any time better,
looking back, nor Hodges either. One season the Christmas
trees would be up, and then before we knew it the ice would
be out of the brooks, and there would be crocus and daffodils
for Mr. Childress' grave.

She and I took all the care of it, and the key to the iron
gate of it lay out on her low work-table, and one or other
of us always passing through; but one afternoon in summer
when I went with a basket of June roses, she being not quite
up to it that day, there on the flat stone I saw with my own
eyes a little crumpled bunch of daisies—all nipped off short,
such as children pick, and crushed and wilted in their hot
little hands! And on no other tomb but his. But I was used to
such as that by then. . . .

Margaret was handy with her needle, and I remember well
the day she made the linen garden hat with a knot of rose-
color under the brim.

"You don't think this will be too old, do you, ma'am?"

she said when she showed it to my mistress, and the dear lady was that pleased!

"Not a bit, Margaret," she said, and I carried it off to Miss Winifred's closet. Many's the time I missed it after that, and knew too much to hunt. It was hunting that spoiled all, for we tried it.

And yet, we didn't half believe. Heaven help us, we knew, but we didn't believe: St. Thomas was nothing to us.

Margaret was with us three years when the new family came. Hodges told us that Hudson River property was looking up and land was worth more every year. Anyway, in one year two families built big houses within a mile of us, and we went to call, of course, as in duty bound. John grumbled at getting out the good harness and having the carriage relined, but my mistress knew what was right, and he had no choice. I dressed her very careful and we watched her off from the door, a thought too pale in her black, but sweet as a flower, and every inch full of breeding, as Hodges said.

I never knew what took place at that visit, but she came back with a bright-red circle in each cheek and her head very high, and spent all the evening in the nursery. Alone, of course, for I heard little quick sounds on the piano in the drawing-room, and the fairy-books were gone from the children's bookshelves, and Margaret found them in front of the fire and brought them to me. . . .

It was only three days before the new family called on us (a pair of ponies to a basket-phaeton—very neat and a nice little groom), and my heart jumped into my mouth when I saw there were two children in with the lady: little girls of eight and twelve, I should say. 'Twas the first carriage callers that ever I'd seen in the place, and Hodges says to me as he goes toward the hall:

"This is something like, eh, Mrs. Umbleby?"

But I felt odd and uncertain, and when from behind the library door I heard the lady say,

"You see, I've kept by word and brought my babies,

Mrs. Childress—my son is hardly old enough for yours—
only four—but Helena and Lou can't wait—they are so impatient to see your little girl!''—when I heard that, I saw what
my poor mistress had been at, and the terrible situation we
were in (and had been in for years) flashed over me, and my
hands got cold as ice.

"Where is she?" the lady went on.

At that I went boldly into the library and stood by my
mistress' chair—I couldn't desert her then, after all those
years.

"Where? where?" my poor lady repeated, vague like, and
turned her eyes so piteous at me that I looked the visitor
straight in the face, and getting between her and my mistress,
I said very calmly:

"I think Miss Winifred is in the children's garden, madam;
shall I take the young ladies there?"

For my thought was to get the children out of the way
before it all came out, you see.

Oh, the look of gratitude she gave me! And yet it was a
mad thing to do. But I couldn't desert her—I couldn't.

"There, you see, mamma!" cried the youngest, and the
older one said,

"We can find our way, thank you," very civil, to me.

"Children have sharp eyes," said the lady, laughing; "one
can't hide them from each other—haven't you found it so?"

"Now what the devil does she mean by that?" Hodges
muttered to me as he passed by me with the tray. He always
kept the silver perfect, and it did one's heart good to see his
tray: urn and sugar and cream just twinkling and the toast in a
covered dish—old Chelsea it was—and new cakes and jam
and fresh butter, just as they have at home.

I don't know what they talked of, for I couldn't find any
excuse to stop in the room, and she wouldn't have had it,
anyway. I went around to the front to catch the children when
they should come back, and quiet them, but they didn't
come, and I was too thankful to think much about it.

After about half an hour I saw the oldest one coming slowly along by herself, looking very sulky.

"Where's your sister, dear?" I said, all in a tremble, for I dreaded how she might put it.

"She's too naughty—I can't get her to leave," she says, pettishly, and burst into the library ahead of me. My mistress' face was scarlet and her eyes like two big stars—for the first time I saw that she was a beauty. Her breath came very quick, and I knew as well as if I'd been there all the time that she'd been letting herself go, as they say, and talked to her heart's content about what she'd never have a chance to talk again to any guest. She was much excited, and the other woman knew it and was puzzled, I could see, from the way she looked at her.

Now the girl burst into talk.

"Mamma, Lou is so naughty!" she cried. "I saw the ponies coming up the drive, and I told her it was time, but she wouldn't come!"

"Gently, daughter, gently," said the lady, and put her arm around her and smoothed her hair. "Why won't Lou come?"

I can see that room now, as plain as any picture in a frame: the setting sun all yellow on the gilt of the rows of books, the streak of light on the waxed oak floor, the urn shining in the last rays. There was the mother patting the big girl, there was Hodges with his hand on the tray, and there was me standing behind my mistress, with her red cheeks and her poor heaving bosom.

"Why won't Lou come?" she asked the girl again.

"Because," she says, still fretful, and very loud and clear— "because she is taking a pattern of the little girl's hat and trying to twist hers into that shape! I told her you wouldn't like it."

My mistress sprang up, and the chair fell down with a crash behind her. I turned (Hodges says) as white as a sheet and moved nearer her.

"Hat!" she gasped. "What hat? *Whose hat?*"

There seemed to be a jingling, like sleigh-bells, all through the air, and I thought I was going crazy, till I saw that it came from the tray, where Hodges' hand was shaking so, and yet he couldn't take it off.

"The hat with the rose-colored ribbon on it," said the girl—"the one we saw as we drove in, you know, mamma. It's so becoming."

"Sarah! Sarah! did you hear? Did you hear?" shrieked my mistress. "She saw, Sarah; *she saw!*"

Then the color went out of her like when you blow out a candle, and she put her hand to her heart.

"Oh, oh, what pain!" she said, very quickly, and Hodges cried, "My God, she's gone!" and I caught her as she fell and we went down together, for my knees were shaking.

When I opened my eyes there was only Margaret there, wetting my forehead, for William had gone for a doctor. Not that it was of any use, for she never breathed. But the smile on her face was lovely.

We got her on her bed, and the sight of her there brought the tears to me, and I cried out: "Oh dear, oh dear! She was all I had in the world, and now—"

"Now you've got me, my girl, and isn't that worth anything to you, Sarah?"

That was William Hodges, and he put his arm over my shoulder, right before Margaret, and looked so kind at me, so kind— I saw in a moment that no one else was anything to him and that he had always cared for me. And that, coming so sudden, when I had given up all hope of it, was too much for me, weak as I was, and I fainted off again, and woke up raving hot with fever and half out of my mind; but not quite, for I kept begging them to put off the funeral till I should be able to be up.

But this, of course, was not done, and by the time I was out of hospital the turf was all in place on her dear grave.

William had managed everything and had picked out all the little keepsakes I should have chosen—the heirs were most kind. Indeed, I've felt different toward Jews ever since; for they made it into a children's home for those of their belief as were poor and orphaned, and whatever may have been, the old place will never lack for children now.

I never stepped foot in the grounds again; for William Hodges, though the gentlest and fairest of men, never thwarted me but once, and it was in just that direction. Moreover, he forbade me to speak of what only he and I knew for a certainty, and he was one of that sort that when a command is laid it's best kept.

We've two fine children—girl and boy—and he never murmured at the names I chose for them. Indeed, considering what my mistress' will left me and what his master had done for him, he was as pleased as I.

"They're named after our two best friends, Sarah," he said, looking hard at me once.

And I nodded my head; but if she saw me, in heaven, she knew who were in my heart when I named them!

THE UPPER BERTH

F. Marion Crawford

I

Somebody asked for the cigars. We had talked so long, and the conversation was beginning to languish, the tobacco smoke had got into the heavy curtains, the wine had got into those brains which were liable to become heavy, and it was already perfectly evident, unless somebody did something to rouse our oppressed spirits, the meeting would soon come to its natural conclusion, and we, the guests, would speedily go home to bed, and most certainly to sleep. No one had said anything very remarkable, it may be no one had anything to say. Jones had given us every particular of his last hunting adventure in Yorkshire. Mr. Tompkins, of Boston, had explained at elaborate length those working principles by the due and careful maintenance of which the Atchison, Topeka, and Sante Fe Railroad not only extended its territory, increased its departmental influence, and transported live stock without starving them to death before the day of actual delivery, but also, had for years succeeded in deceiving those passengers who bought its tickets into the fallacious belief that the corporation aforesaid was really able to transport human life without destroying it. Signor Tombola

had endeavored to persuade us, by arguments which we took
no trouble to oppose, that the unity of his country in no way
resembled the average modern torpedo, carefully planned,
constructed with all the skill of the greatest European arse-
nals, but, when constructed, destined to be directed by feeble
hands into a region where it must undoubtedly explode,
unseen, unfeared, and unheard, into the illimitable wastes of
political chaos.

It is unnecessary to go into further details. The conversation had assumed proportions which would have bored
Prometheus on his rock, which would have driven Tantalus
to distraction, and which would have impelled Ixion to seek
relaxation in the simple but instructive dialogues of Herr
Ollendorf, rather than submit to the greater evil of listening
to our talk. We had sat at a table for hours; we were bored,
we were tired, and nobody showed signs of moving.

Somebody called for cigars. We all instinctively looked
toward the speaker. Brisbane was a man of five-and-thirty-
years of age, and remarkable for those gifts which chiefly
attract the attention of men. He was a strong man. The
external proportions of his figure presented nothing extraordinary to the common eye, though his size was above the
average. He was a little over six feet in height, and moder-
ately broad in the shoulder; he did not appear to be stout, but,
on the other hand he was certainly not thin; his small head
was supported by a strong and sinewy neck; his broad,
muscular hands seemed to possess a peculiar skill in breaking
walnuts without the assistance of the ordinary cracker, and,
seeing him in profile, one could not help remarking the
extraordinary breadth of his sleeves and the unusual thickness
of his chest. He was one of those men who are commonly
spoken of among men as deceptive; that is to say, that though
he looked exceedingly strong, he was in reality very much
stronger than he looked. Of his features I need say little. His
head is small, his hair is thin, his eyes are blue, his nose is
large, he has a small mustache and a square jaw. Everybody

knows Brisbane, and when he asked for a cigar everybody looked at him.

"It is a very singular thing," said Brisbane.

Everybody stopped talking. Brisbane's voice was not loud, but possessed a peculiar quality of penetrating general conversation and cutting it like a knife. Everybody listened. Brisbane perceiving that he had attracted their general attention, lighted his cigar with equal equanimity.

"It is very singular," he continued, "that thing about ghosts: People are always asking whether anybody has seen a ghost. I have."

"Bosh! What, you? You don't mean to say so, Brisbane? Well, for a man of his intelligence!"

A chorus of exclamations greeted Brisbane's remarkable statement. Everybody called for cigars, and Stubbs, the butler, suddenly appeared from the depths of nowhere with a fresh bottle of dry champagne. The situation was saved; Brisbane was going to tell a story.

"I am an old sailor," said Brisbane, "and as I have to cross the Atlantic pretty often, I have my favorites. Most men have their favorites. I have seen a man wait in a Broadway bar for three-quarters of an hour for a particular car which he liked. I believe the barkeeper made at least one-third of his living by that man's preference. I have a habit of waiting for certain ships when I am obliged to cross that duckpond. It may be a prejudice, but I was never cheated out of a good passage but once in my life. I remember it very well; it was a warm morning in June, and the custom house officials, who were hanging about waiting for a steamer already on her way up from quarantine, presented a peculiarly hazy and thoughtful appearance. I had not much luggage—I never have. I mingled with the crowd of passengers, porters, and officious individuals in blue coats and brass buttons, who seemed to spring up like mushrooms from the deck of a moored steamer to obtrude their unnecessary services upon the independent passengers. I have often no-

ticed with a certain interest the spontaneous evolution of
these fellows. They are not there when you arrive; five
minutes after the pilot has called 'Go ahead!' they, or at least
their blue coats and brass buttons, have disappeared from
deck and gangway as completely as though they had been
consigned to that locker which tradition unanimously ascribes
to Davy Jones. But, at the moment of starting, they are there,
clean-shaved, blue-coated, and ravenous for fees. I hastened
on board. The 'Kamtschatka' was one of my favorite ships. I
say was, because she emphatically no longer is. I cannot
conceive of any inducement which could entice me to make
another voyage in her. Yes, I know what you are going to
say. She is uncommonly clean in the run aft, she has enough
bluffing off in the bows to keep her dry, and the lower berths
are the most of them double. She has a lot of advantages, but
I won't cross in her again. Excuse the digression. I got on
board. I hailed the steward, whose red nose and redder
whiskers are equally familiar to me.

" 'One hundred and five, lower berth,' said I, in the
business-like tone peculiar to men who think no more of
crossing the Atlantic than taking a whiskey cocktail at down-
town Delmonico's.

"The steward took my portmanteau, great coat, and rug. I
shall never forget the expression on his face. Not that he
turned pale. It is maintained by the most eminent divines that
even miracles cannot change the course of nature. I have no
hesitation in saying that he did not turn pale; but, from his
expression, I judged that he was either about to shed tears, to
sneeze, or to drop my portmanteau. As the latter contained
two bottles of particularly fine old sherry, presented to me
for my voyage by my old friend Snigginson van Pickyns, I
felt extremely nervous. But the steward did none of these
things.

" 'Well, I'll be damned,' said he in a low voice, and led
the way.

"I supposed my Hermes, as he led me to the lower regions, had had a little grog, but I said nothing, and followed him. One hundred and five was on the port side, well aft. There was nothing remarkable about the stateroom. The lower berth, like most of those upon the 'Kamtschatka,' was double. There was plenty of room; there was the usual washing apparatus, calculated to convey an idea of luxury to the mind of a North American Indian; there were the usual inefficient racks of brown wood, in which it is more easy to hang a large-sized umbrella than the common toothbrush of commerce. Upon the uninviting mattresses were carefully folded together those blankets which a great modern humorist has aptly compared to cold buckwheat cakes. The question of towels was left entirely to the imagination. The glass decanters were filled with a transparent liquid faintly tinged with brown, but from which an odor less faint, but not more pleasing, ascended to the nostrils, like a far-off seasick reminiscence of oily machinery. Sad-colored curtains half closed the upper berth. The hazy June daylight shed a faint illumination upon that desolate little scene. Ugh! How I hate that stateroom!

"The steward deposited my traps and looked at me as though he wanted to get away—probably in search of more passengers and more fees. It is always a good plan to start in favor with those functionaries, and I accordingly gave him certain coins there and then.

" 'I'll try and make yer comfortable all I can,' he remarked, as he put the coins in his pocket. Nevertheless, there was a doubtful intonation in his voice which surprised me. Possibly his scale of fees had gone up, and he was not satisfied; but on the whole I was inclined to think that, as he himself would have expressed it, he was 'the better for a glass.' I was wrong, however, and did the man injustice.

II

"Nothing especially noteworthy of mention occurred during the day. We left the pier punctually, and it was very pleasant to be fairly under way, for the weather was warm and sultry, and the motion of the steamer produced a refreshing breeze.

"Everybody knows what the first day at sea is like. People pace the decks and stare at other, and occasionally meet acquaintances whom they did not know to be on board. There is the usual uncertainty as to whether the food will be good, bad, or indifferent, until the first two meals have put the matter beyond a doubt, there is the usual uncertainty about the weather, until the ship is fairly off Fire Island. The tables are crowded at first, and then suddenly thinned. Pale-faced people spring from their seats and precipitate themselves toward the door, and each old sailor breathes more freely as his seasick neighbor rushes from his side, leaving him plenty of elbow room and an unlimited command over the mustard.

"One passage across the Atlantic is very much like another, and we who cross very often do not make the voyage for the sake of novelty. Whales and icebergs are indeed always objects of interest, but, after all, one whale is very much like another whale, and one rarely sees an iceberg at close quarters. To the majority of us, the most delightful moment of the day on board an ocean steamer is when we have taken our last turn on deck, have smoked our last cigar, and having succeeded in tiring ourselves, feel at liberty to turn in with a clear conscience. On that first night of the voyage I felt particularly lazy, and went to bed in one hundred and five rather earlier than I usually do. As I turned in, I was amazed to see that I was to have a companion. A portmanteau, very like my own, lay in the opposite corner, and in the upper berth had been deposited a neatly folded rug with a stick and umbrella. I had hoped to be alone, and I was disappointed; but I wondered who my roommate was to be, and I determined to have a look at him.

"Before I had been long in bed he entered. He was, as far as I could see, a very tall man, very thin, very pale, with sandy hair and whiskers, and colorless gray eyes. He had about him, I thought, an air of rather dubious fashion; the sort of man you might see in Wall Street, without being able precisely to say what he was doing there—the sort of man who frequents the Café Anglais, who always seems to be alone, and who drinks champagne; you might meet him on a race-course, but he would never appear to be doing anything there either. A little overdressed—a little odd. There are three or four of his kind on every ocean streamer. I made up my mind that I did not care to make his acquaintance, and I went to sleep saying to myself that I would study his habits in order to avoid him. If he rose early, I would rise late. I did not care to know him. If you once know people of that kind they are always turning up. Poor fellow! I need not have taken the trouble to come to so many decisions about him, for I never saw him again after that first night in one hundred and five.

"I was sleeping soundly when I was suddenly wakened by a loud noise. To judge from the sound, my roommate must have sprung with a single leap from the upper berth to the floor. I heard him fumbling with the latch and bolt of the door, which opened immediately, and then I heard his footsteps as he ran at full speed down the passage, leaving the door open behind him. The ship was rolling a little, and I expected to hear him stumble or fall, but he ran as though he were running for his life. The door swung on its hinges with the motion of the vessel, and the sound annoyed me. I got up and shut it, and groped my way back to my berth in the darkness. I went to sleep again; but I have no idea how long I slept.

"When I awoke it was still quite dark, but I felt a disagreeable sensation of cold, and it seemed to me that the air was damp. You know the peculiar smell of a cabin which has been wet with sea water. I covered myself up as well as I could and dozed off again, framing compliments to be made the next day, and selecting the most powerful epithets in language. I could hear my roommate turn over in the upper berth. He had probably returned while I was asleep. Once I thought I heard him groan, and I argued that he was seasick. That is particularly unpleasant when one is below. Nevertheless I dozed off and slept till early daylight.

"The ship was rolling heavily, much more than on the previous evening, and the gray light which came in through the porthole changed in tint with every movement according as the angle of the vessel's side turned the glasses seaward or skyward. It was very cold—unaccountably so for the month of June. I turned my head and looked at the porthole, and saw to my surprise that it was wide open and hooked back. I believe I swore audibly. Then I got up and shut it. As I turned back I glanced at the upper berth. The curtains were drawn close together; my companion had probably felt as cold as I. It struck me that I had slept enough. The stateroom was uncomfortable, though, strange to say, I could not smell the dampness which had annoyed me in the night. My roommate was still asleep—excellent opportunity for avoiding him, so I dressed at once and went on deck. The day was warm and cloudy, with an oily smell on the water. It was seven o'clock as I came out—much later than I had imagined. I came across the doctor, who was taking his first sniff of the morning air. He was a young man from the West of Ireland—a tremendous fellow, with black hair and blue eyes, already inclined to be stout; he had a happy-go-lucky, healthy look about him which was rather attractive.

" 'Fine mornin','' I remarked by way of introduction.

" 'Well,' said he, eyeing me with an air of ready interest, 'it's a fine morning and it's not a fine morning. I don't think it's much of a morning.'

" 'Well, no—it is not so very fine,' said I.

" 'It's just what I call fuggly weather,' replied the doctor.

" 'It was very cold last night, I thought,' I remarked. 'However, when I looked about, I found that the porthole was wide open. I had not noticed it when I went to bed. And the stateroom was damp, too.'

" 'Damp!' said he. 'Whereabouts are you?'

" 'One hundred and five—'

"To my surprise the doctor started visibly, and stared at me.

" 'What is the matter?' I asked.

" 'Oh—nothing,' he answered; 'only everybody has complained of that stateroom for the last three trips.'

" 'I shall complain, too,' I said. 'It has certainly not been properly aired. It is a shame!'

" 'I don't believe it can be helped,' answered the doctor. 'I believe there is something—well, it is not my business to frighten passengers.'

" 'You need not be afraid of frightening me,' I replied. 'I can stand any amount of damp. If I should get a bad cold I will come to you.'

"I offered the doctor a cigar, which he took and examined very critically.

" 'It is not so much the damp,' he remarked. 'However, I dare say you will get on very well. Have you a roommate?'

" 'Yes; a deuce of a fellow, who bolts out in the middle of the night and leaves the door open.'

"Again the doctor glanced curiously at me. Then he lighted the cigar and looked grave.

" 'Did he come back?' he asked presently.

" 'Yes. I was asleep, but I waked up and heard him moving. Then I felt cold and went to sleep again. This morning I found the porthole open.'

" 'Look here," said the doctor, quietly, 'I don't care much for this ship. I don't care a rap for her reputation. I tell you what I will do. I have a good-sized place up here. I will share it with you, though I don't know you from Adam.'

"I was very much surprised at the proposition. I could not imagine why he should take such a sudden interest in my welfare. However, his manner as he spoke of the ship was peculiar.

" 'You are very good, Doctor,' I said. 'But really, I believe even now the cabin could be aired, or cleaned out, or something. Why do you not care for the ship?'

" 'We are not superstitious in our profession, sir,' replied the doctor. 'But the sea makes people so. I don't want to prejudice you, and I don't want to frighten you, but if you will take my advice you will move in here. I would as soon see you overboard,' he added, 'as know that you or any other man was to sleep in one hundred and five.'

" 'Good gracious! Why?' I asked.

" 'Just because on the last three trips the people who have slept there actually have gone overboard,' he answered gravely.

"The intelligence was startling and exceedingly unpleasant, I confess. I looked hard at the doctor to see whether he was making game of me, but he looked perfectly serious. I thanked him warmly for his offer, but told him I intended to be the exception to the rule by which everyone who slept in that particular stateroom went overboard. He did not say much, but looked as grave as ever, and hinted that before we got across, I should probably reconsider his proposal. In the course of time we went to breakfast, at which only an inconsiderable number of passengers assembled. I noticed that one or two of the officers who breakfasted with us looked grave. After breakfast I went into my stateroom in order to get a book. The curtains of the upper berth were still closely drawn. Not a word was to be heard. My roommate was probably still asleep.

"As I came out I met the steward whose business it was to look after me. He whispered that the captain wanted to see me, and then scuttled away down the passage as if very anxious to avoid any questions. I went toward the captain's cabin, and found him waiting for me.

" 'Sir,' said he, 'I want to ask a favor of you.'

"I answered that I would do anything to oblige him.

" 'Your roommate has disappeared,' he said. "He is known to have turned in early last night. Did you notice anything extraordinary in his manner?'

"The question coming, as it did, in exact confirmation of the fears the doctor had expressed half an hour earlier, staggered me.

" 'You don't mean to say that he has gone overboard?' I asked.

" 'I fear he has,' answered the captain.

" 'This is the most extraordinary thing—' I began.

" 'Why?' he asked.

" 'He is the fourth, then?' I explained. In answer to another question from the captain, I explained, without mentioning the doctor, that I had heard the story concerning one hundred and five. He seemed very much annoyed at hearing that I knew of it. I told him what had occurred in the night.

" 'What you say,' he replied, 'coincides almost exactly with what was told me by the roommates of two of the other three. They bolt out of bed and run down the passage. Two of them were seen to go overboard by the watch, we stopped, and lowered boats, but they were not found. Nobody, however, saw or heard the man who was lost last night—if he is really lost. The steward, who is a superstitious fellow, perhaps, and expected something to go wrong, went to look for him this morning, and found his berth empty, but his clothes lying about, just as he had left them. The steward was the only man on board who knew him by sight, and he has been searching everywhere for him. He has disappeared! Now, sir, I want to beg you not to mention the circumstance to any of the passengers; I don't want the ship to get a bad name, and nothing hangs about an ocean-goer like stories of suicides. You shall have your choice of any one of the officers' cabins you like, including my own, for the rest of the passage. Is that a fair bargain?'

" 'Very,' I said; 'and I am much obliged to you. But since I am alone, and have the stateroom to myself, I would rather not move. If the steward will take out that unfortunate man's things, I would as lief stay where I am. I will not say anything about the matter, and I think I can promise you that I will not follow my roommate.

"The captain tried to dissuade me from my intention, but I preferred having a stateroom alone to being the chum of any officer on board. I do know know whether I acted foolishly, but if I had taken his advice I should have had nothing more to tell. There would have remained the disagreeable coincidence of several suicides occurring among men who had slept in the same cabin, but that would have been all.

"That was not the end of the matter, however, by any means. I obstinately made up my mind that I would not be disturbed by such tales, and I even went so far as to argue the question with the captain. There was something wrong about the stateroom, I said. It was rather damp. The porthole had been left open last night. My roommate might have been ill when he came on board, and he might have become delirious after he went to bed. He might even now be hiding somewhere on board, and might be found later. The place ought to be aired and the fastening of the port looked to. If the captain would give me leave, I would see that what I thought necessary was done immediately.

" 'Of course you have a right to stay where you are if you please,' he replied, rather petulantly; 'but I wish you would turn out and let me lock the place up, and be done with it.'

"I did not see it in the same light, and left the captain, after promising to be silent concerning the disappearance of my companion. The latter had had no acquaintance on board, and was not missed in the course of the day. Toward evening I met the doctor again, and he asked me whether I had changed my mind. I told him I had not.

" 'Then you will before long,' he said, very gravely.

III

"We played whist in the evening, and I went to bed late. I will confess now that I felt a disagreeable sensation when I entered my stateroom. I could not help thinking of the tall man I had seen on the previous night, who was now dead, drowned, tossing about in the long swell, two or three hundred miles astern. His face rose very distinctly before me as I undressed, and I even went so far as to draw back the curtains of the upper berth, as though to persuade myself that he was actually gone. I also bolted the door of the stateroom. Suddenly I became aware that the porthole was opened and fastened back. This was more than I could stand. I hastily threw on my dressing-gown, and went in search of Robert, the steward of my passage. I was very angry, I remember, and when I found him I dragged him roughly to the door of one hundred and five, and pushed him toward the open porthole.

" 'What the deuce do you mean, you scoundrel, by leaving that port open every night? Don't you know it is against the regulations? Don't you know that if the ship heeled and the water began to come in, ten men could not shut it? I will report you to the captain, you blackguard, for endangering the ship!'

"I was exceedingly wroth. The man trembled and turned pale, and then began to shut the round glass plate with the heavy brass fittings.

" 'Why don't you answer me?' I said roughly.

" 'If you please, sir,' faltered Robert, 'there's nobody on board as can keep this 'ere port shut at night. You can try it yourself, sir. I ain't a-going to stop hany longer on board o' this vessel, sir; I ain't, indeed. But if I was you, sir, I'd just clear out and go and sleep with the surgeon, or something, I would. Look 'ere, sir, is that fastened what you may call securely, or not, sir? Try it, sir, see if it will move a hinch.'

"I tried the port, and found it perfectly tight.

" 'Well, sir,' continued Robert, triumphantly, 'I wager my reputation as an A 1 steward, that in arf an hour it will be open again; fastened back, too, sir, that's the horful thing—fastened back!'

"I examined the great screw and the looped nut that ran on it.

" 'If I find it open in the night, Robert, I will give you a sovereign. It is not possible. You may go.'

"Soverin, did you say, sir? Very good, sir. Thank you, sir. Good-night, sir. Pleasant reepose, sir, and all manner of hinchantin' dreams, sir.'

"Robert scuttled away, delighted at being released. Of course, I thought he was trying to account for his negligence by a silly story, intended to frighten me, and I disbelieved him. The consequence was that he got his sovereign, and I spent a very peculiarly unpleasant night.

"I went to bed, and five minutes after I had rolled myself up in my blankets the inexorable Robert extinguished the light that burned steadily behind the ground-glass pane near the door. I lay quite still in the dark trying to go to sleep, but I soon found that impossible. It had been some satisfaction to be angry with the steward, and the diversion had vanished that unpleasant sensation I had at first experienced when I thought of the drowned man who had been my chum; but I was no longer sleepy, and I lay awake for some time, occasionally glancing at the porthole, which I could just see from where I lay, and which, in the darkness, looked like a faintly luminous soup-plate suspended in blackness. I believe I must have lain there for an hour, and, as I remember, I was just dozing into sleep, when I was roused by a draught of cold air, and by distinctly feeling the spray of the sea blown upon my face. I started to my feet, and not having allowed in the dark for the motion of the ship, I was instantly thrown violently across the stateroom upon the couch which was placed beneath the porthole. I recovered myself immediately,

however, and climbed upon my knees. The porthole was
again wide open and fastened back!

"Now these things are facts. I was wide awake when I got
up, and I should certainly have been waked by the fall had I
had been dozing. Moreover, I bruised my elbows and knees
badly, and the bruises were there on the following morning to
testify to the fact, if I myself had doubted it. The porthole
was wide open and fastened back—a thing so unaccountable,
that I remember very well feeling astonishment rather than
fear when I discovered it. I at once closed the plate again,
and screwed down the loop nut with all my strength. It was
very dark in the stateroom. I reflected that the port had
certainly been opened within an hour after Robert had at first
shut it in my presence, and I determined to watch it and see
whether it would open again. Those brass fittings are very
heavy and by no means easy to move; I could not believe that
the clamp had been turned by the shaking of the screw. I
stood peering out through the thick glass at the alternate
white and gray streaks of the sea that foamed beneath the
ship's side. I must have remained there a quarter of an hour.

"Suddenly, as I stood, I distinctly heard something moving behind me in one of the berths, and a moment afterward,
just as I turned instinctively to look—though I could, of
course, see nothing in the darkness—I heard a very faint
groan. I sprang across the stateroom, and tore the curtains of
the upper berth aside, thrusting in my hands to discover if
there were any one there. There was some one.

"I remember that the sensation as I put my hands forward
was as though I were plunging them into the air of a damp
cellar, and from behind the curtain came a gust of wind that
smelled horribly of stagnant seawater. I laid hold of something that had the shape of a man's arm, but was smooth,
and wet, and icy cold. But suddenly, as I pulled, the creature
sprang violently forward against me, a clammy, oozy mass,
as it seemed to me, heavy and wet, yet endowed with a sort
of supernatural strength. I reeled across the stateroom, and in

an instant the door opened and the thing rushed out. I had not had time to be frightened, and quickly recovering myself, I sprang through the door and gave chase at the top of my speed, but I was too late. Ten yards before me I could see—I am sure I saw it—a dark shadow moving in the dimly lighted passage, quickly as the shadow of a fast horse thrown before a dog-cart by the lamp on a dark night. But in a moment it had disappeared, and I found myself holding on to the polished rail that ran along the bulkhead where the passage turned toward the companion. My hair stood on end, and the cold perspiration rolled down my face. I am not ashamed of it in the least: I was very badly frightened.

"Still I doubted my senses, and pulled myself together. It was absurd, I thought. The Welsh rarebit I had eaten had disagreed with me. I had been in a nightmare. I made my way back to the stateroom, and entered it with an effort. The whole place smelled of stagnant seawater, as it had when I had waked on the previous evening. It required my utmost strength to go in and grope among my things for a box of wax lights. As I lighted a railway reading-lantern which I always carry in case I want to read after the lamps are out, I perceived that the porthole was again open, and a sort of creeping horror began to take possession of me which I never felt before, nor wish to feel again. But I got a light and proceeded to examine the upper berth, expecting to find it drenched with seawater.

But I was disappointed. The bed had been slept in, and the smell of the sea was strong, but the bedding was as dry as a bone. I fancied that Robert had not had the courage to make the bed after the accident of the previous night—it had all been a hideous dream. I drew the curtains back as far as I could, and examined the place very carefully. It was perfectly dry. But the porthole was open again. With a sort of dull bewilderment of horror, I closed it and screwed it down, and thrusting my heavy stick through the brass loop, wrenched it with all my might, till the thick metal began to bend with the pressure. Then I hooked my reading-lantern into the red velvet at the head of the couch, and sat down to recover my senses if I could. I sat there all night, unable to think of rest—hardly able to think at all. But the porthole remained closed, and I did not believe it would now open again without the application of a considerable force.

"The morning dawned at last, and I dressed myself slowly, thinking over all that had happened in the night. It was a beautiful day and I went on deck, glad to get out in the early pure sunshine, and to smell the breeze from the blue water, so different from the noisome, stagnant odor from my state-room. Instinctively I turned aft, toward the surgeon's cabin. There he stood with a pipe in his mouth, taking his morning airing precisely as on the preceding day.

" 'Good-morning,' said he quietly, but looking at me with evident curiosity.

" 'Doctor, you were quite right,' said I. 'There is something wrong about that place.'

" 'I thought you would change you mind,' he answered, rather triumphantly. 'You have had a bad night, eh? Shall I make you a pick-me-up? I have a capital recipe.'

" 'No, thanks,' I cried. 'But I would like to tell you what happened.'

"I then tried to explain as clearly as possible precisely what had occurred, not omitting to state that I had been scared as I had never been scared in my whole life before. I dwelt particularly on the phenomenon of the porthole, which was a fact to which I could testify, even if the rest had been an illusion. I had closed it twice in the night, and the second time I had actually bent the brass in wrenching it with my stick. I believe I insisted a good deal on this point.

" 'You seem to think I am likely to doubt the story,' said the doctor, smiling at the detailed account of the state of the porthole. 'I do not doubt it in the least. I renew my invitation to you. Bring your traps here, and take half my cabin.'

" 'Come and take mine for half of one night,' I said. 'Help me to get at the bottom of this thing.'

" 'You will get at the bottom of something else if you try,' answered the doctor.

" 'What?' I asked.

" 'The bottom of the sea. I am going to leave the ship. It is not canny.'

" 'Then you will not help me to find out—'

" 'Not I,' said the doctor quickly. 'It is my business to keep my wits about me—not to go fiddling about with ghosts and things.'

" 'Do you really believe it is a ghost?' I inquired, rather contemptuously. But as I spoke, I remembered very well the horrible sensation of the supernatural which had got possession of me during the night. The doctor turned sharply on me:

" 'Have you any reasonable explanation of these things to offer?' he asked. 'No, you have not. Well, you say you will find an explanation. I say that you won't, sir, simply because there is not any.'

" 'But, my dear sir,' I retorted, 'do you, a man of science, mean to tell me that such things can not be explained?'

" 'I do,' he answered, stoutly. 'And if they could, I would not be concerned in the explanation.'

" "I did not care to spend another night alone in the stateroom, and yet I was obstinately determined to get at the root of the disturbances. I do not believe there are many men who would have slept there alone, after passing two such nights. But I made up my mind to try it, if I could not get any one to share a watch with me. The doctor was evidently not inclined for such an experiment. He said he was a surgeon, and that in case any accident occurred on board, he must always be in readiness. He could not afford to have his nerve unsettled. Perhaps he was quite right, but I am inclined to think that this precaution was prompted by his inclination. On inquiry, he informed me that there was no one on board who would be

likely to join me in my investigations, and after a little more
conversation I left him. A little later I met the captain, and
told him my story. I said that if no one would spend the night
with me, I would ask leave to have the light burning all
night, and would try it alone.

" 'Look here,' said he, 'I will tell you what I will do. I
will share your watch myself, and we will see what happens.
It is my belief that we can find out between us. There may be
some fellow skulking onboard who steals a passage by frightening the passengers. It is just possible that there may be
something queer in the carpentering of that berth.'

"I suggested taking the ship's carpenter below and examining the place; but I was overjoyed at the captain's offer to
spend the night with me. He accordingly sent for the workman and ordered him to do anything I required. We went
below at once. I had all the bedding cleared out of the upper
berth, and we examined the place thoroughly to see if there
was a board loose anywhere, or a panel which could be
opened or pushed aside. We tried the planks everywhere,
tapped the flooring, unscrewed the fittings of the lower berth
and took it to pieces—in short, there was not a square inch of
the stateroom which was not searched and tested. Everything
was in perfect order, and we put everything back in its place.
As we were finishing our work, Robert came to the door, and
looked in.

" 'Well, sir—find anything, sir?' he asked with a ghastly
grin.

" 'You were right about the porthole, Robert,' I said, and
I gave him the promised sovereign. The carpenter did his
work silently and skilfully, following my directions. When
he had done he spoke.

" 'I'm a plain man, sir,' he said. 'But it's my belief you
had better just turn out your things and let me run half a
dozen four-inch screws through the door of this cabin. There's
no good never came o' this cabin yet, sir, and that's about it.
There's been four lives lost out o' here to my own remem-

brance, and that in four trips. Better give it up, sir—better
give it up!'

" 'I will try it for one night more,' I said.

" 'Better give it up, sir—better give it up! It's a precious
bad job,' repeated the workman, putting his tools in his bag
and leaving the cabin.

"But my spirits had risen considerably at the prospect of
having the captain's company, and I made up my mind not to
be prevented from going to the end of the strange business. I
abstained from Welsh rarebits and grog that evening, and did
not even join in the customary game of whist. I wanted to be
quite sure of my nerves, and my vanity made me anxious to
make a good figure in the captain's eyes.

IV

"The captain was one of those splendidly tough and cheerful specimens of seafaring humanity, whose combined courage, hardihood, and calmness in difficulty leads them naturally
into high positions of trust. He was not the man to be led
away by an idle tale, and the mere fact that he was willing to
join me in the investigation was proof that he thought there
was something seriously wrong, which could not be accounted for on ordinary theories, nor laughed down as a
common superstition. To some extent, too, his reputation
was at stake, as well as the reputation of the ship. It is no
light thing to lose passengers overboard, and he knew it.

"About ten o'clock that evening, as I was smoking a last
cigar, he came up to me and drew me aside from the beat of
the other passengers who were patrolling the deck in the
warm darkness.

" 'This is a serious matter, Mr. Brisbane,' he said. "We
must make up our minds either way—to be disappointed or to

have a pretty rough time of it. You see, I cannot afford to laugh at the affair, and I will ask you to sign your name to a statement of whatever occurs. If nothing happens to-night, we will try it again to-morrow and next day. Are you ready?'

"So we went below and entered the stateroom. As we went in I could see Robert, the steward, who stood a little further down the passage, watching us, with his usual grin, as though certain that something dreadful was about to happen. The captain closed the door behind us and bolted it.

" 'Suppose we put your portmanteau before the door,' he suggested. 'One of us can sit on it. Nothing can get out then. Is the port screwed down?'

"I found it as I had left it in the morning. Indeed, without using a lever, as I had done, no one could have opened it. I drew back the curtains of the upper berth so that I could see well into it. By the captain's advice I lighted my reading lantern, and placed it so that it shone upon the white sheets above. He insisted upon sitting on the portmanteau, declaring that he wished to be able to swear that he had sat before the door.

"Then he requested me to search the state-room thoroughly, an operation very soon accomplished, as it consisted merely in looking beneath the lower berth and under the couch below the porthole. The spaces were quite empty.

" 'It is impossible for any human being to get in,' I said, 'or for any human being to open the port.'

" 'Very good,' said captain calmly. 'If we see anything now, it must be either imagination or something supernatural.'

"I sat down on the edge of the lower berth.

" 'The first time it happened,' said the captain, crossing his legs and leaning back against the door, 'was in March. The passenger who slept here, in the upper berth, turned out to have been a lunatic—at all events, he was known to have been a little touched, and he had taken his passage without the knowledge of his friends. He rushed out in the middle of the night and threw himself overboard, before the officer who had the watch could stop him. We stopped and lowered a boat; it was a quiet night, just before the heavy weather came on; but we could not find him. Of course his suicide was afterwards accounted for on the ground of his insanity.''

" 'I suppose that often happens?' I remarked, rather absently.

" 'Not often—no,' said the captain; 'never before in my experience, though I have heard of it happening on board of other ships. Well, as I was saying, that occured in March. On the very next trip— What are you looking at?' he asked, stopping suddenly in his narration.

"I believe I gave no answer. My eyes were riveted upon the porthole. It seemed to me that the brass loop-nut was beginning to turn very slowly upon the screw—so slowly, however, that I was not sure it moved at all. I watched it intently, fixing its position in my mind, and trying to ascertain whether it changed. Seeing where I was looking, the captain looked, too.

" 'It moves!' he exclaimed, in a tone of conviction. 'No, it does not,' he added, after a minute.

" 'If it were the jarring of the screw,' said I, 'it would have opened during the day; but I found it this evening jammed tight as I left it this morning.'

"I rose and tried the nut. It was certainly loosened, for by an effort I could move it with my hands.

" 'The queer thing,' said the captain, 'is that the second man who was lost is supposed to have got through that very port. We had a terrible time over it. It was in the middle of the night, and the weather was very heavy; there was an alarm that one of the ports was open and the sea running in. I came below and found everything flooded, the water pouring in every time she rolled, and the whole port swinging from the top bolts—not the porthole in the middle. Well, we managed to shut it, but the water did some damage. Ever since that the place smells of seawater from time to time. We supposed the passenger had thrown himself out, though the Lord only knows how he did it. The steward kept telling me that he could not keep anything shut here. Upon my word—I can smell it now, can't you?' he inquired, sniffing the air suspiciously.

" 'Yes—distinctly,' I said, and I shuddered as that same odor of stagnant seawater grew stronger in the cabin. 'Now, to smell like this, the place must be damp,' I continued, 'and yet when I examined it with the carpenter this morning, everything was perfectly dry. It is most extraordinary—hallo!'

"My reading-lantern, which had been placed in the upper berth, was suddenly extinguished. There was still a good deal of light from the pane of ground-glass near the door, behind which loomed the regulation lamp. The ship rolled heavily, and the curtain of the upper berth swung far out into the stateroom and back again. I rose quickly from my seat on the edge of the bed, and the captain at the same moment started to his feet with a loud cry of surprise. I had turned with the intention of taking down the lantern to examine it, when I heard his exclamation, and immediately afterward his call for help. I sprang toward him. He was wrestling with all his might with the brass loop of the port. It seemed to turn against his hands in spite of all his efforts. I caught up my cane, a heavy oak stick I always used to carry, and thrust it through the ring and bore on it with all my strength. But the strong wood snapped suddenly, and I fell upon the couch. When I rose again the port was wide open, and the captain was standing with his back against the door pale to the lips.

" 'There is something in that berth!' he cried, in a strange voice, his eyes almost starting from his head. 'Hold the door, while I look—it shall not escape us, whatever it is!'

"But instead of taking his place, I sprang upon the lower berth and seized something which lay in the upper berth.

"It was something ghostly, horrible beyond words, and it moved in my grip. It was like the body of a man long drowned, and yet it moved and had the strength of ten men living; but I gripped it with all my might—the slippery, oozy, horrible thing. The dead white eyes seemed to stare at me out of the dusk; the putrid odor of rank seawater was about it,

and its shiny hair hung in foul wet curls over its dead face. I
wrestled with the dead thing; it thrust itself upon me and
forced me back and nearly broke my arms; it wound its
corpse's arms about my neck, the living death, and overpow-
ered me, so that I, at last, cried aloud and fell and left my
hold.

"As I fell, the thing sprang across me and seemed to throw
itself upon the captain. When I last saw him on his feet, his
face was white and his lips set. It seemed to me that he
struck a violent blow at the dead being, and then he, too,
fell forward upon his face, with an inarticulate cry of
horror.

"The thing paused an instant, seeming to hover over his
prostrate body, and I could have screamed again for very
fright, but I had no voice left. The thing vanished suddenly,
and it seemed to my disturbed senses that it made its exit
through the open port, though how that was possible, considering the smallness of the aperture, is more than any one can
tell. I lay a long time upon the floor, and the captain lay
beside me. At last I partially recovered my senses and moved,
and I instantly knew that my arm was broken—the small
bone of the left forearm near the wrist.

"I got upon my feet somehow, and with my remaining
hand I tried to raise the captain. He groaned and moved, and
at last came to himself. He was not hurt, but he seemed badly
stunned.

"Well, do you want to hear any more? There is nothing
more. That is the end of my story. The carpenter carried out
his scheme of running half a dozen four-inch screws through
the door of one hundred and five, and if you ever take a
passage in the 'Kamtschatka,' you may ask for a berth in that
stateroom. You will be told that it is engaged—yes—it is
engaged by that dead thing.

"I finished the trip in the surgeon's cabin. He doctored my
broken arm, and advised me not to 'fiddle about with ghosts
and things' any more. The captain was very silent, and never

sailed again in that ship, though it is still running. And I will not sail in her either. It is a very disagreeable experience, and I was very badly frightened, which is a thing I do not like. That is all. That is how I saw a ghost—if it was a ghost. It was dead, anyhow.''

THE NIGHT CALL

Henry Van Dyke

The first caprice of November snow had sketched the world in white for an hour in the morning. After midday the sun came out, the wind turned warm, and the whiteness vanished from the landscape. By evening the low ridges and long plain of Jersey were rich and sad again, in russet and dull crimson and old gold; for the foliage still clung to the oaks and elms and birches, and the dying monarchy of autumn retreated slowly before winter's cold republic.

In the old town of Calvinton, stretched along the highroad, the lamps were aglow early as the saffron sunset faded into humid night. A mist rose from the long, wet street and the sodden lawns, muffling the houses and the trees and the college towers with a double veil, under which a pallid aureole encircled every light, while the moon above, languid and tearful, waded slowly through the mounting fog. It was a night of delay and expectation, a night of remembrance and mystery, lonely and dim and full of strange, dull sounds.

In one of the smaller houses on the main street the light in the window burned late. Leroy Carmichael was alone in his office reading Balzac's story of "The Country Doctor." He was not a gloomy or despondent person, but the spirit of the night had entered into him. He had yielded himself, as young

137

men of ardent temperament often do, to the subduing magic
of the fall. In his mind, as in the air, there was a soft,
clinging mist, and blurred lights of thought, and a still fore-
boding of change. A sense of the vast tranquil movement of
Nature, of her sympathy and of her indifference, sank deeply
into his heart. For a time he realized that all things, and he
too, some day, must grow old; and he felt the universal
pathos of it more sensitively, perhaps, than he would ever
feel it again.

If you had told Carmichael that this was what he was
thinking about as he sat in his bachelor quarters on that
November night, he would have stared at you and then
laughed a little.

"Nonsense," he would have answered, cheerfully. "I'm
no sentimentalist: only a bit tired by a hard afternoon's work
at Cedar Grove and a rough ride home. Then, Balzac always
depresses me a little. The next time I'll take some Dumas: he
is a tonic."

But in fact, no one came in to interrupt his musings and
rouse him to that air of cheerfulness with which he always
faced the world, and to which, indeed (though he did not
know it), he owed some measure of his delay in winning the
confidence of Calvinton. He had come there some five years
ago with a particularly good outfit to practise medicine in that
unique and alluring old burgh, full of antique hand-made
furniture and traditions. He had not only been well trained for
his profession in the best medical school and hospital of New
York, but he was also a graduate of Calvinton College (in
which his father had been a professor for a time), and his
granduncle was a Grubb, a name high in the Golden Book of
Calvintonian aristocracy and inscribed upon tombstones in
every village within a radius of fifteen miles. Consequently
the young doctor arrived well accredited, and was received in
his first year with many tokens of hospitality in the shape of
tea-parties and suppers.

But the final and esoteric approval of Calvinton was a

thing apart from these mere fashionable courtesies and worldly
amenities—a thing not to be bestowed without due consideration and satisfactory reasons. Leroy Carmichael failed, somehow or other, to come up to the requirements for a leading
physician in such a conservative community. He was brilliant, perhaps, a clever young man; but he lacked poise and
gravity. He walked too lightly along the streets, swinging his
stick, and greeting his acquaintances blithely, as if he were
rather glad to be alive. Now this is a sentiment which Calvinton
regards as near akin to vanity, and therefore to be dis-
countenanced in your neighbor and concealed in yourself.
How can a man be glad that he is alive, and frankly show it,
without a touch of conceit and a reprehensible forgetfulness
of the presence of original sin even in the best families? The
manners of a professional man, above all, should at once
express and impose humility. Young Dr. Carmichael had
been spoiled by his life in New York. It had made him too
gay, light-hearted, almost frivolous. It was possible that he
might know a good deal about medicine, though doubtless
that had been exaggerated; but it was certain that his temperament needed chastening before he could win the kind of
confidence that Calvinton had given to the venerable Dr.
Coffin, whose face was like a tombstone, and whose practice
rested upon the two pillars of podophyllin and predestination.

So Carmichael still felt, after his five years' work, that he
was an outsider; felt it rather more indeed than when he had
first come. He had enough practice to keep him in good
health and spirits. But his patients were along the side streets
and in the smaller houses and out in the country. He was not
called, except in a chance emergency, to the big houses with
the white pillars. The inner circle had not yet taken him in.

He wondered how long he would have to work and wait
for that. He knew that things in Calvinton moved slowly; but
he knew also that its silent and subconscious judgments
sometimes crystallized with incredible rapidity and hardness.
Was it possible that he was already classified in the group

that came near but did not enter, an inhabitant but not a real burgher, a half-way citizen and a life-long new-comer? That would be rough; he would not like growing old in that way. But perhaps there was no such invisible barrier hemming in his path. Perhaps it was only the naturally slow movement of things that hindered him. Some day the gate would open. He would be called in behind those white pillars into the world of which his father had often told him stories and traditions. There he would prove his skill and his worth. He would make himself useful and trusted by his work. Then he could marry the girl that he loved, and win a firm place and a real home in the old town whose strange charm held him so strongly even in the vague sadness of this autumnal night.

He turned again from these musings to his Balzac, and read the wonderful pages in which Benassis tells the story of his consecration to his profession and Captain Genestas confides the little Adrien to his care, and then the beautiful letter in which the boy describes the country doctor's death and burial. The simple pathos of it went home to Carmichael's heart.

"It is a fine life, after all," said he to himself, as he shut the book at midnight and laid down his pipe. "No man has a better chance than a doctor to come close to the real thing. Human nature is his patient, and each case is a symptom. It's worth while to work for the sake of getting nearer to the reality and doing some definite good by the way. I'm glad that this isn't one of those mystical towns where Buddhism and all sorts of vagaries flourish. Calvinton may be difficult, but it's not obscure. And some day I'll feel its pulse and get at the heart of it."

The silence of the little office was snapped by the nervous clamor of the electric bell, shrilling with a night call.

Dr. Carmichael turned on the light in the hall and opened the front door. A tall, dark man of military aspect loomed out of the mist, and, behind him, at the curbstone, the outline of a big motorcar was dimly visible. He held out a visiting-card inscribed "Baron de Mortemer," and spoke slowly and courteously, but with a strong nasal accent and a tone of insistent domination.

"You are the Dr. Carmichael, yes? You speak French—no? It is a pity. There is a want of you at once—a patient—it is very pressing. You will come with me, yes?"

"But I do not know you, sir," said the doctor; "you are—"

"The Baron de Mortemer," broke in the stranger, pointing to the card as if it answered all questions. "It is the Baroness who is very suffering—I pray you to come without delay."

"But what is it?" asked the doctor. "What shall I bring with me? My instrument-case?"

The Baron smiled with his lips and frowned with his eyes. "Not at all," he said. "Madame expects not an arrival—it is not so bad as that—but she has had a sudden access of anguish—she has demanded you. I pray you to come at the instant. Bring what pleases you, what you think best, but come!"

The man's manner was not agitated, but it was strangely urgent, overpowering, constraining; his voice was like a pushing hand. Carmichael threw on his coat and hat, hastily picked up his medicine-satchel and a portable electric battery, and followed the Baron to the motor.

The great car started almost without noise and rolled softly purring, with unlit lamps, down the deserted streets. The houses were all asleep, and the college buildings dark as empty fortresses. The moon-threaded mist clung closely to the town like a shroud of gauze, not concealing the form beneath, but making the immobility more mysterious. The trees drooped and dripped with moisture, and the leaves seemed ready, almost longing, to fall at a touch. It was one of those nights when the solid things of the world, the houses and the hills and the woods and the very earth itself, grow unreal to the point of vanishing; while the impalpable things, the presences of life and death which travel on the unseen air, the influences of the far-off starry lights, the silent messages and presentiments of darkness, the ebb and flow of vast currents of secret existence all around us, seem so close and vivid that they absorb and overwhelm us with their intense reality.

Through this realm of indistinguishable verity and illusion, strangely imposed upon the familiar, homely street of Calvinton, the machine ran smoothly, faintly humming, as the Frenchman drove it with master-skill—itself a dream of incarnate power and speed. Gliding by the last cottages of Town's End where the street became the highroad, the car ran swiftly through the open country for a mile until it came to a broad entrance. The gate was broken from the leaning posts and thrown to one side. Here the machine turned in and labored up a rough, grass-grown carriage-drive.

Carmichael knew that they were at Castle Gordon, one of the "old places" of Calvinton, which he often passed on his country drives. The house stood well back from the road, on a slight elevation, looking down over the oval field that was once a lawn, and the scattered elms and pines and Norway firs that did their best to preserve the memory of a noble plantation. The building was colonial; heavy stone walls covered with yellow stucco; tall white wooden pillars ranged along a narrow portico; a style which seemed to assert that a Greek temple was good enough for the residence of an American gentleman. But the clean buff and white of the house had long since faded. The stucco had cracked, and, here and there, had fallen from the stones. The paint was dingy, peeling in round blisters and narrow strips from the gray wood underneath. The trees were ragged and untended, the grass uncut, the driveway overgrown with weeds and gullied by rains—the whole place looked forsaken. Carmichael had always supposed that it was vacant. But he had not passed that way for nearly a month, and, meantime, it might have been tenanted.

The Baron drove the car around to the back of the house and stopped there.

"Pardon," said he, "that I bring you not to the door of entrance; but this is the more convenient."

He knocked hurriedly and spoke a few words in French. The key grated in the lock and the door creaked open. A withered, wiry little man, dressed in dark gray, stood holding a lighted candle, which flickered in the draught. His head was nearly bald; his sallow, hairless face might have been of any age from twenty to a hundred years; his eyes between their narrow red lids were glittering and inscrutable as those of a snake. As he bowed and grinned, showing his yellow, broken teeth, Carmichael thought that he had never seen a more evil face or one more clearly marked with the sign of the drug-fiend.

"My chauffeur, Gaspard," said the Baron, "also my valet, my cook, my chambermaid, my man to do all, what you call factotum, is it not? But he speaks not English, so pardon me once more."

He spoke a few words to the man, who shrugged his shoulders and smiled with the same deferential grimace while his unchanging eyes gleamed through their slits. Carmichael caught only the word "Madame" while he was slipping off his overcoat, and understood that they were talking of his patient.

"Come," said the Baron. "He says that it goes better, at least not worse—that is always something. Let us mount at the instant."

The hall was bare, except for a table on which a kitchen lamp was burning, and two chairs with heavy automobile coats and rugs and veils thrown upon them. The stairway was uncarpeted, and the dust lay thick along the banisters. At the door of the back room on the second floor the Baron paused and knocked softly. A low voice answered, and he went in, beckoning the doctor to follow.

*   *   *

If Carmichael lived to be a hundred he could never forget that first impression. The room was but partly furnished, yet it gave at once the idea that it was inhabited; it was even, in some strange way, rich and splendid. Candelabra on the mantelpiece and a silver traveling-lamp on the dressing-table threw a soft light on little articles of luxury, and photographs in jeweled frames, and a couple of well-bound books, and a gilt clock marking the half-hour after midnight. A wood fire burned in the wide chimney-place, and before it a rug was spread. At one side there was a huge mahogany four-post bedstead, and there, propped up by the pillows, lay the noblest-looking woman that Carmichael had ever seen.

She was dressed in some clinging stuff of soft black, with a diamond at her breast, and a deep-red cloak thrown over her feet. She must have been past middle age, for her thick, brown hair was already touched with silver, and one lock of snow-white lay above her forehead. But her face was one of those which time enriches; fearless and tender and highspirited, a speaking face in which the dark-lashed gray eyes were like words of wonder and the sensitive mouth like a clear song. She looked at the young doctor and held out her hand to him.

"I am glad to see you," she said, in her low, pure voice, "very glad! You are Roger Carmichael's son. Oh, I am glad to see you indeed."

"You are very kind," he answered, "and I am glad also to be of any service to you, though I do not yet know who you are."

The Baron was bending over the fire rearranging the logs on the andirons. He looked up sharply and spoke in his strong nasal tone.

"*Pardon! Madame la Baronne de Mortemer, j'ai l'honneur de vous presenter Monsieur le Docteur Carmichael.*"

The accent on the "doctor" was marked. A slight shadow came upon the lady's face. She answered, quietly:

"Yes, I know. The doctor has come to see me because I was ill. We will talk of that in a moment. But first I want to tell him who I am—and by another name. Dr. Carmichael, did your father ever speak to you of Jean Gordon?''

"Why, yes," he said, after an instant of thought, "it comes back to me now quite clearly. She was the young girl to whom he taught Latin when he first came here as a college instructor. He was very fond of her. There was one of her books in his library—I have it now—a little volume of Horace, with a few translations in verse written on the flyleaves, and her name on the title-page—Jean Gordon. My father wrote under that, 'My best pupil, who left her lessons unfinished.' He was very fond of the book, and so I kept it when he died.''

The lady's eyes grew moist, but the tears did not fall. They trembled in her voice.

"I was that Jean Gordon—a girl of fifteen—your father was the best man I ever knew. You look like him, but he was handsomer than you. Ah, no, I was not his best pupil, but his most wilful and ungrateful one. Did he never tell you of my running away—of the unjust suspicions that fell on him—of his voyage to Europe?''

"Never," answered Carmichael. "He only spoke, as I remember, of your beauty and your brightness, and of the good times that you all had when this old house was in its prime.''

"Yes, yes," she said, quickly and with strong feeling, "they were good times, and he was a man of honor. He never took an unfair advantage, never boasted of a woman's favor, never tried to spare himself. He was an American man. I hope you are like him.''

The Baron, who had been leaning on the mantel, crossed the room impatiently and stood beside the bed. He spoke in French again, dragging the words in his insistent, masterful voice, as if they were something heavy which he laid upon his wife. Her gray eyes grew darker, almost black, with enlarging pupils. She raised herself on the pillows as if about to get up. Then she sank back again and said, with an evident effort:

"René, I must beg you not to speak in French again. The doctor does not understand it. We must be more courteous. And now I will tell him about my sudden illness to-night. It was the first time—like a flash of lightning—an ice-cold flame of pain—"

Even as she spoke a swift and dreadful change passed over her face. Her color vanished in a morbid pallor; a cold sweat lay like death-dew on her forehead; her eyes were fixed on some impending horror; her lips, blue and rigid, were strained with an unspeakable, intolerable anguish. Her left arm stiffened as if it were gripped in a vise of pain. Her right hand fluttered over her heart, plucking at an unseen weight. It seemed as if an invisible, silent death-wind were quenching the flame of her life. It flickered in an agony of strangulation.

"Be quick," cried the doctor; "lay her head lower on the pillows, loosen her dress, warm her hands."

He had caught up his satchel, and was looking for a little vial. He found it almost empty. But there were four or five drops of the yellowish, oily liquid. He poured them on his handkerchief and held it close to the lady's mouth. She was still breathing regularly though slowly, and as she inhaled the pungent, fruity smell, like the odor of a jargonelle pear, a look of relief flowed over her face, her breathing deepened, her arm and her lips relaxed, the terror faded from her eyes.

He went to his satchel again and took out a bottle of white tablets marked "Nitroglycerin." He gave her one of them, and when he saw her look of peace grow steadier, after a minute, he prepared the electric battery. Softly he passed the sponges charged with their mysterious current over her temples and her neck and down her slender arms and blue-veined wrists, holding the electrodes for a while in the palms of her hands, which grew rosy.

In all this the Baron had helped as he could, and watched closely, but without a word. He was certainly not indifferent;

neither was he distressed; the expression of his black eyes and heavy, passionless face was that of presence of mind, self-control covering an intense curiosity. Carmichael conceived a vague sentiment of dislike for the man.

When the patient rested easily they stepped outside the room together for a moment.

"It is the *angina,* I suppose," droned the Baron, "*hein?* That is of great inconvenience. But I think it is the false one, that is much less grave—not truly dangerous, *hein?*"

"My dear sir," answered Carmichael, "who can tell the difference between a false and a true *angina,* except by a postmortem? The symptoms are much alike, the result is sometimes identical, if the paroxysm is severe enough. But in this case I hope that you may be right. Your wife's illness is severe, dangerous, but not necessarily fatal. This attack has passed and may not recur for weeks or even months."

The lip-smile came back under the Baron's sullen eyes.

"Those are the good news, my dear doctor," said he, slowly. "Then we shall be capable to travel soon, perhaps to-morrow or the next day. It is of an extreme importance. This place is insufferable to me. We have engagements in Washington—a gay season."

Carmichael looked at him steadily and spoke with deliberation.

"Baron, you must understand me clearly. This is a serious case. If I had not come in time your wife might be dead now. She cannot possibly be moved for a week, perhaps it may take a month to restore her strength. After that she must have a winter of absolute quiet and repose."

The Frenchman's face hardened; his brows drew together in a black line, and he lifted his hand quickly with a gesture of irritation. Then he bowed.

"As you will, doctor! And for the present moment, what is it that I may have the honor to do for your patient?"

"Just now," said the doctor, "she needs a stimulant—a glass of sherry or of brandy, if you have it—and a hotwater

bag—you have none? Well, then, a couple of bottles filled
with hot water and wrapped in a cloth to put at her feet. Can
you get them?''

The Baron bowed again, and went down the stairs. As
Carmichael returned to the bedroom he heard the droning,
insistent voice calling "Gaspard! Gaspard!"

The great gray eyes were open as he entered the room, and
there was a sense of release from pain and fear in them that
was like the deepest kind of pleasure.

"Yes, I am much better," said she; "the attack has passed.
Will it come again? No? Not soon, you mean. Well, that is
good. You need not tell me what it is—time enough for that
to-morrow. But come and sit by me. I want to talk to you.
Your first name is—"

"Leroy," he answered. "But you are weak; you must not
talk much."

"Only a little," she replied, smiling; "it does me good.
Leroy was your mother's name—yes? It is not a Calvinton
name. I wonder where your father met her. Perhaps in France
when he came to look for me. He did not find me—no,
indeed—I was well hidden—but he found your mother. You
are young enough to be my son. Will you be a friend to me
for your father's sake?"

She spoke gently, in a tone of infinite kindness and tender
grace, with pauses in which a hundred unspoken recollections
and appeals were suggested. The young man was deeply
moved. He took her hand in his firm clasp.

"Gladly," he said, "and for your sake too. But now I
want you to rest."

"Oh," she answered, "I am resting now. But let me talk a
little more. It will not harm me. I have been through too
much! Twice married—a great fortune to spend—all that the
big world can give. But now I am very tired of the whirl.
There is only one thing I want—to stay here in Calvinton. I
rebelled against it once; but it draws me back. There is a
strange magic in the place. Haven't you felt it? How do you
explain it?"

"Yes," he said, "I have felt it surely, but I can't explain it, unless it is a kind of ancient peace that makes you wish to be at home here even while you rebel."

She nodded her head and smiled softly.

"That is it," she said, hesitating for a moment—"but my husband—you see he is a very strong man, and he loves the world, the whirling life—he took a dislike to this place at once. No wonder, with the house in such a state! But I have plenty of money—it would be easy to restore the house. Only, sometimes I think he cares more for the money than— but no matter what I think. He wishes to go on at once—to- morrow, if we can. I hate the thought of it. Is it possible for me to stay? Can you help me?"

"Dear lady," he answered, lifting her hand to his lips, "set your mind at rest. I have already told him that it is impossible for you to go for many days."

A sound in the hallway announced the return of the Baron and Gaspard with the hot-water bottles and the cognac. The doctor made his patient as comfortable as possible for the night, prepared a sleeping-draught, and gave directions for the use of the tablets in an emergency.

"Good night," he said, bending over her. "I will see you in the morning. You may count upon me."

"I do," she said, with her eyes resting on his; "thank you for all. I shall expect you—*au revoir.*"

As they went down the stairs he said to the Baron, "Re- member, absolute repose is necessary. With that you are safe enough for to-night. But you may possibly need more of the nitrite of amyl. My vial is empty. I will write the prescrip- tion, if you will allow me."

"In the dining-room," said the Baron, taking up the lamp and throwing open the door of the back room on the right. The floor had been hastily swept and the rubbish shoved into the fireplace. The heavy chairs stood along the wall. But two of them were drawn up at the head of the long mahogany table, and dishes and table utensils from a traveling-basket were lying there, as if a late supper had been served.

"You see," said the Baron, drawling, "our banquet-hall! Madame and I have dined in this splendor to-night. Is it possible that you write here?"

His secret irritation, his insolence, his contempt spoke clearly enough in his tone. The remark was almost like an intentional insult. For a second Carmichael hesitated. "No," he thought, "why should I quarrel with him? He is only sullen. He can do no harm."

He pulled a chair to the foot of the table, took out his tablet and his fountain-pen, and wrote the prescription. Tearing off the leaf, he folded it crosswise and left it on the table.

In the hall, as he put on his coat he remembered the paper.

"My prescription," he said, "I must take it to the druggist to-night."

"Permit me," said the Baron, "the room is dark. I will take the paper, and procure the drug as I return from escorting the doctor to his residence."

He went into the dark room, groped about for a moment, and returned, closing the door behind him.

"Come, Monsieur," he said, "your work at the Château Gordon is finished for this night. I shall leave you with yourself—at home, as you say—in a few moments. *Gaspard— Gaspard, fermez la porte à clé!*"

The strong nasal voice echoed through the house, and the servant ran lightly down the stairs. His master muttered a few sentences to him, holding up his right hand as he did so, with the five fingers extended, as if to impress something on the man's mind.

"Pardon," he said, turning to Carmichael, "that I speak always French, after the rebuke. But this time it is of necessity. I repeat the instruction for the pilules. One at each hour until eight o'clock—five, not more—it is correct? Come, then, our equipage is always harnessed, always ready—how convenient!"

The two men did not speak as the car rolled through the brumous night. A rising wind was sifting the fog. The moon had set. The loosened leaves came whirling, fluttering, sinking through the darkness like a flight of huge dying moths. Now and then they brushed the faces of the travelers with limp, moist wings.

The red night-lamp in the drug-store was still burning. Carmichael called the other's attention to it.

"You have the prescription?"

"Without doubt!" he answered. "After I have escorted you. I shall procure the drug."

The doctor's front door was lit up as he had left it. The light streamed out brightly and illumined the Baron's sullen black eyes and smiling lips as he leaned from the car, lifting his cap.

"A thousand thanks, my dear doctor; you have been excessively kind; yes, truly of an excessive goodness for us. It is a great pleasure—how do you tell it in English?—it is a great pleasure to have met you. *Adieu.*"

"Till to-morrow morning!" said Carmichael cheerfully, waving his hand.

The Baron stared at him curiously, and lifted his cap again.

"*Adieu!*" droned the insistent voice, and the great car slid into the dark.

The next morning was of crystal. As Carmichael drove his electric phaeton down the leaf-littered street, where the country wagons and the decrepit hacks were already meandering placidly, and out along the highroad, between the still green fields, it seemed to him as if the experience of the past night were "such stuff as dreams are made of." Yet the impression of what he had seen and heard in that firelit chamber—of the eyes, the voice, the hand of that strangely lovely lady—of her vision of sudden death, her essentially lonely struggle with it, her touching words to him when she came back to life—all this was so vivid and unforgettable that he drove straight to Castle Gordon.

The great house was shut up like a tomb; every door and window was closed, except where half of one of the shutters had broken loose and hung by a single hinge. He drove around to the back. It was the same there. A slight cobweb was spun across the lower corner of the door and tiny drops of moisture jeweled it. Perhaps it had been made in the early morning. If so, no one had come out of the door since night.

Carmichael knocked, and knocked again. No answer. He called. No reply. Then he drove around to the portico with the tall white pillars and tried the front door. It was locked. He peered through the half-open window into the drawing-room. The glass was crusted with dirt and the room was dark. He was trying to make out the outlines of the huddled furniture when he heard a step behind him. It was the old farmer from the nearest cottage on the road.

"Mornin', Doctor! I seen ye comin' in, and tho't ye might want to see the house."

"Good morning, Scudder! I do, if you'll let me in. But first tell me about these automobile tracks in the drive."

The old man gazed at him with a kind of dull surprise as if the question were foolish.

"Why, ye made 'em yerself, comin' up, didn't ye?"

"I mean those larger tracks—they were made by a much heavier car than mine."

"Oh," said the old man, nodding, "them was made by a big machine that come in here las' week. You see this house's bin shet up 'bout twenty-five years, ever sence ol' Jedge Gordon died. B'longs to Miss Jean—her that run off with the Eye-talian—she kind er wants to sell it, and kind er not—ye see—"

"Yes," interrupted Carmichael, "but about that big machine—when did you say it was here?"

"P'raps four or five days ago; I think it was a Wednesday. Two fellers from Philadelfy—said they wanted to look at the house, tho't of buyin' it. So I bro't 'em in, but when they seen the outside of it they said they didn't want to look at it no more—too big and too crumbly!"

"And since then no one has been here?"

"Not a soul—leastways nobody that I seen. I don't s'pose you think o' buyin' the house, Doc'! It's too lonely for an office, ain't it?"

"You're right, Scudder, much too lonely. But I'd like to look through the old place, if you will take me in."

The hall, with the two chairs and the table, on which a kitchen lamp with a half-inch of oil in it was standing, gave no sign of recent habitation. Carmichael glanced around him and hurried up the stairway to the bedroom. A tall four-poster stood in one corner, with a dingy coverlet apparently hiding a mattress and some pillows. A dressing-table stood against the wall, and in the middle of the floor there were a few chairs. A half-open closet door showed a pile of yellow linen. The daylight sifted dimly into the room through the cracks of the shutters.

"Scudder," said Carmichael, "I want you to look around carefully and tell me whether you see any signs of any one having been here lately."

The old man stared, and turned his eyes slowly about the room. Then he shook his head.

"Can't say as I do. Looks pretty much as it did when me and my wife breshed it up in October. Ye see it's kind er clean fer an old house—not much dust from the road here. That linen and that bed's bin here sence I c'n remember. Them burnt logs mus' be left over from old Jedge Gordon's time. I b'lieve he died in here. But what's the matter, Doc'? Ye think tramps or burglars—"

"No," said Carmichael, "but what would you say if I told you that I was called here last night to see a patient, and that the patient was the Miss Jean Gordon of whom you have just told me?"

"What d'ye mean?" said the old man, gaping. Then he gazed at the doctor pityingly, and shook his head. "I know ye ain't a drinkin' man, Doc', so I wouldn't say nothin'. But I guess ye bin dreamin'. Why, las' time Miss Jean writ to me—her name's Mortemer now, and her husband's a kind er Barrin or some sort er furrin noble—she was in Paris, not mor'n two weeks ago! Said she was dyin' to come back to the ol' place ag'in, but she wa'n't none too well, and didn't guess she c'd manage it. Ef ye said ye seen her here las' night—why—well, I'd jest think ye'd bin dreamin'. P'raps ye're a little under the weather—bin workin' too hard?''

"I never was better, Scudder, but sometimes curious notions come to me. I wanted to see how you would take this one. Now we'll go down-stairs again."

The old man laughed, but doubtfully, as if he was still puzzled by the talk, and they descended the creaking, dusty stairs. Carmichael turned at once into the dining-room.

The rubbish was still in the fireplace, the chairs ranged along the wall. There were no dishes on the long table; but at the head of it two chairs; and at the foot, one; and in front of that, lying on the table, a folded bit of paper.

Carmichael picked it up and opened it. *It was his prescription for the nitrite of amyl.*

He hesitated a moment; then refolded the paper and put it in his vest-pocket.

Seated in his car, with his hand on the lever, he turned to Scudder, who was watching him with curious eyes.

"I'm very much obliged to you, Scudder, for taking me through the house. And I'll be more obliged to you if you'll just keep it to yourself—what I said to you about last night."

"Sure," said the old man, nodding gravely. "I like ye, Doc', and that kind er talk might do ye harm here in Calvinton. We don't hold much to dreams and visions down this way. But, say, 'twas a mighty interestin' dream, wa'n't it? I guess Miss Jean hones for them white pillars many a day—they sort er stand for old times. They draw ye, don't they?"

"Yes," said Carmichael, "they speak of the past. There is a magic in those white pillars. They draw you."

THE TRANSFERRED GHOST

Frank R. Stockton

The country residence of Mr. John Hinckman was a delightful place to me, for many reasons. It was the abode of a genial, though somewhat impulsive, hospitality. It had broad, smooth-shaven lawns and towering oaks and elms; there were bosky shades at several points, and not far from the house there was a little rill spanned by a rustic bridge with the bark on; there were fruits and flowers, pleasant people, chess, billiards, rides, walks, and fishing. These were great attractions, but none of them, nor all of them together, would have been sufficient to hold me to the place very long. I had been invited for the trout season, but should probably have finished my visit early in the summer had it not been that upon fair days, when the grass was dry, and the sun was not too hot, and there was but little wind, there strolled beneath the lofty elms, or passed lightly through the bosky shades, the form of my Madeline.

This lady was not, in very truth, my Madeline. She had never given herself to me, nor had I, in any way, acquired possession of her. But, as I considered her possession the only sufficient reason for the continuance of my existence, I called her, in my reveries, mine. It may have been that I would not have been obliged to confine the use of this possessive pronoun to my reveries had I confessed the state of my feelings to the lady.

But this was an unusually difficult thing to do. Not only did I dread, as almost all lovers dread, taking the step which would in an instant put an end to that delightful season which may be termed the ante-interrogatory period of love, and which might at the same time terminate all intercourse or connection with the object of my passion, but I was also dreadfully afraid of John Hinckman. This gentleman was a good friend of mine, but it would have required a bolder man than I was at that time to ask him for the gift of his niece, who was the head of his household, and, according to his own frequent statement, the main prop of his declining years. Had Madeline acquiesced in my general views on the subject, I might have felt encouraged to open the matter to Mr. Hinckman; but, as I said before, I had never asked her whether or not she would be mine. I thought of these things at all hours of the day and night, particularly the latter.

I was lying awake one night, in the great bed in my spacious chamber, when, by the dim light of the new moon, which partially filled the room, I saw John Hinckman standing by a large chair near the door. I was very much surprised at this, for two reasons: in the first place, my host had never before come into my room, and, in the second place, he had gone from home that morning, and had not expected to return for several days. Therefore it was that I had been able that evening to sit much later than usual with Madeline on the moonlit porch. The figure was certainly that of John Hinckman in his ordinary dress, but there was a vagueness and indistinctness about it which presently assured me that it was a ghost. Had the good old man been murdered, and had his spirit come to tell me of the deed, and to confide to me the protection of the dear—? My heart fluttered, but I felt that I must speak. "Sir," said I.

"Do you know," interrupted the figure, with a countenance

that indicated anxiety, "whether or not Mr. Hinckman will return to-night?"

I thought it well to maintain a calm exterior, and I answered: "We do not expect him."

"I am glad of that," said he, sinking into the chair by which he stood. "During the two years and a half that I have inhabited this house, that man has never before been away for a single night. You can't imagine the relief it gives me."

As he spoke he stretched out his legs and leaned back in the chair. His form became less vague, and the colors of his garments more distinct and evident, while an expression of gratified relief succeeded to the anxiety of his countenance.

"Two years and a half!" I exclaimed. "I don't understand you."

"It is fully that length of time," said the ghost, "since I first came here. Mine is not an ordinary case. But before I say anything more about it, let me ask you again if you are sure Mr. Hinckman will not return to-night."

"I am as sure of it as I can be of anything," I answered. "He left to-day for Bristol, two hundred miles away."

"Then I will go on," said the ghost, "for I am glad to have the opportunity of talking to some one who will listen to me. But if John Hinckman should come in and catch me here, I should be frightened out of my wits."

"This is all very strange," I said, greatly puzzled by what I had heard. "Are you the ghost of Mr. Hinckman?"

This was a bold question, but my mind was so full of other emotions that there seemed to be no room for that of fear.

"Yes, I am his ghost," my companion replied, "and yet I have no right to be. And this is what makes me so uneasy and so much afraid of him. It is a strange story, and, I truly believe, without precedent. Two years and a half ago, John Hinckman was dangerously ill in this very room. At one time he was so far gone that he was really believed to be dead. It was in consequence of too precipitate a report in regard to this matter that I was, at that time, appointed to be his ghost.

Imagine my surprise and horror, sir, when, after I had accepted the position and assumed its responsibilities, that old man revived, became convalescent, and eventually regained his usual health. My situation was now one of extreme delicacy and embarrassment. I had no power to return to my original unembodiment, and I had no right to be the ghost of a man who was not dead. I was advised by my friends to quietly maintain my position, and was assured, that, as John Hinckman was an elderly man, it would not be long before I could rightfully assume the position for which I had been selected. But I tell you, sir," he continued with animation, "the old fellow seems as vigorous as ever, and I have no idea how much longer this annoying state of things will continue. I spend my time trying to get out of that old man's way. I must not leave this house, and he seems to follow me everywhere. I tell you, sir, he haunts me."

"That is truly a queer state of things," I remarked. "But why are you afraid of him! He couldn't hurt you."

"Of course he couldn't," said the ghost. "But his very presence is a shock and terror to me. Imagine, sir, how you would feel if my case were yours."

I could not imagine such a thing at all. I simply shuddered.

"And if one must be a wrongful ghost at all," the apparition continued, "it would be much pleasanter to be the ghost of some man other than John Hinckman. There is in him an irascibility of temper, accompanied by a facility of invective, which is seldom met with; and what would happen if he were to see me, and find out, as I am sure he would, how long and why I had inhabited his house, I can scarcely conceive. I have seen him in his bursts of passion, and although he did not hurt the people he stormed at any more than he would hurt me, they seemed to shrink before him."

All this I knew to be very true. Had it not been for this peculiarity of Mr. Hinckman, I might have been more willing to talk to him about his niece.

"I feel sorry for you," I said, for I really began to have a sympathetic feeling toward this unfortunate apparition. "Your case is indeed a hard one. It reminds me of those persons who have had doubles; and I suppose a man would often be very angry indeed when he found that there was another being who was personating himself."

"Oh, the cases are not similar at all," said the ghost. "A double, or doppelganger, lives on the earth with a man, and being exactly like him, he makes all sorts of trouble, of course. It is very different with me. I am not here to live with Mr. Hinckman. I am here to take his place. Now, it would make John Hinckman very angry if he knew that. Don't you know it would?"

I assented promptly.

"Now that he is away, I can be easy for a little while," continued the ghost, "and I am so glad to have an opportunity of talking to you. I have frequently come into your room and watched you while you slept, but did not dare to speak to you for fear that if you talked with me Mr. Hinckman would hear you, and come into the room to know why you were talking to yourself."

"But would he not hear you?" I asked.

"Oh, no!" said the other. "There are times when any one may see me, but no one hears me except the person to whom I address myself."

"But why did you wish to speak to me?" I asked.

"Because," replied the ghost, "I like occasionally to talk to people, and especially to some one like yourself, whose mind is so troubled and perturbed that you are not likely to be frightened by a visit from one of us. But I particularly want to ask you to do me a favor. There is every probability, so far as I can see, that John Hinckman will live a long time, and my situation is becoming insupportable. My great object at present is to get myself transferred, and I think that you may, perhaps, be of use to me."

"Transferred!" I exclaimed. "What do you mean by that?"

"What I mean," said the other, "is this: now that I have

started on my career, I have got to be the ghost of somebody, and I want to be the ghost of a man who is really dead."

"I should think that would be easy enough," I said. "Opportunities must continually occur."

"Not at all! not at all!" said my companion, quickly. "You have no idea what a rush and pressure there is for situations of this kind. Whenever a vacancy occurs, if I may express myself in that way, there are crowds of applications for the ghostship."

"I had no idea that such a state of things existed," I said, becoming quite interested in the matter. "There ought to be some regular system, or order of precedence, by which you could all take your turns, like customers in a barber's shop."

"Oh, dear, that would never do at all!" said the other. "Some of us would have to wait forever. There is always a great rush whenever a good ghostship offers itself—while, as you know, there are some positions that no one would care for. It was in consequence of my being in too great a hurry on an occasion of the kind that I got myself into my present disagreeable predicament, and I have thought that it might be possible that you would help me out of it. You might know of a case where an opportunity for a ghostship was not generally expected, but which might present itself at any moment. If you would give me a short notice, I know I could arrange for a transfer."

"What do you mean?" I exclaimed. "Do you want me to commit suicide or to undertake a murder for your benefit?"

"Oh, no, no, no!" said the other, with a vapory smile. "I mean nothing of that kind. To be sure, there are lovers who are watched with considerable interest, such persons having been known, in moments of depression, to offer very desirable ghostships, but I did not think of anything of that kind in connection with you. You were the only person I cared to speak to, and I hoped that you might give me some information that would be of use; and, in return, I shall be very glad to help you in your love affair."

"You seem to know that I have such an affair," I said.

"Oh, yes!" replied the other, with a little yawn. "I could not be here so much as I have been without knowing all about that."

There was something horrible in the idea of Madeline and myself having been watched by a ghost, even, perhaps, when we wandered together in the most delightful and bosky places. But then, this was quite an exceptional ghost, and I could not have the objections to him which would ordinarily arise in regard to beings of his class.

"I must go now," said the ghost, rising, "but I will see you somewhere to-morrow night; and remember—you help me, and I'll help you."

I had doubts the next morning as to the propriety of telling Madeline anything about this interview, and soon convinced myself that I must keep silent on the subject. If she knew there was a ghost about the house, she would probably leave the place instantly. I did not mention the matter, and so regulated my demeanor that I am quite sure Madeline never suspected what had taken place.

For some time I had wished that Mr. Hinckman would absent himself, for a day at least, from the premises. In such case I thought I might more easily nerve myself up to the point of speaking to Madeline on the subject of our future collateral existence. But now that the opportunity for such speech had really occurred, I did not feel ready to avail myself of it. What would become of me if she refused me?

I had an idea, however, that the lady thought that if I were going to speak at all, this was the time. She must have known that certain sentiments were afloat within me, and she was not unreasonable in her wish to see the matter settled one way or the other. But I did not feel like taking a bold step in the dark. If she wished me to ask her to give herself to me, she ought to offer me some reason to suppose that she would make the gift. If I saw no probability of such generosity, I would prefer that things should remain as they were.

*   *   *

That evening I was sitting with Madeline on the moonlit porch. It was nearly ten o'clock, and ever since supper-time I had been working myself up to the point of making an avowal of my sentiments. I had not positively determined to do this, but wished gradually to reach the proper point when, if the prospect looked bright, I might speak. My companion appeared to understand the situation—at least, I imagined that the nearer I came to a proposal the more she seemed to expect it. It was certainly a very critical and important epoch in my life. If I spoke; I should make myself happy or miserable forever; and if I did not speak, I had every reason to believe that the lady would not give me another chance to do so.

Sitting thus with Madeline, talking a little, and thinking very hard over these momentous matters, I looked up and saw the ghost, not a dozen feet away from us. He was sitting on the railing of the porch, one leg thrown up before him, the other dangling down as he leaned against a post. He was behind Madeline, but almost in front of me, as I sat facing the lady. It was fortunate that Madeline was looking out over the landscape, for I must have appeared very much startled. The ghost had told me that he would see me some time this night, but I did not think he would make his appearance when I was in the company of Madeline. If she should see the spirit of her uncle, I could not answer for the consequences. I made no exclamation, but the ghost evidently saw that I was troubled.

"Don't be afraid," he said; "I shall not let her see me, and she cannot hear me speak unless I address myself to her, which I do not intend to do."

I suppose I looked grateful.

"So you need not trouble yourself about that," the ghost continued. "But it seems to me that you are not getting along very well with your affair. If I were you, I should speak out without waiting any longer. You will never have a better chance. You are not likely to be interrupted, and, so far as I can judge, the lady seems disposed to listen to you favorably— that is, if she ever intends to do so. There is no knowing when John Hinckman will go away again; certainly not this summer. If I were in your place, I should never dare to make love to Hinckman's niece if he were anywhere about the place. If he should catch any one offering himself to Miss Madeline, he would then be a terrible man to encounter."

I agreed perfectly to all this.

"I cannot bear to think of him!" I ejaculated aloud.

"Think of whom?" asked Madeline, turning quickly toward me.

Here was an awkward situation. The long speech of the ghost, to which Madeline paid no attention, but which I heard with perfect distinctness, had made me forget myself.

It was necessary to explain quickly. Of course, it would not do to admit that it was of her dear uncle that I was speaking, and so I mentioned hastily the first name I thought of.

"Mr. Vilars," I said.

This statement was entirely correct, for I never could bear to think of Mr. Vilars, who was a gentleman who had, at various times, paid much attention to Madeline.

"It is wrong for you to speak in that way of Mr. Vilars," she said. "He is a remarkably well educated and sensible young man, and has very pleasant manners. He expects to be elected to the legislature this fall, and I should not be surprised if he made his mark. He will do well in a legislative body, for whenever Mr. Vilars has anything to say he knows just how and when to say it."

This was spoken very quietly, and without any show of resentment, which was all very natural, for if Madeline thought at all favorably of me she could not feel displeased that I should have disagreeable emotions in regard to a possible rival. The concluding words contained a hint which I was not slow to understand. I felt very sure that if Mr. Vilars were in my present position he would speak quickly enough.

"I know it is wrong to have such ideas about a person," I said, "but I can't help it."

The lady did not chide me, and after this she seemed even in a softer mood. As for me, I felt considerably annoyed, for I had not wished to admit that any thought of Mr. Vilars had ever occupied my mind.

"You should not speak aloud that way," said the ghost, "or you may get yourself into trouble. I want to see everything go well with you, because then you may be disposed to help me, especially if I should chance to be of any assistance to you, which I hope I shall be."

I longed to tell him that there was no way in which he could help me so much as by taking his instant departure. To make love to a young lady with a ghost sitting on the railing near by, and that ghost the apparition of a much-dreaded uncle, the very idea of whom in such a position and at such a time made me tremble, was a difficult, if not an impossible, thing to do. But I forbore to speak, although I may have looked my mind.

"I suppose," continued the ghost, "that you have not heard anything that might be of advantage to me. Of course, I am very anxious to hear, but if you have anything to tell me, I can wait until you are alone. I will come to you to-night in your room, or I will stay here until the lady goes away."

"You need not wait here," I said; "I have nothing at all to say to you."

Madeline sprang to her feet, her face flushed and her eyes ablaze.

"Wait here!" she cried. "What do you suppose I am waiting for? Nothing to say to me, indeed! I should think so! What should you have to say to me?"

"Madeline," I exclaimed, stepping toward her, "let me explain."

But she had gone.

Here was the end of the world for me! I turned fiercely to the ghost.

"Wretched existence!" I cried, "you have ruined everything. You have blackened my whole life! Had it not been for you—"

But here my voice faltered. I could say no more.

"You wrong me," said the ghost. "I have not injured you. I have tried only to encourage and assist you, and it is your own folly that has done this mischief. But do not despair. Such mistakes as these can be explained. Keep up a brave heart. Good-by."

And he vanished from the railing like a bursting soap-bubble.

I went gloomily to bed, but I saw no apparitions that night except those of despair and misery which my wretched thoughts called up. The words I had uttered had sounded to Madeline like the basest insult. Of course, there was only one interpretation she could put upon them.

As to explaining my ejaculations, that was impossible. I thought the matter over and over again as I lay awake that night, and I determined that I would never tell Madeline the facts of the case. It would be better for me to suffer all my life than for her to know that the ghost of her uncle haunted the house. Mr. Hinckman was away, and if she knew of his ghost she could not be made to believe that he was not dead. She might not survive the shock! No, my heart might bleed, but I would never tell her.

The next day was fine, neither too cool nor too warm. The breezes were gentle, and nature smiled. But there were no walks or rides with Madeline. She seemed to be much engaged during the day, and I saw but little of her. When we met at meals she was polite, but very quiet and reserved. She had evidently determined on a course of conduct, and had resolved to assume that, although I had been very rude to her, she did not understand the import of my words. It would be quite proper, of course, for her not to know what I meant by my expressions of the night before.

I was downcast and wretched, and said but little, and the only bright streak across the black horizon of my woe was the fact that she did not appear to be happy, although she affected an air of unconcern. The moonlit porch was deserted that evening, but wandering about the house, I found Madeline in the library alone. She was reading, but I went in and sat down near her. I felt that, although I could not do so fully, I must in a measure explain my conduct of the night before. She listened quietly to a somewhat labored apology I made for the words I had used.

"I have not the slightest idea what you meant," she said, "but you were very rude."

I earnestly disclaimed any intention of rudeness, and assured her, with a warmth of speech that must have made some impression upon her, that rudeness to her would be an action impossible to me. I said a great deal upon the subject, and implored her to believe that if it were not for a certain obstacle I could speak to her so plainly that she would understand everything.

She was silent for a time, and then she said, rather more kindly, I thought, than she had spoken before:

"Is that obstacle in any way connected with my uncle?"

"Yes," I answered, after a little hesitation, "it is, in a measure, connected with him."

She made no answer to this, and sat looking at her book, but not reading. From the expression of her face, I thought she was somewhat softened toward me. She knew her uncle as well as I did, and she may have been thinking that if he were the obstacle that prevented my speaking (and there were many ways in which he might be that obstacle), my position would be such a hard one that it would excuse some wildness of speech and eccentricity of manner. I saw, too, that the warmth of my partial explanations had had some effect on her, and I began to believe that it might be a good thing for me to speak my mind without delay. No matter how she should receive my proposition, my relations with her could not be worse than they had been the previous night and day, and there was something in her face which encouraged me to hope that she might forget my foolish exclamations of the evening before if I began to tell her my tale of love.

I drew my chair a little nearer to her, and as I did so the ghost burst into the room from the doorway behind her. I say burst, although no door flew open and he made no noise. He was wildly excited, and waved his arms above his head. The moment I saw him, my heart fell within me. With the entrance of that impertinent apparition, every hope fled from me. I could not speak while he was in the room.

I must have turned pale, and I gazed steadfastly at the ghost, almost without seeing Madeline, who sat between us.

"Do you know," he cried, "that John Hinckman is coming up the hill? He will be here in fifteen minutes, and if you are doing anything in the way of lovemaking, you had better hurry it up. But this is not what I came to tell you. I have glorious news! At last I am transferred! Not forty minutes ago a Russian nobleman was murdered by the Nihilists. Nobody ever thought of him in connection with an immediate ghostship. My friends instantly applied for the situation for me, and obtained my transfer. I am off before that horrid Hinckman comes up the hill. The moment I reach my new position, I shall put off this hated semblance. Good-by! You can't imagine how glad I am to be, at last, the real ghost of somebody."

"Oh!" I cried, rising to my feet and stretching out my arms in utter wretchedness, "I would to Heaven you were mine!"

"I *am* yours," said Madeline, raising to me her tearful eyes.

THE MYSTERY OF SHAFT NO. 6

John A. Foote

I have always maintained that many, so-called, ghostly manifestations could be properly attributed to natural causes, if they were thoroughly investigated; and it was this unyielding scepticism of mine that enabled me to solve the apparently preternatural mystery of Shaft No. 6.

In the year 1867 I stepped out from the portals of an Eastern medical college with little else beside a brand-new diploma and a determination to work. The newly developed anthracite coal region of Pennsylvania seemed a promising field, and I decided to locate at the growing village of Carbondale. I did so, and suffered the experience of nearly every young physician in trying to establish a practice. Time hung heavily on my hands, and as I was something of an amateur botanist, I passed some of my idle moments in wandering among the beautiful forests that surrounded the town, collecting specimens of plants and ferns. Of the latter I discovered and classified several hitherto unknown varieties.

Several times during my wanderings I encountered a tall, gray-haired man who was invariably accompanied by a large St. Bernard dog. But my attention was more particularly drawn to this man by the peculiar expression of his face. He was very pale, and deeply pitted with small-pox marks. His

169

features were irregular and coarsely moulded, and his eyes, deep set under beetling brows, had a furtive, sinister look that was intensified by a peculiar twitching of the muscles controlling his thin, bloodless lips.

I made inquiries at the town, and found that this person was Captain William Galt, general superintendent of the mines of the Pennsylvania Coal Company, and one of the most wealthy and influential residents of Carbondale. My informants also said that he was a most peculiar man, very taciturn and reserved, and that few of the people of the town had ever seen the interior of his residence. All agreed that he was highly valued by his employers.

What I heard served to arouse my curiosity, and I only waited for an opportunity to form his acquaintance. I was not obliged to wait long. One day while in the woods I heard a dog barking violently, and when I stepped out of the thicket I saw Captain Galt's St. Bernard facing a large rattlesnake that had coiled ready to spring. I stepped behind the reptile and stunned it with a blow of my cane, so that its killing became an easy matter. The captain, who had come up just in time to witness the affair, thanked me with great sincerity for my timely action.

So our acquaintance began, and after this incident I met him often and found him a well-informed man and an agreeable companion. We had many tastes in common, and I became a frequent caller at his residence, first to help him in some investigations which he was pursuing regarding the chemistry of mine gases, and later, at his expressed wish that I would continue my visits, "for the sociability of the thing."

During the period of our acquaintance I was twice called to see him professionally. Each time I found him in an extreme state of nervous exhaustion, the twitching of his facial muscles much intensified, and his mental condition bordering on delirium, in which an overpowering fear seemed to be the dominating symptom. This led me to suspect that he had passed through a terrible mental ordeal at some former period; but on inquiring I found that he had lived an apparently uneventful life.

On June fourth, 1870, I was hurriedly summoned to the captain's residence. I had not seen him for over a week, and I knew that he had been very busy superintending the draining and pumping of some old, water-filled mines, in which a large amount of good coal had been left in the days of primitive coal-mining. This work had demanded close attention, and I was prepared to find that he had broken down under the severe strain on his energies. I made all haste to reach him, and was ascending the steps leading to his residence when I met T. J. Murray, the captain's legal adviser, coming down.

"Is he dangerously ill?" I asked anxiously. Mr. Murray looked at me with surprise.

"Ill?" he said. "Why no! I don't think I ever saw him looking better in his life. Don't look so disappointed," he added, laughingly, as I passed in.

Murray's statements relieved my anxiety, and my fears were entirely dispelled when I greeted the captain in his library. He was seated at his desk, amidst a confusion of documents and papers of various kinds, and there were no signs of illness on his face. After a few commonplaces had been exchanged he said, in an abrupt manner, which was not uncommon with him:

"You met Murray outside?"

"Just as I was about to come in," I answered.

"Did he tell you anything?"

"Nothing, excepting that you were in good health."

"Hum?" said the captain, nervously chewing the end of an unlit cigar. "Well, he might have told you that I have just drawn up my will, and that you are named as the executor." Then, noticing the look of surprise that had come into my face, he continued hastily:

"Now don't say that you will not serve me, for there is more involved in this matter than you suspect."

"I will gladly do anything that may be of service to you,"
I said.

The captain thanked me, and then there ensued an uncomfortable pause. After awhile he spoke again, saying:

"Perhaps you remember telling me that I am likely to succumb to one of my periodical nervous attacks. Did you notice that both of my past attacks began on June fifth?"

"No," I answered, "but now that you speak of it I recall the coincidence. Do you think that you will have an attack to-morrow?"

"I am almost certain that it will come," he replied. "I know that you have a theory that these spells of nervousness are nothing more than physical manifestations of a severe mental strain that I am compelled to undergo at certain periods. Your theory is correct: I have placed greater confidence in you during our brief acquaintance than I have in many of my reputed friends whom I have known for years, and now that I have named you for my executor it will be necessary for me to make certain revelations to you, in order that you may fully understand the provisions of my will."

"I trust that you may not find me unworthy of your confidence—" I began; but the captain, seeming not to have heard me, continued:

"You are a prudent man, and of course you will understand that what I am about to tell you must remain a secret between us until my death. After that you may act as you see fit. The incidents which I will relate occurred about fifteen years ago, when I first came to Carbondale. At that time I was foreman in these mines, and I had for an assistant a young man named Thomas Burke. We were both of about the same age, and, as was natural, we became fast friends. Burke possessed a happy, even-tempered disposition; he was the kind of a man that people call a 'good fellow.' Unfortunately for myself, I was not at all like him, being then, as now, excessively nervous and prone to fly into a passion at trifles.

"It was a woman that caused all of the subsequent mis-

ery, and impelled me to the terrible act which I committed.
Her name was Mary Miller, and she was the daughter of an
old German shoemaker. I had earned for myself the reputation of being a woman-hater, and I will confess that I was not
the kind of a man that would find great favor with the ladies;
but I fell desperately in love with this girl. I earned her
gratitude by giving her father, who was very poor, a position
as a pump engineer in the new mines. Her gratitude, I say
now; but at that time, unhappily, I mistook gratitude for love.

"One day I brought Burke to Mary's home and introduced
him to her. He was much better company than I, and I was
glad when I found that Mary enjoyed his lively talk. After
that he became a frequent visitor; but, although the affair was
town gossip, I did not suspect his motives until the fateful
night of June fifth.

"Mary's father was willing and anxious that I should
marry her, and I felt that she did not dislike me; so it was
with a light and confident heart that I called at her home that
night, with the purpose of asking her to become my wife.

"I found her alone, and she seemed to have guessed the
object of my visit by that subtle instinct which women possess, for she wore an air of restraint that was totally unlike
her usual manner. I will not weary you with details; it is
enough to say that she refused to marry me, and said that it
would be impossible for her even to consider the matter. I
was stunned with amazement, and I asked her for her reasons
in thus treating me. She smilingly told me that, if I had
patience, I would learn some day.

"At this my devilish temper broke down my self-control,
and I accused her, in heated language, of trifling with my
affections. She laughed at my jealous rage, and told me that
she had never loved me, or even liked me, and that she had
promised to marry Thomas Burke. These last words of hers
crushed out every feeling of humanity that was in me. Choking with chagrin, I rushed from the house and tried to drown
the recollections of my unhappiness in a near-by saloon,

while I brooded in impotent rage on the perfidy of my treacherous friend.

"I have no remembrance of what occurred after that until I experienced the thrill of horror that overcame me when I found myself in a thicket near the Miller cottage, with the body of a man at my feet. The moon made it as bright as day, and a vague, terrifying instinct told me, even before I had seen its features, that the body was Burke's. Moved by an unaccountable impulse, I stooped down to smooth the tangled, yellow hair, and my hand became clotted with a warm, sticky fluid. It was blood!

"I was sick with fear, and horror, and regret when I realized the enormity of the crime which I had committed. I could not believe that he was dead, and I made frantic efforts to revive him; but even while I worked with him, his body grew cold and his limbs began to stiffen. Then, as the fumes of what I had drunk began to pass away, all of my emotions were consumed in a terrible, overmastering fear. What if some other person had seen my deed? My cowardly thoughts rendered me almost helpless, and I crouched in silence over the body, while I strained my ears to catch any sound that might betray the presence near by of another person. My teeth chattered with nervousness, and I felt impelled to shout, or do something to break the awful silence that prevailed. A cricket chirped behind me, and I leaped to my feet in alarm. Gradually, my spasm of fear passed away, and I determined to hide the body.

"I remembered that the opening to an abandoned water-filled mine was not far away, so I carried the corpse to this place and weighted it with several heavy stones. A sort of a shed had been built over this place, which was known as Shaft No. 6; a roof-like structure of rough boards erected so as to prevent unwary travellers from falling into the old mine. With a strength that my fears stimulated, I tore two of the boards from the roofing and threw the body through the aperture which I had made. I was, by this time, fairly self-possessed, and I watched it as it sank feet downwards. For an instant the glassy eyes seemed to reproach me, and then the murky, yellow water closed over the head and it disappeared from view. I carefully fastened the boards in place.''

A spasm of nervousness, induced by his terrible recollections, seized the captain at this point, and I could see that he was in the throes of another attack.

"I cannot finish,'' he said weakly. "I cannot!''

I hastily laid him on the sofa, and gave him a hypodermic dose of morphia to quiet him. For nearly an hour he writhed in convulsions, but by degrees the soporific influence of the drug gained ascendency, and he dropped into a fitful slumber. I left him then, and told his housekeeper to send for me if his condition should become critical during the night.

The following morning I called to see him, and was surprised to learn that he was not at home. Late that night Mrs. Drew, his housekeeper, came to my office and told me that the captain had not yet returned. She was much alarmed about his absence, and she besought me to try and find him. I made an exhaustive search for him all that night and the following morning, but to no avail; I could find no trace of him. Two days passed, and then I went to Scranton in the hope that I might find him at some of the hotels. I stopped at the Forest House, and at eight o'clock that night I received a telegram:

"Come at once: captain found.

"MRS. DREW.''

I left for Carbondale on the 8:20 train, and when I reached the town it was buzzing with the details of the story. The captain had been found in a branch of the old mine which had recently been pumped dry, and he was said to be in a critical condition. But when I saw him I was shocked at his emaciated appearance. A frightful delirium had seized him, and he shrieked almost continuously in a paroxysm of fright, and sought to shut out the fearful delusions of his brain by covering his head with the pillows of the bed. Father Daly, the parish priest of Carbondale, was at his bedside, and assured me that he had done all that lay in his power for the captain's spiritual comfort. He left shortly after my arrival, promising to return as soon as possible. After about an hour the captain grew calmer, and recognized me. He was comparatively lucid for a little while, but seemed too weak to talk. Then, suddenly, with a vigorous twist, he raised himself on one elbow, and his sunken eyes took on the despairing glare of a madman.

"O God!" he shrieked, "the conscience of a murderer is hell." Then he went on with feverish rapidity: "You remember what I told you a few days ago? I knew then that I would not live much longer. Was I not right? What is death but peace?—peace from the fear, the haunting dread in which I lived; the dread that I should see him as I saw him on that night; the dread lest he should rise and accuse me of my hidden crime. And in the end of all *I saw him!*"

A soul-harassed wail came from the despairing man, and he rocked to and fro in the bed and placed his wasted hands over his eyes. He was silent for a few minutes, and then, with a fierce gesture, he grasped the lapel of my coat and drew me towards him until his sallow, drawn face was close to me, and his sickly breath fanned my cheek. Talking eagerly, and in hoarse whispers, he went on:

"It was in the old mine—the mine that is connected with Shaft No. 6. Some force that I could not resist impelled me to steal out at midnight and go there. . . . So, stealthily, stealthily I crept through the new workings, and then I came to where the props were rotten and covered with strange growths, and the coal was slimy and yellow. . . . And I saw him, as he stood near a pool of putrid water, all dripping with ooze and slime; and the coal was yellow, and the water dripped from his fingers as he pointed at me, and—*O God, look!*"

While he shrieked this out his features worked convulsively, and with a tetanic spasm he rose and pointed over my shoulder. Involuntarily I turned my head, and in that instant he fell back, limp and unconscious. The tell-tale rattle began in his throat; in a little while he was dead!

After the funeral I opened his will, and found, not to my surprise, that the bulk of his property, aggregating nearly $40,000, had been bequeathed to Mary Miller, who was supposed to be living in Pittsburg. If it could be shown that she was dead, part of the estate would go to several charities and part to me.

I found it a difficult matter to obtain any clue to the whereabouts of Mary Miller, and, after some well-nigh useless correspondence with a firm of Pittsburg detectives, I started for that city to conduct the inquiry in person. To guide me in my search I took a great part of the captain's letters and papers with me. Among the latter I found a clipping, taken from the Scranton *Star*, and evidently inspired by the captain, stating that "Thomas Burke, treasurer of the Miners' Accident Fund of Carbondale, had disappeared, with $232 belonging to the society." After ten days of unavailing inquiry at Pittsburg, I secured evidence that Mary Miller had died in an almshouse some miles from the city. This accomplished, I returned to Carbondale.

It was Lawyer Murray who first told me of the mystery of Shaft No. 6. He called on me shortly after my return from Pittsburg, and took the depositions and other papers I had obtained to prove the death of Miss Miller. When he was about to leave me he said, with a half-smile:

"I suppose you heard the ridiculous story that some of the miners circulated, about having seen the captain's ghost in the workings under the old shaft?"

I said that I had heard nothing of it, and he gave me the particulars as he had learned them. Ordinarily a story of this kind would not have caused me a second thought; but now the strange circumstances of the captain's death, and his vivid description of his experience in the mine, came back to me, and the miners' story seemed to confirm as truth what I had considered the ravings of a demented man.

"You are not afraid of ghosts?" said the lawyer, as he noticed my abstraction.

"No," I said, rather ashamed that I had shown such signs of mental perturbation; "not, at least, of imaginary ones."

"It's very likely that it's all bosh," continued Murray. "Anything bearing the faintest resemblance to a human being, coupled with a little superstition, will make a ghost in a coal mine. But dead men tell no tales!"

He laughed at his sombre joke and departed, but I could not dismiss from my mind what he had told me. "Dead men tell no tales!" I repeated to myself. Could it be true that Captain Galt had seen a dead man standing in the mine near the foot of the shaft; a dead man preserved from decay through all these years that he might at last bear evidence to the gruesome tale of murder?

The more I thought on the matter the more I became convinced that the miners had seen, not a ghost but the body of Thomas Burke. It was only natural that they should connect the supposed apparition with Captain Galt, and say that his spirit was haunting the mine that had caused his death.

That evening I sent for the two persons who were said to have seen the apparition. One was a driver boy about eighteen years of age; the other an experienced and fairly intelligent miner. Both described accurately the location of the quarter of the mine in which they had encountered the supposed spirit, and both said that it was the figure of a man dripping with sulphurous water, and standing near a decayed prop. Both said they were certain that it could not have been the body of any human being, because the mine had been filled with water until the day preceding the disappearance of the captain. After considerable urging on my part, and the promise of a reward, the miner agreed to guide me to the place.

Having secured two mine lamps, we immediately set out, and to quiet the nervous fears of my companion I told him all that I could reveal with safety of my theory regarding the supposed mystery. The mine under Shaft No. 6 had been abandoned because the coal was "rusty"—that is, because it contained an unusually large amount of the sulphur salts of iron. Another, though less urgent, reason for its abandonment was the fact that pumps were needed to work continuously in order to prevent it from filling with water. All mine water contains some of these astringent mineral salts, but the water here was almost saturated with them. What he had seen, I told him, was in all likelihood, the body of some unfortunate man who had fallen into the shaft, and had become imbedded in a thick layer of the sulphur and iron salts that collected in the bottom of the mine. The antiseptic and astringent properties of these salts had preserved a certain resemblance to human likeness in the body and prevented it from wholly decaying. When the mine was pumped dry the body was carried with the current of water from the bottom of the shaft toward the direction in which the pumps lay.

But with all my assurances and explanations I could see that he did not feel at ease when we entered the mine. Presently we came to the wet and slippery chambers of the old workings, where the mine water had dyed everything an ochre tint. We were now quite near to the baleful spot, and my companion refused to go any further. I went forward alone, lamp in hand, and a moment later I stood, shivering with a strange terror, and looking at the mute witness to the captain's guilt.

The sight was a horrible one. There was just the form of a man—a bag of leathery skin and bone wrapped up in tattered rags, and all covered with the yellow-sulphur-slime of the mine. It was in an upright position behind an old and fungus-covered wooden prop, where the outgoing waters had left it. While I looked a portion of the rotten prop gave way and the body fell towards me with an almost life-like motion. Thoroughly unnerved, I turned and ran, almost forgetting my companion in my strange terror.

When I came out of the mine I lost no time in reporting the matter to the proper authorities, although I did not then reveal any of the knowledge I had obtained concerning the identity of the body with the murdered Thomas Burke.

But in order that justice may be done to all, and in compliance with the wish expressed by Captain Galt to me shortly before his death, I, Arthur Phillips, have prepared this statement to be read when I, like the others, shall have passed beyond human judgment.

THE RINGING OF THE BELL

Richard F. Woods

They were talking on the deck of the club, the roof garden. The city streets stretched out in glittering, glimmering lines, below them, and their noises came up strangely clear. It was a close, dry evening, heavy with the smell of newly-watered streets and hot asphalt. The city seemed panting from a hard day's work, and its warm breath hung in a misty smoke above the chimneys and stretched far to the west, mingling with the sky-line, which paled frequently with flashes of heat lightning. They had dined on the roof of the club, these three, all through the hot weather.

"Jack," said one, finishing his coffee and pushing the cup away, to make room for his elbow; "I saw Archer to-day; he's been every place in the world; he says the hottest place is hell, then comes Philadelphia, and then Singapore."

"Well, if this continues," said the one addressed, "we'll begin to have the heat cases at the hospital. I took Williams down to the heat tent last summer and he didn't seem to relish the experience. Do you remember, Williams?"

"Do I remember? Will I ever forget it?" he answered. "I had never seen death before that night, and there I saw three men die all at once, as dogs die of fits in the street, with

181

foam and blood-streaked lips, and gray-blue faces. I'll never forget that night; it gives me the horrors to think of it now.''

A man emerged from the darkness, bearing a tray on which could be heard the clinking of ice in glasses. ''Oh! by the way, Jack,'' said Williams, reaching for the check and signing it; ''speaking of hospitals, you promised to tell me some time about Miss Knerr's death. This was when I was a reporter on the *Review*,'' he continued, in an explanatory way to the other; ''a nurse committed suicide and I was placed on the case. I interviewed Jack, but could get nothing from him save the bare facts. He intimated that there was something mysterious and promised to tell me the whole story some time in the future, but I have never heard anything about it since.''

''Well,'' said Jack, taking a sip of the cool drink before him, ''it is true I have kept silent about the matter. It was so mysterious and strange that I have not told it to any one. I have an inborn fear of being laughed at. I suppose this is the reason I have been so silent, but if you and Raines are sure you would like to have the story, and will promise to be as credulous as you can, and will interrupt me when you have had enough, I am willing to tell you my own experience at that time and what I know of the death of the nurse.

''It all happened when I was in the Pencoyed Hospital,'' he began, biting off the end of his cigar and lighting it. ''Let me see; it was about twelve years ago. So many things have occurred since that time, it is rather hard to fix the date, but I think it was in '96; however, the date is of little moment, as you will find my unreliability of memory does not extend to the story. Every incident and action of what I am about to relate is very firmly fixed in my mind. I had almost completed my term at the hospital, and was senior resident, with about five months more to serve, and the importance of my position was, I think, more appreciated by myself than others. The head nurse in one of my wards was a Miss Knerr. She had been in my ward about a month. She was an excellent nurse in many respects, and had the ability and adaptability of a man, combined with the quick, nervous energy of a woman. There was one virtue she lacked, however, and that was sympathy. I never saw her exhibit those little touches of human kindness one expects from a nurse. She was never seen consoling the friends of a dying patient or looking with pity even on a suffering child. She performed every act mechanically, and dressed a wound with the same stolid indifference that she would dress her hair. Mind you, things were well done and quickly done, but sometimes painfully done; the patients noticed it, too; they realized that they were well nursed, but there was something they missed.

" 'Oh, sir,' said an old man, with a bad crush of the leg, 'ef she'd only 'ave given me some 'opeful words instead of tha drug last night, I could 'ave stood the night better; she's fingers like moss but a chunk of wood for a 'art.'

"She was of valuable assistance to me sometimes as an interpreter and could speak French, German, and Italian fluently. We had a great many patients of all nationalities in the hospital, and their English, when they spoke it, being very poor, I found it almost impossible to get an authentic history without Miss Knerr's help. She could speak rapidly and correctly even the patois and seemed to be able to worm out of the patients just the things I wished to know. She was scrupulously neat, but there was nothing out of the ordinary in her personal appearance to attract attention. The only thing one would notice was her hair, which was superbly luxuriant in its growth and dark red in color; otherwise she was quite plain and looked the typical neat nurse.

"One of my duties as senior resident was to take charge of the nurses when they were sick, and it was in the capacity of a patient that Miss Knerr came to consult me one morning. 'I have been counting my pulse,' she said, 'and I find that it is invariably intermittent, and has been for some time. I am very much worried about it; I suppose unnecessarily so—but the death of Number Twelve, who had a pulse similar to mine, has made me anxious. I wish you would examine it and tell me what you think.' I felt her pulse and found that it was as she had said. Her heart ran regularly enough for a time, and then would halt, and miss a beat, and continue as before. This condition occurs quite frequently, especially among smokers and in people who are run down and nervous. The mechanism of the heart gets out of order. It does not necessarily mean that there is anything organically wrong, but, like a machine, it is apt to get awry sometimes.

"I explained this to Miss Knerr, after listening carefully to her heart and finding it healthy as I supposed. She was so anxious about her condition, however, that I questioned her closely as to the length of time she had noticed it, and so forth, and tried to get some knowledge of her previous history, but she was as silent as the grave on everything pertaining to her former life.

"A physician, after long association with all classes in a hospital, has his instincts sharpened, he suspects things without any definite grounds, and I felt that there was something peculiar about Miss Knerr's former life and about her present condition. I felt sure that there was something she was concealing, something I could not definitely determine. The following day I asked my chief, while he was making his rounds, if he would not examine Miss Knerr with me. Together we went to her room in the Nurses' Home, and together we made a thorough examination of her heart, and could find nothing save the irregularity. She was again questioned closely by both of us and my chief (I remember well) said as we were leaving the building: 'Mark my words, there is something peculiar about that young woman, which I can't fathom. I feel sure she is holding something back.' I was very busy that day, and was up until after twelve, dressing a bad burn case, which had been brought into the receiving ward by the patrol, and when I went to bed I was completely tired out. It seemed that I had hardly been asleep five minutes when I became dimly conscious of a sensation of light. It became associated with my dream in some manner, then I

felt my shoulder gently shaken and my name called. I sat up
in bed, blinking at a large candle which an orderly held by
the side of my bed. 'What is it?' I asked, shading my eyes
from the flickering light. 'The night nurse told me to tell
you,' the orderly began, repeating the words slowly as if he
had memorized them, 'that one of the nurses has had a fit in
your ward, and they want you down there as soon as you can
come.'

" 'All right,' I answered, jumping out of bed; 'I'll come
down as soon as possible.' I hurriedly dressed and descended
the stairs (we roomed on the top floor of the main building at
that time), crossed the main corridor, and entered the ward.
The few gray streaks of early dawn, which came through the
closed windows, were enough to let me see from the condition of the patients that something unusual had happened. I
glanced down the long row of white beds and found that
almost every occupant was erect, gazing with frightened face
toward the other end of the ward. My glance followed theirs
and I saw that one of the large white ward screens had been
placed about something on the floor. I could not see under
the screen sufficiently to make out what the object was, but a
candle held behind the screen illuminated it like a transpar-
ency; save at the bottom, where the figure of a nurse was
silhouetted sharply. I walked the length of the ward and,
pushing the wing of the screen aside, saw that Miss Knerr
had fallen on the floor and was quite still. Her dress was
open at the throat and waist, her face was damp from being
bathed in cold water, while from both angles of her closely
clenched mouth, something brown marked a line to her chin.
I was on the floor at her side in an instant, with my finger on
her pulse, and my ear to her heart. There was silence at my
ear, and no pulsation betrayed itself at my finger tips. 'Miss
Knerr is dead,' I said, arising and turning to the night nurse.
'Tell me how it happened?'

" 'I was at the other end of the hall outside of the ward,'
the nurse explained, desisting from arranging the dead nurse's

dress and arising, 'when I heard a short, sharp cry. I hurried to the ward and met the orderly who told me that Miss Knerr had fallen in a fit in the medicine room; I entered the door and found her lying on the floor at the end of the ward—she had evidently crawled from the medicine room to the place we found her. I rushed to her side and sent for you. She had one or two convulsions and then was still. It all occurred so suddenly we had scarcely time to give her anything, although I tried to force some whisky down her throat. It is certainly an awful thing, doctor; what do you think she died of?'

" 'I don't know,' I answered; 'probably her heart.' She questioned me in regard to another patient who was worse, and then left my side to quiet an hysterical woman in the nearest bed, who was laughing wildly, while the orderly and I lifted the body on a stretcher and carried it from the ward.''

"What was the matter with her?'' asked Raines, leaning forward and interrupting the story.

"Hydrocyanic acid poisoning; I made the autopsy myself,'' the speaker continued, pulling at his lightless cigar, "and found distinct evidence of poisoning, which the chemical analysis afterward verified; otherwise we found all the organs perfectly healthy, and not a suggestion of a lesion of the heart. There was the most peculiar life-like appearance after death. It reminded one of the old vampire stories about the undead. Even after the autopsy there was a rosy color in the cheeks and a healthy hue to the skin, with the eyes looking at the ceiling in a living sort of way. By George, she looked so natural that when we were covering her with a sheet, I came near feeling for a pulse at the wrist, even after the post-mortem. Perhaps it was the fading sun that gave the natural color to the skin, for we worked late in the afternoon, and I remember it was a crimson sunset.

"The body was placed in one of the private rooms in 'A' ward, and in order that you may understand thoroughly what follows, I will have to describe the position of the ward and the rooms accurately. Some few weeks before the death of the nurse, we had a slight epidemic of rotheln, or German measles, among the nurses, six or seven being taken sick at the same time. As the disease is contagious, and there was no proper place for caring for these cases in the Nurses' Home, they were placed in the rooms in this ward. After the recovery and removal of the nurses the ward could not be occupied for some time. It was, therefore, thought a proper place for the body of the nurse. 'A' ward projects as a square wing from the main building and contains, on the first floor, four private rooms, two on each side of a long hall. The only entrance into 'A' ward, from the main building, was through a door at the end of this hall. The bedrooms were numbered 1, 2, 3, and 4, and each room was provided with an electric bell, a long wire running from a connection in the wall and ending in a wooden bulb, with a button on the end. This bulb was placed on the bed and could be rung by the patient. The indicator, placed just outside the hall door, was a large black dial, marked with the numbers of the rooms and a silver arrow pointing to each.

"The night after the death of the nurse, I was awakened by a severe storm. The wind had risen to terrific violence, and the rain, which had started in earlier in the evening, was blown by fierce gusts wildly down the street, and smashed against my rattling windows like showers of steel. The thunder succeeding the sharp flashes of lightning was frightful, and if I dozed would suddenly startle me into wakefulness with its loud crashes. I remember sitting up in bed and listening to the wind howling round the eaves and chimneys and slamming the blinds against the side of the house. It must have been a thick night on the river, for I could hear the constant tooting of the river craft in a mournful way borne on each wave of wind. At length my restlessness attained to such a pitch that I rose from the bed and went to the window to look out at the storm, but could see nothing save the tops of wildly waving trees, a low-browed sky, and my own face

looking in at me from the black void. I returned to bed, but
not to sleep.

"As I was sinking into a doze, my door creaked, was
pushed suddenly open, and an orderly came rapidly into the
room. 'Doctor!' he cried. 'Doctor!'

" 'All right,' I answered: 'I'm awake; what is it?'

" 'The bell's ringing down stairs, and they want you right
away.'

" 'What are you talking about?' I questioned. 'What bell?'

" 'I don't know, but I think it has something to do with
Miss Knerr.'

"He was evidently much frightened, and started violently
as a loud crash of thunder shook the building.

" 'I don't know what you are talking about, but you can
tell the nurse that I will come down,' I answered, getting out
of bed and lighting my light. I supposed he had delivered the
message wrong. The orderly declared he had not heard the
bell ring, but suggested that I hurry as quickly as possible for
they were all very much frightened. He was out the door and
into the hall before I could ask him anything further.

"There was in those days an open bridge or passageway
connecting the surgical building, which contained 'A' ward,
and the main building, where our rooms were located. It was
perhaps fifty feet long and entirely without cover. I received
the storm in all its fury when I crossed the bridge. It was like
the deck of an ocean steamer in a heavy gale. At last I
managed to reach the opposite side and entered the hall. They
were waiting for me, all standing in a little group outside of
'A' ward—the ward nurse, the night nurse, and the orderly—
and before I reached them the night nurse turned and advanced to meet me; she was chalk-white and talked nervously.

" 'Oh, doctor! I am so glad you have come,' were her first
words. 'I thought you could not understand the message; I
should have written it, I know, but we wanted you so quickly.'

" 'I certainly did not understand why you sent for me,' I

remarked, walking by her side to the door, 'and still am in doubt.'

" 'It is most peculiar,' the nurse explained, 'and I am frightened. I was making my rounds with the ward nurse, and we were both at the upper end of the surgical ward, when we heard clearly and sharply the sound of a bell. We hurried to the end of the ward and into the hall, when the bell was again rung, this time for a longer period, and we discovered that it was coming from the private rooms in "A" ward. We went to the door leading into the ward, thinking we must be mistaken, and we were about to open it when the bell rattled again immediately above our heads. We looked at the indicator and there was the arrow pointing to room Number One. Doctor, we both knew that there was no living person in that ward and the only occupant of room Number One was a dead body. I called the orderly and sent for you.'

"While she was talking I was gazing at the dial of the indicator and found each arrow pointing downwards in its proper place.

" 'We have pushed the under catch,' the nurse continued, noticing the direction of my glance.

" 'Well, of course you know, Miss Farr,' I stated reassuringly, 'that there is nothing—' I stopped suddenly. With a burr, sharp and metallic, the bell went off, continued for some seconds, and then ceased. I looked at the dial; the silver arrow pointed to Number One. I must confess I was startled; the hour, the storm, everything stimulated my imagination; as for the others, they were frightened almost to the stage of desertion. 'I am going into that room, something may have happened,' I said, trying to control my voice which in spite of my efforts trembled. 'Give me the candle, and you follow,' I commanded the orderly. I could hear the orderly panting over my shoulder as we advanced down the dark hall. At last we reached room Number One. I pushed open the door with some difficulty—it seemed to resist my efforts—and was greeted by such a burst of storm and wild wind that I started back; my candle was immediately extinguished and I was left in utter darkness. The orderly cried out, and actually ran down the hall when he found that we were in the dark. I called on him to return but my voice received no answer. I heard the hall door close on the sound of his footsteps, then there was silence, and I was alone. I searched my pockets for matches. At last I found one and advanced, feeling around the wall for the gas, when the door of the room slammed with sudden violence. I was in pitch darkness and the un-lighted candle in my hand. I struck a match, the head flew, sputtered a moment on the floor, and then went out. I was standing with my back to the wall, vainly trying to peer through the darkness in order to locate the door; my only desire now was to get out of the room. There was a slight lull in the storm, and the wind, instead of roaring, had sunk into a whining outside of the window, when I distinctly heard something move in the bed, something move again, making the mattress wheeze and the bed creak, something slid off the bed to the polished floor, a soft pit-pat, sounding strangely like some one getting out of bed in bare feet, and then it came round the end of the bed and towards me, nearer and nearer, and I had the strange sensation that something was standing directly in front of me and looking at me; then, sounding miles away, came the jingle of the bell in the hall. It ceased, and for a moment there was not a sound, and then the frightful stillness and blackness were broken by a crash of thunder, the like of which had never been heard before, and which seemed to shatter the foundations of the hospital like an earthquake, and the room, the whole hospital, and the street outside were filled with a glare of vivid, blinding light.

"I was filled with fear, the kind that comes in the night, with things you can't see, or feel, or know; the horrible terror I had heard about but never had, the kind that grasps you by the throat and makes your ears pulsate from holding in your breath and straining to catch sounds you are afraid to hear. Then the orderly, bringing exquisite relief, appeared with

another candle. He was evidently ashamed of his lack of
courage and had summoned up nerve to return. I could not
speak to him; my mouth was dry, and my tongue seemed
swollen. I motioned him to remain outside, however, keeping
the door wide open, while I closed the windows. The rain
had poured in at both windows during the night in a deluge.
After closing the window I lit the gas, and turned towards the
bed. The sheet which had covered the body lay in a wet pile
on the floor. The body was undisturbed, but still preserved
the life-like appearance we had noticed at the autopsy. The
head, from the relaxation of the muscles of the neck, had
fallen over to one side, and was gazing at us with partially
separated lips and healthy blood-charged cheeks. I picked up
the sheet from the floor, and was about to replace it over the
body, when an exclamation from the orderly startled me.
'My God, doctor! look at that!' he cried, pointing towards
the bed, gray-lipped, and with staring eyes. I looked to where
his finger pointed, and there, clasped tight in the fingers of
that wax-like hand, was the bulb of the electric bell. I know
not how long we both stood breathlessly waiting and watching for the sound of the bell, but it seemed hours. I advanced
to the bed at last, grasped the wire and gave it a fierce jerk;
the force of it did not pull the bulb from the fingers as I
expected, but pulled the bulb and hand still clasping it from
the bed, and the arm dropped and swung like a pendulum
from the shoulder. I grasped the hand and unwound the
fingers from the bell. They were tight and stiff, and opened
like bending lead pipe. The hand was cold and claw-like, and
I thought held on to the bulb with all its force. I replaced the
arm on the bed but it swung off with, I imagined, some
movement, as if it wanted the bell again. I placed the bell
well out of reach over the head of the bed and spread the wet
sheet over the corpse; it stuck closely to the outlines of the
body and covered up the face with its red hair. The orderly
left the room before me and I turned out the light. As I
passed the bed in the dark, walking towards the door, I could

have sworn I heard a faint sigh and some one whisper, like a
breath, something I could not understand. I rushed out into
the hall and closed and locked the door securely.

"The coroner made an examination the next day and rendered a verdict of suicide. She was buried quietly, and there
was no one outside of the hospital who seemed to have any
interest in her. I offered the night nurse the explanation that I
had tried to persuade myself to accept: that the insulation had
worn from the wires and the ringing of the bell was the
result. The orderly, I found, had left the hospital suddenly
after our experience in the night, leaving no explanation of
his departure; otherwise things resumed their usual course
again. I was far too busy during the day to bother much about
what I had been through, but during the night I frequently
would waken from a sound sleep and hear a bell ringing far
off, as if the nurse was calling me from her grave. This wore
on my nerves and, after a time, I caught myself listening for
it during the day.

"Six months afterwards two new doctors were elected to
the hospital and, the resident rooms being all occupied, two
of us were moved out to make accommodations for the new
men. I was one of the two who were obliged to move and,
'A' ward being unoccupied, we were placed in the private
rooms on that floor. The room I occupied was directly opposite the one where the dead nurse had lain. I did not like my
quarters, but I had not heard the bell for some months. I was
sleeping well and regaining my nerves. Then came the dream.
I had gone to sleep quietly enough, but I dreamt that suddenly I heard the bell in the hall ring. I seemed to be in my
bed, as I was in fact. I sat up in bed and listened; again the
bell rang. I got out of bed and again listened; perfect silence.
I must have been dreaming, but I could in my dream hear the
gentle part of the shade blown by the wind against my
window. I went to the door of the room where my companion
was and I looked in; he was sleeping soundly, for I could
hear his slow, hard breathing. 'It's a shame to wake him,' I

thought. I softly closed his door, walked to the end of the hall and, opening the door, looked at the indicator. The arrow pointed to room Number One. I became suddenly very angry. 'Why do you annoy my sleep in this manner,' I cried loudly, looking at the bell; then, being ashamed of my anger and thinking some one would hear me, I whispered the words again: 'Why do you annoy me.' The bell, I imagined, answered with an irritating little ring of just one beat; this so enraged me that I smashed my fist bravely into the glass over the indicator and splintered it all over the floor.

" 'Now you will be quiet,' I cried, entering the ward again. The hall seemed changed and much lengthened and very narrow, and was suffused with a peculiar blue light which flickered irregularly, like an arc light when the carbons burn badly. Instead of two rooms on each side there were twenty or thirty in all, and I had great trouble in picking out my room from the rest. The first one I opened was like a window and looked directly out on the street, but high above it, and extending to the horizon, as far as my vision carried, there were hundreds and hundreds of hospitals, arranged regularly in squares like a checker-board, each surrounded by four streets. On the corner of each street was a lamp post burning brightly, and directly beneath it, lying prone, was a body covered with a white sheet, altogether covered, except at one end where a bunch of red hair was exposed. I tried to count the bodies; there seemed myriads of them, but the cold air blowing in strongly made me desist. I shut the door and, turning, found the ward had assumed its natural proportions. Then suddenly everything snapped dark like the shutter of a camera and I found that the muscular power had entirely disappeared from my lids and I could not open them. By raising them, however, with my fingers, I managed to see, although dimly. My room I found was now directly in front of me and, as the door was open, I entered. Now I will get some sleep, I thought; there will be no more ringing of that bell; then, just as I was getting into bed, I heard my name called, softly, like a whisper, at first close to my ear and then in a pleading way at some distance—'Doctor, Doctor, Doctor' —three times and sounding like the soft murmur I had heard when I left the room of the dead six months before. I arose from the bed and went into the hall again and listened with straining ears. I was certain some one was in trouble and I wanted so much to help. 'Poor thing,' I called; 'poor thing.' Again the soft 'Doctor' came to me in a pleading way. This time I traced it to room Number One. I looked towards the room and heard a strange noise like a key being turned quietly, like the creaking of a bolt, and the door swung slowly open, and again some one called from within the room. I hastened towards it and crossed the threshold; the room was lighted by the same blue light I had noticed in the hall. The door of the room opened inwards and was drawn back, forming an angle with the wall, as if to conceal something. 'I am sure some one is behind that door,' I said to myself. I tried to close it and found it resisted. I pulled harder, when it yielded suddenly, and behind it I saw Miss Knerr, looking as she looked the day she died, wrapped in the damp white sheet, standing motionless against the wall— only her eyes had been removed, and she looked at me with cave-like sockets white as polished bone. I tried to push the door and crush her in the corner, but the fingers of an ice-cold hand closed on mine. The intense horror of nightmare came over me. 'Let me go!' I cried, trying to draw back my arm, but the hand clung to it, and a most melancholy voice sobbed: 'Oh, listen to me; oh, listen to me!'

" 'Who are you?' I asked, struggling meanwhile to disengage myself.

" 'Josephine Knerr; I have been murdered. Please listen to me and I will tell you all.'

"Terror made me quiet, and I listened to her story, with her skull-like eyes gazing into mine and her cold fingers grasping my arm like four ice bands.

" 'I have been murdered,' she continued; 'cruelly murdered, and I am unable to rest until my story is told. John Holl, the orderly, did it. He followed me about all the time, and the evening that I died, when I was alone in the ward, he came into the office and told me that he was in love with me and wished me to marry him. I nearly fainted from fright and called loudly for help; his appearance terrified me. He turned and left the ward quickly, but as he was leaving, he said, at any rate, no one else should have me. Oh, why did I take the coffee?' she asked, moaning in a sobbing way. 'I generally take coffee when I go on duty in the early morning. It was poisoned. John Holl always brought it up from the diet kitchen. I became sick as soon as I reached the ward, and hurriedly returned to the medicine room to get something to help me. I entered suddenly and found John Holl on his knees in front of the register in the wall; he had pulled out the whole frame and was pouring something from a bottle down the dark hole in the register pipe. When he saw me he started and dropped the bottle, and I heard it fall and break below. He rose and came towards me, and the room, the floor, and the building went round and round; I had a terrific pain and fell and all was dark. I struggled and opened my eyes, only to find his repulsive face bending over mine. Then he kissed me and I died.'

" 'You must come out and tell it to someone else,' I said, pulling at her arm. She did not move. I pulled again with all my force. The arm came off from the shoulder and swung at my feet, with its fingers soft like putty in my hand. She started for me with a horrible, wild cry, and I stepped back off a great height, and fell, down, down, down, into darkness. I looked up and saw her falling too, distinctly above me, and I was wild with terror. She was falling faster than I, and was coming nearer and nearer. I found that I was not falling through the air, but under water, and I was choking. I started from my sleep, shivering like one with ague, and screaming aloud. It was bright daylight—thank God for that— but all the dream was so vividly impressed on my mind that I could at first hardly persuade myself that I was awake. I started to get out of bed; my hand pained me and I found it covered with dried blood and cut in many places. I must have broken the glass after all. A look at the indicator in the hall showed that its glass was shattered into many pieces. There was blood on the floor and a track of drops led down the hall. I followed the blood stains; they led into my room and stopped at the door, but from this point, traveling across the hall, was another trail, leading directly to room Number One. I had walked across the hall in my dream. I went to the door of the room. It was locked. I can't tell you how glad I was to find the door securely locked. It had been so for many months, but somehow I expected to find it open. But I must see the interior of that room. You may think I was foolish or mad but, try as I would, I could not banish the impression that I had been in that room some time in the night.

"After binding up my hand and having breakfast I procured the key. The lock was rusty and the key worked with difficulty; at last it opened, and, well, you may not believe it, and remember it was morning, with God's daylight shining in, banishing every superstitious fear and freak of the imagination, but when I entered the room the blood tracks crossed the threshold and ended behind the door. I had been in that room. How I entered through a locked door, how the blood drops happened there, I do not explain, but they were there and I saw them as plainly and as true, drop after drop, behind the door, as I see the lights from yonder building." The speaker paused, wiped the moisture from his face, and then continued. "I went to the medicine room, about which the dead nurse had spoken in her dream. I found the register and, pulling out the frame, thrust my hand in and groped about as far as I could reach. Finding nothing, I descended to the lower ward. I found in this ward that the register was directly below the one above; I removed the frame and entered my hand as I had done on the upper floor. The tin pipe made a right angle turn before it descended and formed a small platform immediately back of the opening. Directly my hand encountered dust and some soft cobwebs. I felt carefully about, until I felt something hard and round, just on the edge of the pipe; blowing the dust from it I held it to the light. It was the broken neck of a medicine bottle with the cork intact. I smelt it to see if I could detect by the odor what had been the contents of the bottle, but there was nothing that I could discover. For a long time I was uncertain what course I should pursue. I was sure that if I told my story I should be disbelieved. Who would place any reliance in a dream and the neck of a broken bottle in a heater pipe?

"The more I thought of it the more foolish it seemed, so I decided to keep the mystery to myself. You may think I should have told some one, and had the occurrence probed to the bottom. Perhaps I was unwise; but, at any rate, I was constant in my resolve. All my inquiries about the orderly, John Holl, were negative. The hospital authorities knew absolutely nothing about him since he had left the institution. I asked the superintendent if Miss Knerr had ever spoken to him about being annoyed by the actions of the orderly; he answered in the negative. He had come to the hospital, the superintendent told me, only a month before the nurse's death, and said he was a sailor from Finland. He had a letter from the captain of a Danish bark, on which he had been working, testifying to his good character. As sailors generally make good helpers about a hospital, being obedient and industrious, he was taken in without a question. While in the hospital he made an excellent record, being quiet and well-behaved, and every one was very much surprised at his sudden departure.

"Well, my story is nearly told. That is all I found out about John Holl while he was in the hospital, and I learned nothing of him after his departure until about three years ago; then I read a short item in the New York *Herald* about a sailor committing suicide in the bay, from one of the Cunarders. His name was John Holl The reporter had done what he

could to make an interesting story of the item, though his
material was scanty; he told, however, that the sailor was a
Finlander, and that his acquaintances had long thought him
wrong in his head, for the man was forever starting in terror
of something no one else could see or hear; and as the years
had passed his sufferings, which he tried in vain to conceal,
had become keener and more continual. He tried to find
peace, it seems, by jumping in the water; whether he did or
not—who knows?''

A TOUGH TUSSLE

Ambrose Bierce

One night in the autumn of 1861 a man sat alone in the heart of a forest in Western Virginia. The region was one of the wildest on the continent—the Cheat Mountain country. There was no lack of people close at hand, however; within a mile of where the man sat was the now silent camp of a whole Federal brigade. Somewhere about—it might be still nearer—was a force of the enemy, the numbers unknown. It was this uncertainty as to its numbers and position that accounted for the man's presence in that lonely spot; he was a young officer of a Federal infantry regiment and his business there was to guard his sleeping comrades in the camp against a surprise. He was in command of a detachment of men constituting a picket-guard. These men he had stationed just at nightfall in an irregular line, determined by the nature of the ground, several hundred yards in front of where he now sat. The line ran through the forest, among the rocks and laurel thickets, the men fifteen or twenty paces apart, all in concealment and under injunction of strict silence and unremitting vigilance. In four hours, if nothing occurred, they would be relieved by a fresh detachment from the reserve now resting in care of its captain some distance away to the left and rear. Before stationing his men the young officer of whom we are writing had pointed out to his two sergeants the spot at which he would be found if it should be necessary to consult him, or if his presence at the front line should be required.

It was a quiet enough spot—the fork of an old wood-road, on the two branches of which, prolonging themselves deviously forward in the dim moonlight, the sergeants were themselves stationed, a few paces in rear of the line. If driven sharply back by a sudden onset of the enemy—and pickets are not expected to make a stand after firing—the men would come into the converging roads and naturally following them to their point of intersection could be rallied and "formed." In his small way the author of these dispositions was something of a strategist; if Napoleon had planned as intelligently at Waterloo he would have won that memorable battle and been overthrown later.

Second-Lieutenant Brainerd Byring was a brave and efficient officer, young and comparatively inexperienced as he was in the business of killing his fellow-men. He had enlisted in the very first days of the war as a private, with no military knowledge whatever, had been made first-sergeant of his company on account of his education and engaging manner, and had been lucky enough to lose his captain by a Confederate bullet; in the resulting promotions he had gained a commission. He had been in several engagements, such as they were—at Philippi, Rich Mountain, Carrick's Ford and Greenbrier—and had borne himself with such gallantry as not to attract the attention of his superior officers. The exhilaration of battle was agreeable to him, but the sight of the dead, with their clay faces, blank eyes and stiff bodies, which when not unnaturally shrunken were unnaturally swollen, had always intolerably affected him. He felt toward them a kind of reasonless antipathy that was something more than the physical and spiritual repugnance common to us all. Doubtless this feeling was due to his unusually acute sensibilities—his keen sense of the beautiful, which these hideous things outraged.

Whatever may have been the cause, he could not look upon a
dead body without a loathing which had in it an element of
resentment. What others have respected as the dignity of
death had to him no existence—was altogether unthinkable.
Death was a thing to be hated. It was not picturesque, it had
no tender and solemn side—a dismal thing, hideous in all its
manifestations and suggestions. Lieutenant Byring was a braver
man than anybody knew, for nobody knew his horror of that
which he was ever ready to incur.

Having posted his men, instructed his sergeants and retired
to his station, he seated himself on a log, and with senses all
alert began his vigil. For greater ease he loosened his sword-
belt and taking his heavy revolver from his holster laid it on
the log beside him. He felt very comfortable, though he
hardly gave the fact a thought, so intently did he listen for
any sound from the front which might have a menacing
significance—a shout, a shot, or the footfall of one of his
sergeants coming to apprise him of something worth knowing. From the vast, invisible ocean of moonlight overhead
fell, here and there, a slender, broken stream that seemed to
splash against the intercepting branches and trickle to earth,
forming small white pools among the clumps of laurel. But
these leaks were few and served only to accentuate the
blackness of his environment, which his imagination found it
easy to people with all manner of unfamiliar shapes, menacing, uncanny, or merely grotesque.

He to whom the portentous conspiracy of night and solitude and silence in the heart of a great forest is not an
unknown experience needs not to be told what another world
it all is—how even the most commonplace and familiar
objects take on another character. The trees group themselves
differently; they draw closer together, as if in fear. The very
silence has another quality than the silence of the day. And it
is full of half-heard whispers—whispers that startle—ghosts
of sounds long dead. There are living sounds, too, such as
are never heard under other conditions: notes of strange

night-birds, the cries of small animals in sudden encounters
with stealthy foes or in their dreams, a rustling in the dead
leaves—it may be the leap of a wood-rat, it may be the
footfall of a panther. What caused the breaking of that twig?
—what the low, alarmed twittering in that bushful of birds?
There are sounds without a name, forms without substance,
translations in space of objects which have not been seen to
move, movements wherein nothing is observed to change its
place. Ah, children of the sunlight and the gaslight, how little
you know of the world in which you live!

Surrounded at a little distance by armed and watchful
friends, Byring felt utterly alone. Yielding himself to the
solemn and mysterious spirit of the time and place, he had
forgotten the nature of his connection with the visible and
audible aspects and phases of the night. The forest was
boundless; men and the habitations of men did not exist. The
universe was one primeval mystery of darkness, without form
and void, himself the sole, dumb questioner of its eternal
secret. Absorbed in thoughts born of this mood, he suffered
the time to slip away unnoted. Meantime the infrequent
patches of white light lying amongst the tree-trunks had
undergone changes of size, form and place. In one of them
near by, just at the roadside, his eye fell upon an object that
he had not previously observed. It was almost before his face
as he sat; he could have sworn that it had not before been
there. It was partly covered in shadow, but he could see that
it was a human figure. Instinctively he adjusted the clasp of
his sword-belt and laid hold of his pistol—again he was in a
world of war, by occupation an assassin.

The figure did not move. Rising, pistol in hand, he approached. The figure lay upon its back, its upper part in
shadow, but standing above it and looking down upon the
face, he saw that it was a dead body. He shuddered and
turned from it with a feeling of sickness and disgust, resumed
his seat upon the log, and forgetting military prudence struck
a match and lit a cigar. In the sudden blackness that followed

the extinction of the flame he felt a sense of relief; he could no longer see the object of his aversion. Nevertheless, he kept his eyes set in that direction until it appeared again with growing distinctness. It seemed to have moved a trifle nearer.

"Damn the thing!" he muttered. "What does it want?"

It did not appear to be in need of anything but a soul.

Byring turned away his eyes and began humming a tune, but he broke off in the middle of a bar and looked at the dead body. Its presence annoyed him, though he could hardly have had a quieter neighbor. He was conscious, too, of a vague, indefinable feeling that was new to him. It was not fear, but rather a sense of the supernatural—in which he did not at all believe.

"I have inherited it," he said to himself. "I suppose it will require a thousand ages—perhaps ten thousand—for humanity to outgrow this feeling. Where and when did it originate? Away back, probably, in what is called the cradle of the human race—the plains of Central Asia. What we inherit as a superstition our barbarous ancestors must have held as a reasonable conviction. Doubtless they believed themselves justified by facts whose nature we cannot even conjecture in thinking a dead body a malign thing endowed with some strange power of mischief, with perhaps a will and a purpose to exert it. Possibly they had some awful form of religion of which that was one of the chief doctrines, sedulously taught by their priesthood, as ours teach the immortality of the soul. As the Aryans moved slowly on, to and through the Caucasus passes, and spread over Europe, new conditions of life must have resulted in the formulation of new religions. The old belief in the malevolence of the dead body was lost from the creeds and even perished from tradition, but it left its heritage of terror, which is transmitted from generation to generation—is as much a part of us as are our blood and bones."

In following out his thought he had forgotten that which suggested it; but now his eye fell again upon the corpse. The shadow had now altogether uncovered it. He saw the sharp profile, the chin in the air, the whole face, ghastly white in the moonlight. The clothing was gray, the uniform of a Confederate soldier. The coat and waistcoat, unbuttoned, had fallen away on each side, exposing the white shirt. The chest seemed unnaturally prominent, but the abdomen had sunk in, leaving a sharp projection at the line of the lower ribs. The arms were extended, the left knee was thrust upward. The whole posture impressed Byring as having been studied with a view to the horrible.

"Bah!" he exclaimed; "he was an actor—he knows how to be dead."

He drew away his eyes, directing them resolutely along one of the roads leading to the front, and resumed his philosophizing where he had left off.

"It may be that our Central Asian ancestors had not the custom of burial. In that case it is easy to understand their fear of the dead, who really were a menace and an evil. They bred pestilences. Children were taught to avoid the places where they lay, and to run away if by inadvertence they came near a corpse. I think, indeed, I'd better go away from this chap."

He half rose to do so, then remembered that he had told his men in front and the officer in the rear who was to relieve him that he could at any time be found at that spot. It was a matter of pride, too. If he abandoned his post he feared they would think he feared the corpse. He was no coward and he was unwilling to incur anybody's ridicule. So he again seated himself, and to prove his courage looked boldly at the body. The right arm—the one farthest from him—was now in shadow. He could barely see the hand which, he had before observed, lay at the root of a clump of laurel. There had been no change, a fact which gave him a certain comfort, he could not have said why. He did not at once remove his eyes; that which we do not wish to see has a strange fascination, sometimes irresistible. Of the woman who covers her eyes with her hands and looks between the fingers let it be said that the wits have dealt with her not altogether justly.

Byring suddenly became conscious of a pain in his right hand. He withdrew his eyes from his enemy and looked at it. He was grasping the hilt of his drawn sword so tightly that it hurt him. He observed, too, that he was leaning forward in a strained attitude—crouching like a gladiator ready to spring at the throat of an antagonist. His teeth were clenched and he was breathing hard. This matter was soon set right, and as his muscles relaxed and he drew a long breath he felt keenly enough the ludicrousness of the incident. It affected him to laughter. Heavens! what sound was that? what mindless devil was uttering an unholy glee in mockery of human merriment? He sprang to his feet and looked about him, not recognizing his own laugh.

He could no longer conceal from himself the horrible fact of his cowardice; he was thoroughly frightened! He would have run from the spot, but his legs refused their office; they gave way beneath him and he sat again upon the log, violently trembling. His face was wet, his whole body bathed in a chill perspiration. He could not even cry out. Distinctly he heard behind him a stealthy tread, as of some wild animal, and dared not look over his shoulder. Had the soulless living joined forces with the soulless dead?—was it an animal? Ah, if he could but be assured of that! But by no effort of will could he now unfix his gaze from the face of the dead man.

I repeat that Lieutenant Byring was a brave and intelligent man. But what would you have? Shall a man cope, single-handed, with so monstrous an alliance as that of night and solitude and silence and the dead,—while an incalculable host of his own ancestors shriek into the ear of his spirit their coward counsel, sing their doleful death-songs in his heart, and disarm his very blood of all its iron? The odds are too great—courage was not made for so rough use as that.

One sole conviction now had the man in possession: that the body had moved. It lay nearer to the edge of its plot of

light—there could be no doubt of it. It had also moved its
arms, for, look, they are both in the shadow! A breath of
cold air struck Byring full in the face; the boughs of trees
above him stirred and moaned. A strongly defined shadow
passed across the face of the dead, left it luminous, passed
back upon it and left it half obscured. The horrible thing was
visibly moving! At that moment a single shot rang out upon
the picket-line—a lonelier and louder, though more distant,
shot than ever had been heard by mortal ear! It broke the
spell of that enchanted man; it slew the silence and the
solitude, dispersed the hindering host from Central Asia and
released his modern manhood. With a cry like that of some
great bird pouncing upon its prey he sprang forward, hot-
hearted for action!

Shot after shot now came from the front. There were
shoutings and confusion, hoof-beats and desultory cheers.
Away to the rear, in the sleeping camp, were a singing of
bugles and grumble of drums. Pushing through the thickets
on either side the roads came the Federal pickets, in full
retreat, firing backward at random as they ran. A straggling
group that had followed back one of the roads, as instructed,
suddenly sprang away into the bushes as half a hundred
horsemen thundered by them, striking wildly with their sa-
bres as they passed. At headlong speed these mounted mad-
men shot past the spot where Byring had sat, and vanished
round an angle of the road, shouting and firing their pistols.
A moment later there was a roar of musketry, followed by
dropping shots—they had encountered the reserve-guard in
line; and back they came in dire confusion, with here and
there an empty saddle and many a maddened horse, bullet-
stung, snorting and plunging with pain. It was all over—"an
affair of out-posts."

The line was reestablished with fresh men, the roll called,
the stragglers were re-formed. The Federal commander with
a part of his staff, imperfectly clad, appeared upon the scene,
asked a few questions, looked exceedingly wise and retired.

After standing at arms for an hour the brigade in camp "swore a prayer or two" and went to bed.

Early the next morning a fatigue-party, commanded by a captain and accompanied by a surgeon, searched the ground for dead and wounded. At the fork of the road, a little to one side, they found two bodies lying close together—that of a Federal officer and that of a Confederate private. The officer had died of a sword-thrust through the heart, but not, apparently, until he had inflicted upon his enemy no fewer than five dreadful wounds. The dead officer lay on his face in a pool of blood, the weapon still in his breast. They turned him on his back and the surgeon removed it.

"Gad!" said the captain—"It is Byring!"—adding, with a glance at the other, "They had a tough tussle."

The surgeon was examining the sword. It was that of a line officer of Federal infantry—exactly like the one worn by the captain. It was, in fact, Byring's own. The only other weapon discovered was an undischarged revolver in the dead officer's belt.

The surgeon laid down the sword and approached the other body. It was frightfully gashed and stabbed, but there was no blood. He took hold of the left foot and tried to straighten the leg. In the effort the body was displaced. The dead do not wish to be moved—it protested with a faint, sickening odor. Where it had lain were a few maggots, manifesting an imbecile activity.

The surgeon looked at the captain. The captain looked at the surgeon.

CALEB THORNE'S DAY

Elizabeth Coatsworth

The day was warm and a heat mirage hung over the waters of the Sound. The houses of Rhodanthe seemed to stand out of the sea, bare outlines of houses supported on nothing but their own reflections. Jim Midgett, sitting at the bow of his grandfather's fishing boat, half leaning against a coil of rope, was used to the sight, but it always gave him the feeling of being in a dream. His grandfather and his own younger brother Jo, aft in the cockpit, were silent. He could hear the flapping of fish against the boards, a little creaking of ropes, and the sigh of the water along their slowly moving keel. That was all. Behind them, thirty-five miles away, lay the low shore of Carolina, hidden far beyond sight. In front of them lay the great Atlantic and, apparently rising from the waves, this group of squares and oblongs that meant home, cutting the huge, lonely horizon of the sky. Nowhere was there the smallest glimpse of land.

"Reckon the Sound's covered the Banks again, Jo," said Jim.

"Reckon you're crazy," said Jo.

"Reckon the Sound *can* cover the Banks, can't it, granddad?" argued Jim.

"Reckon it can, Jim," said his grandfather, "but it's a

long string of years since it did. I was about Jo's age here
when it happened last, and I'll never forget it, if I live to be a
hundred. Terrible wind from the southwest piled up the
Sound water till it came over like a wall, clear to the sea. All
heaving water as far as the eye could make out, with wreckage and chicken coops and the poor critters tossing about.
Carried off the kitchen just after mother had put some ham on
the stove to fry. She was laying the table, I recollect, and
there was a crack to split your head, and the whole ell ripped
off. Father cussed about that ham, more to keep up mother's
spirits than anything else, I reckon. We none of us knew if
the house wouldn't go next, but it held. Mother never was
the same after that. When the waters parted again and the
Banks showed up, same as ever, the rest of us went about our
business, but mother kept the doors and windows shut ever
after. Couldn't bear the sound of the waves on the beach, she
said.''

"Reckon she wasn't a real Banker," remarked Jo, a little
scornfully.

"Yes, she was, too," answered his grandfather, sharply.
"Born between tide and tide like the rest of us. But it's
harder on the women. They don't get out in the boats as we
do.''

Old Captain Midgett grew silent, and Jim went on with his
thoughts.

Yes, he thought to himself, it was a fine thing to be a
Banker. Why, their family had been on the Banks ever since
Sir Walter Raleigh's lost colony came there from Roanoke to
get away from the Indians. Twenty miles of shore, past the
bend of Hatteras, what more could a man need to stretch his
legs? And then there were always the boats. But the women
stayed at home all day long, and the sand covered their little
gardens and drifted under the sills of the doors. He remembered his mother saying once that she treasured the rooster
more than a brooch of gold. "Something to listen to other
than those screeching gulls," she had said. He secretly de-

cided to bring her back a posy in a pot next time he went to Roanoke. He even pitied his younger sister Joanna a little, until he saw her standing on the shore in a faded red dress, skipping stones.

"Wake up, Jim! Wake up!" she cried, in her shrill little voice. "Pitch me the painter, Jim, quick!"

Jo, nearly a head shorter than Jim, was already nimbly over the side, wading to join her. Jim tumbled after him, his face reddening at being caught daydreaming again.

"Never you mind, Jim," said old Captain Midgett. "Reckon you got things going on inside your head that those young ones don't know anything about."

As they came up the steps, the old cock crowed; Ginger, the cat, rose slowly, arched her back, stretched each hind leg, and came forward at her own pace to be petted; while Spot, the hound, thumped the porch with his tail until it resounded like a drum.

Young Captain Midgett, the children's father, appeared from indoors, filling the doorway with his bulk.

"Hello, dad," he said. "Good fishing?"

"Nothing to complain of," answered old Captain Midgett.

"Had a good catch, myself," said young Captain Midgett. "Reckon we'll take the pink [a small, light fishing vessel] up to Norfolk. They say there's a good market right now up there."

Joanna whistled. Usually her father and the other men waited for the buyers, or occasionally went to Roanoke. Norfolk was quite another matter. They would be gone four or five days at least.

"Take me, too, dad?" she cried, swinging on his hand.

"What should I be doing with a big girl like you?" he asked. "You stay and help your mother."

"I could do a lot on the pink," said Jim, "and run errands in Norfolk."

"So could I," said Jo, not to be behind.

"Both of you stay right here, looking after things, while granddad and I are away," said young Captain Midgett, with a glance that warned them he would have no argument. "After supper I want you to take a letter for me to Captain Prudden about an errand I'm to do for him in the city."

That meant riding, for the captain lived four miles or more away in the next neighborhood. First the boys had to catch their ponies, which were grazing with the rest of the town horses and cows on the coarse beach grass. The little animals let themselves be caught and bridled easily enough, and trotted off side by side, with the boys on their backs, over the sand which would have brought an ordinary horse to a walk. But the Banks ponies were as used to the sand as the Bankers were, and had been there even longer. Their ancestors had been put ashore centuries before by the Spanish explorers in order to raise a supply of horses for their expeditions on the mainland.

It was getting dusk, and where the going was good the boys cantered the ponies. At one piece of broken wreckage on the beach, both animals shied violently. When they were by, Jim called to his brother, "Reckon it was a ghost they saw, Jo?"

"Reckon not," Jo called back, in his matter-of-fact way. "Horse will shy at most anything."

"Mighty lot of ghosts of drowned sailors along the beach, Jo," Jim argued.

"Didn't see nary ghost," said Jo.

"Horse can see a ghost before ever a man can," said Jim, and became silent. Looking over his shoulder, he saw that Spot, who was following them, avoided the wreckage, too; but there was no use arguing with a boy like Jo.

They were among the dead oaks now, great trees, whitened as driftwood, but standing upright in the sand, their broken stumps of branches jagged against the evening sky. A cow with a white face and long, twisted horns rose from a dune and gave them a wild, mournful stare.

"Reckon this is where they used to hang the pirates, Jo," said Jim.

"They always hung pirates on the mainland, and you know it," said Jo, somewhat annoyed at Jim's gloomy conversation.

"Then reckon this is where the pirates used to hang other folks. Granddad says Blackbeard used to be hereabouts, with his long black beard combed and braided into two braids and their ends looped up over his ears. You've heard of Blackbeard, Jo?"

"Can't you talk of anything except ghosts and Blackbeards at this time of the night, Jim Midgett?" demanded Jo angrily, switching his pony into a canter to stop all possibility of further conversation.

They made good time to Captain Prudden's, and reached his doorstep just as Mrs. Prudden was lighting the lamp in the kitchen.

It seemed to both boys that Captain Prudden took a long time to find his glasses and read their father's letter, and then an even longer time to get out ink and paper and to write a slow reply. By the time that Jim, as the oldest, had the letter safely in his pocket, it was nearly dark, and the waves gleamed a dim white along the resounding beaches. This time it was Jo who walked wide of the Prudden graves by the front fence as they unhitched their ponies.

"Oh, *they* don't walk," Jim reassured him. "They're at home. It's those on the beaches that no one ever found."

The night was full of sounds and the vague movement of water. A sleeping seal woke and flopped awkwardly down the dark beach. The ponies snorted and threw up their heads. A piece of driftwood, ending in a knot of whitened roots, for a moment seemed to reach toward them like a skeleton hand. Both the ponies and their riders were out of breath by the time they drew down to a walk in the shelter of the scattered lights of Rhodanthe.

*   *   *

The next day the pink sailed, and Jim and Jo and Joanna and Spot were all down on the shore to see it off. Just before he left, young Captain Midgett put his hand for a moment on Jim's shoulder.

"You're the oldest, Jim," he said. "You're in charge."

"Just keep off the water on Caleb Thorne's day, and I reckon you young ones can take care of yourselves," said old Captain Midgett.

With the men of the family gone, the children were on their best behavior. Joanna's curly head could be seen at the kitchen window, where she stood washing dishes instead of vanishing like quicksilver the moment the last spoon was laid down and the last mouthful eaten. The boys took the small boat fishing on Pamlico Sound, but for the first two days their luck was bad. They had been particularly anxious to make a good showing while their father was away.

The third day was Caleb Thorne's day, a fine blue day with just enough wind for good sailing.

"Reckon we'll mend nets today," said Jim at breakfast, regretfully, eating his tenth pancake.

"Whyever can't we go fishing just because of old Caleb Thorne?" asked Jo, rebelliously kicking at the leg of the table.

"Just stop that, Jo Midgett," said his mother. "No one goes fishing on Caleb Thorne's day, and you know it."

"If no one ever does, how does anyone know they'd get drowned if they did?" asked Joanna, who loved to argue.

"Because people *have* gone and they *have* been drowned," said Mrs. Midgett firmly.

"Well, but who, mother?" said Jo. "Who? I dare you to say who."

"There was a man named Will Elwell when I was a girl," replied Mrs. Midgett somberly. "He went out on Caleb Thorne's day. It was a fine day like today, and it stayed fine and stayed fine. Everyone began to say, 'Reckon maybe Will Elwell's right.' Then along about four o'clock there came a burst of wind out of nowhere. Didn't blow more than five minutes, but no one ever saw Will Elwell again.''

Mrs. Midgett's story was followed by silence. Even Jo and Joanna were convinced for the time at least. But sitting on the warm sand, the big net across their knees, the light wind blowing by them, Joanna returned to the discussion in a roundabout way.

"Reckon lots of people been drowned who weren't fishing on Caleb Thorne's day and never had nary glimpse of Caleb Thorne.''

"Reckon,'' said Jim, working steadily.

There was a long silence while three sea gulls winged their way overhead, crossing from the Sound to the sea.

"Reckon lots of people fish on Caleb Thorne's day and don't get drowned,'' went on Joanna in a low voice.

"Reckon they *don't*, Joanna,'' said Jim, looking up. "Didn't you hear what mother said?''

"That was only one man, and it might have happened anyway,'' said Jo, coming into the discussion.

"It mightn't,'' said Jim.

"It might, too,'' said Jo and Joanna together.

"Happens every time,'' said Jim.

"Who else ever got drowned?'' asked Jo.

"Lots,'' said Jim.

"Name them!'' cried Joanna, triumphantly.

"I can't, but I know it's true. None of the men go out,'' replied Jim stanchly.

Joanna again returned to the attack from a different angle. "If Will Elwell got drowned, who knows he saw Caleb Thorne's boat?''

"They know right enough.''

"How do they know, Jim Midgett?''

"Because they do, that's all.''

They all went on mending the net for a while longer. It was Jo who broke the silence.

"I don't believe there ever was any Caleb Thorne, anyhow, and if there was, I don't believe he ever said, 'I'll finish my catch if I have to fish till judgment day'; and if he did, I don't believe he disappeared in a gale of wind; and if he did disappear, I don't believe that he still fishes every year on that day and that if anyone sees him they'll be drowned too, so there! It's just as Joanna says. If they're drowned, how can they tell they've seen Caleb Thorne fishing? It's just a story some one made up, and everyone's scared for fear it *might* be true."

"You think you know everything, Jo Midgett," said Jim. "You think you know more than dad and granddad and all the Bankers put together. It's only one person *has* to be drowned, I reckon. Maybe some of them get back to shore and tell."

By this time Jo and Joanna were in open rebellion. Eyes shining with excitement, they had dropped work on the net. They exchanged glances.

"Reckon I'll go fishing," said Jo, in what he hoped was his everyday voice.

"Reckon I'll come with you," said Joanna. "Must have fish to show dad when he gets back."

"Reckon you won't, either of you!" said Jim. "You heard what granddad said. Why, even father doesn't go out on Caleb Thorne's day, and he isn't afraid of anything on land or sea. You can't go, I say!"

"Who's going to stop us, then?" asked Jo, getting up and squaring off. He was shorter and younger than Jim, but he was more heavily built, and the boys were nearly an even match.

"Mother'll stop you."

"Tattletale, tattletale," shrieked Jo and Joanna.

No, Jim must see it through himself. Helplessly he followed the other two down to the shore and watched them make ready. Not a soul was in sight. Spot stood wagging his tail hopefully. He didn't care with whom he went, so long as he could go sailing. As the children pushed off, he jumped

over the side and landed in the cockpit, with a great scraping
of claws. Joanna was already in, pulling up the sail. Jo was
scrambling in after her.

The blackness of despair closed over Jim. His father had
left him in charge. How could he ever face him and tell him
that the other children had been lost on Caleb Thorne's day?
Quickly he waded after the boat and, just as it steadied to the
breeze, pulled himself over the stern.

Jo grinned impishly. "Hello," he said, "who's here?"

Jim grinned back. He was in for whatever was to happen.
The decision had been taken out of his hands. Now matters
were up to Caleb Thorne.

All day long not a cloud crossed the sky, and there was
only enough breeze for sailing. The fishing was better than
any they had ever known.

"Won't dad be surprised?" Joanna kept asking excitedly.
"Aren't the others foolish to stay ashore when they could be
getting a catch like this?"

Fishing was in their blood. And soon they had almost
forgotten that this was a day with a curse on it, for, after all,
they came of a people who lived always under the threat of
danger. There were fresh water and biscuits stowed away
under one of the seats, and when they were hungry they ate
and drank quickly, begrudging every minute lost from their
lines. Only Jim kept an anxious eye on the sky, an anxious
ear intent on the quality of the wind. But hour followed hour,
and sky and sea remained calm and clear. The boat rose and
dipped quietly on an untroubled swell, while the cockpit
grew heavier and heavier with its load of fish.

Old Spot rose, shook himself, and climbed to the decked-in
space by the mast to get the last of the sun. The light had not
grown less, but the breeze was cooler.

"Better be getting home," said Jim.

"Reckon we had," said Jo. After all, enough was enough

of a good thing, and he, too, had heard about Caleb Thorne ever since he was born.

Only Joanna wanted to catch a few more.

"Just like a girl, never knowing when to quit," said Jo. Joanna stuck out her tongue at him, but drew in her line. Jim swung the boat toward Rhodanthe, which appeared more like a distant fleet of vessels on the horizon than the homes of human beings. The breeze which they had had all day held steady—a following breeze which every minute brought them nearer home. The houses of Rhodanthe grew larger; the beach appeared. They could even make out the distant boats pulled up on the shore.

Jim gave an unconscious sigh of relief. There was a whine from Spot and a sudden chill in the air.

"What's that astern?" asked Joanna in a whisper, pale with terror. Jim saw Jo's eyes look past him, fixed and staring, and swung his own head over his shoulder. A low fog had come in behind them and was moving down upon them with terrifying speed, rushing over the water, which was whipped into one long sheet of spray.

"A white squall," thought Jim, sitting paralyzed at the tiller.

A white squall, coming so suddenly out of perfect weather, was unearthly and horrible enough, but in the whiteness he thought he saw something whiter still, the shape of a sail, the outline of an onward-driven boat.

Jo was praying loudly. The outskirts of the wind had struck them, the water hissed about them.

"Take the tiller, Joanna!" Jim screamed, pushing the handle into her cold hand and stumbling forward to where Spot was crouched in the cockpit near the stern.

Images stabbed his mind: Dad, Caleb Thorne— Something had to be drowned. He caught the struggling hound, lifted him, and with a great effort succeeded in pushing him overboard. Then he let go the halyards, which brought down their single sail in a pile of fluttering canvas, and was back in time to catch the tiller as the squall struck them. All was whiteness about them and a shrieking of icy wind, and their boat tore ahead under its bare pole. Fast as they went, something passed by them faster still, something that looked like a small fishing vessel, almost lost to sight in the spray and fog. In a breathtakingly short time the squall had passed them and they were left drenched and shaken in a boat rocking crazily.

"We've seen Caleb Thorne," said Joanna, first to recover her power of speech.

"Poor old Spot," said Jo, beginning to cry. "I wouldn't have lost him for ten catches of fish! It's all my fault that Spot's drowned."

Jim was busy with the sail, so that they could get home as soon as possible. He could still feel Spot's weight in his arms, and his heart was heavier than Jo's.

"Spot isn't drowned," said Joanna in surprise. "Didn't you see Caleb Thorne pull him aboard? Reckon he wanted company, and Spot always was one to like sailing."

"I didn't see any such thing," said Jo. "Just something white a-driving by, lickety-cut."

"Reckon you were too scared to see," said Joanna with a touch of satisfaction. "Reckon my eyes are sharper than yours. Won't it make a tale on the Banks, though, us meeting with Caleb Thorne and bringing home our catch of fish, anyhow?"

The beach stretched before them. They saw people running toward them down the sand. Their mother was there, waving a red tablecloth, and around their feet were the fish floating about in a cockpit half-filled with water. All the rest seemed a sudden nightmare, come and gone like a clap of thunder. Even Joanna began to doubt her own senses.

"I did see Spot pulled aboard, Jim, didn't I?" asked Joanna beseechingly. All that had been so clear to her five minutes before now seemed hazy and uncertain.

"Reckon you did, Joanna," said Jim, reassuring her. "It did just tear me to do that, but if I hadn't, we'd *all* have been drowned together. As it was, the center of the squall never struck us. We just got the edge of it.''

''And that was squall enough,'' said Jo. ''Everything was white. I wonder, did we really see another boat?''

''As sure as we're alive this minute,'' said Jim stoutly. ''And somehow I reckon we'll know for sure about Spot.''

And Jim proved to be right. They never found Spot's body, but it was Jim who came across his old collar washed up on the shore. Caleb Thorne had let them know for sure that Spot was safe with him.

GRAYLING: OR, "MURDER WILL OUT."

William Gilmore Simms

Chapter 1

My grandmother was an old lady who had been a resident cf the seat of most frequent war in Carolina during the Revolution. She had fortunately survived the numberless atrocities which she was compelled to witness; and, a keen observer, with a strong memory, she had in store a thousand legends of that stirring period, which served to beguile me from sleep many a long winter night. The story which I propose to tell was one of these, which I heard more than once in my boyhood. She not only devoutly believed it herself, but it was believed by sundry of her contemporaries, who were privy to the circumstances as could be known to third parties, and whose gravity I found difficult to doubt.

The revolutionary war had but a little while been concluded. The British had left the country; but peace did not imply repose. The community was overrun by idlers, adventurers, profligates, and criminals. Disbanded soldiers, half-starved and reckless, occupied the highways—outlaws skulked about the settlements with an equal sentiment of hate and fear in their hearts; patriots were clamoring for justice upon the tories, and sometimes anticipating its course by judgments of their own; while the tories against whom the proofs were too strong for denial or evasion, buckled on their armor for a renewal of the struggle.

Life and property lacked many of their necessary securities. Men generally travelled with weapons which were displayed on the smallest provocation: and few who could provide themselves with an escort ventured to travel any distance without one.

There was, about this time, a family of the name of Grayling, that lived somewhere upon the skirts of "Ninety-six" district. Old Grayling, the head of the family, was dead. He was killed in Buford's massacre. His wife was a fine woman, not so very old, who had an only son named James, and a little girl, only five years of age, named Lucy. James was but fourteen when his father was killed, and that event made a man of him. He went out with his rifle in company with Joel Sparkman, who was his mother's brother, and joined himself to Pickens' Brigade. Here he made as good a soldier as the best. He had no sort of fear. He was always the first to go forward; and his rifle was always good for the enemy's button at a long hundred yards. He was in several fights both with the British and tories; and just before the war was ended he had a famous brush with the Cherokees, when Pickens took their country from them. But though he had no fear, and never knew when to stop killing while the fight was going on, he was the most bashful of boys that I ever knew; and so kind-hearted that it was almost impossible to believe all we heard of his fierce doings when he was in battle. But they were nevertheless quite true for all his bashfulness.

Well, when the war was over, Joel Sparkman, who lived with his sister, Grayling, persuaded her that it would be better to move down into the low country. I don't know what reason he had for it, or what they proposed to do there. They had very little property, but Sparkman was a knowing man, who could turn his hand to a hundred things; and as he was a bachelor, and loved his sister and her children just as if they had been his own, it was natural that she should go with him wherever he wished. James, who was restless by nature—and the taste he had enjoyed of the wars had made him more so—decided to go too.

And so, one sunny morning in April, their wagon started for the city. It was driven by a Negro fellow named Clytus, and carried Mrs. Grayling and Lucy. James and his uncle loved the saddle too well to shut themselves up in such a vehicle; and both were mounted on fine horses which they had won from the enemy.

The roads were excessively bad, for the rains of March had been frequent and heavy, the track was very cut up, and the red clay gullies of the hills of "Ninety-six" were washed so much that it required shoulders, twenty times a day, to get the wagon-wheels out of the bog. This made them travel very slowly—perhaps, not more than fifteen miles a day.

Also, there was the necessity for great caution. James and his uncle took turns to ride ahead, keeping a constant lookout for enemies both up and down the road, precisely as they did when scouting in war.

They had gone on this way for two days, and saw nothing to trouble and alarm them. There were few persons on the high-road, and these seemed as shy of them as they were in return.

But on the evening of the second day, while they were splitting light wood, and getting out the kettles and the frying pan, a person rode up and joined them without much ceremony. He was a short thickset man, somewhere between forty and fifty, wearing very coarse and common garments, though he rode a fine black horse of remarkable strength and vigor. He was very civil of speech, though he had little to say, and that little showed him to be a person without much education or refinement. He begged permission to stay, and his manner was very respectful and even humble; but there

was something dark and sullen in his face—his eyes, which
were of a light gray color, were very restless, and his nose
turned up sharply, and was very red. His forehead was
excessively broad, and his eyebrows thick and shaggy—white
hairs being freely mingled with the dark, both in them and
upon his head. Mrs. Grayling did not like this man's looks,
and whispered her dislike to her son; but James, who felt
himself equal to any man, said, promptly—

"What of that, mother! We can't turn the stranger off and
say 'no;' and if he means any mischief, there's two of us,
you know."

The man had no weapons—none, at least, which were
visible; and deported himself so humbly that the prejudice
which the party had formed against him dissipated slowly.
He was very quiet, did not mention an unnecessary word,
and seldom permitted his eyes to rest upon those of any of
the party, the females not excepted.

In a little while the temporary encampment was put in a
state equally social and warlike. The wagon was wheeled a
little way into the woods, and off the road; the horses fastened behind it in such a manner that any attempt to steal
them would be difficult of success, even were the watch
neglectful. Extra guns, concealed in the straw at the bottom
of the wagon, were kept well loaded. In the foreground,
between the wagon and the highway, a fire was soon blazing
with a wild but cheerful gleam; and the worthy dame, Mrs.
Grayling, assisted by the little girl, Lucy, lost no time in
setting on the frying pan, and cutting into slices the haunch
of bacon, which they had carried with them. James Grayling
patrolled the woods for a mile or two round the encampment,
while his uncle, Joel Sparkman sat foot-to-foot with the
stranger, chatting in what seemed a happy, carefree manner.
But Joel was very far from being a careless person. Like an
old soldier, he simply hung out false colors, and concealed
his real timidity by an extra show of confidence and courage.
He did not relish the stranger from the first, anymore than his

sister, and subjected him to a searching examination, such as was considered, in those days of peril and suspicion, not inconsistent with courtesy.

"You are a Scotchman, stranger," said Joel, suddenly drawing up his feet, and bending forward to the other with an eye like that of a hawk swooping over a covey of partridges. It was a wonder that he had not made the discovery before. The broad dialect of the stranger was not to be subdued; but Joel made slow stages and short progress in his mental journeyings. The answer was given with evident hesitation, but it was affirmative.

"Well, now, it's mighty strange that you should ha' fou't with us and not agin us," responded Joel Sparkman. "There was a precious few of the Scotch, and none that I knows on—saving yourself, perhaps—that didn't go dead agin us, and for the tories, through thick and thin. That 'Cross Creek settlement' was a mighty ugly thorn in the sides of us whigs. It turned out a real bad stock of varmints. I hope—and reckon, stranger—you ain't from that part."

"No," said the other; "oh no! I'm from over the other quarter. I'm from the Duncan settlement above."

"I've hearn tell of that other settlement, but I never know'd as any of the men fou't with us. What gineral did you fight under? What Carolina gineral?"

"I was at Gum Swamp when General Gates was defeated;" was the still hesitating reply of the other.

"Well, I thank God, I warn't there, though I reckon things wouldn't ha' turned out quite so bad, if there had been a lettle sprinking of Sumter's, or Pickens' or Marion's men, among them two-legged critters that run that day. They did tell that some of the regiments went off without ever once emptying their rifles. Now, stranger, I hope you warn't among them fellows."

"I was not," said the other with something more of promptness.

"I don't blame a chap for dodging a bullet if he can, or

being too quick for a bagnet, because, I'm thinking, a live
man is always a better man than a dead one, or he can
become so; but to run without taking a single crack at the
inimy, is downright cowardice. There's no two ways about
it, stranger.''

This opinion, delivered with considerable emphasis, met
with the ready assent of the Scotchman, but Joel Sparkman
was not to be diverted, even by his own eloquence, from the
object of his inquiry.

"But you ain't said," he continued, "who was your Carolina gineral. Gates was from Virginny, and he stayed a mighty
short time when he come. You didn't run far at Camden, I
reckon, and you joined the army ag'in and come in with
Greene? Was that the how?''

To this the stranger assented, though with evident disincli-
nation.

"Then, mou'tbe, we sometimes went into the same scratch
together? I was at Cowpens and Ninety-Six, and seen sarvice
at other odds and eends, where there was more fighting than
fun. I reckon you must have been at 'Ninety-Six'—perhaps
at Cowpens, too, if you went with Morgan?''

The unwillingness of the stranger to respond to these questions appeared to increase. He admitted, however, that he
had been at "Ninety-Six," though, as Sparkman afterwards
remembered, in this case, as in that of the defeat of Gates at
Gun Swamp, he had not said on which side he had fought.
Joel, as he discovered the reluctance of his guest to answer
his questions, and perceived his growing doggedness, forbore
to annoy him, but mentally resolved to keep a sharper lookout than ever upon his motions. His examination concluded
with an inquiry, which in the plain dealing regions of the
south and southwest, is not unfrequently put first.

"And what mout be your name, stranger?''

"Macnab," was the ready response, "Sandy Macnab.''

"Well, Mr. Macnab I see that my sister's got supper ready
for us; so we mou't as well fall to upon the hoecake and
bacon.''

Sparkman rose while speaking, and led the way to the spot, near the wagon, where Mrs. Grayling had spread the feast. "We're pretty nigh on to the main road, here, but I reckon there's no great danger now. Besides, Jim Grayling keeps watch for us, and he's got two as good eyes in his head as any scout in the country, and a rifle that, after you once know how it shoots, 'twould do your heart good to hear its crack, if so be that twa'n't your heart that he drawed sight on. He's a perdigious fine shot, and as ready to shoot and fight as if he had a nateral calling that way."

"Shall we wait for him before we eat?" demanded Macnab, anxiously.

"By no sort o' reason, stranger," answered Sparkman. "He'll watch for us while we're eating, and after that I'll change shoes with him. So fall to, and don't mind what's a coming."

Sparkman had just broken the hoecake, when a distant whistle was heard.

"Ha! That's the lad now!" he exclaimed, rising to his feet. "He's on trail. He's got a sight of an eminy's fire, I reckon. 'Twon't be onreasonable, friend Macnab, to get our we'pons in readiness;" and, so speaking, Sparkman bid his sister get into the wagon, where the little Lucy had already placed herself, while he threw open the pan of his rifle, and turned the priming over with his finger. Macnab, meanwhile, had taken from his holsters, which he had before been sitting upon, a pair of horseman's pistols, richly mounted with figures in silver. These were large and long, and had evidently seen service. Unlike his companion, his proceedings occasioned no comment. What he did seemed a matter of habit, of which he himself was scarcely conscious. Having looked at his priming, he laid the instruments beside him without a word, and resumed the bit of hoecake which he had just before received from Sparkman. Meanwhile, the signal whistle, supposed to come from James Grayling, was repeated. Silence ensued then for a brief space, which Sparkman employed in perambulating the grounds immediately contiguous. At length, just as he had returned to the fire, the sound of a horse's feet was heard, and a sharp quick hallow from Grayling informed his uncle that all was right. The youth made his appearance a moment after, accompanied by a stranger on horseback; a tall, fine-looking young man, with a keen flashing eye, and a voice whose lively clear tones, as he was heard approaching, sounded cheerily like those of a trumpet after victory. James Grayling kept along on foot beside the newcomer; and his hearty laugh and free, glib, garrulous tones, betrayed to his uncle, long ere he drew nigh enough to declare the fact, that he had met unexpectedly with a friend, or, at least, an old acquaintance.

"Why, who have you got there, James?" was the demand of Sparkman, as he dropped the butt of his rifle upon the ground.

"Why, who do you think uncle? Who but Major Spencer—our own major?"

"You don't say so!—what!—well! Li'nel Spencer, for sartin! Lord bless you, major, who'd ha' thought to see you in these parts; and jest mounted too, for all natur, as if the war was to be fou't over ag'in. Well, I'm real glad to see you. I am, that's sartin!"

"And I'm very glad to see you, Sparkman," said the other, as he alighted from his steed, and yielded his hand to the cordial grasp of the other.

"Well, I knows that, major, without you sayin it. But you've jest come in the right time. The bacon's frying, and here's the bread;—let's down upon our haunches, in right good airnest, camp fashion, and make the most of what God gives us in the way of blessings. I reckon you don't mean to ride any further tonight, major?"

"No," said the person addressed, "not if you'll let me lay my heels at your fire. But who's in your wagon? My old friend, Mrs. Grayling, I suppose?"

"That's a true word, major," said the lady herself, making

her way out of the vehicle with good-humored agility, and
coming forward with extended hand.

"Really, Mrs. Grayling, I'm glad to see you." And the
stranger, with the blandness of a gentleman and the hearty
warmth of an old neighbor, expressed his satisfaction at once
more finding himself in the company of an old acquaintance.
Their greetings once over, Major Spencer readily joined the
group about the fire, while James Grayling—though with
some reluctance—disappeared to resume his toils of the
scout while the supper proceeded.

"And who have you here?" demanded Spencer, as his eye
rested on the dark, hard features of the Scotchman. Sparkman
told him all that he himself had learned of the name and
character of the stranger, in a brief whisper, and in a moment
after formally introduced the parties in this fashion—

"Mr. Macnab, Major Spencer. Mr. Macnab says he's true
blue, major, and fou't at Camden, when general Gates run so
hard to 'bring the d—d militia back.' He also fou't at Ninety-
Six, and Cowpens—so I reckon we had as good as count him
one of us."

Major Spencer scrutinized the Scotchman keenly—a scrutiny which the latter seemed very ill to relish. He put a few
questions to him on the subject of the war, and some of the
actions in which he allowed himself to have been concerned;
but his evident reluctance to unfold himself had the natural
effect of discouraging the young officer, whose sense of
delicacy had not been materially impaired amid the rude
jostlings of military life. But, though he forbore to propose
any other questions to Macnab, his eyes continued to survey
the features of his sullen countenance with curiosity and a
strangely increasing interest. This he subsequently explained
to Sparkman, when, at the close of supper, James Grayling
came in, and the former assumed the duties of the scout.

"I have seen that Scotchman's face somewhere, Sparkman,
and I'm convinced at some interesting moment; but where,
when, or how, I cannot call to mind. The sight of it is even

associated in my mind with something painful and unpleasant; where could I have seen him?''

"I don't somehow like his looks myself,'' said Sparkman,
"and I mislists he's been rether more of a tory than a whig;
but that's nothing to the purpose now; and he's at our fire,
and we've broken hoecake together: so we cannot rake up the
old ashes to make a dust with.''

"No, surely not,'' was the reply of Spencer. "Even though
we knew him to be a tory, that cause of former quarrel
should occasion none now. But it should produce watchfulness
and caution. I'm glad to see that you have not forgot your old
business of scouting in the swamp.''

"Kin I forget it, major?'' demanded Sparkman, in tones
which, though whispered, were full of emphasis, as he laid
his ear to the earth to listen.

"James has finished supper, major—that's his whistle to
tell me so; and I'll just step back to make it cl'ar to him how
we're to keep up the watch tonight.''

"Count me in your arrangements, Sparkman, as I am one
of you for the night,'' said the major.

"By no sort of means,'' was the reply. "The night must
be shared between James and myself. Ef so be you wants to
keep company with one or t'other of us, why, that's another
thing, and of course, you can do as you please.''

"We'll have no quarrel on the subject, Joel,'' said the
officer, good naturedly, as they returned to the camp together.

Chapter II

The arrangements of the party were soon made. Spencer
renewed his offer at the fire to take his part in the
watch; and the Scotchman, Macnab, volunteered his
service also; but the offer of the latter was another reason
why that of the former should be declined. Sparkman was

resolute to have everything his own way; and while James Grayling went out upon his lonely rounds, he busied himself in cutting bushes and making a sort of tent for the use of his late commander. Mrs. Grayling and Lucy slept in the wagon. The Scotchman stretched himself with little effort before the fire; while Joel Sparkman, wrapping himself up in his cloak, crouched under the wagon body, with his back resting partly against one of the wheels. From time to time he rose and thrust additional brands into the fire, looked up at the night, and round upon the little encampment, then sunk back to his perch and stole a few moments, at intervals, of uneasy sleep.

The first two hours of the watch were over, and James Grayling was relieved. The youth, however, felt in no mood for sleep, and taking his seat by the fire, he drew from his pocket a little volume of Easy Reading Lessons, and by the fitful flame of the resinous light-wood, he prepared, in this ruse manner, to make up for the precious time lost during the seven years of war. He was surprised at this employment by his late commander, who, himself sleepless, now emerged from the bushes and joined Grayling at the fire.

The youth had been rather a favorite with Spencer. They had both been reared in the same neighborhood, and the first military achievements of James had taken place under the eye and with the approbation of his officer. The difference of their ages was just such as to permit of the warm attachment of the lad without diminishing any of the reverence which should be felt by the inferior. Grayling was not more than seventeen, and Spencer was perhaps thirty-four—the very prime of manhood.

They sat by the fire and talked with the hearty glee and good-nature of the young. Their mutual inquiries led to the revelation of their several objects in pursuing the present journey. Those of James Grayling were the plans and purposes of his uncle, and it does not concern this narrative that we should know more of their nature than has already been revealed. But, whatever they were, they were as freely un-

folded to his hearer as if the parties had been brothers, and
Spencer was quite as frank in his revelations as his companion. He, too, was on his way to Charleston, from whence he
was to take passage for England.

"I am rather in a hurry to reach town," he said, "as I
learned that the Falmouth packet is preparing to sail for
England in a few days, and I must go in her."

"For England, major!" exclaimed the youth with unaf-
fected astonishment.

"Yes, James, for England. But why—what astonishes you?"

"Why, lord!" exclaimed the simple youth, "if they only
knew there what a cutting and slashing you did use to make
among their red coats, I reckon they'd hand you to the first
hickory."

"Oh, no! Scarcely," said the other, with a smile.

"But I reckon you'll change your name, major?" continued the youth.

"No," responded Spencer, "if I did that, I should lose the
object of my voyage. You must know, James, that an old
relative has left me a good deal of money in England, and I
can only get it by proving that I am Lionel Spencer; so you
see I must carry my own name, whatever may be the risk."

"Well, major, you know best; but I do think if they could
only have a guess of what you did among their sodgers at
Hobkirk's and Cowpens, and Eutaw, and a dozen other
places, they'd find some means of hanging you up, peace or
no peace. But I don't see what occasion you have to be going
cl'ar away to England for money, when you've got a sight of
you own already."

"Not so much as you think," replied the major, giving an
involuntary and uneasy glance at the Scotchman who was
seemingly sound asleep on the opposite side of the fire.
"There is you know, but little money in the country at any
time, and I must get what I want for my expenses when I
reach Charleston. I have just enough to carry me there."

"Well, now, major, that's mighty strange. I always thought

that you was about the best-off of any man in our parts; but if you're strained so close, I'm thinking, major—if so be you wouldn't think me too presumptuous—you'd better let me lend you a guinea or so that I've got to spare, and you can pay me back when you get the English money."

And the youth fumbled in his bosom for a little cotton wallet, which, with its limited contents, was displayed in another instant to the eyes of the officer.

"No, no, James," said the other, putting back the generous tribute; "I have quite enough to carry me to Charleston, and when there I can easily get a supply from the merchants. But I thank you, my good fellow, for your offer. You *are* a good fellow, James, and I will remember you."

It was needless to pursue the conversation farther. The night passed away without any alarms, and at dawn of the next day the whole party was engaged in making preparation for a start. Mrs. Grayling was soon busy in getting breakfast in readiness. Major Spencer consented to remain with them until it was over; but the Scotchman, after returning thanks very civilly for his accommodation of the night, at once resumed his journey. His course seemed, like their own, to lie below; but he neither declared his route nor betrayed the least desire to know that of Spencer. The latter had no disposition to renew those inquiries from which the stranger seemed to shrink the night before, and he accordingly suffered him to depart with a quiet farewell, and the utterance of a good-natured wish, in which all the parties joined, that he might have a pleasant journey. When he was fairly out of sight, Spencer said to Sparkman,

"Had I liked that fellow's looks, nay, had I not positively disliked them, I should have gone with him. As it is, I will remain and share your breakfast."

The repast being over, all parties set forward; but Spencer, after keeping along with them for a mile, took his leave also. The slow wagon-pace did not suit the high-spirited cavalier; and it was necessary, as he assured them, that he should

reach the city in two nights more. They parted with many
regrets, as truly felt as they were warmly expressed; and
James Grayling never felt the tedium of wagon travelling to
be so severe as throughout the whole of that day when he
separated from his favorite captain. But he was too stout-
hearted to make any complaint; and his dissatisfaction only
showed itself in his unwonted silence, and an over-anxiety,
which his steed seemed to feel in common with himself, to
go rapidly ahead. Thus the day passed, and the wayfarers at
its close had made a progress of some twenty miles from sun
to sun. The same precautions marked their encampment this
night as the last, and they rose in better spirits with the next
morning the dawn of which was very bright and pleasant, and
encouraging. A similar journey of twenty miles brought them
to the place of bivouac as the sun went down; and they
prepared as usual for their securities and supper. They found
themselves on the edge of a very dense forest of pines and
scrubby oaks, a portion of which was swallowed up in a deep
bay—so called in the dialect of the country—a swamp-bottom,
the growth of which consisted of mingled cypresses and
bay-trees, with tupola, gum, and dense thickets of low stunted
shrubbery, cane grass, and dwarf willows, which filled up
every interval between the trees, and to the eye most effectually barred out every human intruder. This bay was chosen as
the background for the camping party. Their wagon was
wheeled into an area on a gently rising ground in front, under
a pleasant shade of oaks and hickories, with a lonely pine
rising loftily in occasional spots among them. Here the horses
were taken out, and James Grayling prepared to kindle up a
fire; but, looking for his axe, it was unaccountably missing,
and after a fruitless search of half an hour, the party came to
the conclusion that it had been left on the spot where they
had slept last night. This was a disaster, and, while they
meditated in what manner to repair it, a Negro boy appeared
in sight, passing along the road at their feet, and driving
before him a small herd of cattle. From him they learned that

they were only a mile or two from a farmstead where an axe might be borrowed; and James, leaping on his horse, rode forward in the hope of obtaining one. He found no difficulty in his quest; and, having obtained it from the farmer, who was also a tavern-keeper, he casually asked if Major Spencer had not stayed with him the night before. He was somewhat surprised when told that he had not.

"There was one man stayed with me last night," said the farmer, "but he didn't call himself a major, and didn't much look like one."

"He rode a fine sorrel horse—tall, bright color, with white fore foot, didn't he?" asked James.

"No, that he didn't! He rode a powerful black, coal black, and not a bit of white about him."

"That was the Scotchman! But I wonder the major didn't stop with you. He must have rode on. Isn't there another house near you, below?"

"Not one. There's ne'er a house either above or below for a matter of fifteen miles. I'm the only man in all that distance that's living on this road; and I don't think your friend could have gone below, as I should have seen him pass. I've been all day out there in that field before your eyes, clearing up the brush."

Chapter III

Somewhat wondering that the major should have turned aside from the track, though without attaching any importance to it, James Grayling took up the borrowed axe and hurried back to the encampment, where the toil of cutting an extra supply of lightwood to meet the exigencies of the ensuing night, sufficiently exercised his mind as well as his body, to prevent him from meditating upon the seeming strangeness of the circumstance. But when he sat down to supper over the fire he had kindled, his fancies crowded

thickly upon him, and he felt a confused doubt and suspicion
that something was to happen, he knew not what. His conjec-
tures and apprehensions were without form, though not altogether void; and he felt a strange sickness and sinking of
the heart which was very unusual with him. He had, in short,
that lowness of spirits, that cloudy apprehensiveness of soul
which takes the form of presentiment, and makes us look out
for danger even when the skies are without a cloud, and the
breeze is laden with balm and music. His moodiness found
no sympathy among his companions. Joel Sparkman was in
the best of humors, and his mother was so cheery and happy,
that when the thoughtful boy went off into the woods to
watch, he could hear her at every moment breaking out into
little catches of a country ditty, which the gloomy events of
the late war had not yet obliterated from her memory.

"It's very strange!" soliloquized the youth, as he wandered along the edges of the dense bay or swamp-bottom,
which we have passingly referred to. "It's very strange what
troubles me so! I feel almost frightened, and yet I know I'm
not to be frightened easily, and I don't see anything in the
woods to frighten me. It's strange the major didn't come
along this road! Maybe he took another higher up that leads
by a different settlement. I wish I had asked the man at the
house if there's another road. I reckon there must be, however, for where could the major have gone?"

The unphilosophical mind of James Grayling did not, in
his farther meditations, carry him much beyond this starting
point; and with its continual recurrence in soliloquy, he
traversed the margin of the bay, until he came to its termina-
tion at the high-road. He wandered on and on, as he himself
described it, without any power to restrain himself. Instead of
maintaining his watch for two hours only, he was gone more
than four; and, at length, a sense of weariness which over-
powered him all of a sudden, caused him to seat himself at
the foot of a tree, and snatch a few moments rest. He was
conscious of fatigue and exhaustion, but not drowsiness—and

that this fatigue was so numbing as to effectually keep him
from any sleep. While he sat thus beneath the tree, with a
body weak and nerveless, but a mind excited, he heard his
name called by the well-known voice of his friend, Major
Spencer. The voice called him three times—"James Grayling! James! James Grayling!"—before he could muster
strength enough to answer. It was not courage he wanted—of
that he was positive, for he felt sure, as he said, that something had gone wrong, and he was never more ready to fight
in his life than at that moment, could he have commanded the
physical capacity; but his throat seemed dry to suffocation—
his lips sealed as if with wax, and when he did answer, the
sounds seemed as fine and soft as the whisper of some newly
born.

"Oh! major, is it you?"

The answer was instantaneous, though the voice came
from some little distance in the bay, and his own voice he did
not hear. He only knew what he meant to say. The answer
was to this effect.

"It is I, James!—It is your own friend, Lionel Spencer,
that speaks to you; do not be alarmed when you see me. I
have been shockingly murdered!"

James tried to tell him he would not be frightened, but his
own voice was still a whisper, which he himself could scarcely
hear. A moment later, he heard something like a sudden
breeze rustling through the bay bushes at his feet, and his
eyes were closed without his effort, and indeed in spite of
himself. When he opened them, he saw Major Spencer standing at the edge of the bay, about twenty steps from him.
Though he stood in the shade of a thicket, and there was no
light in the heavens save that of the stars, he was yet able to
distinguish perfectly, and with great ease, every lineament of
his friend's face.

He looked very pale, and his garments were covered with
blood; and James said that he strove to rise from the place
where he sat and approach him. "For, in truth," said the lad,

"instead of fear, I felt nothing but fury in my heart; but I could not move a limb. I felt as if I should have died with vexation that I could not rise; but a power I could not resist, made me motionless, and almost speechless. I could only say, 'Murdered!' "

"Yes, murdered!—murdered by the Scotchman who slept with us at your fire the night before last. James, I look to you to have the murderer brought to justice! James!—do you hear me, James?"

"These," said James, "I think were the very words, or near about the very words, that I heard: and I tried to ask the major to tell me how it was, and how I could do what he required; but I didn't hear myself speak, though it would appear that he did, for almost immediately after I had tried to speak what I wished to say, he answered me just as if I had said it. He told me that the Scotchman had waylaid, killed, and hidden him in that very bay; that his murderer had gone to Charleston; and that if I made haste to town, I would find him on the Falmouth packet, which was then lying in the harbor and ready to sail for England. He farther said everything depended on my making haste—that I must reach town by tomorrow night if I wanted to board the vessel and charge the criminal with the deed. 'Do not be afraid,' said he, when he had finished; 'be afraid of nothing, James, for God will help and strengthen you to the end.' When I heard all, I felt strong. I felt I could talk, or fight, or do almost anything; and I jumped up to my feet, and was just about to run down to where the major stood, but, with the first step which I made forward, he was gone. I stopped and looked all around me, but I could see nothing; and the bay was just as black as midnight. But I went down to it, and tried to press in where I thought the major had been standing; but I couldn't get far, the brush and bay bushes were so close and thick. I was not bold and strong enough, and I called out, loud enough to be heard half a mile. I didn't exactly know what I called for, or what I wanted to learn, or I have forgotten. But I heard nothing more.

"Then I remembered the camp, and began to fear that something might have happened to mother and uncle, for I now felt, what I had not thought of before, that I had gone too far round the bay to be of much assistance, or, indeed, to be in time for any, had they been suddenly attacked. Besides, I could not think how long I had been gone; but it now seemed very late. The stars were shining their brightest, and the thin white clouds of morning were beginning to rise and run towards the west. Well, I bethought me of my course—for I was a little bewildered and doubtful where I was; but, after a little thinking, I took the back track, and soon got a glimpse of the campfire, which was nearly burnt down; and by this I reckoned I was gone considerably longer than my two hours.

"When I got back into the camp, I looked under the wagon, and found uncle in a sweet sleep, and though my heart was full almost to bursting with what I had heard, and the cruel sight I had seen, yet I wouldn't waken him; and I beat about and mended the fire, and watched, and waited, until near daylight, when mother called to me out of the wagon, and asked who it was. This wakened my uncle, and then I up and told all that had happened, for if it had been to save my life, I couldn't have kept it in much longer. But though mother said it was very strange, Uncle Sparkman considered that I had been only dreaming; but he couldn't persuade me of it; and when I told him I intended to be off at daylight, just as the major had told me to do, and ride my best all the way to Charleston, he laughed, and said I was a fool. But I felt that I was no fool, and I was solemn certain that I hadn't been dreaming; and though both mother and he tried their hardest to make me put off going, yet I made up my mind to it, and they had to give up. For, wouldn't I have been a pretty sort of a friend to the major, if, after what he told me, I should have stayed behind, and gone on only at a wagon-pace to chase the

murderer! I don't think if I had done so that I should ever
have been able to look a man in the face again.

"Mother was mighty sad, and begged me not to go, but
Uncle Sparkman was mighty sulky, and kept calling me fool
upon fool, until I was almost angry enough to forget we were
blood kin. But all his talking did not stop me, and I reckon I
was five miles on my way before he had his team in traces
for a start. I rode as briskly as I could without hurting my
nag. I had a smart ride of more than forty miles before me,
and the road was very heavy. But it was a good two hours
from sunset when I got into town, and the first question I
asked of the people I met was, to show me where the ships
were kept. When I got to the wharf they showed me the
Falmouth packet, where she lay in the stream, ready to sail as
soon as the wind should favor."

Chapter IV

James Grayling, with the same eager impatience he has
described in his own language, had already hired a boat
to go on board the British packet, when he remembered
that he had neglected all those means, legal and otherwise,
by which his purpose might be properly effected. He did not
know much about legal process, but had common sense
enough to know that some such process was necessary. This
conviction produced another difficulty; he knew not in which
quarter to turn for counsel and assistance; but here the boat-
man came to his relief and gave him directions where to find
the merchants with whom his uncle, Sparkman, had done
business in former years. To them he went and told the story
of his ghostly visitation. Even as a dream, which these
gentlemen conjectured it to be, the story of James Grayling
was equally clear and curious; and his intense warmth and the
entire absorption, which the subject had effected, of his mind
and soul, was such that they judged it not improper, at least

to carry out the search of the vessel which he contemplated. It would certainly, they thought, be a curious coincidence—believing James to be a veracious youth—if the Scotchman should be found on board. But another test of his narrative was proposed by one of the firm. It so happened that the business agents of Major Spencer, who was well known in Charleston, kept their office but a few rods distant from their own; and to them all parties at once proceeded. But here the story of James was encountered by a circumstance that made somewhat against it. These gentlemen produced a letter from Major Spencer, intimating the utter impossibility of his coming to town for the space of a month, and expressing his regret that he should be unable to make the foreign vessel, of whose arrival in Charleston, and proposed time of departure, they had advised him. They read the letter aloud and with difficulty suppressed their smiles at the gravity with which James related and insisted upon the particulars of his vision.

"He has changed his mind," returned the impetuous youth: "He was on his way down, I tell you—a hundred miles on his way—when he camped with us. I know him well, I tell you, and talked with him myself half the night."

"At least," remarked the gentlemen who had gone with James, "it can do no harm to look into the business. We can procure a warrant for searching the vessel after this man, Macnab; and should he be found on board the packet, it will justify having the magistrates detain him until we can ascertain where Major Spencer really is."

This measure was accordingly adopted, and it was nearly sunset before the warrant was procured, and the proper officer in readiness. The impatience of spirit so eager and so devoted as James Grayling, under these delays, may be imagined; and when in the boat, and on his way to the packet where the criminal was to be sought, his blood became so excited that it was difficult for him to keep his seat. His quick, eager action continually disturbed the trim of the boat, and one of his mercantile friends, who had accompanied him, with that interest in the affair which curiosity alone inspired, was under constant apprehension Grayling would plunge overboard in his impatient desire to shorten the space which lay between. The same impatience enabled the youth, though never on shipboard before, to grasp the rope which had been flung at their approach, and to mount her sides with catlike agility.

Without waiting to declare himself or his purpose, he ran from one side of the deck to the other, greedily staring, to the surprise of officers, passengers, and seamen, in the faces of all of them, and surveying them with an almost offensive scrutiny. He turned away from the search with disappointment. There was no face like that of the suspected man among them. By this time, his friend, the merchant, with the sheriff's officer, had entered the vessel, and were in conference with the captain. Grayling drew nigh in time to hear the latter affirm that there was no man of the name of Macnab, as stated in the warrant among his passengers or crew.

"He is—he must be!" exclaimed the impetuous youth. "The major never lied in his life, and couldn't lie after he was dead. Macnab is here—he is a Scotchman—"

The captain interrupted him—

"We have, young gentleman, several Scotchmen on board, and one of them is named Macleod—"

"Let me see him—which is he?" demanded the youth.

By this time, the passengers and a goodly portion of the crew were collected about the little party. The captain turned his eyes upon the group, and asked,

"Where is Mr. Macleod?"

"He is gone below—he's sick!" replied one of the passengers.

"That's he! That must be the man!" exclaimed the youth. "I'll lay my life that's no other than Macnab. He's only taken a false name."

It was now remembered by one of the passengers, and remarked, that Macleod had expressed himself as unwell, but a few moments before, and had gone below even while the boat was rapidly approaching the vessel. At this statement, the captain led the way into the cabin, closely followed by James Grayling and the rest.

"Mr. Macleod," he said with a voice somewhat elevated, as he approached the berth of that person, "you are wanted on deck for a few moments."

"I am really too unwell, captain," replied a feeble voice from behind the curtain of the berth.

"It will be necessary," was the reply of the captain. "There is a warrant from the authorities of the town, to look after a fugitive from justice."

Macleod had already begun a second speech declaring his feebleness, when the fearless youth, Grayling, bounded before the captain and tore away, with a single grasp of his hand, the curtain which concealed the suspected man from their sight.

"It is he!" was the instant exclamation of the youth, as he beheld him. "It is he—Macnab, the Scotchman—the man that murdered Major Spencer!"

Macnab—for it was he—was deadly pale. He trembled like an aspen. His eyes were dilated with more than mortal apprehension, and his lips were perfectly livid. Still, he found strength to speak, and to deny the accusation. He knew nothing of the youth before him—nothing of Major Spencer— his name was Macleod, and he had never called himself by any other. He denied, but with great incoherence, everything which was urged against him.

"You must get up, Mr. Macleod," said the captain; "the circumstances are very much against you. You must go with the officer!"

"Will you give me up to my enemies?" demanded the culprit. "You are a countryman—a Briton. I have fought for the king, our master, against these rebels, and for this they seek my life. Do not deliver me into their bloody hands!"

"Liar!" exclaimed James Grayling. "Didn't you tell us at

our own campfire that you were with us? That you were at
Gates' defeat, and Ninety-Six?''

"But I didn't tell you,'' said the Scotchman, with a grin,
"which side I was on!''

"Ha! Remember that!'' said the sheriff's officer. "He
denied just a moment ago, that he knew this young man at
all; now, he confesses that he did see and camp with him.''

The Scotchman was aghast at the strong point which, in
his inadvertence, he had made against himself; and his stam-
mering and contradictory efforts to excuse himself served
only to involve him ever more deeply in his difficulty. Still
he continued his urgent appeals to the captain of the vessel,
and his fellow-passengers, as citizens of the same country,
subjects to the same monarch, to protect him from those who
equally hated and would destroy them all. In order to move
their national prejudices in his behalf, he boasted of the
immense injury he had done, as a tory, to the rebel cause and
insisted that the murder was only a pretext, by which to gain
possession of his person, and wreak upon him the revenge his
own fierce performances during the war had provoked. Two
of the passengers joined with him in entreating the captain to
set the accusers adrift and make sail at once; but the stout
Englishman who was in command, rejected the unworthy
counsel. He was better aware of the dangers which would
follow such rash action. Fort Moultrie, on Sullivan's Island,
had been already refitted and prepared for an enemy; and he
was lying, at that moment, under the formidable range of
grinning teeth, which would have opened upon him, at the
first movement, from the jaws of Castle Pinckney.

"No, gentlemen,'' said he, "you mistake your man. God
forbid that I should give shelter to a murderer, though he
were from my own parish.''

"But I am no murderer,'' said the Scotchman.

"You look cursedly like one, however,'' was the reply of
the captain. "Sheriff, take your prisoner.''

The base creature threw himself at the feet of the English

officer and clung, with piteous entreaties, to his knees. The
latter shook him off, and turned away in disgust.

"Steward," he cried, "bring up this man's luggage."

He was obeyed. The luggage was brought up from the
cabin and delivered to the sheriff's officer, by whom it was
examined in the presence of all, and an inventory made of its
contents. It consisted of a small new trunk, which it afterwards appeared, he had bought in Charleston, soon after his
arrival. This contained a few changes of raiment, twenty-six
guineas in money, a gold watch, not in repair, and the two
pistols which he had shown while at Joel Sparkman's campfire; but, with this difference, that the stock of one was
broken off short just above the grasp, and the butt was
entirely gone. It was not found among his chattels. A careful
examination of the articles in his trunk did not result in
anything calculated to strengthen the charge of his criminal-
ity; but there was not a single person present who did not feel
as morally certain of his guilt as if the jury had already
declared the fact. That night he slept—if he slept at all—in
the common jail of the city.

Chapter V

Macnab or Macleod—and it is possible that both names
were fictitious—as soon as he recovered from his
first terrors sought the aid of an attorney—one
of those acute, small, chopping lawyers, to be found in
almost every community, who are willing to serve with equal
zeal the sinner and the saint, provided that they can pay with
equal liberality. The prisoner was brought before the court
under *habeas corpus,* and several grounds submitted by his
counsel with the view to obtaining his discharge. It became
necessary to ascertain, among the first duties of the state,
whether Major Spencer, the alleged victim, was really dead.
Until it could be established that a man should be impris-

oned, tried, and punished for a crime, it was first necessary
to show that a crime had been committed, and the attorney
made himself exceedingly merry with the ghost story of
young Grayling. In those days, however, the ancient Superstition was not so feeble as she has subsequently become.
The venerable judge was one of those good men who had a
decent respect for the faith and opinions of his ancestors: and
though he certainly would not have consented to the hanging
of Macleod under the sort of testimony which had been
adduced, he yet saw enough, in all the circumstances, to
justify his present detention. In the meantime, efforts were
made, to ascertain the whereabouts of Major Spencer; though,
were he even missing—so the counsel for Macleod contended—
his death could be by no means assumed in consequence. To
this the judge—who it must be understood was a real existence, and who had no small reputation in his day in the
south—shook his head doubtfully. '' 'Fore God!'' said he,
''I would not have you to be too sure of that. A man may
properly be hung for murdering another, though the murdered
man be not dead; aye, before God, even though he be
actually unhurt and uninjured, while the murderer is swinging
by the neck for the bloody deed!'' He then proceeded to
establish the correctness of his opinions by authorities and
argument, with all of which, doubtlessly, the bar were exceedingly delighted.

James Grayling, however, was not satisfied to wait the
slow processes which were suggested for coming at the truth.
Even the wisdom of the judge was lost upon him, possibly,
for the simple reason that he did not comprehend it. But the
ridicule of the culprit's lawyer stung him to the quick, and he
muttered to himself, more than once, a determination ''to
lick the life out of that impudent chap's leather.'' But this
was not his only resolve. There was one which he proceeded
to put into instant execution, and that was to seek the body of
his murdered friend in the spot where he fancied it might be
found—namely, the dark and dismal bay where the spectre
had made its appearance to his eyes.

The suggestion was approved—though he needed no sanctions—by his mother and uncle Sparkman. The latter determined to be his companion, and he was farther accompanied by the sheriff's officer who had arrested the suspected felon. Before daylight, on the morning after the examination before the judge had taken place, and when Macleod had been remanded to prison, James Grayling started on his journey. His fiery zeal received additional force at every added moment of delay, and his eager spurring brought him at an early hour after noon, to the neighborhood of the spot through which his search was to be made. When his companions and himself drew nigh, they were all at a loss in which direction first to proceed. The bay was one of those massed forests, whose wall of thorns, vines, and close tenacious shrubs, seemed to defy invasion. To the eye of the townsman it was so forbidding that he pronounced it absolutely impenetrable. But James was not to be baffled. He led them round it, taking the very course which he had pursued the night when the revelation was made him; he showed them the very tree at whose foot he had sunk when the supernatural torpor—as he himself esteemed it—began to fall upon him; he then pointed out the spot, some twenty steps distant, at which the spectre made his appearance. To this spot they then proceeded in a body, and essayed an entrance, but were so discouraged by the difficulties at the outset that all, James not excepted, concluded that neither the murderer nor his victim could possibly have found entrance there.

But lo! A Marvel! Such it seemed, at the first blush, to all the party. While they stood confounded and indecisive, undetermined in which way to move, a sudden flight of wings was heard, even from the center of the bay, at a little distance above the spot where they had striven for entrance. They looked up, and beheld about fifty buzzards—those notorious domestic vultures of the south—ascending from the interior of the bay, and perching along upon the branches of the loftier trees by which it was overhung. Even were the character of these birds less known, the particular business in which they had just then been engaged, was betrayed by huge gobbets of flesh which some of them had borne aloft in their flight, and still continued to rend with beak and bill, as they tottered upon the branches where they stood. A piercing scream issued from the lips of James Grayling as he beheld this sight, and strove to scare the offensive birds from their repast.

"The poor major! The poor major!" was the involuntary and agonized exclamation of the youth. "Did I ever think he would come to this!"

The search, thus guided and encouraged, was pressed with renewed diligence and spirit; and, at length, an opening was found through which it was evident that a body of considerable size had but recently gone. The branches were broken from the small shrub trees, and the undergrowth trodden into the earth. They followed this path, and, as is the case commonly with waste tracts of this description, the density of the growth diminished sensibly at every step they took, till they reached a little pond, which, though circumscribed in area, and full of cypresses, yet proved to be singularly deep. Indeed, it was an alligator-hole, where, in all probability, a numerous tribe of these reptiles had their dwelling. Here, on the edge of the pond, they discovered the object which had drawn the keen-sighted vultures to their feast, in the body of a horse, which James Grayling at once identified as that of Major Spencer. The carcass of the animal was already very much torn and lacerated. The eyes were plucked out, and the animal completely disembowelled. Yet, on examination, it was not difficult to discover the manner of his death. This had been effected by fire-arms. Two bullets had passed through his skull, just above the eyes, either of which must have been fatal. The murderer had led the horse to the spot, and committed the cruel deed where his body was found.

The search was now continued for that of the owner, but for some time it proved ineffectual. At length, the keen eyes of James Grayling detected, amidst a heap of moss and green sedge that rested beside an overthrown tree, whose branches jutted into the pond, a whitish, but discolored object, that did not seem native to the place. Bestriding the fallen tree, he was enabled to reach this object, which, with a burst of grief, he announced to the distant party was the hand and arm of his unfortunate friend, the wristband of the shirt being the conspicuous object which had first caught his eye. Grasping this, he drew the corpse, which had been thrust beneath the branches of the tree, to the surface; and, with the assistance of his uncle, it was finally brought to the dry land. Here it underwent a careful examination. The head was very much disfigured; the skull was fractured in several places by repeated blows of some hard instrument, inflicted chiefly from behind. A closer inspection revealed a bullet-hole in the abdomen, the first wound, in all probability, which the unfortunate gentleman received, and by which he was perhaps, tumbled from his horse. The blows on the head would seem to have been unnecessary, unless the murderer—whose proceedings appeared to have been singularly deliberate—was resolving upon making "assurance doubly sure." But, as if watchful Providence had meant that nothing should be left doubtful which might tend to the complete conviction of the criminal, the constable stumbled upon the butt of the broken pistol which had been found in Macleod's trunk. This he picked up on the edge of the pond in which the corpse had been discovered, and while James Grayling and his uncle Sparkman, were engaged in drawing the body from the water. The place where the fragment was discovered at once denoted the pistol as the instrument by which the final blows were inflicted.

" 'Fore god," said the judge to the criminal, as those proofs were submitted at the trial, "you may be a very innocent man after all, as, by my faith, I do think there have been many innocent men convicted as murderers before you; but you ought, nevertheless, to be hung as an example to all other persons who suffer such strong proofs of guilt to follow their innocent misdoings. Gentlemen of the jury, if this person, Macleod or Macnab, didn't murder Major Spencer, either you or I did; and you must now decide which of us it is! I say, gentlemen of the jury, either you, or I, or the prisoner at the bar, murdered this man; and if you have any doubts which of us it was, it is but justice and mercy that you should give the prisoner the benefit of your doubts; and so find your verdict. But, before God, should you find him not guilty, Mr. Attorney there can scarcely do anything wiser than put us all on trial for the deed.''

The jury, it may be scarcely necessary to add, perhaps under fears of an alternative such as his honor had suggested, brought in a verdict of ''Guilty,'' without leaving the panel; and Macnab, *alias* Macleod, was hanged at White Point, Charleston, somewhere about the year 178-.

Chapter VI

"And here," said my grandmother, devoutly, "you behold a proof of God's watchfulness to see that murder should not be hidden, and that the murdered should not escape. You see that he sent the spirit of the murdered man—since, by no other mode could the truth have been revealed—to declare the crime, and to discover the criminal. But for that ghost, Macnab would have got off to Scotland, and probably have been living to this very day on the money that he took from the person of the poor major.''

As the old lady finished the ghost story, which, by the way, she had been tempted to relate for the fiftieth time in order to combat my father's ridicule of such superstitions, the latter took up the thread of the narrative.

"Now, my son," said he, "as you have heard all that your grandmother has to say on this subject, I will proceed to show you what you have to believe, and what not. It is true that Macnab murdered Spencer in the manner related; that

James Grayling made the discovery and prosecuted the pursuit; found the body and brought the felon to justice; that Macnab suffered death, and confessed the crime; alleging that he was moved to do so because of the money that he suspected Spencer to have in his possession and because of the hate he felt for a man who had been particularly bold and active in cutting up a party of Scotch loyalists to which he belonged, on the borders of North Carolina. But the appearance of the spectre was nothing more than the work of a quick imagination, added to the shrewd and correct judgment. James Grayling saw no ghost, in fact, but such as was in his own mind; and, though the instance was one of a most remarkable character, one of singular combination, and well depending circumstances, still, I think it is to be accounted for by natural and very simple laws.''

The old lady was indignant.

''And how could he see the ghost just on the edge of the same bay where the murder had been committed, and where the body of the murdered man even then was laying?''

My father did not directly answer the demand, but proceeded thus:

''James Grayling, as we know, mother, was a very ardent, impetuous, sagacious man. He had the sanguine, the race-horse temperament. He was generous, always prompt and ready, and one who never went backward. What he did, he did quickly, boldly, and thoroughly! He never shrank from trouble of any kind: nay, he rejoiced in the constant encounter with difficulty and trial; and his was the temper which commands and enthralls mankind. He felt deeply and intensely whatever occupied his mind, and when he parted from his friend he brooded over little else than their past communion and the great distance by which they were to be separated. The dull travelling wagon-gait at which he himself was compelled to go, was a source of annoyance to him; and he became sullen, all the day, after the departure of his friend.

"When, on the evening of the next day, he came to the house where it was natural to expect that Major Spencer would have slept the night before and learned the fact that no one stopped there but the Scotchman, Macnab, we see that he was struck with the circumstance. He mutters it over to himself, "Strange, where the major could have gone!" His mind then naturally reverts to the character of the Scotchman: to the opinions and suspicions which had been already expressed by his uncle, and felt by himself. They had all, previously, come to the full conviction that Macnab was, and had always been, a tory, in spite of his protestations. His mind next, and very naturally, reverted to the insecurity of the highways; the general dangers of travelling at that period; the frequency of crime, and the number of desperate men who were everywhere to be met with. The very employment in which he was then engaged, in scouting the woods for the protection of the camp, was calculated to bring such reflections to his mind. If these precautions were considered necessary for the safety of persons so poor, so wanting in those possessions which might prompt cupidity to crime, how much more necessary were precautions in the case of a wealthy gentlemen like Major Spencer! He then remembered the conversation with the major at the campfire, when they fancied that the Scotchman was sleeping. How natural to think that he was all the while awake and must have heard him speak of the wealth of his companion. True, the major, with more prudence than himself, denied that he had any money about him, more than would bear his expenses to the city; but such an assurance was natural enough to the lips of a traveller who knew the dangers of the country.

"That the man, Macnab, was not a person to be trusted, was the equal impression of Joel Sparkman and his nephew from the first. The probabilities were strong that he would rob and perhaps murder, if he might hope to do so with impunity; and as the youth made the circuit of the bay in the darkness and solemn stillness of the night, its gloomy depths and mournful shadows, naturally gave rise to such reflections as would be equally active in the mind of a youth familiar with the arts and usages of strife. He would see that the spot was just the one in which a practiced partisan would delight in ambushing an unwary foe. There ran the public road, with a little sweep, around two-thirds of the extent of its dense and impenetrable thickets. The ambusher could lie concealed and at ten steps command the bosom of his victim.

Here, then, you perceive that the mind of James Grayling, stimulated by an active and sagacious judgment, had by gradual and reasonable stages come to these conclusions: that Major Spencer was an object to tempt a robber; that this was the very spot in which a deed of blood could be most easily committed, and most easily concealed; and that Major Spencer had not reached a well-known point of destination, while Macnab had.

"With these thoughts, thus closely linked together, the youth forgets the limits of his watch and his circuit. This fact, alone, proves how active his imagination had become. It leads him forward, brooding more and more on the subject, until, in the very exhaustion of his body, he sinks down beneath a tree. Hie sinks down and falls asleep; and in his sleep, what before was plausible conjecture, becomes fact, and the creative properties of his imagination give form and vitality to all his fancies. These forms are bold, broad, and deeply colored, in due proportion with the degree of force which they receive from probability. Here, he sees the image of his friend; but, you will remark—and this should almost conclusively satisfy any mind that all that he sees is the work of his imagination—that, though Spencer tells him that he is murdered, and by Macnab, he does not tell him how, in what manner, or with what weapons. Though he sees him pale and ghostlike, he does not see, nor can he say, where his wounds are! He sees his pale features distinctly, and his garments are bloody. Now, had he seen the spectre in the true appearances of death, as he was subsequently found, he would not have been able to discern his features, which were battered, according to his own account, almost out of all shape of humanity, and covered with mud; while his clothes would have streamed with mud and water, rather than with blood.''

''Ah!'' exclaimed the old lady, my grandmother, ''it's hard to make you believe anything that you don't see; you are like Saint Thomas in the Scriptures; but how do you propose to account for his knowing that the Scotchman was on board the Falmouth packet? Answer to that!''

''That is not a more difficult matter than any of the rest. You forget that in the dialogue which took place between James and Major Spencer at the camp, the latter told him that he was about to take passage for Europe in the Falmouth packet, which then lay in Charleston harbor, and was about to sail. Macnab heard all that.''

''True enough, and likely enough,'' returned the old lady; ''but, though you show that it was Major Spencer's intention to go to Europe in the Falmouth packet, that will not show that it was also the intention of the murderer.''

''Yet how probable and natural for James Grayling to imagine such a thing! In the first place he knew that Macnab was a Briton; he felt convinced that he was a tory; and the inference was immediate, that such a person would scarcely have remained long in a country where such characters labored under so much odium, disfranchisement, and constant danger from popular tumults. The fact that Macnab was compelled to disguise his true sentiments, and affect those of the people against whom he fought so vindictively, shows what was his sense of the danger which he incurred. Now, it is not unlikely that Macnab was quite as well aware that the Falmouth packet was in Charleston, and about to sail, as Major Spencer. No doubt he was pursuing the same journey, with the same object, and had he not murdered Spencer, they would, very likely, have been fellow passengers together to Europe. But, whether he knew the fact before or not, he probably heard it stated by Spencer while he seemed to be sleeping; and, even supposing that he did not then know, it was enough that he found this to be the fact on reaching the city. It was an afterthought to fly to Europe with his illgotten spoils; and whatever may have appeared a politic course to the criminal, would be a probable conjecture in the mind of him by whom he was suspected. The whole story is one of strong probabilities which happened to be verified; and if proving anything, proves only that which we know—that James Grayling was a man of remarkably sagacious judgment, and quick, daring imagination. This quality of imagination, by the way, when possessed very strongly in connection with shrewd common sense and well balanced general faculties, makes that particular kind of intellect which, because of its promptness and powers of creation and combination, we call genius. It is genius only which can make ghosts, and James Grayling was a genius. He never, my son, saw any other ghosts than those of his own making!''

*   *   *   *   *

I heard my father with great patience to the end, though he seemed very tedious. He had taken a great deal of pains to destroy one of my greatest sources of pleasure. I need not add that I continued to believe in the ghost, and, with my grandmother, to reject the philosophy. It was more easy to believe the one than to comprehend the other.

A TRAGEDY OF SOUTH CAROLINA

Mrs. F. W. Dawson

Then why did she not keep the pigs from his cotton-patch? He had warned her! No man of his race ever failed to keep his word! By the eternal powers of mud and the State of South Carolina, he was a gentleman! He never said a thing he did not mean! This thing had gone on long enough. Again and again he had said, "Sure as you let those hogs of yours in my cotton, I'll blow your brains out!" Did they believe him? Well, they knew now whether he kept his word or not! Thank themselves for playing with fire once too often! Why did he not kill the pigs? Well! he had not thought of that. He had remembered he had to keep his word. By the powers of mud, a gentleman has to think of that first!

But this was in his twilight, whisky-strengthened meditation on the broad piazza.

When the sun had been overhead, hours ago, he was standing there looking at Scipio, who had fallen asleep bolt upright, sustained by the handle of his hoe, which had ceased to turn the soil. The colonel had retired to the house to fortify himself with his midday toddy. Scipio took the next best thing, from his point of view—a nap. As the colonel, mellowed by the subtle influence of the old corn whisky, stepped out on the sunlit piazza, those depraved pigs, before his very eyes, were ravaging his one hope of earning a living. Scipio, with a jerk that made the hoe scatter the soil, awakened at the ringing cry, "Here! you, Scipio!" He sprang forward briskly.

The colonel advanced with compressed lips and resolute stride. His hands grasped a gun. "Come along!" was his brief command.

Scipio followed, neither demurring nor questioning. Indeed, a bolder man than Scipio would have shrunk from inquiring the meaning of that deadly and intense silence. The colonel's fixed eyes and martial stride inspired caution. A clear, young voice rang out on the silence:

"Pa-a!"

The colonel half turned, without looking at the speaker. Waving the hand that was not clutching the gun, he tenderly cried: "You go back, Lorena! I'll come back, by and by!"

"Well, pa-a! What you goin' to shoot?"

"Hogs, child!"

"I'll go, too!"

"No you won't! You go just where I tell you: right in that house. And stay there, too!"

She was a strange, frail, elf-like child; tall, slender, on the debatable land between childhood and girlhood. Her threadbare, outgrown garments accentuated, in rents, the poverty sufficiently proclaimed by the naked feet and long stretch of stockingless legs. The mass of black hair hanging raggedly over her shoulders betrayed the absence of a mother's care. The pose and tone of this fresh, young creature bespoke a freedom and self-reliance rarely found in one of so few years. Her mother had passed away within her brief span of memory. Young as she was, she remembered the patient endurance, the poverty, toil, and humiliation that had been the portion of that mother in those latter days. "Befoh de wah," the colonel had been the owner of more lands and of nearly as many "subjects" as fall to the lot of some European kings. The bride he had enthroned in his ancestral home was envied by all the maidens of the land, because of the rare fortune that had come to her. No matrimonial candidate of the country could rank with the colonel. The wife never forgot this when poverty and degradation banished from the fine old house every sound of mirth and almost every trace of pardonable pride. It was her misfortune to fade with his waning fortunes. Loyally she ministered, as servant, to him who had crowned her queen of his princely home. But her fragile physique was ill-suited to rough fare and coarse work. She sank visibly and without a murmur. She would have held herself as unworthy, had she failed to conceal from him the burden under which she was crushed. The end was sudden, fortunately. She died in a superhuman effort to accomplish some menial task beyond her strength.

Only then did the colonel fully understand what her life had been. Henceforth, he was more than ever silent, and more than ever devoted to the one living child. His library, which had been his delight in days of luxury, was still his favorite retreat. But external contact with books now sufficed him. Rarely were they touched, save by the child who lay on the well-trodden carpet, striving to unravel their secrets. Her singular inspiration in drawing was his chief interest. Untaught, she had mastered the art of reproducing her childish fancies with wonderful ability. Her father was her sole companion. She was not aware that the demon drink did not always leave him in a state for ideal intercourse. Drunk or sober, she never saw the difference. And he had the grace to save his deeper potations for the night, when they would kill him more speedily and make him less offensive. Through the day, he merely drank enough to deaden himself to the memory of the galling poverty that had blasted his life. All the tenderness lavished on his wife was now centered on the child. She followed him afield; she ran beside him as he hunted the game that occasionally varied their common fare. In earliest youth she learned to light his pipe, bring his whisky, and to discharge the household duties within her limits. The toil of others was the play of this little one. Apart from the whole unheeding world, father and child clung to each other. They neither knew nor cared for other interests. Had she died, he would have avenged himself on an unjust omnipotence by rushing unbidden into the awful mysteries of the unseen. In the elementary instructions unconsciously bestowed upon the child he had never included the knowledge of a Heavenly Father. Long ago she had ceased to repeat the half-forgotten prayers her mother had taught her. If the name of God suggested anything to her mind, it was chiefly as a potent curse of her father's when things went wrong in the field. And so the little weed grew with its own peculiar use and beauty, neither knowing nor caring that development, fruition, and decay were the inscrutable laws illustrated in its obscure sphere.

Hearing the beloved father order her to the house, she turned without demur and busied herself with her daily duties.

Meanwhile, the stern, silent man stalked on, bearing his gun, and followed by Scipio, who reluctantly dragged behind. It was but two hundred yards to the next house, a rough log structure which stood bleak and somber in its few acres of neglected land. The poor dwelling consisted of two rooms, divided by a broad, open passage. A single mud chimney relieved the dark outline; a thin wreath of smoke arose in delicate waves in the limpid atmosphere. On this balmy day, it could only be a kitchen fire that was needed within.

The mistress of this lowly home was standing on the porch. Three rough steps led down to the littered ground. She had stepped from the room that served as kitchen, bed-room, parlor, and work-room. Glancing through the rude opening that served as a window, she had seen the colonel and his dusky attendant in their singular progress. Curiosity prompted her to leave the double rasher of bacon frying in the skillet, and made her hasten out to watch them pass. Her son, a gaunt, tall youth of twenty, collapsed, rather than crouched on the hearth to take her place. No word of explanation passed between them. His lank, yellow hair crowned him as the stubble crowns the neglected field. The coarse, homespun shirt of dubious tint served alike as coat and shirt. Certainly they are never worn together. One broken and patched suspender held his recalcitrant butternut trousers as much in place as they ever would be. A pair of suspenders was never owned in its entirety by any one of his caste. "Galluses" they called them; if originally purchased, they could only have been to divide between father and son, or near neighbors; they twain were never again one flesh.

The youth raked hotter embers on the sweet potatoes banked in the ashes that ever lay half a foot deep in the yawning fireplace. A few more minutes, and the last crisp, brown shade would touch the frying bacon. Already the hoe-cake was firmly crusted on the side presented to the live coals opposite the board on which it was spread. The primitive table with its yellow earthenware stood near the fire. The loom, with its half-finished cloth, was at one end of the room, and the bed, with its dingy appurtenances, was at the other. Half-way between these two prominent pieces, knelt the young "cracker" on the hearth. His protruded tongue was held upside down between his discolored teeth as he thrust his iron fork in the hoe-cake, the bacon, or the potatoes, to test their fitness for serving. Absorbed in this critical examination, he hardly heeded when his mother suddenly called, "Teddy!" Turning the last slice of bacon in its dripping fat, he laid the fork on the ashes and reluctantly arose to join her. As he shambled to the porch through the open hallway, once more his mother cried, "Teddy!"

No one ever called him again—not even to dinner!

The bacon sizzled angrily in its neglect; fretted and puckered up its edges, and burned away to crisp, black ashes. The hoe-cake baked through to the board, which slowly and sullenly charred and crumbled in hot resentment. The sweet potatoes, but now luscious with their hidden sugar exuding on the skin in soft candy, stiffened, hardened, and burned in their stifling bed, unseen and untasted.

For the colonel had kept his word as a gentleman, "by the eternal powers of mud and the State of South Carolina!"

When Teddy's mother had abandoned her cooking duties to her son, she had stepped out wearing that calico sunbonnet, without which this peculiar class of women are never seen. Sometimes strips of pasteboard serve to give those shapeless hoods an evanescent form. But these soon collapse and dangle helplessly around the face. The next device is to wear them loosely folded over backward, and drawn forward to fall in any random plait that calico can assume. So decked, the southern "cracker," or "sand-hiller," is apparently unconscious of the lack of any other garment, at home or abroad. These bonnets are worn afield, to keep off heat, cold, sun, rain. They are worn in the house, to be prepared for any of these possibilities in their constant visits to the outer air. Whether it be a stroll to the woodpile, or to the pigsty, or to the "branch," or to the corner where the daintiest bit of clay lies hidden for the dirt-eater's delectation, the sunbonnet crowns the woman from the cradle to the grave.

So Teddy's mother stepped from the hearth to the porch, the sunbonnet that shielded her from the fire, still falling around her eyes. From under its shadow she glanced at the colonel, who was now some paces from the wooden steps, Scipio respectfully halting in the rear.

"Them hogs of yourn," said the colonel, adopting the vernacular familiar to Teddy's mother, "have got in my cotton again."

She looked at him in silence. To her dull mind it must have seemed unimportant where they "got," provided they got enough to fatten them for killing. It did not matter to her; she planted no cotton herself. Indeed, she planted nothing that required care.

The colonel was very quiet—frightfully so, had she been intelligent enough to see the danger signal. Then he said deliberately:

"I told you I'd blow your brains out if you let your hogs in my patch again. I'm going to keep my word. Here, Scipio, shoot that old hag! Quick, fool! before I brain you!"

"Fore God, colonel, I kint! O Lawd! Maussa, don't mek po' Scip shoot buckra same like 'possum! You kin shoot bes', colonel! Shoot, please, maussa! Let Scip go!"

The colonel saw crimson. Purple veins distended his temples; crimson veins swelled in his eyeballs; a Niagara of curses burst from his livid lips. His hand was raised with the gun pointed at the Negro who groveled at his feet.

"Teddy!" cried the motionless woman, just as she would have said, "Teddy, dig some more 'taters!"

"Take it, you fool, or I'll shoot you! Shoot and be—"

"Teddy!" monotonously repeated the mother the second time.

Teddy had shuffled out, one hand grasping his sagging trousers, the other shading his fishy eyes from the noontide glare. In a flash he had seen more than living man can boast; for the swift bullet that pierced his mother's body had sped through his yokel heart. Together they fell on the rough flooring, he already seeing with eyes that were not of the flesh; and she, poor soul, doomed to a brief space of horror and pain—a sense of awful isolation and merciful oblivion at last.

The colonel turned stoically away, mindful to take his gun from Scipio's trembling hands. He gave neither look nor regret to the dead, nor yet to the death in life lying in a long, ghastly, straggling line along the porch and gaping passage. Scipio's slouch became grotesque as he followed his master home. Fear suggested flight; but the innate instinct of the former slave recognized that the colonel was his refuge and the arbiter of his fate. His ashen face expressed abject terror and a passive irresponsibility to leave "consequences" to higher natures; for, even in his mortal panic, he felt that he and the gun had nothing to do with the murder. It was the colonel who had "gone off!" And the colonel was the big-

gest man in the county: twice as big as the sheriff and the
jailor. The colonel would "fix it."

Within a few steps of home the colonel halted. Scipio
shifted from one foot to the other, an ebony image of degradation and helplessness. The colonel was strangely touched
by this silent appeal. "Scipio," he said kindly, almost tenderly, "there will be some talk about this, and I don't want
you to get in trouble. You know the cane-brake; and if you
don't get victuals enough, you know where to find more.
You are welcome to all you can take of mine. But cane-
brakes are not always safe. Travel on; better go when you
can, than run when you must. You are too good a Negro to
waste on a hanging, and you have done nothing to deserve
hanging,—only some people are born fools and think they
can carry things as they please! It is all right; you had it to
do. Don't worry about it any more than I shall. I have no
money; and money won't help you. Take my flask, though;
you'll need that. And be off while the coast is clear."

"Thankee, colonel! I'll go. 'Tain' like I had a fambly. I
kin git up an' git. No one ain' gwine find me. Goodby,
colonel! Thankee kindly!"

The colonel gazed calmly at the retreating form of the lithe
Negro who swung lightly along the untraced path to the cane-
brake. Fresh life had clearly been awakened in his downtrodden
breast by the prospect of travel and new scenes unconnected
with any prospect of toil.

Lorena came dancing from the house.

"Did you shoot the pigs, pa-a?"

"Yes; both."

"Why, there was lots of them, pa-a! Two ain't shakes to
what's in the patch now!"

"The worst are done for; the rest don't matter," said the
colonel, indifferently.

She caught the gun to relieve him of the burden. Quickly
he held it above her grasp.

"Look out; you'll get hurt!"

"O pa-a! would you take me for a pig?" she laughed.

Echoing the laugh tenderly, he led her by the hand to the place where the gun habitually rested, and then to the frugal dinner she had prepared for his return.

The disheveled chicken with the disjointed leg had grown weary of the social void in its haunts. There had been no implied invitation to potato peelings and hoe-cake crumbs. The land around was too poor to offer spontaneous hospitalities of attractive character. Chickie felt that an unwonted gloom had settled on its limited prospects. At best, life held no charms for her. "Cracker" chickens are so imbued with the shiftlessness and indolence of their owners that they speedily lose even the instinct of laying eggs. Poultry can hardly be said to be "cultivated" in such circles. No energy remains. Enough chickens to pick the casual worm from the neglected path, or clear the refuse from the family living-rooms,—enough to spare for the hawks and the wild things that prowl in the night,—these amply content the modest aspirations of the "cracker." If they ever vary the monotony of bacon and corn-bread by an occasional ration of chicken, no stranger has yet witnessed the orgy.

The frowzy little pullet fluttered up from step to step, ever pausing for a remark from the mother and son who lay supinely motionless in the rays of the sinking sun. Within the compass of her chicken life, familiar as she was with their idleness, never had she known them to be as lazy as this. Clucking and peeping in a shrill falsetto, vainly she interrogated them as to their eccentricity. Bright eyes blinking, head askew, feathers apparently developed during a stiff gale which had impelled her ever forward, she circled around and around the twain in irritating inquiry. Suddenly, a satisfactory reply seemed vouchsafed. The raw dough of the hoe-cake still clung to the dead woman's hands. Going from the hearth to her death, there had been no thought of the toilet observances all too rare among "crackers." The chicken accepted the dough as an answer to prayer for enlightenment and suste-

nance. It solaced itself pecking the stiff cold fingers clean of
every trace of meal. While thus actively engaged a man
passed by. Attracted by the extraordinary situation, he drew
near the porch. To glance, to shudder, to fly was the work of
half a minute. Nor had he run far when he met another "one
gallus" man, hands in pocket, slouch hat drawn over his
eyes, sauntering toward him.

"Bill! Teddy an' his ma-a is lyin' there dead. Murdered!"

The other nodded: "Knowed it sence noon. Been awaitin'
to see who's goin' to tell on the colonel."

"The colonel! Did he do it?"

"N-o-o-o! Yes! Leastways, he made Scipio do the shootin'.
I was outside the fence, an' I took keer to lay low. Jim an'
Pete was along. They've done gone. Reckon I'll go, too."

"Well, we won' git our heads blowed off for tellin' on
Scipio!"

"Tell an' be blowed, if you've a min' to. I'm goin' to
min' my own business an' git out! I ain't fool enough to stay
here an' tackle the colonel."

"Bill! You won' leave 'em there, an' all these pigs an'
things a-roamin' in the night?"

"Well, you go tell the sheriff, kin' er keerless like, he
better ride out this way. He'll think it means whisky, an'
he'll ride fast enough. I'm off for a run up the country." And
even as he spoke he strode past the frightened man. The latter
sauntered to town and intimated to the sheriff that some
interest might attend a ride out that road. The story was
whispered as he went along. When the sheriff arrived in the
fast-falling twilight, pine torches flared their banners of crimson and yellow and smoke over the dreary scene. Hemmed in
by the living half circle, the faces of the dead seemed to
mock and mow in answer to fearful comments and vain
queries. Those who pressed too near, in their curiosity, or
urged by eager neighbors, struggled back to place a barrier of
life between themselves and the dead.

From his broad piazza, where he sat smoking and meditating on the events of the day, the colonel saw the fitful light and wavering forms so near. If any one wanted him they knew where to find him.

Presently the sheriff walked up the avenue and respectfully accosted him. The colonel received him as though this were his reception evening and the sheriff his first and most honored guest. The sheriff began painfully:

"Of course, colonel, it's all nonsense them fellows is talkin'; but you'll not think hard of me for askin' you—"

"Anything you like, sheriff! Take your time. Anything!"

The sheriff, with a gasp, seized the other horn of the dilemma: "They say, colonel, that Scipio killed Teddy and his ma-a yonder."

"Indeed!" said the colonel.

"Yes, sir; and I hope you don't min' our ketchin' an' hangin' him so close to your house, sir?"

"Oh! hang him, by all means, if you catch him!" said the colonel cordially.

"An' you won't take no offense, colonel? 'Most on your place; one of your hands, too! It's hard on me, colonel, to have to do things displeasin' to you! You know my duty—"

"No one knows better than I, sheriff! Do what you think best. Have a drink? Well! Here's to you sheriff!"

Drink was never far from the colonel's hand. It was only decorum with him to drink with any chance visitor, and any number of them, night or day. So with the glow of the corn whisky in their veins, he and the sheriff considerately told each other as little as the law required under the awkward circumstances. Each was ready to declare that the other was a "perfect gentleman," warranted to evince no conscientious scruples in critical moments. The colonel had merely sanctioned the lawful prosecution of Scipio,—if he could be found, and if guilt attached to him. The sheriff thanked him effusively and returned to the seething crowd around the two cadavers.

"Where's Scipio?" he called in a voice mellow with recent whisky.

Silence was only broken by the thick utterance of Negro whispers. Again he called: "Come here, Scipio!"

A skinny old Negress drew near.

"Law, maussa! Scipio done dead long time. 'Fo' freedom come."

"Who are you?" roared the sheriff.

"I Scipio ma-a! He ain't never live here, no how," she sturdily asserted. The black faces remained unshaken in their gravity. Some of the white men laughed aloud, even in the presence of death, at this astounding invention.

"We'll find him when we want him," said the sheriff curtly. "But first, we'll have an inquest. Any of you got an opinion about this here murder—if it is a murder?"

"No, sir!" "I ain't!" " 'Taint no murder!" "Serve 'em right!" "Nuffin' but poo' white trash!" "Buckra." "Does de jury git pay same like de court-house?" These, simultaneously, from many voices.

"Well, all you who don't know and don't keer, step up an' form the jury."

"Mebbe dey is playin' 'possum," suggested a wary African.

"Dey's dead sure 'nuff!" replied another, stirring the old woman tentatively with his distorted shoe end.

"Who am dat say Scipio shoot 'em?"

There was an implied menace in this question which led to silence. No man cared to make himself responsible for the rumor in the face of unknown possibilities. White men stood stolidly; Negroes shifted restlessly, eager for a pretext for a row.

"If Scipio ain't here, an' no one ain't see him shoot, den Scipio ain't do it."

"Bress God! Dat so!" groaned the religious element.

"An' if Scipio ain't shoot, dey ain't shoot!" logically deducted an old ebon Solon.

"Amen! Dat so, Lawd! Black man, white man can't tell by de bullet who pull de trigger."

This audaciously irrelevant insinuation was greeted with a gasp of amazement. Mindful of late hospitalities, the sheriff was equal to the emergency.

"See here, Joe Saunders! an' you, Pompey; an' you fellows there! You ain't got nothin' to do with who did it, nor why it was done! That's none of your business; you've only got to say they were shot. The law does the rest."

On this simple basis, the jury was rapidly impaneled. As quickly the stereotyped verdict was formulated: "Came to their death by gunshot wounds inflicted by a person or persons unknown to the jury."

Time flies rapidly, even with those who chide its droning. But to Lorena, transformed into an ideal nymph of seventeen, time had brought no solace nor prosperity. She still roamed the woods, barefooted, driving cows which neither increased nor profited. Her father, her books, her sketches, these formed her world. Her drawing was inspired. She had no training, no theories to follow; she obtained results as the bird learns to sing, as the bee learns to make honey. On that plane, there was no room for improvement.

The colonel kept aloof from the world and sought no sympathy. But the girl's isolation weighed heavily upon him. Still more and more he resorted to the grave of his beloved wife, as though she could give him the help he dared not ask of heaven and would not ask of men. But he ever returned home bowed down by a burden that only increased with years.

Though he never spoke of it, whispers were afloat of a ghastly woman with a calico sunbonnet drawn over her eyes, who daily, in the gloaming, walked around the colonel's once beautiful home. It was not a pleasant topic; but there were those who averred that they had seen the gruesome vision. Under the seal of secrecy, scores likewise confessed

that they, also, had met a woman in that peculiar guise, silent
and intent on her mission. No one could question the colonel;
but no one could doubt that he, also, was conscious of her
presence. He never complained, whatever the mortal stress
laid upon him. Year after year, he endeavored to wrest from
the earth the return other men could so confidently expect,
—always meeting with loss, or at best, a scanty return. And
ever, in the twilight, as he sat on the wide piazza, while
Lorena prepared the meager supper, his meditations were
disturbed by the quiet apparition of a woman, who glided out
of the surrounding shadows and came toward him. The form
was the homely one so familiar to him in life. The routine
never varied. Up to where he sat, then around and around the
house—the face in the limp sunbonnet felt rather than seen.
While he remained without, she walked her weary round;
when he entered the library, she peered into each window as
she passed. The monotonous tramp continued until he fled
from the house. She never spoke. She seemed merely a
typical "cracker," indifferent to surroundings, shielded by
the calico sunbonnet that drooped over her eyes. Her face
was ever turned on the colonel, though she uttered no word.

The colonel stoically accepted this as one of the incompre-
hensible hostilities with which an inscrutable fate had long
pursued him. When the monotony became intolerable he
withdrew from the piazza, where he had passed his evenings
for a lifetime, and retreated to the library. But in the twilight
within he still listened acutely for the familiar step on the
crisp leaves or on the rain-soaked earth. He learned to shrink
nervously from the faint sound and from the shadowy form
that flitted past each window, the face with the unseen eyes
always turned fixedly toward him. Finally, he learned to
close the great shutters before sunset. It was unendurable
suspense waiting for the unwelcomed form that never failed
to glide by. His ear, grown doubly acute, learned all that his
eyes refused to look upon. So that his soul loathed life and
chose rather strangling and death. He dreaded the day; but

the night was still more awful. He would leave the house when Lorena slept, and walk all night, never resting, save when he could throw himself on his wife's grave. Earth held no other refuge for him. By and by, he intuitively understood that the woman in the sunbonnet was familiar to all who passed him by. No one dared tell him; yet he knew that she was so notorious that no one cared to pass his house after sunset. He only grew more reticent and more lonely.

After some years of stoic endurance, the strain could no longer be borne. The colonel nailed the doors and windows of his ancestral home and abandoned the place to ruin. He moved to a poor cottage on the outskirts of a large village some miles away. Isolation was still their portion. Poor as they were, he would take almost nothing from his beloved home. The associations which he sought to escape were too closely entwined with all that house contained. Nameless treasures, ancient furniture that had survived the wreck of fortune—all were left to molder in the deserted house. Lorena made no protest. The books dearest to her he transferred to the cottage. One drawing, which revealed her singular genius, he carried away with him. This erratic sketch which so impressed him, long survived him. It remains a singular memento of the family history. He wanted no other token from that once happy home. His whole mind was absorbed by the one image he sought to flee—the ghastly woman in the sunbonnet. Remorse needed no external suggestion to feed the fire that ever burned in his heart.

Far from the home he loved, in this new and humble shelter, fate might well have sent some respite to the broken and desolate man. But a Nemesis who never relented stalked beside him when he fled from his past, and ruthlessly she scourged him to the bone. She was neither triumphant nor aggressive. She merely conveyed the impression that somewhere from the remote depths of that limp, calico cavern, her dead eyes were fixed on him. When he could endure no more, the colonel stalked in grim despair to the grave of his wife, where the woman in the sunbonnet never came. Exhaustion always brought him merciful sleep on that desolate mound of earth. The villagers whispered of the new sentry-round followed by the silent woman who watched over the colonel in the gloaming.

Five years more of this unsought and undesirable companionship proved the limit of endurance for the colonel. The last time came for him as it comes for all. Whether, that night, the eyes finally gleamed from the depths of that shabby bonnet, or whether she had summoned him to confront them elsewhere, cannot be known. Only, the night came when he kissed Lorena with more than usual tenderness, and, as she left the room with the step of a young goddess, followed her with loving gaze. Presently he passed out of the cottage for the last time. He was not alone. He carried the gun which Scipio had so ably handled on that memorable day. And as he walked down the path, clutching the gun with an iron grip, the woman in the sunbonnet followed him. Where he went—what he felt—what he saw—remains untold.

It was Lorena who traced him to her mother's grave in the early morning. Often she had found him there, oblivious of all pain and sorrow, pillowed on the only refuge he had known in weary years. She caroled on her way, through field and woods, knowing where she would find him sleeping. The voice he so loved would awaken him with no startling consciousness of new torment to be faced.

Stooping over, the more gently to arouse him, she tripped on a gun lying by his side. With a stifled cry the girl fell on the still heart of the desolate suicide.

She did not long survive him; nor did she make her moan to heaven above or earth beneath. She held aloof, as ever, from the compassion that would gladly have encircled her. For a brief space, she roamed the woods and old haunts alone, Silent, now, she lived her life of isolation. refusing all proffer of companionship or sympathy. And one morning those who pitied her from afar found her lying at the foot of a slight precipice, her faultless face with its inscrutable smile turned to the sky. One beautiful arm was thrown over her head; the dead hand grasped trailing vines and wild flowers that delicately traced a shrine around the exquisite form. There was no indication of struggle, no evidence of pain. Was it accident? Was it design? Did a demon force or did a spirit lure her to her doom? Who knows?

They carried her to the deserted cottage, and there they stood astounded before the sketch her father had loved best of all. It was hanging just over the couch where she lay in her final sleep. Years before, in her elfin girlhood, she had with unconscious and prophetic hand sketched her young divinity that was to be and its pathetic end.

The picture represented a girl in the dawn of womanhood, of rarest beauty, lying dead at the base of the crag they had just seen. The faultless arm was tossed upward, a long spray of vines and wild flowers had encircled the radiant sylph-like form. In awe-stricken whispers they noted every strange detail of the singular coincidence. Nor did any false sympathy murmur, "Would she could have tarried with us!" If ever a hope had crossed her piteous life, it could only have gleamed from the unknown beyond the grave.

Near a well-known town of to-day, the old ancestral residence of the colonel stands deserted and shunned. No one loiters near it or cares to fathom the mysteries within. The faded carpets and dusty furniture and books may still be discerned through the slats of the window-shutters which were so firmly nailed by the colonel, when he hoped to escape the memory of the past. What was once luxury, is now the haunt of uncanny things that scurry through the obscurity and decay. No one dares penetrate within the silent house. It is the haunt of the woman in the sunbonnet, keeping watch and ward over the phantom of her murderer. Only a soul as vacuous as hers, as idle and as lonely, would brave the lion in his den! Only the tranquil ghost of the woman in the sunbonnet would venture to encounter the shade of the colonel in that moldering house! To-day he is still shrinking, yet eagerly listening for the unfaltering footstep that hounded him to suicide.

A STRANGE ARRIVAL

John William DeForest

Brig Betsy Jane, of New Haven, Connecticut, bound for Jamaica, is doing her best to get there.

It is not by any means her "level best," for a fresh tornado has burst from his lair in the Gulf of Mexico, and is blowing all his great guns and marline-spikes down the course of the Gulf Stream, as if he were totally out of patience with that venerable current, and meant to hurricane it off the face of the planet.

The waves rush, rear, tumble, howl, and froth at the mouth, like a mad herd of immeasurable buffaloes. Up goes one to a quivering peak; for a moment it stands, shaking its maniacal head of spray at the heavens; then, with a dying roar, it is trampled upon by its comrades. Onward they climb, roll, reel, topple, and wallow; their panting sides marbled with long streaks and great splashes of foam; their bluish masses continually throwing out new outlines of jagged, translucent edges; their sullen bellows and sharp gasps defying the beak and scream of the tornado. It is a combat which makes little account of man if he comes within range of its fury.

At a distance, the brig appears a stumpy black speck, buffeted, jerked, submerged, and then tossed upward. Now it plunges clean out of sight, as if the depths had gaped beneath it to their trembling base; now it crawls slowly into view again, as if a miracle had saved it for just another moment. You can see, misty miles away, that the craft has lost her topmasts, and that she is in dire trouble.

At hand things appear even worse than afar. The forty horses and mules, which were being transported for hard labor to the sugar-mills of the West Indies, have been drowned at their fastenings, thrown overboard by the sailors, dragged overboard by the billows. Short, frayed tatters of canvas, and loose, unstranding ends of rope, flutter and snap from the remaining yards. The caboose is gone; the bulwarks have taken to swimming; the water sweeps clean from stem to stern. Under a storm-jib, the only sail that can hold, the only sail that the reeling craft can bear, she is running before the gale. Worst of all, one of the dragging topmasts made a parting, traitorous rush at the stern, and stove a fracture through which the Atlantic spurts and foams.

We will wait a night and day, while the tornado dies into a half-gale, and the sea changes from toppling mountains to the sliding hills. Around the wheel, the only upright object on deck, sits a little group of drenched forms and haggard faces, staring with reddened eyes at the restless deserts of ocean. We will spend few words on the black cook, the mulatto cabin-boy, the six gaunt and brown New England sailors, the broad-shouldered, hard-featured mate. Our story more nearly concerns Captain Phineas Glover, and his daughter, Mary Anne Glover.

If the little oyster-planting suburb of Fair Haven ever produced a purer specimen of the old-fashioned, common-place stock Yankee than "Capm Phin Glover," let Fair Haven stand forth and brag of her handiwork in that line, secure from competition. It passed understanding how he could be so yellow, so sandy, so flaxen, after thirty years of exposure to sun, wind, and sea. How was it that pulling at tackles in his youth had left his shoulders so scant, his chest

so hollow, and his limbs so lean? We must conclude that
Captain Glover was Yankee all through, and that his soul was
too stubborn for the forces of nature, beating them in their
struggle to refashion his physique.

But tough as was his individuality, a due proportion of it
had melted into paternity. As he looked at Mary Anne's
round, blond face and ringlets of draggled flaxen, he was
evidently thinking mainly of her peril. "O Lord! what made
me fetch her?" was the all-absorbing thought of Phineas
Glover. The girl, eighteen years old perhaps, was still child-
like enough to have implicit trust in a father, and she returned his gaze with a confiding steadiness which enhanced
his trouble.

"Pumps are played out, Capm," said the mate, in the
hoarse tone of an over-fatigued and desperate man. "The
brig will go down in two hours. We must take to the boat."

"It's lucky we had one stowed away," replied Glover, and
paused to meditate, his eyes on the waves.

"Shall we get her up and launch her?" asked the mate,
sharply, impatient at this hesitation.

"I wish we had n't cut the masts away," sighed the captain, after another pause. "If we had n't, I'd make a sail."

"Make sail to Davy Jones's locker? I tell you we see the
Dutchman last night. More 'n one of us see him."

"I seen him," said the cook, with a deprecatory grin.
"An' so did Jimmy."

"Ordinarily I don't mind such stories," continued the
mate. "But now you see how things is for yourself; you see
that something out o' the common has been afoul of us; and
my opinion is that it hain't done with the brig yet. Anyway,
Dutchman or no Dutchman, this brig is settling."

"I don't believe it, Mr. Brown. Them staves an' bar'ls is a
floatin' cargo. She 'll go to the water's edge, mebbe, but she
won't go a mite farther."

"Now look a here, Capm. I, for one, don't want to resk
it."

"Nor I," struck in the sailors, and, in a more humble tone, the black cook.

"Wal," decided the captain, "I sha' n't put my daughter in a boat, in this sea, a thousan' miles from land. She an' I'll stay aboard the brig. If you want to try the boat, try it. I don't say nothin' agin it."

A brief silence, a short, earnest discussion, and the thing was thus settled. The boat was dragged out of the hold and launched; two or three barrels of provisions and water were embarked; the crew, one by one, slid down into the little craft; presently it dropped away to leeward. Phineas and Mary Anne Glover called to the adventurers, "Look us up, if you find help," and waved them a sad farewell. The seamen rose from their seats and returned three encouraging cheers. A little sail was set in the bow of the boat, and it stole, rising and falling, toward the setting sun. Night came down on the rolling, waterlogged, but still floating brig.

"I tell ye them boys had better a great sight hung by us," said Captain Glover to Mary Anne, as they sat on the upper steps of the gangway and looked down upon the water swashing about the cabin. "She hain't settled a hair in the last two hours. The' ain't a speck o' danger o' founderin'. I knew the' wa'n't. Noah's flood could n't founder them staves an' bar'ls."

"Oh dear! I wish I was in Fair Haven," blubbered Mary Anne. "If I could only git back there, I'd stay there."

"Come now, cheer up," returned the father, doing his best to smile. "Why, I've been a sight wus off than this, an' come out on't with the stars an' stripes a flyin'. Las' time I was wrecked, I had to swim ashore on a mule,—swum a hundred miles in three days, with nothin' to eat but the mule's ears,—an' as for sleepin', sho! Tell ye that mule *was* a kicker. A drove o' sharks was right after us, an' he kicked out the brains o' th' whole boodle of 'em. Stands to reason I could n't sleep much."

"O pa! You *do* tell such stories! I sh'd think you'd be afraid to tell 'em now."

"Wal, you don't b'lieve it. But live an' learn. Tell you, b'fore you git home, you'll b'lieve things you never b'lieved b'fore. Why, I got a new wrinkle no later 'n day b'fore yesterday. Many strange things 's I've seen, I never b'lieved till now in the Flyin' Dutchman. You heard what the men said. Wal, I saw him 's plain 's they did. I'm obleeged to b'lieve in him. I sighted him comin' right up on our larboard bow, 's straight in the wind's eye 's he could steer. He run up till he was a cable's length from us, an' I was jest about to hail him, when he disappeared. Kind o' went up or down, I could n't say which. Anyhow, next minute, he was n't there."

This time Captain Glover spoke with such earnestness that his daughter put faith at least in his sincerity.

"O pa! I wish you would n't scare me so," she whimpered. "It's awful."

"Lord bless you! never mind it, Mary Anne," chirruped the father. "The critter 's done all the harm he 's allowed to do. 'Tain't in his pea-jacket to do wus 'n he has. That's jest the reason why he up helm and put out o' sight. Come now, we'll have supper; lots to eat aboard. I reckon we've provisions enough to last three years, an' have a big tuck-out every Thanksgiving. Come, chirk up, Mary Anne. I wish them poor boys was half 's well off's we be. Why, we can be as happy 's Robinson Crusoe."

All night Mary Anne, as she afterwards related, dreamed about the Flying Dutchman. She saw him steer straight over the meadows to the Fair Haven steeple, and knock it prostrate with one glance through his telescope. He carried her away to caverns under the sea which were encrusted with pearls and stored with treasure. He sailed with her so fast around the world that the sun was always setting and yet never got out of sight. His canvas was made of moonbeams, and his hull of the end of a rainbow. When she awoke at daylight, the first words that she heard from her father were, "Wal, if that ain't the Dutchiest Dutchman that ever I did see!"

Leaping up, and steadying herself against the paternal shoulder, she looked across the now gently heaving waters. Was there witchcraft in the world? Had they slept a hundred years in a night, and slept backward at that? Not for two centuries, not since the days of Hendrik Hudson and De Ruyter, had earthly eyes beheld such a sight as now bewildered these two human oysters from Fair Haven. The wildest fancies, the most improbable invention of Capm Phin Glover were left a long ways astern by the spectacle before him.

"I never see the like," he said, quite forgetting his need of rescue in his wonder. "Dunno whether it's a Dutchman or a Chinaman. The' was a Chinee junk brought to New York that was a mite like it."

Here he suddenly remembered that he was a shipwrecked unfortunate, and burst into a series of shrill yellings, emphasized by wavings of his tarpaulin.

A hundred fathoms distant, right against the broad, dazzling halo of the rising sun, slowly bowing and curvetting on the long, low swell, lay a craft of six or eight hundred tons burden, with a perfectly round bow capped by a lofty forecastle, and a stern which ran up into something like a tower. Two huge but stumpy masts supported the yards of four enormous square sails, while a third mast, singularly short and slender, rose from near the tiller. Two short jibs ran down to a bowsprit which pointed upward at an angle of forty-five degrees. two monstrous tops, fenced around with bulwarks, looked like turrets on stilts. The whole pompous, grotesque edifice was painted bright red, with a wide streak of staring yellow.

It seemed to swarm with men, and they were all in strange, old-fashioned costumes, as if they were revellers in a masked ball, or wax-figures escaped out of museums. The queerest hats and high-colored jackets and knickerbocker breeches and long stockings went up and down the shrouds, and glided about the curving decks, and stole out on the pug-nosed bowsprit. On the castle-like poop stood three men in richer vesture than the others, whose hats showed plumes of feathers. Presently these three uncovered their heads, and set their faces steadfastly toward heaven, as if engaging in some act of devotion. This ended, the tallest turned toward the sufferers of the Betsy Jane, made them a solemn bow and waved his hand encouragingly.

"Wal, if this don't beat all!" said Phin Glover to his daughter. "Now tell me nothin' happens at sea but what happens in Fair Haven. Now tell me I never swum ashore on a mule."

"What is it, pa?" demanded Mary Anne. "Is it a ship, or a house?"

"I declare I dunno whether it's a meetin'-house afloat or Noah's Ark," responded the hopelessly bewildered skipper. "I never hailed the like before, not even in picters."

By this time a round-shouldered, full-breasted boat, high out of water fore and aft, had been let down the bulging sides of the stranger. Half a dozen of the grotesque sailors swung themselves into it; then came the tall personage who had made the cheering signals to our shipwrecked couple; in another minute the goose-fashioned craft was bobbing under the quarter of the Betsy Jane. Phin Glover looked at his rescuers in such amazement that he forgot to speak to them. Even when the tall man stepped from his seat upon the deck of the waterlogged brig, the Yankee skipper could only continue to stare with his mouth open.

The visitor was in every way a remarkable object. A sugar-loaf hat with a feather, a close-fitting doublet of purple velvet, loose breeches of claret-colored silk tying below the knee, silk stockings of a topaz or sherry yellow, broad, square-toed shoes decked with a bow, and a long, straight sword hanging from a shoulder-belt, constituted a costume which even the wonder-hunting Phin Glover had never before beheld, nor so much as constructed out of the rich wardrobe of his imagination. Moreover, this man had a noble form, a stately bearing, and a countenance which was at once stern

and sweet. His gray eyes set forth a melancholy yet hopeful
light, which seemed to tell a history beyond the natural
experience of humanity.

His conduct was as singular as his appearance. After one
glance at the Glovers, he knelt down upon the damp deck of
the brig, removed his hat, and uttered a prayer in some
unknown language. Rising, with a face moistened by tears,
he approached Mary Anne, took her trembling hand in his,
bowed over it in profound humility and kissed it. Then,
before he could be prevented, he in the same manner kissed
the horny fist of Captain Glover.

"Seems to me this is puttin' on a leetle too many airs,
ain't it?" was the remark of our astonished countryman.

"You are English," returned the other, with a pronuncia-
tion which was foreign, and even stranger than foreign. It
seemed as if the mould of ages clogged it, as if the dead who
have been buried for centuries might have uttered those
tones, as if they were meant for ears which have long since
been stopped by the fingers of decay.

"No, *sir!*" responded Phin Glover, emphatic with national
pride. "Americans! United States of America! Dunno's you
ever sailed there," he added, startled and somewhat humbled
by a suspicion that there might be countries or ages in which
his beloved Union was not, or had not been, famous. He was
a good deal confused by what was happening, and could not
think in perfectly clear grammar or sense.

"You speak English," continued the stranger. "I also
have learned it. During five years I abode in London. Inform
me of the state of the gracious Queen Elizabeth."

"Queen Elizabeth!" echoed Captain Phin Glover. "Why,
good gracious! you don't mean the old Queen Elizabeth!
Come now, you don't mean to say you mean *her!* Why,
bless your body! that's all gone by; improved off the face of
the earth; holystoned out of creation. Queen Elizabeth! She's
dead. Been dead ever s'long. Did n't you know it? Shipmate,

tell a fellah; ain't you a jokin'? Where upon earth do you hail from?"

"From Amsterdam. I have voyaged to the Indies and am returning to Amsterdam."

"Amsterdam! Queen Elizabeth—The Flyin' Dutchman, as I'm a sinner!" exclaimed Phineas. "Shipmate, *be* you the Flyin' Dutchman?"

"I know not what you mean," answered the stranger. "I am, however, a Hollander, and I am flying from the wrath to come. I am a great criminal who hopes forgiveness."

"That's right,—that's orthodox," chimed in Glover, who always went to church in Fair Haven, though indifferent to divine service in foreign parts. "But bless my body! Queen Elizabeth! The Flyin' Dutchman! If this don't beat all! Now tell me I did n't swim ashore on a mule. Tell me I never rigged a jury-mast on an iceberg, an' steered it into the straits of Newfoundland. Shipmate, I'm glad to see ye. What's the news from Amsterdam?"

"Alas! it is long since I was there. I know not how long. When I left, Antwerp had lately been overcome by the Spaniards."

"By the Spaniards? Never heerd of it. Wal, cheer up, shipmate. Since you quit, the Dutch have taken Holland, every speck an' scrap of it."

The stranger's eyes beamed with a joy which was at once patriotic and religious.

"What might your name be?" was the next remark of our countryman.

"Arendt Albertsen Van Libergen."

Captain Glover was silent; such a long title awed him, as being clearly patrician; moreover, he did not feel capable of pronouncing it, and that was embarrassing.

"You must now come upon my vessel," continued the Hollander. "Yours cannot be got to land."

"How 'bout the cargo?" queried Glover. "Bar'ls 'n staves—

wal, no use, I s'pose—can't be got up. Some provisions, though. Might take 'em along, 'n allow somethin' for 'em.''

"Our provisions never fail," returned Captain Van Libergen. "Come."

They stepped into the boat; the old-time sailors fell back on their old-time oars; in two minutes they were mounting the sides of the Flying Dutchman. If Phineas and Mary Anne Glover had been led into the Tower of London or the Museum of Dresden, they could hardly have discovered a more curious medley of antiques than saluted their gaze on this singular craft.

"The bul'arks was five feet high," our countryman subsequently related. "The' was at least three inches through, —made for fightin', I should jedge. The' was four big iron guns, 'bout the size o' twenty-four pounders, but the curiousest of shape y' ever see, an' mounted, Lord bless you! Sech carriages 'd make a marine laugh now-a-days. Then the' wa' n't less 'n a dozen small brass pieces, dreadful thin at the breech, an' with mouths like a bell. I see some blunderbusses, too, with thunderin' big butts, an' muzzles whittled out like the snouts of dragons. Fact is, the' had all sorts of arms, spears, an' straight broadswords, an' battle-axes on long poles, an' crossbows, —y' never see such crossbows in Fair Haven.

"The decks was a sight," our narrator proceeded. "They run scoopin' up for'ard an' scoopin' up aft. The fo'kesle an' the quarter-deck looked at each other like two opposition meetin'-houses. The fore an' main masts was as stumpy's cabbage-stalks. As for her riggin', she was a ship, an' yet she wa' n't a ship. However, on the whole, might 's well call her a ship, considerin' the little mizzen by the tiller. But the' ain't a boy in Fair Haven don't draw better ships on his slate in school-time, when he oughter be mindin' his addition 'n substraction. As for the crew, y' never see such sailors now-a-days, not even in picter-books. The' looked more like briguns in a play than like real seamen. A Weathersfield

onion-sloop would n't ship such big-trousered, long stock-
inged lubbers. Put me in mind o' Greeks, most of anything
human. But the' was discipline among 'em. Tell ye the' was
mighty ceremonious to the skipper an' his mates. Must allow
'em that credit. The' was discipline.''

Phineas Glover's wonder did not abate when he was con-
ducted into the cabin of the Flying Dutchman. All was
antique,—the carved oaken wainscoting, the ponderous side-
board of Indian wood, the mighty table, set with Delft ware
and silver flagons. Amid this venerable, severe elegance
stood two gentlemen and a beautiful lady; the former attired
much like Van Libergen, the latter in what seemed a court
costume of other days.

"These are Adraien Van Vechter and Dircksen Hybertzen,
my cousins," said the Flying Dutchman. "And this is Cornelie
Van Vechter, the wife of my cousin. They speak no English,
but they desire me to say that they rejoice in your deliverance, and that they are your humble servants."

"When a woman 's as putty as that, an' can smile as sweet
as that, she don't need no English to make herself understood," returned Captain Glover, gallantly. "Tell 'em they
can't be no humbler servants to us than we be to them."

The lady now advanced to Mary Anne, took her hand with
another charming smile, and placed her at table. Van Libergen
went through the same gracious formality with Phineas; and
the other two Hollanders, after bowing to right and left,
seated themselves.

"But before we took a mouthful," relates our minute and
veracious countryman, "the Flying Dutchman stood up an'
asked a blessing which I thought would last till we got to
Amsterdam. Never see a more pious critter. If he could
manhandle a blessing that long, he must have had a monstrous gift at prayer."

By the way, Captain Glover was boggled, as we may
suppose, by the outlandish names of his new acquaintance,
and especially by that of the commandant. The title of a

celebrated cheese, which he had partaken of in lager-bier saloons, came to the aid of his memory; and he found it convenient, during his stay on the famous sea-wanderer, to address Arendt Van Libergen as Capm Limburgher.

The meal was served by dark men in white apparel, whom Mary Anne took to be "some kind of Negroes," but whom her father guessed to be "Lascars." In place of tea and coffee, there were vintages of Spain, taken perhaps from some captured galleon. The glorious old wine! Captain Glover had never tasted the like before, not even at his owner's in New Haven. Under its incitation, he came out strong as a conversationalist, telling the story of his shipwreck and not a little of his previous life, and throwing in some of those apocryphal episodes for which he was celebrated. He was particularly splendid in describing a religious procession which he had seen in Havana.

"Most wonderful sight!" he said. "Two miles of priests, and every one of 'em with a wax-candle in his hand, as big—as big as the pillars in front of the State-House."

"O pa!" protested the abashed Mary Anne, with an alarmed glance at her august hosts, "you don't mean as big as the pillars in front of the State-House."

"Yes, by thunder!" insisted the captain; "*and* fluted from top to bottom."

But, if our countryman slightly surprised his entertainers, they prodigiously and perpetually puzzled him. Their inquiries were all concerning matters so out of date, so far beyond his tether! They asked about the siege of Antwerp, the surrendry of Brussels and Ghent, the reported mutinies of Walloons, the prospect of armed succors from England. After endeavoring to draw some information on these subjects from the abysses of his subjective, and finding that he was floundering into various geographical and chronological errors, he frankly acknowledged that he was not logged up in Dutch politics, having had little chance of late at the newspapers. And when they spoke of the Prince of Parma, William of Orange,

Maurice of Nassau, the Earl of Leicester, and Henry of
Navarre, he feared that he was not making things very clear
to them in asserting that those old cocks were all as dead as
General Washington. This statement, however, produced a
painful impression upon his auditors.

"Dead!" sighed the beautiful lady. "Then others also
have passed away. Are we only to find those we love in the
grave?"

"And are we not dead ourselves?" sadly yet firmly replied
Captain Van Libergen. "Did not our due term of life long
since close? Only the signal mercy of Heaven has preserved
us on earth until we could repent of our great sin. Perhaps,
when the expiation is complete, we also shall suddenly cease
to be."

"Let's hope not," replied Phineas Glover, always cheerful
in his views. "But come, about the dates; time of Queen
Elizabeth, you say. Why that was settlement of Virginny.
That was 1587, wa' n't it, Mary Anne? Wal, if 't was 1587,
then as this is the year 1867, 't was two hundred 'n eighty
years ago. Why, shipmates, if your log is correct, if you left
Amsterdam when you say, you've been on the longest cruise
ever I heard of. Two hundred 'n eighty years out o' sight o'
land! Jerusalem! I'd ruther live ashore all the while."

When these words were translated to Cornelie Van Vechter,
she covered her face with her hands, moaning, "All dead! all
dead!"

"I knew it was thus," sighed Arendt Van Libergen; "and
yet I weakly hoped that it might be otherwise."

"What! hain't you kep' no log, shipmate?" demanded
Phineas Glover.

"How could we believe it?" replied the Hollander. "How
could we believe that we were even as the Everlasting Jew?"

"Everlasting Jew? Wandering Jew, s'pose ye mean. Wal
now, Capm Van Limburgher, I'll tell ye what it all means.
You're the Flyin' Dutchman; that 's just what you are; now
take my word for it, an' be easy; I've heard of ye often, an'

dunno but what I've seen ye. You 're monstrous well known
to sailors; an' on the whole I 'm glad I 've come acrost ye;
though seems to me, 't wa n't quite han'some to sink the
Betsy Jane; that is, unless you was under some kind o'
necessity o' doin' it. Yes, *sir*; you're the Flyin' Dutchman;
bet your pile on it, if you're a bettin' man.''

''But what in the name of thunder is it all for?'' he added,
after a moment of curious and puzzled staring at the famous
wanderer; ''what makes ye go flyin' round, sinkin' ships an'
sailin' in the wind's eye, an' raisin ' Nipton generally? Why
don't ye go into port? Tell ye the whole United States would
turn out to give ye receptions an' hear ye lecter! The Ledger
'd give ye a hundred thousan' dollars for your biography,
written by your own fist. Might pile up a million in five
years. Must be mighty fond o' cruisin'. Make money by it?
Sh'd think y'd want to slosh round on shore, once in a
century, at least.''

''It is my punishment,'' replied the rover, with an affect-
ing solemnity and humanity. ''I am a great criminal.''

''Waterlogged the Betsy Jane, certin,'' muttered Glover,
in spite of a jog on the elbow from Mary Anne.

''You shall hear our tale,'' said Captain Van Libergen,
signing to the Hindoo servants to leave the cabin.

''Sh'd be delighted to put it in the papers,'' observed our
countryman. ''The Palladium or the Journal would either of
'em snap at it.''

''I was mad to be rich,'' began the Flying Dutchman. ''I
desired wealth, not for its luxury, but for its power. Sometimes, in the midst of my hardness towards other men as I
grasped at gold, it occurred to me that some day a fitting
retribution would descend upon my head. A voice within
sometimes whispered, 'In that thou art living for thyself
alone, thou art denying Him who died for thee; an appointed
hour will come when thou wilt be subjected to a last trial; and
then, if thou choose the evil, thy punishment will be great.'

''Yet I continued covetous and pitiless, and I made these

men who voyage with me like myself. This vessel is freighted
with the tears and sweat of the Indies, wrung out by me into
gold and precious merchandise. Knowing that the sooner I
gained my native land the greater would be my profit, I
swore that nothing should detain me on my voyage. Horrible
oath! kept with the faith of a demon! punished with the
wrath of God! On the ninetieth day, when we were within a
hundred leagues of Amsterdam, I saw a wreck with two
persons upon it. My cousin Cornelie Van Vechter implored
me with tears to turn aside and save them. Monstrously cruel,
I refused to waste the time, and steered onward. Then, even
as we passed, a far-sounding voice, surely not the voice of a
mortal, called from the sinking-ship, 'Sail forever, without
reaching port, until you repent!'

"Cornelie Van Vechter cried: 'It was Christ upon that
wreck, and you have forsaken him, and he has doomed you.'
Had she been a man, I would have stricken her down, I was
so hardened in heart. But she had perceived the truth; she had
divined our punishment. Alas! she, the innocent, as so often
happens on earth, was fated to share the reward of the guilty.
Since that time we have sailed, we have sailed, we have
sailed. No land. Nothing but sea. We cannot anywhere find
the blessed land. We find nothing but a vast hell of ocean. O,
the hell of illimitable ocean! Time, too, was no more. We
have kept record of time, without faith in it. For a while we
laughed at our calamity, as we had mocked at our sin. We
could not believe that our friends were dead; that the world of
our time had passed away; that we were strangers to the
human race.

"Another horror! we were fated to witness all wrecks that
be upon the sea. Wherever a vessel went down, amid howl-
ings of waves and shrieks of sailors, thither we were borne at
the speed of lightning, always in the teeth of gales. No
struggling and crying of desperate men on the ocean for near
three centuries but what these eyes have seen and these ears
heard. From tempest to tempest we have flown, always,

always beaten by opposing billows, discovering strange seas only to find new horrors. And amidst all this, my heart has remained so hardened that I would not wish to succor one perishing soul.

"At last, wearied with struggling against the Almighty, crazed to see once more the sweet earth for which Christ died, we repented. Yesternight I called my crew together and confessed my sin and besought the mercy of God. A voice answered me from the abysses of the stars, saying, 'Succor those whom I shall send, and find grace!'

"At dawn this morning I beheld you on your wreck, and I turned aside to save you."

During this relation Cornelie Van Vechter wept so piteously that Mary Anne Glover cried aloud in sympathy. Even the commonplace soul of Phineas Glover was moved to suitable thoughts.

"Wal, Capm, it's a most surprisin' providence," he remarked, with solemnity. "An' the' 's one thing, at the end on 't, that p'r'aps you don't see. It 's consid'able of a come-down for you to pick up an' make so much of two poor critters like us. We 're middlin' sort o' folks, Capen; we ain't lords an' ladies, like what you've asked about; we're no great shakes, an' that 's a fact. I begun my seafarin' life as a cabinboy, an' Mary Anne has shelled her heft in oysters, over an' over. Pickin' *us* up, an' kissin' our hands an' all that, is a kind o' final test of your humility.

"Wal, it 's a most edifyin' narrative," he continued, after a thoughtful pause. "It's better 'n many a sermon that I've sot under. I see the moral of it, as plain as a marline-spike in my eye. You want to git to port; you won't help a feller-critter in distress; consequently you don't git to port. Why, our great Republic, the United States of America, —dunno 's you ever heerd of it,—has had some such dealin's. We run alongside them poor Negroes: we might 'a' helped 'em an' sent 'em to school an' civilized 'em; but all we did was to use em in puttin' money into our puss. Consequently we've had a dreadful long voyage over a sea of troubles, an' hain't got quite into port yit. However, you don't know what I'm jawin' about; an', besides, I'm takin' up the time of the company. Gentlemen, go on!''

No one responding, Captain Glover raised his flagon of Manzanilla to his lips, with the words, "Here's better luck nex' time!''

Thus closed this remarkable breakfast, seldom paralleled, we venture to say, on this planet, however it may be on the others.

Now came an interesting week on the Flying Dutchman. What most struck Captain Glover, as he has repeatedly informed us, was the solemnity and religious aspect of all on board.

"They seemed to be awfully convicted, and yet they seemed to entertain a hope," were his words. "They had a kind 'o tender, humble look, mixed with a sort o' trustin' joy. Certinly it was the most interestin' occasion that I ever see or expec' to see. Jest think of the Flyin' Dutchman an' his whole crew gittin' religion together. Father Taylor would 'a' given his head to be aboard o' that ship in such a season.''

Our level-headed skipper took a deep interest also in an examination of the far-famed wanderer's cargo. Arendt Van Libergen led the two Glovers through what portion of the hold was accessible, and showed them such treasures of spice, gums, India silks, gold-dust and ornaments, pearls and precious stones, as no Fair-Havener ever gazed upon before.

"Beats the oyster trade, don't it, Mary Anne?'' remarked our countryman. "Capen Limburgher, you probably don't realize the value of our American oyster. It's the head sachem of shell-fish for cookin' pupposes. Every free white native American citizen eats his forty bushels annually. You can estimate by that the importance of the openin' business; an' Fair Haven is the very hub an' centre an' stronghold of it. Nary gal in the village but can knife her sixty quarts daily. Mary Anne here is a splitter at it. It's made heaps of money for the place. But compared with your trade, compared with dealin' in the gold an' silver an' diamond line, sho! why, Capm Limburgher, you're one of the merchant princes of the earth. Your ship puts me in mind of Zekiel's description of the galleys of Tyre and Sidon. Model about the same, too, I sh'd reckon.''

Except by a profound sigh, Arendt Van Libergen made no response to these flatteries. He pushed aside with his foot a bag of gold-dust, as if he considered it dross indeed, and ensnaring dross.

"S'prisin' how well preserved things be," continued Glover. "Now here's this alspice, 's fresh 's if 't was picked this year, 'stead of two hundred an' eighty years ago."

"It is a part of our punishment," returned the Flying Dutchman. "Our wealth was forbidden to decay, and yet we were forbidden to use it. We could gaze upon it in all its freshness, and yet we could not land it at our homes. In the midst of it, we have known that it was not ours. Surrounded by the fruit of our desires, we were under a curse of barrenness."

"And here am I, under a cuss, without a red cent," was the natural reply. "Capm, I declare I'd like to swap cusses with ye."

"Take what pleases you," answered Arendt Van Libergen. "It is now of no value to me."

"Now, really, Capm, don't want to rob ye," protested Phineas Glover. But, bent downward by his poverty and his avarice, he commenced filling his pockets with gold.

"Catch hold, Mary Anne," he whispered. "Take what's offered ye, 's a good old text."

But in the girl's soul there was a fine emotion which would not permit her to clutch at the wealth which dazzled her eyes. A profound pity for the woes of these fated wanderers had rapidly risen into love as she had watched from day to day the noble bearing and mournful beauty of Arendt Van Libergen. Not for all the treasures that were in his galleon would she have grasped for greed in his presence. She stood up-right, her lashes gemmed with tears, gazing at this strangely doomed being.

He caught her glance; he gave her one sad, sweet smile in reward for it; then he selected a string of priceless pearls and placed it around her neck. One of her tears wet his hand, and he murmured, ''Thanks for pity.''

They now went on deck, Captain Glover's numerous pockets cumbrously stuffed with gold-dust and idols, and Mary Anne beating naught but the string of pure pearls.

Meantime the Flying Dutchman is sailing before a fair wind towards Amsterdam. The curse is lifted; the vessel is not now different from all earthly craft; she no longer flies in the teeth of gales, surrounded forever by billows; she is like other ships in her dependence upon the laws of nature; but she is favored with fortunate breezes and a smooth sea; she seems to know that at last she is bound home.

On a sunlit summer morning—on such a cloudless and dewy morning of grace as forgiven phantom ships are wont to enter port—the Flying Dutchman arrived off a low, green coast, within sight of the masts, roofs, and towers of a great city.

''That's Amsterdam,'' confidently declared Captain Glover, who had never before crossed the ocean. ''There the old town is, jest as I left it last, an' jest as you left it, I'll bet a biscuit. There's the State-House—I s'pose it is—an' all the meetin'-houses,—the 'Piscopal 'n' the Methodis' 'n' the Congregational. Take the word of an old sailor, you'll find it all right ashore, an' everybody turnin' out to shake hands with ye. See all your friends an' family before night, Miss Van Vechter.''

''Will the dead arise to greet us?'' sighed Cornelie Van Vechter, when this cheerful prophecy was translated to her.

''Wal, now 'tain't certin they be dead,'' argued Captain Glover. ''There was Joyce Heth, in our country,—Barnum did say an' swear she was a hundred an' thirty-two year

old,—an' she but a Negro, with no chance for proper eatin'
an' no medicines to speak of. An' there was old Tom John-
son of Fair Haven. *I* never heerd anybody pretend to deny
that he was less 'n two hundred. That's a positive, solemn
fact,'' declared the cheerful captain, looking a little embar-
rassed under the lady's mournful gaze.

"Now in your time,'' he continued, "folks had powerful
constitutions, an' necessarily lived to a good old age. Why, it
stands to reason you'll find *some* of 'em all alive an' frisky.
An' glad to see ye? Sho!''

"Alas!'' murmured the beautiful Hollander, "if they live,
they will be broken with years, and they will not know us.''

"Let us deceive ourselves with no false hopes,'' said
Ardent Van Libergen. "We are the dead going to the dead.''

"Now that ain't my style, Capm Limburgher,'' protested
Glover. "Hope on, hope ever, is my motto. If't had n't been,
I never sh'd 'a' come ashore many a time when I've gone to
the bottom, or fit with white bears for a squattin' right on an
iceberg.''

A glance, not of disdain, but of devout pity, fell from the
rover's eyes, and silenced the babbling skipper.

A Dutch pilot, who now boarded the vessel, was so
dumbfounded at its build and the appearance of its crew,
that, while he remained upon it, he did not utter one syllable.
He stood blanched with fright at the clumsy tiller, and made
signs as to the management of the nondescript rigging. Our
garrulous countryman sidled up to him, and sought to engage
him in conversation. Whether the pilot understood English or
not, he made no reply further than to clatter his teeth with
terror.

And now, as they approached the wharves, a strange,
awful transformation began to steal upon the crew of the
Flying Dutchman. The green water of the harbor seemed to
commence the dissolution of that charm which had kept them
youthful through nearly three centuries. Phineas Glover, glancing at Arendt Van Libergen, noticed that his chestnut hair

was streaked with silver, and that his face, lately so smooth
and hale, was seamed with wrinkles. Turning to Cornelia
Van Vechter, he saw that she too had lost the freshness of her
young beauty, and taken on the tints and bearing of middle
age.

"I've heerd o' folks gittin' gray in a night," muttered the
startled skipper; "but this is the first time I ever see it. Tell
me now I never steered an iceberg."

Moment by moment this fearful change of youth into age
proceeded. Soon Arendt Van Libergen sat feebly down on
the gangway steps, a decrepit, snowy-haired old man, with
no beauty but a smile of devout resignation. Cornelie Van
Vechter, now an ancient matron, clung to the shoulder of her
suddenly venerable husband. Gray-headed sailors, their locks
momentarily growing whiter, and their bronzed faces paling
to the ashy hue of age, slowly and weakly coiled away ropes
which seemed to be falling into dust. The change reached the
ship; every fathom toward land opened cracks in the bulwarks; the masts began to drop in dry-rotted slivers; the sails
lay on the yards in mouldering rags.

Suddenly terrified, Captain Glover seized Mary Anne, rushed
with her to the castle-like quarter-deck, and sought refuge
behind the trembling pilot. The girl was crying. "O, he must
die!" she whispered; "I shall never see him again."

Looking towards Arendt Van Libergen, Glover beheld him,
feeble with extreme age, deadly pale and gasping. Beyond
him lay Cornelie Van Vechter, Adraien Van Vechter, Dircksen
Hybertzen, and all the sailors, all prostrate, all breathing out
their little remaining life, yet all with a sweet smile of
resignation on their indescribably ancient features.

At this moment the vessel neared the wharf. With a loud
scream the Dutch pilot sprang across decaying timbers, leaped
the space between the bulwarks and the shore, and disappeared in the labyrinth of the living city. Over the dust of
vanishing planks Phineas Glover and his daughter followed,
tumbling upon the flagging of the landing-place. They heard

the ship touch behind them, with a soft, rustling noise, as of
mere mould and fungus. They turned to gaze at her, but she
had disappeared. A great dust filled the air; it hid her, as they
thought, from their sight; it descended slowly and noiselessly
into the green waters; and when it was gone, nothing was
left; the Flying Dutchman was no more. But, high above the
spot where she had been, sweeping first clearly and then
faintly into the heavens, rang a sweet music of many joyous
voices, a chant of gratitude and of deliverance.

The Glovers, staring down into the mysteriously whisper-
ing wavelets, saw only a cloudy settling of pulverous matter,
which each instant grew thinner, and soon was naught. Clear
green water, woven through with strands of sunlight, rolled
over the last mooring-place of the famous sea-wanderer.

"Wal, that beats square-rigged icebergs," mumbled Captain Glover. "Lord! how full the world is of wonders! yes,
and of disappointments! I did expec' to git some kind of
commission out of that chap, an' make my fortune. However, I've got some gold-dust an' idols."

He touched his pockets; they were flat against his ribs. He
rammed his hands into them; they contained only a corroded
solution. He looked for the chain of pearls; it was still around
Mary Anne's neck. The wealth which he had hinted his
desire for, and which he had so eagerly clutched at, had
vanished. Naught remained but the pure offering of gratitude
to pity.

Such is the story of the return of the Flying Dutchman
from his long cruise, as related to us by the worthy and
reliable Captain Phineas Glover of Fair Haven.

THE LEGEND OF
JOE LEE

John D. MacDonald

"Tonight," Sergeant Lazeer said, "we get him for sure."

We were in a dank office in the Afaloosa County Courthouse in the flat wetlands of south central Florida. I had come over from Lauderdale on the half chance of a human interest story that would tie in with the series we were doing on the teenage war against the square world of the adult.

He called me over to the table where he had the county map spread out. The two other troopers moved in beside me.

"It's a full moon night and he'll be out for sure," Lazeer said, "and what we're fixing to do is bottle him on just the right stretch, where he got no way off it, no old back country roads he knows like the shape of his own fist. And here we got it." He put brackets at either end of a string-straight road.

Trooper McCollum said softly, "That there, Mister, is a eighteen mile straight, and we cruised it slow, and you turn on off it you're in the deep ditch and the black mud and the 'gator water."

Lazeer said, "We stake out both ends, hide back good with lights out. We got radio contact, so when he comes whistling in either end, we got him bottled."

He looked up at me as though expecting an opinion, and I said, "I don't know a thing about road blocks, Sergeant, but it looks as if you could trap him."

"You ride with me, Mister, and we'll get you a story."

"There's one thing you haven't explained, Sergeant. You said you know who the boy is. Why don't you just pick him up at home?"

The other trooper Frank Gaiders said, "Because that fool kid ain't been home since he started this crazy business five-six months ago. His name is Joe Lee Cuddard, from over to Lasco City. His folks don't know where he is, and don't much care, him and that Farris girl he was running with, so we figure the pair of them is off in the piney woods someplace, holed up in some abandoned shack, coming out at night for kicks, making fools of us."

"Up till now, boy," Lazeer said. "Up till tonight. Tonight is the end."

"But when you've met up with him on the highway," I asked, "you haven't been able to catch him?"

The three big, weathered men looked at each other with slow, sad amusement, and McCollum sighed, "I come the closest. The way these cars are beefed up as interceptors, they can do a dead honest hundred and twenty. I saw him across the flats, booming to where the two road forks come together up ahead, so I floored it and I was flat out when the roads joined, and not over fifty yards behind him. In two minutes he had me by a mile, and in four minutes it was near two, and then he was gone. That comes to a hundred and fifty, my guess."

I showed my astonishment. "What the hell does he drive?"

Lazeer opened the table drawer and fumbled around in it and pulled out a tattered copy of a hot-rodder magazine. He opened it to a page where readers had sent in pictures of their cars. It didn't look like anything I had ever seen. Most of it seemed to be bare frame, with a big chromed engine. There was a teardrop shaped passenger compartment mounted between the big rear wheels, bigger than the front wheels, and there was a tail-fin arrangement that swept up and out and then curved back so that the high rear ends of the fins almost met.

"That engine," Frank Gaiders said, "it's a '61 Pontiac, the big one he bought wrecked and fixed up, with blowers and special cams and every damn thing. Put the rest of it together himself. You can see in the letter there, he calls it a C.M. Special. C.M. is for Clarissa May, that Farris girl he took off with. I saw that thing just one time, oh, seven, eight months ago, right after he got it all finished. We got this magazine from his daddy. I saw it at the Amoco gas in Lasco City. You could near give it a ticket standing still. Strawberry flake paint it says in the letter. Damnedest thing, bright strawberry with little like gold flakes in it, then covered with maybe seventeen coats of lacquer all rubbed down so you look down into that paint like it was six inches deep. Headlights all the hell over the front of it and big taillights all over the back, and shiny pipes sticking out. Near two years he worked on it. Big racing flats like the drag strip kids use over to the airport."

I looked at the coarse screen picture of the boy standing beside the car, hands on his hips, looking very young, very ordinary, slightly self-conscious.

"It wouldn'd spoil anything for you, would it," I asked, "if I went and talked to his people, just for background?"

"Long as you say nothing about what we're fixing to do," Lazeer said. "Just be back by eight thirty this evening."

Lasco City was a big brave name for a hamlet of about five hundred. They told me at the sundries store to take the west road and the Cuddard place was a half mile on the left, name on the mailbox. It was a shacky place, chickens in the dusty yard, fence sagging. Leo Cuddard was home from work and I found him out in back, unloading cinder block from an ancient pickup. He was stripped to the waist, a lean, sallow man who looked undernourished and exhausted. But the

muscles in his spare back writhed and knotted when he lifted
the blocks. He had pale hair and pale eyes and a narrow
mouth. He would not look directly at me. He grunted and
kept on working as I introduced myself and stated my business.

Finally he straightened and wiped his forehead with his
narrow arm. When those pale eyes stared at me, for some
reason it made me remember the grisly reputation Florida
troops acquired in the Civil War. Tireless, deadly, merciless.

"That boy warn't no help to me, Mister, but he wasn't no
trouble neither. The onliest thing on his mind was that car. I
didn't hold with it, but I didn't put down no foot. He fixed
up that old shed there to work in, and he needed something,
he went out and earned up the money to buy it. They was a
crowd of them around most times, helpin' him, boys workin'
and gals watchin'. Them tight-pants girls. Have radios on
batteries set around so as they could twisty dance while them
boys hammered that metal out. When I worked around and
overheard 'em, I swear I couldn't make out more'n one word
from seven. What he done was take that car to some national
show, for prizes and such. But one day he just took off, like
they do nowadays."

"Do you hear from him at all?"

He grinned. "I don't hear *from* him, but I sure God hear
about him."

"How about brothers and sisters?"

"They's just one sister, older, up to Waycross, Georgia,
married to an electrician, and me and his stepmother."

As if on cue, a girl came out onto the small back porch.
She couldn't have been more than eighteen. Advanced preg-
nancy bulged the front of her cotton dress. Her voice was a
shrill, penetrating whine. "Leo? Leo, honey, that can opener
thing just now busted clean off the wall."

"Mind if I take a look at that shed?"

"You help yourself, Mister."

The shed was astonishingly neat. The boy had rigged up

droplights. There was a pale blue pegboard wall hung with shining tools. On closer inspection I could see that rust was beginning to fleck the tools. On the workbench were technical journals and hot-rodder magazines. I looked at the improvised engine hoist, at the neat shelves of paint and lubricant.

The Farris place was nearer the center of the village. Some of them were having their evening meal. There were six adults as near as I could judge, and perhaps a dozen children from toddlers on up to tall, lanky boys. Clarissa May's mother came out onto the front porch to talk to me explaining that her husband drove an interstate truck from the cooperative and he was away from the next few days. Mrs. Farris was grossly fat, but with delicate features, an indication of the beauty she must have once had. The rocking chair creaked under her weight and she fanned herself with a newspaper.

"I can tell you, it like to broke our hearts the way Clarissa May done us. If'n I told LeRoy once, I told him a thousand times, no good would ever come of her messin' with that Cuddard boy. His daddy is trashy. Ever so often they take him in for drunk and put him on the county road gang sixty or ninety days, and that Stubbins child he married, she's next door to feeble-witted. But children get to a certain size and know everything and turn their backs on you like an enemy. You write this up nice and in it put the message her momma and daddy want her home bad, and maybe she'll see it and come on in. You know what the Good Book says about sharper'n a serpent's tooth. I pray to the good Lord they had the sense to drive that fool car up to Georgia and get married up at least. Him nineteen and her seventeen. The young ones are going clean out of hand these times. One night racing through this county the way they do, showing off, that Cuddard boy is going to kill hisself and my child too."

"Was she hard to control in other ways, Mrs. Farris?"

"No, sir, she was neat and good and pretty and quiet, and she had the good marks. It was just about Joe Lee Cuddard

she turned mulish. I think I would have let LeRoy whale that
out of her if it hadn't been for her trouble.

"You're easier on a young one when there's no way of
knowing how long she could be with you. Doc Mathis, he
had us taking her over to the Miami clinic. Sometimes they
kept her and sometimes they didn't, and she'd get behind in
her school and then catch up fast. Many times we taken her
over there. She's got the sick blood and it takes her poorly.
She should be right here, where's help to care for her in the
bad spells. It was October last year, we were over to the
church bingo, LeRoy and me, and Clarissa May been resting
up in her bed a few days, and that wild boy come in and
taking her off in that snorty car, the little ones couldn't stop
him. When I think of her out there . . . poorly and all. . . ."

At a little after nine we were in position. I was with
Sergeant Lazeer at the west end of that eighteen mile stretch
of State Road 21. The patrol car was backed into a narrow
dirt road, lights out. Gaiders and McCollum were similarly
situated at the east end of the trap. We were smeared with
insect repellent, and we had used spray on the backs of each
other's shirts where the mosquitoes were biting through the
thin fabric.

Lazeer had repeated his instructions over the radio, and we
composed ourselves to wait. "Not much travel on this road
this time of year," Lazeer said. "But some tourists come
through at the wrong time, they could mess this up. We just
got to hope that don't happen."

"Can you block the road with just one car at each end?"

"If he comes through from the other end, I move up quick
and put it crosswise where he can't get past, and Frank has a
place like that at the other end. Crosswise with the lights and
the dome blinker on, but we both are going to stand clear
because maybe he can stop it and maybe he can't. But
whichever way he comes, we got to have the free car run

close herd so he can't get time to turn around when he sees he's bottled.''

Lazeer turned out be a lot more talkative than I had anticipated. He had been in law enforcement for twenty years and had some violent stories. I sensed he was feeding them to me, waiting for me to suggest I write a book about him. From time to time we would get out of the car and move around a little.

"Sergeant, you're pretty sure you've picked the right time and place?''

"He runs on the nights the moon is big. Three or four nights out of the month. He doesn't run the main highways, just these back country roads—the long straight paved stretches where he can really wind that thing up. Lord God, he goes through towns like a rocket. From reports we got, he runs the whole night through, and this is one way he comes, one way or the other, maybe two, three times before moonset. We got to get him. He's got folks laughing at us.''

I sat in the car half listening to Lazeer tell a tale of blood and horror. I could hear choruses of swamp toads mingling with the whine of insects close to my ears, looking for a biting place. A couple of times I had heard the bass throb of a 'gator.

Suddenly Lazeer stopped and I sensed his tenseness. He leaned forward, head cocked. And then, mingled with the wet country shrilling, and then overriding it, I heard the oncoming high-pitched snarl of high combustion.

"Hear it once and you don't forget it," Lazeer said, and unhooked the mike from the dash and got through to McCollum and Gaiders. "He's coming through this end, boys. Get yourself set.''

He hung up and in the next instant the C.M. Special went by. It was a resonant howl that stirred echoes inside the inner ear. It was a tearing, bursting rush of wind that rattled fronds and turned leaves over. It was a dark shape in the moonlight, slamming by, the howl diminishing as the wind of passage died.

Lazeer plunged the patrol car out onto the road in a screeching turn, and as we straightened out, gathering speed, he yelled to me, "Damn fool runs without lights when the moon is bright enough."

As had been planned, we ran without lights too, to keep Joe Lee from smelling the trap until it was too late. I tightened my seat belt and peered at the moonlit road. Lazeer had estimated we could make it to the far end in ten minutes or a little less. The world was like a photographic negative—white world and black trees and brush, and no shades of grey. As we came quickly up to speed, the heavy sedan began to feel strangely light. It toe-danced, tender and capricious, the wind roar louder than the engine sound. I kept wondering what would happen if Joe Lee stopped dead up there in darkness. I kept staring ahead for the murderous bulk of his vehicle.

Soon I could see the distant red wink of the other sedan, and then the bright cone where the headlights shone off the shoulder into the heavy brush. When my eyes adjusted to that brightness, I could no longer see the road. We came down on them with dreadful speed. Lazeer suddenly snapped our lights on, touched the siren. We were going to see Joe Lee trying to back and turn around on the narrow paved road, and we were going to block him and end the night games.

We saw nothing. Lazeer pumped the brakes. He cursed. We came to a stop ten feet from the side of the other patrol car. McCollum and Gaiders came out of the shadows. Lazeer and I undid our seat belts and got out of the car.

"We didn't see nothing and we didn't hear a thing," Frank Gaiders said.

Lazeer summed it up. "OK, then. I was running without lights too. Maybe the first glimpse he got of your flasher, he cramps it over onto the left shoulder, tucks it over as far as he dares. I could go by without seeing him. He backs around and goes back the way he came, laughing hisself sick. There's the second chance he tried that and took it too far, and he's wedged in a ditch. Then there's the third chance he lost it. He could have dropped a wheel off onto the shoulder and tripped hisself and gone flying three hundred feet into the swamp. So what we do, we go back there slow. I'll go first and keep my spotlights on the right, and you keep yours on the left. Look for that car and for places where he could have busted through.''

At the speed Lazeer drove it took over a half hour to traverse the eighteen mile stretch. He pulled off the road where we had waited. He seemed very depressed, yet at the same time amused.

They talked, then he drove me to the courthouse where my car was parked. He said, ''We'll work out something tighter and I'll give you a call. You might as well be in at the end.''

I drove sedately back to Lauderdale.

Several days later, just before noon on a bright Sunday, Lazeer phoned me at my apartment and said, ''You want to be in on the finish of this thing, you better do some hustling and leave right now.''

''You've got him?''

''In a manner of speaking.'' He sounded sad and wry. ''He dumped that machine into a canal off Route 27 about twelve miles south of Okeelanta. The wrecker'll be winching it out anytime now. The diver says he and the gal are still in it. It's been on the radio news. Diver read the tag, and it's his. Last year's. He didn't trouble hisself getting a new one.''

I wasted no time driving to the scene. I certainly had no trouble identifying it. There were at least a hundred cars pulled off on both sides of the highway. A traffic control officer tried to wave me on by, but when I showed him my press card and told him Lazeer had phoned me, he had me turn in the park beside a patrol car near the center of activity.

I spotted Lazeer on the canal bank and went over to him.

A big man in face mask, swim fins and air tank was preparing to go down with the wrecker hook.

Lazeer greeted me and said, "It pulled loose the first time, so he's going to try to get it around the rear axle this time. It's in twenty feet of water, right side up, in the black mud."

"Did he lose control?"

"Hard to say. What happened early this morning a fellow was goofing around in a little airplane, flying low, parallel to the canal, the water like a mirror, and he seen something down in there so he came around and looked again, then he found a way to mark the spot, opposite those trees away over there, so he came into his home field and phoned it in, and we had that diver down by nine this morning. I got here about ten."

"I guess this isn't the way you wanted it to end, Sergeant."

"It sure God isn't. It was a contest between him and me, and I wanted to get him my own way. But I guess it's a good thing he's off the night roads."

I looked around. The red and white wrecker was positioned and braced. Ambulance attendants were leaning against their vehicle, smoking and chatting. Sunday traffic slowed and was waved on by.

"I guess you could say his team showed up," Lazeer said.

Only then did I realize the strangeness of most of the waiting vehicles. The cars were from a half-dozen counties, according to the tag numbers. There were many big, gaudy, curious monsters not unlike the C.M. Special in basic layout, but quite different in design. They seemed like a visitation of Martian beasts. There were dirty fenderless sedans from the thirties with modern power plants under the hoods, and big rude racing numbers painted on the side doors. There were other cars which looked normal at first glance, but then seemed to squat oddly low, lines clean and sleek where the Detroit chrome had been taken off, the holes leaded up.

The cars and the kids were of another race. Groups of

them formed, broke up and re-formed. Radios brought in a
dozen stations. They drank Cokes and perched in dense
flocks on open convertibles. They wandered from car to car.
It had a strange carnival flavor, yet more ceremonial. From
time to time somebody would start one of the car engines,
rev it up to a bursting roar, and let it die away.

All the girls had long burnished hair and tidy blouses or
sun tops and a stillness in their faces, a curious confidence of
total acceptance which seemed at odds with the frivolous and
provocative tightness of their short shorts, stretch pants, jeans.
All the boys were lean, their hairdos carefully ornate, their
shoulders high and square, and they moved with the lazy
grace of young jungle cats. Some of the couples danced
indolently, staring into each other's eyes with a frozen and
formal intensity, never touching, bright hair swinging, girls'
hips pumping in the stylized ceremonial twist.

Along the line I found a large group. A boy was strum-
ming slow chords on a guitar, a girl making sharp and erratic
fill-in rhythm on a set of bongos. Another boy, in nasal and
whining voice, seemed to improvise lyrics as he sang them.
"C.M. Special, let it get out and *go*./C.M. Special, let it way
out and *go*./Iron runs fast and the moon runs slow."

The circle watched and listened with a contained intensity.

Then I heard the winch whining. It seemed to grow louder
as, one by one, the other sounds stopped. The kids began
moving toward the wrecker. They formed a big silent semi-
circle. The taut woven cable, coming in very slowly, stretched
down at an angle through the sun glitter on the black-brown
water.

The snore of a passing truck covered the winch noise for a
moment.

"Coming good now," a man said.

First you could see an underwater band of silver, close to
the drop-off near the bank. Then the first edges of the big
sweeping fins broke the surface, then the broad rear bumper,
then the rich curves of the strawberry paint. Where it wasn't

clotted with wet weed or stained with mud, the paint glowed
rich and new and brilliant. There was a slow sound from the
kids, a sigh, a murmur, a shifting.

As it came up further, the dark water began to spurt from
it, and as the water level inside dropped, I saw, through a
smeared window, the two huddled masses, the slumped boy
and girl, side by side, still belted in.

I wanted to see no more. Lazeer was busy, and I got into
my car and backed out and went home and mixed a drink.

I started work on it at about three thirty that afternoon. It
would be a feature for the following Sunday. I worked right
on through until two in the morning. It was only two thousand words, but it was very tricky and I wanted to get it just
right. I had to serve two masters. I had to give lip service to
the editorial bias that this sort of thing was wrong, yet at the
same time I wanted to capture, for my own sake, the flavor
of legend. These kids were making a special world we could
not share. They were putting all their skills and dreams and
energies to work composing the artifacts of a subculture,
power, beauty, speed, skill and rebellion. Our culture was
giving them damned little, so they were fighting for a world
of their own, with its own customs, legends and feats of
valor, its own music, its own ethics and morality.

I took it in Monday morning and left it on Si Walther's
desk, with the hope that if it were published intact, it might
become a classic. I called it "The Little War of Joe Lee
Cuddard."

I didn't hear from Si until just before noon. He came out
and dropped it on my desk. "Sorry," he said.

"What's the matter with it?"

"Hell, it's a very nice bit. But we don't publish fiction.
You should have checked it out better, Marty, like you
usually do. The examiner says those kids have been in the
bottom of that canal for maybe eight months. I had Sam check
her out through the clinic. She was damn near terminal eight

months ago. What probably happened, the boy went to see her and found her so bad off he got scared and decided to rush her to Miami. She was still in her pajamas, with a sweater over them. That way it's a human interest bit. I had Helen do it. It's page one this afternoon, boxed.''

I took my worthless story, tore it in half and dropped it into the wastebasket. Sergeant Lazeer's bad guess about the identity of his moonlight road runner had made me look like an incompetent jackass. I vowed to check all facts, get all names right, and never again indulge in glowing, strawberry flake prose.

Three weeks later I got a phone call from Sergeant Lazeer.

He said, "I guess you figured out we got some boy coming in from out of county to fun us these moonlight nights.''

"Yes, I did.''

"I'm right sorry about you wasting that time and effort when we were thinking we were after Joe Lee Cuddard. We're having some bright moonlight about now, and it'll run full tomorrow night. You want to come over, we can show you some fun, because I got a plan that's dead sure. We tried it last night, but there was just one flaw, and he got away through a road we didn't know about. Tomorrow he won't get that chance to melt away.''

I remembered the snarl of that engine, the glimpse of a dark shape, the great wind of passage. Suddenly the backs of my hands prickled. I remembered the emptiness of that stretch of road when we searched it. Could there have been that much pride and passion, labor and love and hope, that Clarissa May and Joe Lee could forever ride the night roads of their home county, balling through the silver moonlight? And what curious message had assembled all those kids from six counties so quickly?

"You there? You still there?''

"Sorry, I was trying to remember my schedule. I don't think I can make it."

"Well, we'll get him for sure this time."

"Best of luck, Sergeant."

"Six cars this time. Barricades. And a spotter plane. He hasn't got a chance if he comes into the net."

I guess I should have gone. Maybe hearing it again, glimpsing the dark shape, feeling the stir of the night wind, would have convinced me of its reality. They didn't get him, of course. But they came so close, so very close. But they left just enough room between a heavy barricade and a live oak tree, an almost impossibly narrow place to slam through. But thread it he did, and rocket back onto the hard top and plunge off, leaving the fading, dying contralto drone.

Sergeant Lazeer is grimly readying next months's trap. He says it is the final one. Thus far, all he has captured are the two little marks, a streak of paint on the rough edge of a timber sawhorse, another nudge of paint on the trunk of the oak. Strawberry red. Flecked with gold.